# ZIVA'S CHALLENGE

# ZIVA'S CHALLENGE

## MONICA FLORES

This book is dedicated to Kate, my young beta reader, whose enthusiastic response regarding my first book moved me to write this one. Thank you, Kate.

# CONTENTS

# ACKNOWLEDGEMENTS

An attitude of gratitude is magical for both the person who has the gratitude and the person receiving it. Creating a book takes a bunch of time and people, and it's always good to acknowledge them. First and foremost, I have to thank my family for their continued support throughout this process.

I have to thank the tireless efforts of those who have edited my writing and enhanced my writing skills: Jessica McNair, Henry Bausman, and my copyeditor, Rachel Hulet. I learn much from them each and every time.

Thank you to my beta readers Dorine Campsey, Kendra Harvey, and Kendra's daughters, Kate and Macy. Their attitude of gratitude brought to pass this second book. Thank you to my friends, Cindy Anderson and Wendy Passantino, who encourage me forward.

Finally, a very grateful thank you to all who read this book. I hope it may uplift you and help you forward with your journey called life.

The most beautiful people . . . are those who have known defeat, known suffering, known struggle, known loss, and have found their way out of the depths. These persons have an appreciation, a sensitivity, and an understanding of life that fills them with compassion, gentleness, and a deep loving concern. Beautiful people do not just happen.

Elisabeth Kübler-Ross

# PROLOGUE

*34 BC*

ZIVA, ANGRY WITH HER FATHER'S plans, sits next to him on the stool in his workshop. As he works his skill on the jewelry he creates, she glares at him through big brown eyes, pouting, with her arms crossed. "Why do I have to again go with you to the market? I want to stay home and play with Tokal."

Emer sighs, puts down his tools, and turns toward her. "Because you need to start learning how to interact with others. You're growing up."

Ziva pouts, muttering, "I don't like going to the market. People don't like me. I can see it in their faces."

"Their reaction is caused by the fact that what you feel about a person comes out of your mouth. It makes them nervous. You have no filter, Ziva. The Great Spirit blessed you with this. Your friends will be those that recognize it as a gift, as your mother and I do. Your mouth has saved us from being robbed many times, but we also need to refine it so that you can socialize with other people."

"I would rather work in the shop with the pearls and shells." Ziva looks down and murmurs, "I don't like it when I upset people."

Emer thoughtfully gazes at his daughter. Taking out a carefully folded cloth from his pocket, he places it in Ziva's hand and crouches down to his daughter's eye level. "Carefully open it, Ziva." With a questioning look, she meets his eyes before following his instructions. Inside the simple, dark-colored cloth is a large freshwater pearl. She looks up at her father with wide eyes. "I found this pearl many years ago. It has great value. Your mother and I have kept it to remind us of what is truly important.

You are our only child, our greatest creation. Though the pearl in your hand holds great value, you are worth more to us—our pearl of great price. I know your heart, and I know you do not like to upset people. That is why we must practice talking with others so that you can improve. Part of being a parent is helping you learn so that one day, you can prosper without us. Will you please come to the market with your father and keep me company?"

Ziva gazes at the pearl, evaluating his words before looking into her father's gray eyes. "I love you, Father. I will do as you ask. Can Tokal join us?"

"Only if his parents approve." Emer winks at his daughter and stands up. Ziva folds the cloth around the pearl and hands it to her father. "The pearl is yours, Ziva. May it always remind you how very special you are, my daughter."

Jumping off the stool, Ziva rushes to her father to give him a big heartfelt hug. She disappears out the door, tucking the treasure in her pocket, and with Emer's laughter following her, heads toward the neighbor's home.

ZIVA AND TOKAL ARRIVE AT Uthal's marketplace to set up their stall with the assorted jewelry. Uthal is a commerce city with a Lamanite king, where merchants and traders alike come to the market to buy and sell. The two different factions of people that come to this city are Nephites, who come from the North, and the Lamanites, who live in this region. Even though their ancestors were brothers, there has been a blood feud over the generations that has ebbed and flowed based on the beliefs of the clans and the current threat they face.

After the stall is set up, Emer pulls out the bag of dried fruit and nuts to eat. Ziva and Tokal dig in, filling their bellies.

Emer watches the two children with dark brown hair as they share the meal and is grateful that Ziva has Tokal as a friend. Still, he frowns as he looks at the boy. Tokal is three years older than Ziva and will be starting his training with the army soon. He will no longer be there to protect Ziva from the other children. As the first customer of the day arrives at the stall, Emer turns away, changing his face to a smile and concentration on the task at hand.

While Emer works on specially requested items, Ziva and Tokal greet the Lamanite and Nephite customers, answer questions, and exchange commodity. If the stall gets busy; Emer steps in to assist.

Late in the morning, a woman covered in fine clothing and jewelry walks with her guard toward the table.

Another woman, humbly dressed, comes toward the rich woman, only to be forcibly pushed away by her guard.

Ziva frowns, watch the scene unfold. When the haughty woman arrives in front of her, Ziva greets her. "You are very rich."

"I am, indeed," the woman proudly says.

"Why don't you help those that are less fortunate than you, such as that poor woman who approached you?" Ziva innocently queries.

Surprised at the child's words, she asks, "What makes you assume that I don't help the poor?"

Ziva looks at the woman for a moment and cocks her head, innocently stating, "You don't. You're more focused on yourself than on others, which makes you ugly."

The woman's proud face scowls, and a hand lashes out.

Tokal steps in the way, shielding Ziva from the blow.

Emer moves forward in front of the children, trying to diffuse the situation. "What Ziva meant to say is, for one so rich, you have the capability for helping others—like us—with a small purchase from our stand."

"Your daughter needs to be beaten for her insolent mouth. Perhaps cutting out her tongue would be even better. You are a highly favored craftsman, which brings me to your table," the irate woman returns.

Emer frowns at the woman's words. "Find what you want, but never lay another hand on the children, or you will not be able to purchase within this stall. I don't care if you are the market manager's wife."

The woman huffs, glaring at the vendor, but doesn't leave from the stall. She looks through the display and picks out some earrings. Money is exchanged and the woman moves on.

After she departs, Emer looks at Tokal with concern. "Are you all right?"

Tokal nods smartly at Emer.

Ziva smiles at Tokal. "Thank you for protecting me."

Emer hands the money from the sale to Ziva. "Find the woman."

Smiling broadly at her father, she nods her head and grabs the currency, quickly leaving the stall with Tokal to go in search of the poor woman.

A little time later, Ziva and Tokal return, taking up where they left off in helping the customers.

When a lag in patrons occurs, Emer whispers to his daughter, "Did you find her?"

"Yes," she reports softly. "She says thank you for helping her so that her family has food."

"Thank you for pointing out the need. I'm glad we can help." He lovingly flicks the end of her nose, causing Ziva to smile.

Looking around her, she warns her father, "I overheard someone say they were going to steal from the king."

He nods, asking her, "If you saw them again, would you be able to point them out?"

Ziva nods.

"Very good, daughter," he acknowledges proudly.

Sometime later, a man dressed in fine linen comes to the stall to look at their goods. He strikes up a casual dialogue with Emer. When a lull in the conversation occurs, Ziva interrupts, "Why do you steal when you don't have a need?"

The man's face turns red, and he stares angrily at the little girl. "How dare you accuse me of stealing!"

"Perhaps you would like to purchase something from a different vendor," Emer calmly asserts.

Offended, the man replies, "Your daughter accuses me of being a thief."

Calmly, Emer stands up straighter, dismissing the man. "She speaks only the truth. Take your business elsewhere. If not, I will call the guards."

"How dare you!" The man growls, moving away from the table.

"How do you know he is a thief?" Tokal whispers confidentially to Ziva as he stands next to her. "He looks just like any other rich man."

"I don't know," she shrugs. "I just do and can't keep quiet."

When a lull between customers arrives, Emer gently touches his daughter's shoulder while facing her. "Thank you, daughter, for saving us again from being robbed, but perhaps we can work on trying to remember to notify me with the signal rather than confronting the thief."

"Oh." Ziva, head falling, feels incompetent. "I'm sorry, Father. I couldn't keep quiet."

Emer crouches down to her level and puts a finger under her chin, making her look at him. "Remember, you are a pearl of great price. What we learn at the market will only help us."

Ziva smiles lovingly at her father's understanding.

Emer reciprocates the smile before standing up as the next customer comes their way.

As time at the market nears the end and they are packing up the stall, a man walks by the table. Ziva tugs on her father's arm and points at the man, stating a little too loudly, "That's the man who is going to steal from the king."

The man, hearing the allegation and seeing Ziva's finger pointing at him, comes toward the stall with a knife drawn.

Emer stands in front of the children, explaining, "Disregard what she says. She means you no harm."

The man doesn't stop.

Ziva's mouth drops open to scream, but nothing comes out. Her mind tells her legs to move, but they stand rooted to the spot.

She watches in horror as the man repeatedly stabs her father, knocking him out of the way. He continues to move toward her as her heart hammers in her chest.

Tokal grabs Ziva's arm, pulling her to action. "Come on!"

They rush out of the stall. The man chases after them.

Tokal weaves through groups of people but is unable to lose the murderer.

Ziva continues to run as fast as her little legs can carry her.

Tokal pulls her up and down the streets, and they are finally halted by guards at King Gilgal's gate.

Knowing the man is quickly descending upon them, the scared children swallow, looking up at the big, hulking guards that block the way each one holding sharp weapons.

Breathing hard, Tokal courageously spits out, "That man following us is planning on stealing from the king. He killed her father."

The guards quickly take action. Several of them chase after the man who is hunting the children, while others usher the children forward into the king's domain.

The children are marched down the aisle of a large room, between tables and benches, toward a large, muscular man sitting in one of several ornate, gold-encrusted chairs.

Upon wood benches that line the sides of the large chamber, people sit, observing the activity within and whispering to each other. Guards and servants stand around the perimeter, following the beck and call of the man sitting in the chair.

To be brought before King Gilgal's presence is a frightening experience. Neither child speaks, but they stand hand in hand, looking down at the floor.

Gilgal speaks kindly to them. "I am told you had a man chasing after you? That a father is stabbed? If that is the case, he may yet be alive and able to regain his health, but we need to know where this took place?"

Tokal, the first to recover, takes the lead. He looks at Ziva, who is silently weeping with her eyes to the floor. Turning to face the king, he confirms, "He's not alive. The man made sure of that. Ziva overheard the man's plan to steal from the king."

"Your name?" the king questions.

"Tokal."

The king replies sadly, "I am sorry about your father."

"It happened to her father," Tokal corrects, cocking his head toward Ziva.

"Ziva, is it?"

Ziva nods as she looks at the floor.

"I am sorry about your father. Can you tell me what happened?" Gilgal gently urges.

Ziva looks up at the king with tears coursing down her face. "I saw a man walking by the stall. I knew he was the same man who planned to steal from the king. I told my father, but the man . . . he overheard. He . . . he . . . he stabbed my father and continued toward us. We ran."

Gilgal exhales sadly. "It is good you came here. Tokal, are you well enough to take us to her father?"

Tokal nods, looking at the king.

"Ziva, please stay with the queen while we sort this out," Gilgal softly orders.

She nods in response, obeying him. She wonders what will happen to her now that she's caused her father's death. Will her mother even still want her?

# THE STAND

*28 BC*

ZIVA BLINKS, PULLED BACK TO the present by the male voice beside her. She realizes where she is, sitting on a hillside, watching the sheep graze while absently stroking a lamb asleep on her lap. The gentle spring breeze plays with some flyaway, dark-brown hair that has escaped her braids and tickled her face. "What did you say?"

"Tomorrow, you take the Journey with your mother?" The old shepherd confirms while looking out at the sheep nearby.

Pulled from her musings by the question, Ziva turns to him as he sits down next to her. "Yes, although I'm not fond of leaving this place."

"Why is that?" he probes.

Ziva sits and ponders for a minute, absently stroking the lamb on her lap.

The old shepherd's brown eyes pivot to her, awaiting a response.

"Because it feels safe."

The shepherd looks back at the herd he protects. "When you came here, you were a skittish little thing, hiding behind your mother's skirt."

Ziva frowns, "I remember."

"I know you don't like change, and to compound that, you still have an underlying mistrust of people. Why?"

"Because of my mouth. When I open my mouth, words flow out, and people don't always like it. I don't always like it."

"That is true," he confirms.

Ziva's head drops as her face turns red.

The old shepherd chuckles at her expression. "What comes out of your mouth are not bad things."

She pets the lamb in her lap and mutters, "My mouth got my father killed."

"Your mouth didn't get your father killed. A man took your father's life and, from what you've stated before, was coming after you too."

Defending her statement, she fixes her fiery brown eyes at the shepherd and juts her chin out defiantly. "After I spoke."

"Ah, I see." The shepherd's eyes home in on her. "You still feel responsible for your father's death?"

She nods and drops her eyes, petting the lamb again.

"Ziva, at some point in your life, you're going to have to forgive yourself in order to move forward. You're also going to have to come to terms that how you talk is something that is not to be feared but something to be treasured. I always know where I stand with you because your words hold no malice, only honesty within them. All of us shepherds and our families are grateful you are here among us, and we'll miss you." He smiles at her. "Tomorrow will be a change, but take it from an old man, it will be a good thing in your life."

She frowns and mutters, "I don't like it, and I don't want to go."

"I understand that, Ziva," the old shepherd sighs, "but change will still happen whether you want it to or not. Change can be a good thing."

Ziva sighs, continuing to pet the lamb in her lap. She looks up at the old shepherd, who smiles kindly at her. "I will miss all of you."

"That's the spirit," he encouragingly returns. "This is a good thing for you. You're no longer a little girl. Stand up and take your place as a woman." The old man leaves her side and walks a short distance away, leaving Ziva with her thoughts.

After a time, "Ziva" blows to her on the breeze. She turns her head to see her mother waving at her in the distance. Getting up, she returns the lamb to the shepherd, petting the creature a final time. "Mother's calling. Thank you for letting me care for him."

The old shepherd nods his head.

Turning her back to the man, Ziva makes her way across the meadow to her and her mother's small home.

Khatoon, Ziva's mother, watches her daughter pick her way gracefully across the meadow with brown braids dancing behind her. She smiles.

When the petite, slender girl reaches Khatoon, she inquires, "Yes, Mother?"

"Ziva, time for food." Khatoon greets her daughter, who looks like a much younger version of herself. "Tomorrow will be a big day for you." Khatoon gives her a hug and pulls her inside their small home.

Ziva goes and dips a rag in the water to wash her hands and feet before moving further into the small hut.

"I know you're scared. When you stand before the city, look at something other than the people. I will speak for you—and we have time to figure out what to do when we return."

Ziva nods as she goes to the pot, smelling the savory aroma of mutton stew, and dishes out two bowls while her mother speaks. After Khatoon is seated on the rug in front of the fire, Ziva passes a bowl to her.

Khatoon continues to talk in between bites of food. "King Gilgal has been good to us by moving us to live here with the shepherds. Their families have been kind and helpful. You haven't had to deal with a lot of people, and they have been patient with you."

*It has kept us safe*, Ziva admits as she stirs the contents within her bowl.

They continue to eat in silence, each one immersed in her own thoughts.

When Khatoon is done eating, Ziva breaks the silence. "I'm sorry about Father."

Surprised, Khatoon gazes at her daughter. "What brought this up?"

Ziva shrugs. "I miss him."

Khatoon touches her daughter's hand. "I miss him too. But you're not responsible."

Ziva looks up at her mother. "If I had only spoken softer, it wouldn't have happened."

"Do you have it?"

Confused, Ziva questions, "Have what?'

"The pearl."

Ziva nods.

"Can you show me?" Khatoon encourages.

Ziva sighs, putting her nearly full bowl on the ground. She reaches into her pocket and pulls out the dark, folded cloth.

Carefully, she lays the cloth on her open hand, revealing the luminescent pearl within.

"Do you recall what your father told you about this pearl?"

Ziva nods, again recalling his words six years ago when he first said them.

"Your father willingly gave his life to protect yours. I know he would do the same again if he had to."

Responding to her mother's gentle caress, Ziva looks up at her.

"I do not blame you. Please don't blame yourself. You are our greatest treasure. Please remember that." Khatoon closes Ziva's hand over the pearl and gives her daughter a hug.

Ziva wraps up the little treasure, returning it to its home, and wipes her eyes.

"Try to eat, Ziva."

Khatoon sews while Ziva sits watching the fire the rest of the evening; immersed in their own thoughts.

ZIVA ROUSES FROM A FITFUL sleep. She moves outside to sit and watch the light break through the darkness, a sight that usually speaks peace to her heart.

Today, she's filled with sadness knowing this is a last among the sheep and shepherds. After she completes her morning chores, she slowly returns to the little hut where her mother hands her a bowl of mush once her hands and feet are clean. Ziva eats without saying a word, not even tasting the food. When the meal is over, both wash their bowls and spoons and store them with their other belongings.

"Ready?" Khatoon asks.

"I'm scared. What if something happens?" Ziva squeaks.

"The king and I will be with you," Khatoon soothes. "Remember to not look at the people. This is your time to stand as a woman." Pulling out an arm hidden behind her back, Khatoon presents the contents in her hand to Ziva. "You will need these on our journey."

Before touching them, Ziva's hand hovers above the new apparel, and she realizes the effort her mother put into the moccasins. "Thank you, Mother."

Khatoon smiles. "Try them on and see if they fit." Ziva sits down and pulls on the shoes, wiggling her toes inside of them.

"They seem to fit," Ziva gratefully informs her mother.

"I'm glad." Helping her daughter stand, Khatoon gives her a hug. "We need to go." She puts on her pack as Ziva nods to her and then walks out the door.

Ziva soon follows, closing it behind her.

Living outside the gates of Uthal with the shepherds has been pleasant for Ziva. The community—as poor as they may be—lives by the standard of honesty and hard work, making it easy for Ziva to fit in. She has done her best to blend in and not be seen, but that has never been accomplished as well as she would like because of her mouth.

The shepherds and their family's wave at them as they begin their walk toward Uthal. Ziva's stomach knots, and her anxiety grows the closer they get to Uthal. "Mother, can we just return home and not go to the Stand?"

"No." Her mother puts an arm around her, encouraging her faltering feet to move faster. "I wouldn't be a good mother if I made you miss this. Furthermore, the queen has requested your presence."

As they walk toward Uthal's front gates, the decorated city wall, with animal scenes upon the vertical posts, looms to life. Uthal is a Lamanite trade city that annually has many visitors, both Nephites and Lamanites, from many other cities.

Ziva's fear of the elusive assassin stops her progress and makes it hard for her to breathe.

Khatoon, understanding Ziva's anxiety, takes her hand to lead her into the city.

Ziva wants to obey her mother, but her reservations stop her. "I don't like this, Mother," she announces fearfully as her mother gently encourages her along.

"I know." She pat's her daughter's hand reassuringly. "We must always move forward in life. You must move forward with your life. There is no need to fear your father's killer. Too many years have gone by, and you have changed from a child into a beautiful woman."

"Can't we continue as we are?" Ziva's voice rises a notch.

Khatoon stands in front of Ziva, gazing at her. "We've had this conversation. You must stand as a woman. You cannot become that unless you move forward." She encourages her with a smile.

Ziva takes a breath and blows it out. "I know." She looks down at the ground and mutters. "I still don't like it, Mother. I don't like being forced. I'm afraid that this will be bad for us."

Khatoon hugs her daughter and chuckles as she wisely says, "You'll never know if you don't try." She pats her daughter's hand encouragingly as they move forward together into the city.

Ziva keeps her eyes down, looking at the ground, following her mother's instructions. The crowded streets of unknown people press around her, causing a claustrophobic effect, and her hand tightens on her mother's as she struggles to breathe.

The multiple contrasting aromas, some foul and some good, attack her nose, causing her stomach to clench as bile rises. She grits her teeth, pressing forward by her mother's side.

The roar of the crowd is sometimes overshadowed by merchants inviting people to their stall.

She concentrates on breathing while putting one foot after another.

Her mother talks soothingly as they travel, letting her know what will be coming next.

Before long, they arrive at the building next to the Stand where Khatoon leads Ziva, placing her at the back of the line next to another young woman.

Ziva exhales deeply, relieved that they've made it where there are a lot fewer people milling around her.

As they stand in a line inside the building, whispers start at one end of the line and move to the other end where they wait. "The queen is coming this way," reaches both sets of ears.

Ziva looks to her mother to find that she is bowing. Ziva looks up to see a beautiful older woman with black hair and intelligent brown eyes, accompanied by three guards.

"Ziva, you look beautiful." The queen approvingly smiles at Ziva as she greets her. "You have grown up."

"I don't want to be here. I'm scared. Why are you making me do this?" flows forcefully out of Ziva's mouth.

Queen Suyana's eyes widen and her mouth pops slightly open before she closes it again. She chuckles. "I have forgotten your candid tongue. First, tell me, have your years been pleasant?"

Having been asked about a subject close to her heart, Ziva enthusiastically responds, "I love being with the kind shepherds and the sheep. They don't judge me. I want to return there."

The queen's eyes smile as she nods. "I'm glad they have been pleasant." Taking a breath, she continues, "Do you not recall, we had this same conversation many years ago when the king and I moved you to that environment for your safety?"

Ziva nods recalling the scared little girl that didn't want to go. Today, the memory is pleasant.

The wise queen continues, "You are of age and need to move forward with your life." Suyana smiles with understanding in her eyes. "The king and I have talked long about this time for you. We have tried to plan accordingly, to let you know that we support you and cherish your gift." She smiles at Ziva again before taking a breath. "My present to you this day comes in the form of this guard."

The mentioned guard steps forward and bows to Ziva. His black hair is neatly pulled away from his strong angular face with a band above his brow and rests slightly below his shoulders. Inquisitive dark eyes stare back at her. His upper body contains well-developed muscles.

"He will be in your service the duration of the Journey and . . . if you choose the Challenge . . . he will go with you."

Fire lights Ziva's eyes as she looks at the queen. Without her thinking, the words rush out of her mouth, "I don't need a guard. I need to go home."

The queen smiles patiently at Ziva's outburst and in a soft one laced with firmness remarks, "All children grow up, and you are no exception. You must stand and take your place as a woman." The stern manner in her voice changes as she smiles at her again. "Would your father be proud of you if you hid from the world?"

Ziva's anger quickly dissipates, and her eyes fall to the floor. "No."

"Stand, my dear, and be counted—for indeed, you are very rare and special."

Ziva looks up at the queen, surprised by her response.

"Good." She nods. "Time to start. When you are called, please go to the Stand."

Ziva humbly nods.

Suyana kindly smiles at Ziva one last time. "Be of good cheer, we are here to help." She leaves the way she came with only two guards following her.

Khatoon whispers to Ziva after the queen's departure, "I don't know why or how you have found favor with the queen, but she is trying to help us. Perhaps you could show a little more respect?"

The young women are called to the Stand.

Ziva and her mother start to follow.

The gifted guard steps in front of them and instructs, "You are to remain here until you are called."

Trying to control her anger, she looks up at the imposing guard blocking their way and notices his bulging muscles. He's tall, too—a full head above her. She stares him down and "I don't like you" flies out of her mouth.

The affronted guard simply replies. "I am only here to help."

Ziva turns her head away, ignoring him as the young women and their mothers disappear from her view.

Khatoon says, "See?" She pats Ziva's hand. "The king and queen are here to help. When you're called, remember what I told you."

In the distance they hear King Gilgal. "Spring has arrived where a young woman takes the Journey to become a woman."

A young woman is called, and she steps forward with her mother. The mother says several things about her daughter to the audience before attaching a bracelet on her daughter's left wrist, signifying she's of age for courting. When all the young women have been introduced, King Gilgal continues, "We have one other young woman who is shy. Please be kind to her. Ziva, would you please take your place on the Stand?" The audience looks to the building.

Ziva frowns and grumbles, "The king lies. I'm not shy."

"Would you rather he tells the world that you state only your truth and you distrust others? Remember what I told you."

Holding Ziva's hand, Khatoon walks Ziva out the door. Trying to keep her anxiety in check, Ziva looks at anything else other than the people. The guard accompanies them to the stairs of the Stand. The closer she gets to the top of the Stand, the tighter Ziva holds onto Khatoon's hand. "You're hurting me, Ziva," her mother fiercely whispers. "You can do this."

Ziva lightens her hold on her mother's hand and looks at the ground, taking deep breaths while her mother helps move her forward. When she stops, she closes her eyes for a moment, facing forward. She grits her teeth and opens her eyes, looking above the crowd as her mother speaks. "Ziva, my beloved daughter, is kind, caring and compassionate. She has a good heart."

Ziva feels her mother step in front of her reaching for her wrist. She looks down to find an exquisite bracelet of pearls and shells placed upon her wrist—her father's handiwork. Tears prick her eyes, and she looks at her mother.

Khatoon nods slightly, confirming that indeed her father created the bracelet, and both embrace, recalling the beloved man.

When the hug is over, Gilgal announces, "Time for Uthal's new women to start their Journey with their mothers. They will return in four moons at which time, each single woman will have to decide whether to take the Challenge or the Joining. The Challenge sends the woman and her guardian outside the gates of the city. They are not able to return to Uthal until after the next season of women return from their Journey. If the single woman is found inside Uthal's walls during her Challenge, then she forfeits her life. On the other hand, if the woman chooses the Joining, then she has this season to decide who she wants for her husband. When the next group of new women return from their Journey and that woman has not been joined, then I will match her to a husband. The women are excused."

The new women and their mothers file off the Stand to the opposite side where their families and a few horses wait.

When Ziva steps off the Stand, the guard is there to greet them. He offers to help Ziva from the Stand, which she ignores, so he assists Khatoon.

"Follow me," he orders. They shadow him to the front of the line where a single horse stands with supplies lashed to its back.

Ziva has never seen a horse before and looks at the animal warily. The horse greets her and tries to nuzzle Ziva's shoulder, but she backs away.

"You can touch her. She's safe. She won't bite you," the guard coaches. "Like this, Ziva." He strokes the horse's neck.

Ziva imitates him, feeling the velvet soft fur. Intrigued, she focuses all her attention on the animal while the other families say their farewells.

Gilgal speaks behind her. "You have grown into a beautiful woman."

Ziva jumps and turns toward him, wide-eyed.

He smiles at her. "Enjoy your time with your mother. We will see you when you return."

Ziva looks pointedly at the king. "You lied!"

The king's eyes as well as his mouth pop open, which he quickly closes as he tries to catch up to what Ziva is telling him. "What?"

"You lied. I'm not shy," she announces.

"Yes." He takes a breath. "I lied for your benefit." The king patiently smiles at her. "I would do it again to help you." Changing the subject, he continues. "You did well on the Stand, but at this moment, you need to go." Turning, he motions the guards to proceed forward.

Soon, Khatoon and the guard gently push Ziva forward, prompting her to start her trek.

With a frown on her face and eyes on the feet of those in front of her, Ziva moves forward, but the war within her continues. Should she trust her mother's decision or give into the fear that this unknown change brings?

# PUDDLE JUMPING

ONE BY ONE, EACH NEW woman and her mother tail those in front of them, moving out Uthal's gates, followed by more guards in the rear. The city of Uthal continues to shrink as they head toward the distant mountain.

"Where are we going, Mother?" Ziva inquires.

"It has been a long time since I went on this journey with my mother. My time at Arnac with her is a pleasant memory." Khatoon sighs. "We're headed for the mountain in the distance. A small city that contains only women exists up there. If memory serves me right, it will take around six or seven days to travel."

"That long?" Ziva's mouth pops open in concern. "We are not prepared with seven days of food."

"It'll be provided. You'll see." Khatoon smiles and pats her daughter's hand.

Ziva focuses her attention on the guard who walks silently on her other side. "If you're going to be my shadow, what shall I call you?"

The guard looks at her for a moment, searching for something, "Whatever you want."

At his answer, confusion washes over Ziva's face as a distant memory flits past. "Do I know you?"

He grins at her. "Perhaps."

Ziva stops in her tracks to look at him better. Something seems familiar, but before she can figure it out, an arm pulls her forward again.

He chuckles. "Don't stop. We need to keep moving."

"I want to look at you closer." She glares at him.

"I know," he laughs again, "but this is not a good time."

"How am I going to figure out what to call you?" she shoots back.

A mischievous grin crosses his face. "You're going to have to figure that one out."

"Tell me something that no one else knows about me," she orders.

"Besides the fact that you have no filter?" He grins at her.

She frowns at him. "Yes, besides that."

"Hmm." They continue in silence as Ziva waits for his reply.

"I think I'm going to have some fun with this." He takes a breath, making up his mind. "I'm not going to tell you. You'll have to figure it out on your own."

Perturbed, she eyes him as they walk. "You know I could ask one of the other guards."

"You could . . . but you won't." He grins and looks at her out of the corner of his eyes.

Frustrated that he won't tell her, she whines, "Why not?"

Because you like the game," he reveals.

She frowns at him again and presses, "How can you be so sure?"

His eyes twinkle as he says, "Because I know you, Ziva."

She quickly peers at him before looking at the road in front of her. "If I figure it out on my own and tell you, will you acknowledge it?"

"Perhaps," he grins watching her irritation grow, "but you'll never know."

Ziva, with a menacing glare, storms, "At this moment, I don't like you."

"Of course you don't," he smirks with twinkling eyes. "You're angry because I'm not telling you what you want to hear."

"Ziva, leave the man alone," Khatoon commands, setting herself between the two of them. "This is going to be a long journey for me if the two of you continue bickering."

"Sorry, Mother," Ziva quickly returns.

"Stop. Time to set up camp," the camp leader shouts. "Separate yourselves into four groups." Once all the women have been divided, their leader points to each group. "The first group will cook our meal tonight. The second group is in charge of water and clean up. The third group is in charge of helping the men with the tents. The fourth group is in charge of gathering firewood. On a daily basis these tasks will rotate to keep our travel varied. The responsibility for any animal brought by you is yours. Get to work."

Ziva and her mother start gathering firewood as instructed, while the guard sets off to tend to his animal.

A young woman approaches Ziva and enthusiastically says, "Hello, I'm Ami."

Ziva, surprised to find someone talking to one so poor, looks at the well-dressed young woman with black braids and sparkly, almost-black eyes. "I'm Ziva. What question do you have?" she frowns in return.

Ami's eyes widen at the unexpected response. After an uncomfortable silence, Ami takes a breath and chitters, "Why did the queen give you a personal guard?"

"I have no idea. I don't like it," Ziva's scoffs before turning away to pick up some more firewood, thinking the woman is done speaking with her.

"He's a very handsome man," Ami continues, following her.

Without looking up, Ziva places another broken stick on her stack. "Didn't notice." Ziva steps further away before adding a stick.

Ami, surprised again by her curt response, frowns and follows Ziva. "You are . . . very honest."

Frowning, Ziva looks at Ami and shrugs. "Sorry," she says before selecting some more firewood, expecting Ami to huff and walk off.

Ami continues following her, picking up a piece of dead wood here and there. "Why are you sorry?"

Ziva stops what she's doing and turns, not believing Ami is still shadowing her. Her pursuer reaches her side, causing Ziva to shield herself from the response that's soon to come. "It has been my experience that people don't like the way I talk."

"I like it," Ami counters.

Ziva stares back in disbelief.

"What's his name?" Ami asks.

Ziva shrugs, deflated. "I don't know." She drops her eyes and picks up another piece of wood. "He won't tell me." A brief pause occurs before Ziva pointedly looks at Ami and probes, "Are you only interested in me because of the guard?"

Ami regards Ziva for a minute. "You're refreshing. At first, you interested me, but now that I've heard you talk, I want to get to know you better."

"Why?" Ziva counters as she picks up another dead branch and adds it to her loaded arm. She starts walking toward a fire pit.

"Wait up," Ami calls as she quickly moves forward, catching up with Ziva. "What's wrong with having me for a friend?"

"A friend? Nothing." Ziva drops her load on the pile of dead branches a few feet away from where a fire is being lit and turns to gather more wood.

Ami follows suit, catching up with Ziva again.

"I think I would like a friend," Ziva says carefully, "but am not sure what that entails."

Ami's brows draw together in disbelief and her mouth drops open with the words, "Haven't you had friends before?"

Ziva shakes her head. "One . . . a long time ago."

"Oh my. Why only one?"

Ziva frowns and shrugs her shoulders. "People don't like the way I speak, and bad things tend to happen to those around me."

"I like the way you speak, and good things happen to me," announces Ami.

Ziva scoffs. "You just met me. You'll probably change your mind."

Ami stands at her full height and stares at Ziva, perturbed at how she is responding. She crosses her arms. "Well, how about this? We continue to be honest with each other and see what happens. Hmm?"

Ziva looks at her for a moment before grinning. "I can do that."

"Good," Ami returns before picking up more dried limbs for the fire.

Ziva joins her.

Together, they each gather another armful of dead sticks and head for the firewood pile.

Ami drops her second load onto the heap. "Are you going to choose the Joining or the Challenge?"

Ziva frowns. "I don't want to gain a husband with the Joining, and I don't want to leave my mother for a year to go on the Challenge. I just don't know. I just want to return home."

Ami smiles at Ziva as they head back to get some more wood. "You don't have to choose at this moment. I'm looking forward to the Journey. I have four younger siblings, so it will be nice to have my mother to myself for a time. I know we're going to miss our family, but uninterrupted time with my mother is nice."

Ziva looks at this happy person who is so very different from herself. "My family is only my mother and me."

Ami, holding a limb in her hand, looks up at Ziva with a surprised look on her face. "What happened to your father?" She adds the limb to her pile.

Ziva turns from her, blinking back the tears that prick, not wanting to share this information with someone she barely knows. "I don't want to talk about it."

Ami's inquisitive, concerned nature takes over. "Why, Ziva?"

"Because," Ziva snaps. She walks away from Ami, trying to stop the conversation.

Ami continues pursuing her. "I didn't mean to upset you, Ziva. We can talk about something else, like your beautiful bracelet," she suggests brightly.

Ziva turns on Ami, showing her upset face. "No!" she spits before walking away, leaving Ami to wonder what she did wrong.

Ziva drops the sticks onto the growing heap created by the women. She marches over to her mother and vehemently cries, "I don't want to be here. I want to go home." Her guard overhears the commotion and comes their way.

Khatoon drops her sticks and wraps a protective arm around Ziva, "What happened?"

"She asked questions about Father and my bracelet," Ziva cries into her mother's shoulder.

"Ziva, I'm sure she wants to get to know you better—not to cause you pain," Khatoon soothingly returns.

"Ziva," Ami pleads behind her, "I didn't mean to make you upset. I am only trying to get to know you better. You can ask me anything you'd like, and I will try to answer you. Please do not be upset."

"See?" Khatoon gives her daughter a hug. "You know you can answer her."

Ziva looks down and grinds out, "I don't want to talk about it."

Khatoon raises her daughter's chin, causing Ziva to open her eyes and look at her mother. In a very soft, loving voice she says, "In order for you to move forward, you must confront the past. Stand, Ziva, and confront your demons." She gently tucks a fly away hair behind her daughter's ear, gives an encouraging smile, and turns

Ziva toward Ami. Khatoon turns her attention toward Ami, saying, "Ziva says you had some questions about her father and her bracelet. What were they?"

Ami, uncomfortable with the situation, swallows and answers, "I meant no disrespect. I wondered why I didn't see her father when we left and who made her bracelet."

"I see. Ziva, would you please answer her?"

Ziva looks to her mother, who smiles reassuringly. Ziva grabs her mother's hand and glances at her guard, only to find a pained expression on his face. Her eyes drop to the ground as she struggles with her own emotions.

Ziva holds her breath as the pain in her chest finally bursts out through her mouth. "He died. I got him killed." Her legs give out and she falls to the ground weeping. "Oh, Mother, I'm so sorry. I didn't mean to be so loud. Mother, please forgive me. I wish I'd died that day so I wouldn't have to carry this burden."

Khatoon sits on the ground, holding her daughter as Ziva's loss pours out of her.

"I'm so sorry," Ami cries, throwing her arms around Khatoon and Ziva as she empathetically joins herself to the two women to mourn their loss.

The commotion gathers a group, and Ziva's guard directs them away, quietly requesting that the others give the women space so they can work this out among themselves.

When Ziva's tears subside, Khatoon gets her daughter's attention and quietly speaks to her. "I love you, Ziva. As many times as we've talked about this, I have never blamed you for what happened. I think the only person who hasn't forgiven you is you.

That is why speaking of this is painful. You must forgive yourself to move forward."

Ami notices Ziva's distressed expression as Ziva looks at her mother. Drying her face, Ami softly says, "I'm so sorry you had to go through that. Did this recently happen?"

"No," Khatoon answers.

"It must be hard without him," Ami returns.

"Yes, very hard without him," Ziva laments, looking to her mother and finding unity there.

"But we have a good life together," Khatoon declares, smiling at her daughter.

"I'm so glad." Ami smiles. "You have a beautiful bracelet, Ziva. Did he get it for you?"

Ziva, still drying her eyes as tears continue to escape, grimaces to herself as this girl continues her unpleasant probing questions, which her mother wants her to answer. Looking at the ground, she responds, "My father made it before he died."

"That makes it even more special." Ami gives Ziva a quick hug of support.

Ziva feels the quick hug and doesn't know what to make of Ami. She glances at her. "Yes, it does."

"I'm sorry for upsetting you. I didn't mean to. I only want to get to know you better," Ami confesses. Changing the subject, she says, "I would like to introduce you to some of my friends."

Ziva stops and looks at her mother for help. "I don't want to go."

"Go, Ziva. It will do you good." Turning to Ami, Khatoon says, "Ami, Ziva is fearful. Please bring her back happy." Ami nods her head and starts to move forward to help Ziva from the ground.

Khatoon stops Ami and looks directly at her. "I'm serious."

Ami swallows as a weight of responsibility falls on her shoulders. She nods again.

Khatoon removes her hand.

Ami pulls a reluctant Ziva from the ground and leads her away.

After a few paces, Ami's curiosity gets the best of her and she cautiously asks, "Are you truly scared to meet other people?"

"Yes." Ziva blows out her pent-up breath. "Can we stop for a minute?"

"Why?"

"This is truly hard for me. Let me have a minute to recover," Ziva pleads. "To add to it, I embarrassed myself by publicly crying."

Ami stops and turns to her. "You have nothing to be embarrassed about—everyone must deal with their emotions. Holding your emotions in will only make them come out later, like they did. I'm glad you got them out. Your mother is right—you must forgive yourself so you can move forward."

"Easier said than done." Ziva frowns.

"I think you've come a long way," Ami comforts. Chuckling with a raised eyebrow, she continues, "You're talking to me." She grins at Ziva. "Keep it up." They stand there quietly for a minute while Ami waits patiently for her new friend to compose herself.

Ziva is amazed at how much better she feels after talking with this easygoing, happy person. On the other hand, Ami wants her to meet new people—scary thought. Will they also accept her for who she is? Gaining strength from Ami's acceptance, Ziva takes a deep breath and blows it out slowly.

Ami stretches and urges, "Ready?" Ziva nods, and they continue forward. "Why are you scared of people?"

"I've had many bad experiences with people," Ziva explains.

"That is a lonely and scary way to live," Ami retorts, frowning. "You've got to trust people, Ziva. Most of them are good and mean well. 'Faith over fear,' my mother always says." Ami's face brightens. "I've been surprised many times by people by doing just that."

Ziva frowns. "My experience has been the opposite. Most people only tolerate me."

"That's because they don't know the real you," Ami remarks.

"We've just met. You don't know me," Ziva returns.

"Yes, we've recently met, and I don't know you all that well, but that is why I ask questions; so, I can get to know you better. I like you."

Ziva looks at her in disbelief. "Why do you like me?"

Ami, surprised by the question, looks at Ziva, and searches for an answer. She shrugs. "Because . . . you are you."

"What does that mean?"

"You're honest. Your mother says, 'you're kind, caring, and compassionate.' I like those characteristics, so I suspect we'll be great friends. You're being prickly because you're trying to protect yourself from dealing with your emotions. You're avoiding being honest with yourself. Once you're honest with yourself, you will be much happier, and I suspect that others will see for themselves those wonderful characteristics your mother mentioned. I like you, Ziva, and hope you will accept me as your friend."

Ziva throws back, "You have a way of getting to the heart of a matter and exposing a wound."

Ami shrugs and smiles at Ziva, letting her words roll off her back. "You're my friend and I'm here to help you," she returns brightly. Ziva glares at her, but Ami's smile and her personality is infectious. Soon, Ziva's frown softens to a smile.

Suddenly, dinner is announced somewhere from camp.

Ami changes direction. "Let's eat."

Ziva's not used to how fast Ami deviates, stands there flummoxed. "What about your friends?"

"They'll find us," Ami trills, coming back and grabbing Ziva's arm, pulling her along as they rush toward the line that is forming.

After receiving bowls of food, the new women sit around one of the camp's fire rings. Before long, their mothers find them and sit to eat their food. Soon, four other women with their mothers arrive. They adjust the seating arrangements so that the new women sit on one side of the fire while their mothers sit on the other side and converse.

Khatoon makes sure she remains next to Ziva to keep a close eye on her since she isn't used to such a large group of people.

Ami points to each of her friends as she introduces them. "Ziva, this is Tovah, Frema, Chaya, and Mazal. I know them from school." Ziva notices that their hair and eye colors are similar, but their facial features differ.

"So nice to meet you, Ziva." Tovah smiles at Ziva before taking a bite of food.

Mazal finally puts the pieces together regarding Ziva, "You're the girl who has a personal guard."

"He's so good looking," Chaya gushes.

"And tall," Frema adds, pointing her spoon at them.

"How did you get the queen to assign *him* to you?" Mazal questions between bites.

Ziva frowns at Mazal's question. "You . . ." she cocks her head thinking, "like to stand out. I don't. I didn't do anything. The queen just . . . did it. I don't want him."

"I'll take him," Mazal mischievously offers.

Ziva laughs, not giving it another thought. "You can have him."

"Stop it, Mazal," Ami interjects. "I don't think the guard will change his duty even if Ziva orders him."

Mazal pouts. "It doesn't hurt to try."

Ziva sighs, realizing Ami is correct. "I agree, but will ask."

Mazal's face lights up. Ziva looks at the group. "How long have you been friends?"

"We live near each other, so we grew up playing together," Ami answers.

"Each of you is so different." Ziva cocks her head again, looking at each of them. "Ami is curious. Tovah is confident. As I have mentioned, Mazal likes to stand out. Chaya is boy crazy, and Frema is . . . shy." Ziva turns, pointing at each of them as she speaks their characteristics.

"Yes, we're all very different," Tovah chuckles, "but ultimately, we care about each other, and that's what keeps us close." Heads nod all around.

That night, games are played around the main campfire to help everyone gets to know one another better. The guards watch from the perimeter.

Once in bed, Ziva muses over the day and realizes that no judgement took place, even with her crying fit. Thinking about her new friendships fills her with warmth, and a smile crosses her face as she closes her eyes.

ZIVA STRETCHES AND SMILES KNOWING that dawn is approaching—her favorite time of day. A time of quiet to refresh herself before she deals with people.

She silently puts on her shoes and moves outside the tent door only to have her foot hit something that causes her to fall.

Swallowing back a cry, she hits the dirt with a thud.

With closed eyes, she gathers herself before glaring at a pair of eyes staring back at her from the dark form of her guard. "What . . ." she hisses.

He puts a finger over his lips, silencing her verbal outburst.

She realizes that others are still sleeping.

He quickly arises, coming to help her up, and walks her to the edge of camp away from the others.

"What were you thinking?" she storms in a fierce whisper.

"I didn't want you to wake the others, although I do suspect they will be awake soon." He grins, reminding her of her voice.

She scowls at him and lowers her volume, retorting, "That is not what I meant, and you know it."

His grin deepens as her frustration mounts. "What do you mean?" he inquires, feigning ignorance.

"You . . . you . . . Argh," she hisses. "You're so infuriating!"

She takes a breath before seething, "Why are you sleeping outside the door to my tent?"

"What better place to sleep to guard my charges?" He shrugs simply.

His simple, innocent response aggravates her further. "Why at the door?"

"So, I know who goes in and out." He shrugs and moves his hands out with palms forward. "I'm only doing my job."

Ziva gets close to his face and grinds out, "Don't do it again."

He takes a breath before calmly inquiring, "Why are you leaving the tent, Ziva?"

"My favorite time of day is sunrise. I like the time alone and don't want to be interrupted," she haughtily answers.

Before she can react, he gently moves a piece of hair away from her face, which surprises and disquiets her further. He softly concedes, "You were always an early riser."

Ziva hisses back, "How do you know that?"

The man stares at her, only inches between them, and quietly asks, "Have you figured out my name?"

Her eyes break from his, looking past his shoulder. "Look."

He turns toward the direction she indicates to see the hues of the morning light start off as deep blues above the mountain and, together, they watch the transformation of spectrums until the sun blinks, revealing itself.

"Ladies, time to wake up," breaks the beautiful silence as it echoes through camp. Their leader calls, "We need to get moving."

Brought back to the present, they look at each other. The guard cautions, "I will not change from sleeping at the door of the tent, but feel free to wake me and I will move." He smiles at her. "Thank you for the sunrise." He bumps her nose with a forefinger, like her father used to do, before turning toward camp. Changing the subject, he asks, "Do you know how to start a fire?"

She glares at him again as a memory briefly flickers and the anger leaves her voice, "I know how to start a fire."

He smiles at her reaction. "Good. Follow me." He starts walking back to one of the unlit rings within camp, expecting her to follow.

She catches up, curious as to what he wants from her, "You expect me to start the fire?"

"Of course," he smirks. "Unless you can't."

"I can." She glares at him, jutting out her chin in defiance. "I do it all the time at home."

He stops and looks at her, thoroughly enjoying her defensive reaction. He has no control over the smile that spreads across his face. She frowns at him, so he starts walking again. "Tell me about your home."

Ziva falls into step next to him, "What is there to tell? I love it and I miss it."

"Where do you live?"

They arrive at the fire pit. Ziva looks at him and cocks her head, wondering if this man is truly from her past. "So, I do know you?"

He chuckles before seriously replying, "Yes."

"Can you give me another hint?"

He grins, enjoying his anonymity. "About how to start a fire?"

"No," she huffs, turning her attention to setting up the kindling, "about who you are."

"Hmm. Let me think about that. Take the stones." He hands her the sparking stones to start the fire.

"Thank you." Taking the sparking stones, she hits them together, creating a spark and feeding the new flame. Before long, a good-sized fire burns.

Her guard adds a few more logs to the fire. "Good job."

He nods while looking at her handy work. "Do you have your own sparking stones?"

"We brought everything we own with us," Ziva sadly responds.

The man's face frowns. "So, I assume that is a yes."

Ziva doesn't look at him but throws another stick on the fire. "Can't have a home without sparking stones."

"Where have you been living, Ziva?"

She turns to look at him and realizes he wants answers too. She smirks. "Are you going to at least give me a hint about who you are?"

He's quiet for a moment before looking to the tent Ziva slept in. "Come on. Let's see if your mother is awake." They start walking together toward their destination.

"Women, please gather here," the leader's voice calls again.

Her guard looks at her and leans his head toward the direction of the voice. "Better go. We'll talk later."

Ziva moves toward their leader to hear what he has to say, while her guard continues toward the tent.

Khatoon steps out the tent door and starts walking toward the group that has gathered.

After the women have assembled, their leader commences his speech. "Women, those of you who cleaned up yesterday will be in charge of cooking for today. Those of you who cooked yesterday will, for today, be in charge of helping the men with the tents. Those of you who gathered wood yesterday will be in charge of water and cleanup for today. Those of you that helped the men with tents yesterday will, for today, be in charge of gathering kindling. Get to work. We need to get on the road to reach our next destination as quickly as possible. It looks like we are in for a storm."

Khatoon finds Ziva and they move toward the designated well to gather water for those that are cooking. "What have you and the guard been talking about? Did you find out his name?"

"I haven't found out his name, although I'm pretty sure we have met before," she answers, glancing at her mother.

"So, you were asking him questions to find out who he is?" Khatoon clarifies.

"Trying, but he didn't tell me anything." Ziva frowns, discouraged.

After delivering the water, mother and daughter return to their tent to find that it has already been taken down and packed. "Let's go back to the fire and I will fix your hair," Khatoon suggests.

CLOUDY SKIES AND THE SMELL of rain fill the air as a cool breeze touches Ziva's skin. She shivers, walking next to Ami and her friends while their mothers are behind. Ziva notices that Ami has a way of including everyone and making them feel wanted. She wishes she had that characteristic and starts to observe what Ami subconsciously does. The storm starts as a mist with very little lightning but soon turns to a drizzle. They continue to travel, but the conversation deteriorates along with the weather, starting with complaints about being wet.

"Why is our leader making us walk in the rain? I'm soaked," Mazal whines.

"You look like a wet dog," Chaya teases before gasping, "which means I look like a wet dog."

"This is a light rain, which is not worth complaining about even though we're wet," Ziva informs them.

"You may be used to it, but we are not," Frema storms haughtily.

"I look ugly." Chaya pouts. "The men won't be attracted to me," she whines, stomping her foot.

Mazal's mouth drops open and she pushes Chaya further away. "You splashed mud on me, Chaya."

"Don't push her into us," Frema chides as Chaya bumps into her, pushing her into Ami.

"I would like to be inside, around a nice, warm fire. I'm cold," Ami sullenly returns, shivering and drawing closer to Mazal to keep warm.

"Wouldn't we all," Mazal sarcastically quips. "But that's not happening. Instead, we're having to walk in this rain," Mazal rants as she pushes Ami away from her. "You're wet. Move away from me."

Ziva, who started off the day feeling part of a positive group, doesn't like the contention she's now surrounded with.

She recalls when she moved to the hut near the shepherds, being unhappy then. For a long time, she didn't talk—before her sadness overflowed to words. Once, after saying unkind things all day to the other children and their mothers, another mother had marched her to Khatoon while tweaking her ear.

After hearing what the mother had to say about Ziva's behavior, Khatoon had apologized. The other mother finally left and Khatoon sat down with a frown on her face.

"We don't need them," had bitterly fallen out of Ziva's mouth. "Any of them. I'm perfectly fine without them."

Her mother's downcast head had whipped up, and she looked sharply at Ziva. Very quietly, she stated, "We do need them, Ziva. Survival is difficult without others, let alone having a happy life. The shepherds have kept us safe. One day, I will not be here anymore, and what will you do when that occurs?" She sighed. "The only way we succeed is with each other. Words and actions can just as quickly destroy. Anyone can destroy, but it takes a stronger person to choose to build. Your father was a builder. Both your father and I liked it when you were a builder. Life is a very lonely road if you choose to destroy. You must choose who you will be."

Ziva recalls her mother's loving hug before she departed the hut, leaving Ziva to her thoughts. That day became a defining point in her life; she had decided life would be better as a builder.

Ziva grimaces, recalling that she hasn't been much of a builder recently.

Life didn't get better for her overnight in the small community, but through patience and kindness, she finally became accepted within it.

She frowns to herself, thinking of home and wishing to be back there. She decides to work on being more positive.

Finding herself at the back of the pack of women, Ziva is alone and happy with her thoughts. She soon finds puddles in the path and adjusts her pace to distance herself from the women in front of her and the men behind her. She starts a game of puddle jumping. Occasionally, as the mood hits her, she jumps into a puddle—just for the fun of the splash—oblivious of the laughing eyes of the men that follow.

Here and there, she skips along, jumping over a good-sized puddle before jumping high in the air and coming down to splash hard on a smaller puddle, then quickly jumping out of it. Her face lights up in delight as the muddy water flies around her, inducing her to giggle.

"What are you doing?" The male voice stops her in her tracks and wipes the smile from her face. She looks up to find her guard next to her, looking innocently at her. She smiles brightly. "I'm puddle jumping."

"It looks more like puddle splashing," he blandly returns.

She gazes at him for a moment and cocks her head to one side. "I suppose it does. Puddle jumping is fun."

"Start walking. We need to stay with the group." Ziva starts moving again, and her guard joins her. "Why are you not with the group of women?"

She shrugs looking at another puddle, which she hops over before jumping in the following puddle, splashing mud on her guard. I didn't much like it when they were arguing and complaining."

"And puddle jumping is better?" he asks.

She grins at him. "By far. You should try it."

"It has been many years since I've done this." He scratches his chin. "I may have forgotten how," he absently interjects, hopping over a puddle and jumping into the next puddle, sending a spray of water around the perimeter as he jumps out of it. His face lights up and he chuckles. "I forgot how much fun this is."

After hearing the statement and his laughter, she stops in her tracks as the revelation hits her.

# REUNION



Ziva stares at him as he continues jumping. "You're Tokal!" explodes from her.

He stops and turns, facing her with a funny look on his face.

She inspects his features, recognizing the little boy that meant so much to her, hidden inside the face of the grinning man in front of her.

"Took you long enough."

Her feet transport her into his arms as she grabs his neck, thankful to have her friend with her again. "Where have you been?" she demands.

"I've been with the military. One of us had to grow up." He gently separates her from him. "We can talk, and I will tell you all. Shall we continue our puddle jumping?"

A smile lights her face and they both turn, hopping over the first puddle and into and out of the second as laughter rolls from their throats.

"Where did you move to, Ziva? After that dreadful day . . . you disappeared."

Ziva stops and frowns at the mention of the past, "King Gilgal hid us with the shepherds." He pushes her forward and she hops over another puddle. "I was safe with them and had to deal with only a few people. Did they ever catch the man who did it?"

"No." Tokal frowns. "He got away, so we were hidden to protect us." Tokal jumps over a puddle, lands with the splash, and looks at her. "Were you happy?"

She smiles. "Eventually. Not when I arrived—I wasn't for a long time. Mother worried about me. My unhappiness ultimately overflowed into everything I did, which got me in more trouble. I had to change and found help in an old shepherd whose kindness and patience with me helped. Little by little, more people accepted me into the close-knit community. I enjoyed spending time outdoors with the sheep."

"That's good," Tokal returns, hopping over another puddle. Stopping for a moment, Ziva looks at Tokal. The delight is gone from her face and her laughter changes to a serious tone. "What about you? What have you been doing all these years?"

"After that day?" Tokal clarifies.

Ziva nods.

Tokal touches her arm, moving her forward again. "The king took me to the palace guards, and I began my training. I guess he felt that being with the guards kept me and my family safe." He shrugs. "It was time to start my training anyway."

By the time their leader calls for the group to stop, a small assortment of very muddy men and a few new women located in the back of the group are in a similar condition as Ziva and Tokal.

Tokal takes Ziva and has her start a fire in the rain—not an easy task, but he shows her how. Soon, several fires are lit and beckon to everyone with their light and warmth. After the women quickly complete their chores and the rain stops, they huddle around the fire to warm themselves while they dry off. "Mother, I figured it out," Ziva excitedly announces around the campfire.

"Figured out what?" Khatoon returns, lifting up a wet foot toward the fire to help dry it.

"Mother." She waits until she has Khatoon's attention, "my guard is Tokal."

"Tokal?" Surprised, Khatoon scrambles to her feet to greet him. She pierces him with probing eyes, searching for the little boy she once knew. Finding him, she smiles and nods.

"You're all grown up."

He chuckles at Ziva's introduction and Khatoon's reaction. "I have indeed, Khatoon. It makes me happy to see you again. You have done a good job raising Ziva."

"She's a good girl, even with her challenges." Khatoon grins.

"I like her the way she is," Tokal returns, smiling back.

Irritated, Ziva waves her hands, trying to get their attention. "I'm right here." Ziva stands looking at them pointedly. "You can talk about me when I'm not around," Ziva huffs.

Khatoon and Tokal look at each other before chuckling, watching as Ziva turns and stomps away.

Dinner is called, and everyone quickly gathers to get their food. Lightning flashes in the sky, and dark heavy clouds fill the air, blowing a cold wet wind the travelers' way. The leader interrupts people lining up, shouting, "Hurry and eat before finishing what chores you may have. It looks like rain will be arriving again shortly."

Khatoon finds Ziva in the line and stands with her. When their bowls are filled, they return to the fire to eat. Ami and her friends show up a short time later with their meals, and the group adjusts so that mothers and daughters are separated.

Concerned over her friend's earlier disappearance, Ami inquires as she sits down, "Ziva, where did you go? You disappeared from our group." She frowns, declaring, "You scared us."

"How did I scare you?" Ziva cocks her head not understanding the concern in Ami's voice. 'My mother wasn't scared."

"You were part of our group and when we looked again, you disappeared," Tovah clarifies sitting down next to Ami with Frema, Chaya, and Mazal. "What happened?"

Ziva hesitates before lifting her chin. "I learned a long time ago that I prefer to build not destroy." As an afterthought, she continues, "Though my mouth on occasion still gets in the way."

"Huh?" Tovah's face scrunches up trying to figure out what Ziva's saying.

Ami, also confused, says, "You're not making sense Ziva. Please explain."

Looking down, Ziva answers, "I don't like contention. I don't like it when a person tears down another. I like being around those that build others up, not the reverse."

"I think she's talking about earlier today in the rain," Frema translates, frowning.

"Oh, that." Mazal's hand holding a spoon swipes the air as if to remove it. "That is normal. We're like sisters. We love each other, but sometimes we get short tempered."

"And someone gets their feelings hurt," Chaya throws in, pointing out the obvious.

"Afterward, we make up," Mazal reinforces, making light of the whole incident. Tokal walks up interrupting their conversation.

"Guard," Mazal purrs, gazing at Tokal. "Ziva doesn't want you. Why don't you *guard* me?"

"Or me." Chaya bats her eyes at Tokal.

Tokal looks at Mazal and Chaya while he chews his food, thinking of how to respond to the females showing their interest in him. When Tokal is done swallowing, he looks directly at Ziva, "Is this true?"

Surprised by their statements and his direct question, Ziva looks at Tokal and finds probing eyes that make her uncomfortable.

She drops her eyelids, masking her emotions, and sputters, "Before I found out who you are, I didn't want a guard. At this moment, I don't want you to leave."

Tokal nods, understanding her. "Can you introduce your friends?"

"I only met them yesterday."

"I know." Tokal smiles, encouraging her.

Ziva nods to Tokal before pointing to each girl. "This is Mazal, Tovah, Chaya, Frema, and Ami. I met Ami first."

Tokal looks at each girl as they're introduced.

"And you are?" Chaya inquires as she bats her eyes.

"Not of any importance." He smiles sweetly at Chaya's shocked face. Turning toward the women around the fire, he announces,

"Ladies, I'm under direct orders from our king and queen to protect Ziva and Khatoon. I cannot change it, nor will I waiver in that responsibility."

"Why did they assign you to her? A personal guard is very unusual, especially when she is so poor," Mazal loftily simpers.

Ziva cringes, feeling the insult in her words. Ami's eyes fly open, and Frema chokes on a bite of food. Chaya pounds on Frema's back, looking uncomfortable, while Tovah's face turns red.

"Mazal, why are you being so rude?" Ami scolds.

"I'm only asking because I want to know why Ziva has a guard and I don't," Mazal returns in a superior tone as she takes another bite of food.

Tokal looks at Mazal, shocked by her behavior, but determines to put her in her place. "My job is not to question the king—only to do. You will have to ask King Gilgal if you want an answer."

Mazal turns red knowing that she will never ask such an impertinent question of the king. Embarrassed, she turns her attention to her food.

Ami, in an effort to remove the discomfort by changing the subject, asks, "Ziva, what did you do today after you disappeared from the group?"

Ziva grins as she meets Tokal's eyes. "I went puddle jumping."

"Puddle jumping?" the group of new women, except Mazal, boom in unison.

"A game I've played since a child. When it rains, I jump over and into puddles." Ziva shrugs. "Puddle jumping is fun," she reveals before taking another bite of food.

"It sounds messy," Chaya responds, wrinkling her nose and motioning to Ziva's dirty clothes.

Ziva looks down, taking in her appearance, then returns her attention back to Chaya with a big, happy grin covering her face. "I guess puddle jumping is messy, but the rain helps wash away some of the dirt."

A heavy rain starts in earnest, and the women quickly end their meal and remove themselves to find cover or finish their chores, leaving the men to fend for themselves. Khatoon and Ziva are in the group in charge of water and cleanup. By the time they are done with the chores, they are drenched. Arriving at their tent, they quickly disrobe, hanging their wet clothing to dry during the night before snuggling under their blankets.

THEIR LEADER'S BANGING AND SHOUTING, startles them to start their day. After dressing into their slightly damp clothing, Khatoon and Ziva each grab a blanket to wrap around their shoulders before leaving the tent. The ground is muddier than last night. With careful steps, they make their way to the fire.

When they reach their destination, their leader announces their chores. Many groan, redirecting themselves to completing their assignment.

As Ziva makes a meal with Ami, the sun shines bright. The air smells fresh and clean after the rain, causing Ziva to soon be smiling. Ami still frowns as though something bothers her, until she finally speaks. "I'm sorry about Mazal."

"Don't be," Ziva returns. "She spoke the truth. I am very poor."

"Yes, but her words were thoughtless," Ami explains, frowning as she starts chopping up the dried fruit. "I hope she didn't hurt you. I like you, Ziva, and I didn't approve of Mazal's words."

Glancing at Ami's frowning face, Ziva sighs. "It hurt a little," Ziva admits.

Ami lifts her head, looking at Ziva.

"Ami, I could get mad, but what will it help? My mouth has no filter, and I say things that aren't appropriate. I can't get upset over her words when I struggle with the same problem. Even if I didn't struggle with this problem, how will getting mad resolve the issue? She made a mistake, and she understands that."

Understanding hits Ami and she nods. Feeling better, she smiles. "I guess she does." She turns her attention back to chopping before asking, "Where is your guard? I haven't seen him this morning."

"I haven't either, but with the bad weather last night, he had to find some place to sleep other than the ground in front of our tent door. We couldn't allow him in the tent with us, so I hope he found shelter for the night."

"It would not have been appropriate to allow him in your tent unless he is to be your husband." After a pause, Ami asks quietly, "Have you thought anymore about the Joining?"

Ziva looks at Ami for a moment. "No, I haven't." Taking a breath, she changes the subject. "Having my mother and him with me has been a great comfort. Getting to know you has also been nice. I never thought it possible to have friends my age. I mean . . . usually people only . . . tolerate me."

"Yesterday, you wanted nothing to do with him. What changed?"

Ziva chuckles. "That was before I figured out who he is."

Ami looks up from chopping. "Who is he?"

Ziva glances at Ami. "His name is Tokal, and he's an old family friend."

"How long have you known him?"

"I knew him when I was a small child, before my father's death. Being my only friend at the time, he looked out for me." Ziva smiles at the fond memories.

Ami mirrors her expression. "It sounds like he's still looking out for you."

"Yes," Ziva frowns, "but this time by order of the king."

Ziva continues her chopping. "I don't know why."

"Perhaps for you to get reacquainted." Finished with her slicing, Ami takes the dried chopped fruit and puts it in a bowl, moving the container to where it will be served. Ziva follows shortly thereafter with her contribution of chopped nuts.

Mazal interrupts Ami and Ziva as she delivers wood.

"Ziva, I'm . . . uh . . . sorry for what I said yesterday. I didn't mean it," she stammers. "I didn't think."

"Thank you, Mazal." Ziva gratefully smiles. "I appreciate it."

"I hope we can be friends," Mazal pleads.

Ziva nods, reassuring Mazal.

The women eat the morning meal around the fire pits. After their friends join them, Mazal humbly announces, "I'm sorry for how I acted yesterday toward Ziva. I apologized to her earlier."

"Good," Tovah responds, "because, if you hadn't, we would soon be speaking about it."

Their mothers arrive and sit nearby.

Tokal shows up a little later with a few of the other guards, all holding bowls. "These are some friends who would like to get to know you better. This is Tovar, Limhi, Nehor, and Antion."

The girls look to their mothers for approval.

Ami's mother, Segara, takes the lead. "Ladies, move back with us so the men can be closer to the fire and get warm." When everyone is situated, Segara continues, "We are grateful for you looking after our safety. Did you find cover last night?"

Nehor responds, "Thank you for your kindness. We have a tent that we used during the night."

"That's good," Khatoon replies before looking at the clear blue sky. "It looks like it will be a beautiful day."

The group of new women silently continue to eat next to their mothers.

The parents converse with the men. After a little while, Segara introduces their grinning daughters.

The interested men smile back, hoping to be granted more time with their offspring.

Boy-crazy Chaya gushes, "You're all so handsome. It will be difficult for us to choose." Mouths drop open and the men look at each other, not knowing how to respond.

Chaya's mother, red faced and glaring at her daughter, tries to smooth things over, "What my daughter is trying to say is . . . that she hopes to get to know you better."

"Uh, thank you," Nehor returns as the men grin and the rest grimace. A casual conversation starts between both parties, but when the women finish with their meal, they leave the men to complete theirs.

THE JOURNEY CONTINUES AS THEY trudge toward the mountain in the distance.

"The guards we met this morning are walking near us," Chaya hisses to the others before muttering, "I'm so embarrassed by what I said earlier."

Ami and Ziva look around, validating Chaya's first statement.

Frema and Tovah look at one another.

"You should be," Mazal fires back. "You can think it, but don't say it to them."

"What do we do?" Frema squeaks.

Mazal lifts her head a fraction and looks forward. "Act normal. If they speak to us, we respond."

"What if I don't know what to say?" Frema asks, concerned she may say something wrong.

"We will help each other. Agreed?" Ami reinforces, resulting in a quick response in the affirmative.

Tokal, who walks behind the mothers but is a head taller than the others, sees the commotion among the young women and notices where their eyes travel. The mothers see it too but remain silent. He sees the guards he introduced earlier move forward with two on each side of the group, preparing to merge with the young women; the mothers decrease their distance from their daughters. He smiles in anticipation of what will play out.

Nehor speaks first, "It seems that fate has brought us together today while we walk."

"So, it seems," Segara responds.

"Which one of these lovely girl's is yours?" Nehor asks, eyeing the young women.

"My daughter, Ami, walks in front of me."

"She is very beautiful," Nehor returns.

Ami blushes from the compliment.

"Mothers, do you mind if we converse with your daughters?"

"They are of age," Segara says.

Nehor nods his head, and the men move closer to the young women. Nehor falls into step with Ami, leaving Ziva without a man next to her.

Tokal quietly moves up, taking his place next to Ziva. "Do you feel left out, Ziva?" Tokal needles as he comes to her side.

She peers at Tokal from the corner of her eyes, surprised that he would even think that. "No. Why should I?"

"Because they're looking for wives, and you were not among those they chose," he pesters.

Ziva realizes he's trying to rattle her. She grins at him, not taking the bait. "That's because you're my guard, and they know better."

Tokal sheepishly grins. "You caught me." They walk together a few paces. "Last night, I needed a place to shelter, so I talked with them. They agreed I could stay in their tent if I would introduce them. I told them I would if they left you to me."

Ziva eyes him suspiciously. "And why did you say that?"

"Because they will not understand you." He takes a breath before continuing, "I didn't want you to get hurt."

Ziva startles at his response. "You're always protecting me. Why?"

Tokal leans over to Ziva and in a titillating low rumble reveals, "Because I hope you will accept me as your husband."

Ziva stops and stares at him, perplexed. He grabs her arm, prompting her to move again. She frowns and chokes out, "Is this why the king assigned you to me?"

"No," he shoots back.

The mixture of Ziva's emotions confuses her. On one hand, she's giddy, flattered that a man has noticed her, but she also feels awkward. The man is her childhood friend. Scared at the prospect of joining anyone, her eyes narrow and she demands, "Explain why the king assigned you as my guard."

Tokal looks at Ziva, realizing that he may have revealed his plan prematurely. Hiding his emotions behind a bland face, he offers, "I suspect it's because your father's killer hasn't been found. Truthfully, I don't know why I was assigned."

Confusion and anger win out as she struggles with a response. "We're more like brother and sister than husband and wife. I don't understand why you're stating this. We haven't seen each other in many years—"

"And now we can get to know one another again," Tokal finishes for her, touching her shoulder to get her to look at him before he continues. "I want to take care of you, Ziva, and your mother. Will you at least think about it?"

Ziva glares at him. "I'm angry that you dropped this on me when you know this is the last place I want to be. But I'm required to be here, so I am. I'm not ready to even think of choosing the Joining or the Challenge."

Tokal, pushing the subject, continues with his reasoning without paying attention to her words. "I always know where I stand with you and thought you would appreciate the same. When you settle down, think about it, Ziva, we would make a great match."

Before she can respond, Tokal falls back to speak with Khatoon, leaving Ziva to her anger.

During mealtime preparation, Ami works with Ziva chopping some potatoes and carrots.

Ziva uses excessive force on the vegetables.

Ami tentatively asks, "What's wrong, Ziva?"

Ziva doesn't look up but continues to chop. "I'm mad at Tokal."

"Why?"

Ziva's knife comes down forcefully with each word. "Because," she snaps, "he wants me to be his wife." She puts the knife down and takes a cleansing breath.

Ami touches her friend's arm, noticing Ziva's rapid blinking. "Don't you want to be his wife?"

Ziva looks at Ami with a firm jaw as she blinks her tears away. "I don't want to be anyone's wife. I want to go home. I have to be here, so I am—but I don't like the Journey, and I don't like people making choices for me. I'm tired of that."

Ami nods. "Have you told him?"

Understanding hits Ziva. "I've realized I don't want to be Joined," she mumbles, dazed. She looks up at Ami. "How many more days until we reach Arnac?"

Confused, Ami answers her question. "I think three more days."

"Good to know." Ziva smiles and mutters to herself, "Right now, I have to figure out what to do with Tokal." She picks up the knife and continues her task, but she no longer mutilates the potatoes.

That night, the group is tired. Chores are completed with little talking before the women head to their tents and quickly fall asleep. Before bed, Khatoon advises her daughter, pointing out the pros for Joining Tokal, but Ziva doesn't want to hear it.

"Mother, I'm tired. Can we talk about this some other time?" she pleads.

"Ziva, he is a good man who has always had your best interests in mind. Think about his offer."

She still has to figure out what to tell Tokal, so she's technically telling the truth when she answers, "I will, Mother. Please don't talk to me more about it tonight."

ZIVA DISCOVERS TOKAL AT THE front door again, sleeping. She frowns in the dark. Rather than waking him up to escape the tent, she does the cowardly thing and stays within, thinking about his proposal.

When their leader starts his morning cacophony of waking the camp, she waits until Tokal moves away before getting out of the tent and, ignoring him, heads directly to do her daily chores.

This day's chore is to help the men with the tents. She goes up to the first guard she sees. She doesn't know him but cheerfully says, "I'm to help take down the tents today. May I join you?"

Surprised, the man stops what he's doing and smiles at the brown-haired, pigtailed new woman in front of him with friendly dark-brown eyes. He looks around and sees neither Mother nor her ever-present guard nearby. "I'm Kish. Yes, you can join me."

"I'm Ziva. What do I need to do?"

"You can go inside the tent and pack everything up, then bring it outside."

Ziva, preparing to enter the tent, hears footsteps behind her.

"Hi Ziva, are you taking down tents?" Ami asks, finding her friend.

"Yes." Ziva smiles at Ami. "We're about to start."

"Great, I'll help." Ami tightly smiles back at Ziva and walks to her side.

"We will too," Khatoon and Segara forcefully state and, with frowns on their faces, they join the young women.

Kish moves cautiously away as the three pull Ziva their way.

Using terse sentences to communicate, the women quickly pack the inside of the tent. By the time they finish inside, Nehor and Tokal have joined the group, helping with the deconstruction.

When all tents have been taken down, everyone heads off to eat.

Ami pulls Ziva aside and seethes, "What were you doing going off by yourself? Did you know that man?"

Pulling Ami closer, Ziva whispers back, "No! I didn't want to talk with Tokal or my mother this morning, so I went about getting the chores done."

Shaking Ziva's arm, Ami fiercely orders under her breath, "Don't do that again by yourself. That could have ended badly for you—getting you a husband you may not like."

Ziva stops, looking at Ami with wide, innocent eyes. "What do you mean?"

Ami, surprised that Ziva doesn't know, pulls her further away before explaining, "If you were caught in the tent with him alone, it would be assumed that you had chosen him as your husband."

"Great!" Ziva wails bitterly. "What else don't I know?" Grateful, she looks at Ami and breathes, "Thank you."

Ami nods before they walk back to the cooking area, getting in line for bowls of food. "What about Nehor? He seems to be following you around."

"Yes." Ami smugly smiles. "But it doesn't bother me—my Joining is arranged."

Ziva frowns. "Does he know that?"

"Yes, but he still follows me." Ami takes a bowl that is handed to her, and both new women find a place around the fire to eat their food. Ami's face puckers. "Upon thinking about it further, both of us need to be careful."

The Journey continues as the young women walk together with their mothers following. Tokal remains a shadow behind Khatoon. Their journey within the landscape changes with the higher elevation, bringing them into a forest that provides some shade from the sun. Before long, the guards again mix with the young women.

Kish shows up next to Ziva. "Thank you for your help this morning."

"Hi, Kish," Ziva returns. Grabbing Ami's arm for support, she chitters, "Ami, this is Kish, in case you didn't get introduced this morning."

"Hello, Kish. Do you know Nehor?" Ami points to Nehor, who is on her other side.

"Yes, we've met," Kish responds.

"Our other friends are a little further away. Today is a beautiful day," Ami continues.

"Indeed, the day is." Tokal breaks into the conversation, walking closely behind Ziva. "Kish, what brings you to Ziva's side?"

Kish glances at Tokal and grins. "A chance to get to know her better."

"She is not available," Tokal informs Kish.

Ziva begins to push Ami away from both men before Tokal's statement hits her. Her head swivels to the men, surprised at Tokal's words, and her eyes narrow, glittering dangerously at Tokal. "I'm not available to either of you. But we can still be nice," she informs them before transferring her attention to Kish.

Kish, taking the hint, quickly disappears from view. Ziva glares at Tokal, who proudly walks next to her. "Go away. I don't want you next to me at this moment," she orders.

He disappears, becoming Khatoon's shadow again.

Ami takes strength in Ziva's words and, turning toward Nehor, quietly says, "Nehor, I think you need to leave as well."

When both men disappear from view, Ziva snaps to her friend, "I'm furious with him. How dare he limit who I talk with. I'm so glad that we're almost to Arnac."

Ami exhales. "It will be nice to be without the men for a while." They continue walking together, enjoying the silence.

After a time, Khatoon joins them. "Ami, can I talk with my daughter privately?"

"Of course," Ami returns, falling behind to walk with her mother.

Concern covers Khatoon's face. "What happened, Ziva?"

"Where's Tokal?" Ziva softly queries.

"Walking behind us," her mother whispers back.

Ziva looks over her shoulder to see Tokal closely shadowing.

"Go away and let me talk to my mother," she hollers at him.

"I'm only keeping you both safe," Tokal fires back, matching her volume.

"No, you're not," Ziva throws back. "You're not allowing me my space. Leave us!"

Tokal falls a few paces further behind them, allowing them some privacy to talk, and Ziva breathes a sigh of relief.

Khatoon, not liking the confrontation between the two and concerned about their welfare, frowns. "Tell me what's wrong."

"Tokal has changed." Ziva forcefully exhales. "Instead of allowing me space and opportunity to choose, he's making choices for me."

"Ziva, this morning's choice put you in harm of becoming someone's wife without even knowing them. You were lucky that Ami and the rest of us were able to get there quickly to prevent issues," Khatoon reprovingly reminds her daughter. Hugging her to take the bite out of her words, she warns, "Don't do that again."

"I understand, Mother," Ziva returns, accepting her mother's concern for her. "Ami spoke to me about it." Irritated with her ignorance, she asks, "What are the other things that I need to know to keep me from being Joined?"

Ziva's mother proceeds in educating her about the societal city rules she needs to follow that weren't required among the shepherds as a child; giving the example she was able to work with a shepherd without another woman being present. Ziva asks her questions, and her mother answers them. When that conversation ends, Ziva mutters, "But Tokal also won't allow another man to speak with me. His actions are like . . . he is threatened that . . . I'll like someone else."

Khatoon claps her hands together excitedly. "So, you do like Tokal?"

Ziva scoffs. "As a brother," she informs her mother, "but not for a husband." Ziva takes a breath. "I'm not ready for that."

Khatoon nods. "Why do you think he told you that he wants you for his wife?"

Ziva lips thin. "He said he was telling me so I would know where I stood with him."

Khatoon takes her daughter's arm as they continue their journey forward. "Does he want an answer immediately?"

Ziva shakes her head and begrudgingly reports, "He asked me to think about it."

Khatoon eyes her daughter. "Are you?"

Ziva frowns, but nods and says, "I am." She takes a breath again as her brows draw together and her lips flatten. She forcefully mutters, "But he needs to allow me to learn from my experiences."

Khatoon gently squeezes her daughter's arm affectionately. "I will talk with him."

"No," Ziva fiercely returns, turning her head toward her mother. Trying to soften the forcefulness of her response, she smiles. "His interference is my concern. I need to talk with him."

Her mother nods and squeezes her arm again as they continue to walk. The rest of the day is spent by her mother's side.

ZIVA FINDS TOKAL SLEEPING AT the tent door. This time, she wakes him up and they move silently to the edge of camp. Ziva tries to gather her feelings into words.

Before she can say anything, Tokal barks, "What were you thinking, going off by yourself yesterday morning?"

Her chin lifts at his words and any kindness in delivery is forgotten. "I was trying to get away from you."

"Me?" His eyes spring open before scrunching to suspicious slits. "Why?"

"Because you're being domineering—overprotective. I know you want me for your spouse, but I haven't chosen you," she throws back. "I don't want to be Joined with anyone at present."

She takes a breath and exhales slowly. "You must step back and allow me some freedom to make my own choices—to experience things." Poking him in the chest, she continues, "Even when it comes to talking with other men." She drops her hand to her chest. "I'm learning that I can't be afraid of others, and I need to speak up for myself. So," she says, punctuating the next words by poking his chest again, "I'm doing that." She turns and stomps a few steps away, trying to get her emotions under control before turning back to him. "Give me space and time, or the answer you want will not happen."

Tokal, surprised by her anger, rubs the sore spot where she poked him. He pauses a moment, digesting everything, and then answers, "I'll step back."

"Thank you," she sighs. Trying to repair the damage to their relationship she may have caused by her outburst; she looks at him. "You can still teach me things."

He grins, accepting her olive branch. "Good. Because you have much to learn," he teases.

Ziva's mouth drops open to retaliate, but at that moment their leader shouts, waking up those in camp.


THE NEXT COUPLE OF DAYS, Tokal and Ziva's conversation is limited—they barely talk to one another, keeping the subjects to pertinent matters.

"You need to learn how to trap animals for food," Tokal says one late afternoon after they've stopped for the night. "We will start right now." He walks away without waiting for her answer.

Irritated, she glares at him but follows him, greatly anticipating showing him what she knows. Over the years, the shepherds taught

Ziva how to use a sling and how to set traps for quarry like squirrels, fish, and other small rodents. She even knows how to skin an animal.

When he shows her how to tie knots, she listens politely.

When it's her turn, she quickly ties all the knots and sets them. Snickering, Ziva reveals, "The shepherds taught me how to catch game with snares and sling. I also know how to dress a kill." She looks at him seriously and reprimands him with, "All you had to do is ask and I would have told you. What I would like to learn is how to shoot an arrow."

His eyes widen in surprise at her skill, reprimand, and request. She's not the Ziva he knew. She's changed, even over these last few days. He seems to keep underestimating her. He shrugs his shoulders at her unconventional request. "I will be happy to show you how to shoot."

During the day, she still remains close to Khatoon and her friends, leaving Tokal to shadow them, which he doesn't like, but at least he can watch her. At the end of the day, after the chores are completed, he pulls Ziva away from the others, enticing her with archery. Her mother watches from a short distance away, smiling as Tokal instructs Ziva.

He stands close to her as he begins his teaching.

Ziva can smell his odious scent from the many days of travel, and she suspects he can smell her too, but she hopes she's not as repellent. She would so like to bathe. She's glad when he stands downwind from her.

Tokal doesn't reveal to Ziva how much he enjoys standing close to her. Doing so accomplishes his twofold goal: to encourage her to have more affection for him, and as a statement to others that she is his.

"Thank you for introducing this to me before we reach Arnac," Ziva supplies as Tokal standing behind her, improves her handling of the bow, and adjusts her aim. She holds the string carefully in her fingers, ready to shoot. His hand moves with a feather light touch from her shoulder to just under her elbow and slightly pushes upward, lifting her elbow to improve her form.

"After Arnac, we can continue if you would like," he whispers in Ziva's ear, alluding to something more.

Ziva doesn't hear the undertone of his message so focused as she is on learning the skill. "I would like that." Ziva smiles, releasing the bowstring. The arrow hits a tree in the distance, and Ziva, following the arrow's path, moves to retrieve it. Calling back to him over her shoulder, she asks, "So tomorrow we will be at the city?"

"Yes." He frowns as she walks away.

Ziva pulls out the arrow. "What is it like there?" she shouts as she returns, oblivious of Tokal's efforts.

He shrugs. "I've only seen the courtyard."

Ziva takes her position and fires the arrow again. "How many times have you been to Arnac already?" She walks forward to retrieve the arrow.

"Three times. We should be there by the midday meal."

Hauling the arrow from its target, Ziva turns and walks back to her starting point. "Good to know."

After some time watching her practice, Tokal announces, "The day is gone. Time for us to stop." He reaches out his hand, palm up, hoping for hers.

Ziva places the arrow and bow in it.

Tokal gathers up his equipment.

Ziva walks to her mother.

"Tokal says we're done. Are you ready to return?" Ziva asks Khatoon. Before long, Tokal is by their side as they travel back toward the fire where the group gathers for their last night together.

When they near the fire, they separate. Tokal leaves to put his equipment away, and Khatoon continues toward the fire.

Ziva stops in front of Ami, who stands nearby.

"Hi, Ziva. I'm happy to see you. Why is Tokal teaching you how to use a bow and arrow?"

Ziva shrugs. "I asked him to. I truly like it. I think it has become my second favorite thing to do."

Ami frowns and, in case Ziva doesn't know this information, whispers tentatively, "Archery is not a skill for women."

"I know, but I still enjoy the activity," Ziva returns brightly. Ami's eyes widen in surprise, but she chooses to change the subject. "Tomorrow, we'll be at Arnac."

"I'm excited to be done with traveling."

"So am I," Ziva returns. "We smell bad," she whispers.

She glances over to the others in the group that sit around the fire and notices Tovar, Limhi, Nehor, and Antion vying for attention. She points her chin toward the fire. "It seems like Tovah, Frema, Chaya, and Mazal are enjoying the company of the guards."

Ami follows Ziva's chin to her smiling friends. "It does look like it. I can't wait to see who gets whose necklace." Both new women giggle. "You seem pretty friendly with Tokal."

"He's only teaching me how to shoot," Ziva dismisses. "You stated that your husband has already been chosen. Do you know him?"

"Yes, I know him." Ami smiles adoringly and sighs, missing him. "He lives in the city near me. I've liked him since we were small.

I can't see myself with anyone else." She sighs contentedly, recalling her intended. "He's grown up into a very handsome man."

"I'm happy for you. I don't see myself with anyone."

Ami's head swivels toward Ziva as her eyes widen and her mouth drops open. "What about Tokal?" she whispers fiercely.

"I've wondered whether you would be the first to accept a necklace, considering how close he stood next to you during your lesson."

Ziva shakes her head, surprised by Ami's response and retorts, "He's just my friend. He's like a brother to me." She shrugs. "Nothing more."

Ami leans close to Ziva's ear and cautions, "I don't think he feels that you're his sister. He acts as though you're already his. And with him cuddled up behind you as he teaches you to shoot, it sure seems you're quite all right with it."

ALL NIGHT, AMI'S WORDS BOTHER Ziva as the conversation replays in her head, keeping her awake. She didn't think that Tokal would continue to pursue her, but according to Ami, he's doing so without Ziva understanding it. Frowning, she wonders what she needs to do to stop Tokal's advances and to stop the illusion that they are linked together. By morning, her anger is barely kept in check. When she tries to step outside the tent, she of course finds Tokal sleeping there. She kicks his legs, waking him up.

After he stands and moves away, she climbs out and extends to her full height, a head shorter than him, with her arms fisted at her side. Anger pours off her body as she forcefully informs him, not caring who is asleep, "I'm telling you that I will not be your wife." She shivers as the cool morning air kisses her skin. "If you continue to pursue me, I won't speak to you ever again." Ziva stalks away toward the only lit fire, leaving him standing there in stunned silence.

Khatoon climbs out of the tent and straightens in front of Tokal. "No one can sleep after that eruption. Let me go talk with her." She pats Tokal on the arm before wrapping the blanket she brought with her more tightly around her shoulders and heading toward Ziva, who has her arms wrapped around herself, staring into the fire.

Khatoon arrives at Ziva's side and silently waits for her to finish breaking, throwing, and stabbing the wood. "Ziva, why won't you join Tokal?"

"I'm not ready for any of that." Ziva breaks and tosses a stick into the fire.

"You don't need to decide right now. We'll be at Arnac soon. I hope that you can work through your issues." Her mother touches her shoulder. "He means well, Ziva, and will take good care of us."

Ziva sighs. "Yes, Mother, I know. But we first have to work through our issues, and right now, I don't want to be Joined."

THE GROUP EATS AND HEADS toward Arnac. Ziva walks beside Ami as they talk with one another. Ziva continues to ignore Tokal, causing him to frown at her.

A waterfall is seen in the distance as they go around a corner. Flowers dot the ground off the road, and green foliage of ferns and other flora fill in the gaps. A mixture of different trees results in a canopy. Birds sing in the distance, and the air smells fresh and clean, touched with the mist from the cascading liquid.

"The waterfall is so beautiful." Ami sighs, admiring the clear view of the cataract and the adjacent trees. She takes a deep breath, enjoying the splendor surrounding her.

Ziva's eyes narrow and she cocks her head as she asks, "I don't understand how you're so awed. The waterfall is only tumbling river on a large scale. Standing here in the shade with the cool, fragrant air is so much better."

Ami turns her head toward Ziva, looking at her strangely. "The waterfall adds to the picturesque scenery. You truly amaze me with your different viewpoints. This scenery is not something you see every day."

"You are correct," Ziva agrees, "but it doesn't matter. This scenery is only a waterfall and a bunch of trees. What makes it different are the smells and the feeling it gives."

"Well, I like it," Ami returns. "This scenery is something I will remember."

When they move forward again, Ziva and Ami walk through a tunnel made of walls lined with vertical timbers and reinforced with dirt. The tunnel opens to a courtyard containing two buildings on opposite ends and a building built into the far wall in front of them.

Once everyone is inside the courtyard, the gate is closed.

MONICA FLORES

# ARNAC

AFTER A LITTLE TIME, THEY notice a small group of women coming their way. Their traveling leader dismounts from his horse and moves forward a little bit, waiting for the women to arrive. He greets them by raising a hand.

An older woman bows slightly to him, speaking to the group at large. "Women of Uthal, welcome to Arnac. I am Calene. Follow us. Men, you will stay in the courtyard and follow your leader." The Arnac women turn, and the Uthal women fall in behind them, wondering what is going to happen next, while the men head to the opposite building on the other side of the courtyard.

Ziva, not sure what to make of this, grabs her mother's hand as they follow those in front of them. Her mother quickly squeezes her hand to reassure her. They stop near a building that contains animals. The Uthal horses brought to Arnac by the rich women are left here to be cared for. Once all animals have been removed from the group, the women continue through a door and into what looks to be a large building.

The Great Hall contains a spacious room with colorful murals on the walls, and the floors are covered with vibrant rugs around the perimeter. Many beautiful and ornately carved tables and benches are arranged in rows at the center of the room and cover the area. Between the tables stand vertical, carved floor sconces that hold oil and lit wicks, illuminating the tables and room around them. At the other end of the room is a row of perpendicular tables. While most have simple chairs, one table has three ornately carved chairs, making it the head table. Similar floor sconces on each end and between the tables stand lighting the area.

Ziva looks at her mother in surprise. "I've never seen anything like this, except in the palace. We are going to live here?"

"Yes, Ziva, we'll live in Arnac for a short time," Her mother answers.

Once all the women are in the hall, the door is closed. The leading women come to stand behind the ornate chairs at the head table.

Calene looks around at the group of Uthal women. "I am glad that all of you have arrived safely. Please take your seats in the chairs at this table, and we will feed you."

The Uthal women follow her instructions. Khatoon and Ziva wait for a minute before moving forward to take two of the remaining seats.

When everyone is seated, Calene continues. "After you eat, we will get you settled into Arnac. There will be a celebration dinner tonight where you will say goodbye to the men until the time to return to Uthal comes." As Calene sits and claps her hands once, platters of food are set on the table, and all begin helping themselves to the simple meal of succotash, a mixture of squash, corn, and beans.

When the tasty dish has been consumed, Calene stands. "Time to get you settled here at Arnac. Please follow me." Calene walks toward another door that is opened for her, and the women follow with wide-eyed anticipation of what will be seen next.

As Khatoon and Ziva walk through the doors, they find themselves in some sort of wide pathway between buildings. They follow those in front of them, turning several times where pathways intersect. They stop in front of a black rock face.

Calene stands on something that Ziva cannot see but that makes her visible to those in the back.

"The women of Arnac are here to serve you during your stay. You have the opportunity to learn many skills and enhance what you already know. If you need something, please ask. At this time, we will get you settled in your rooms."

KHATOON GENTLY TOUCHES ZIVA'S SHOULDER. "Wake up, Ziva. Time to prepare to go to the Great Hall."

Ziva blinks her eyes a few times and sits up. "I fell asleep!" she exclaims. "I've never taken a nap."

Mother chuckles and pats Ziva's shoulder. "Yes, you did. The nap is probably a good thing. Gather yourself together and take care of your needs. I'll wait for you in the main room."

A few minutes later, Ziva joins the others in the main room. She finds that by good fortune, Ami and Segara are also in the same building. Ami gives Ziva a delighted hug. "I am so glad that we share the same apartment. This is good."

"I'm happy as well. It makes me feel better to have you here," Ziva returns delightedly as they embrace.

Another mother and daughter are also in the room and stand quietly watching the greeting. Ami turns Ziva toward the new people. "Ziva, I think you may have met them before on our journey here, but in case you forgot, this is Shapash and Koki." Shapash' s brown eyes connect with Ziva's. She inclines her head when she is announced, causing her brown hair to spill forward. She raises a hand, pulling it back behind her shoulder. Koki, a younger version of her mother, does the same when her name is presented.

"You have green eyes," Ziva spits out, noticing the unusual color.

Koki smiles, relishing her gift.

"Yes, she does." Ami grins at Ziva's surprised words. "Isn't she beautiful?"

"She is." Khatoon interjects cutting off any response from Ziva. "I'm Khatoon, Ziva's mother. The opportunity to get to know you better is a good one."

Koki lowers her eyes, covering her embarrassment at being the center of attention.

Shapash smiles. "My daughter is indeed beautiful. Thank you, Ami and Khatoon." Turning to look at Ziva, she returns, "So, this is your daughter. Ziva, I'm happy to meet you."

Realizing her mistake during the introduction, Ziva inwardly cringes and outwardly smiles, trying to emulate Ami's friendly attitude. "Likewise."

Titchna, one of the women from Arnac, enters the room dressed in a colorful dress; she has a black braid down her back, and her friendly brown eyes greet the visitors. "Now that everyone is clean, settled, and knows who they room with, are you ready to go to the Great Hall for the feast?"

Segara looks at Titchna and nods. "Please lead the way."

The group follows Titchna out the door, mothers walking behind daughters. The new women continue to chatter with Ami walking in the middle.

"I like meeting new people," Ami starts the conversation.

"Koki, in what part of Uthal do you live?"

Koki looks at Ami, who smiles at her. "I live in the commerce district. Are you familiar with it?"

"I believe the district is near the market, which is near the Stand?"

"That's right," Koki returns. "My father is a merchant."

"What does he sell?" Ami asks.

"He travels to the Nephites and brings back different kinds of Nephite cloth, including their fine linen," Koki returns proudly. "We also create our own cloth."

"Oh, I bet seeing what your father brings back from the Nephites is so much fun." Ami trills excitedly, "Ziva, have you ever been to the market?"

"A long time ago as a child," Ziva answers.

Ami, hearing the sorrow in Ziva's voice, peers at Ziva. "I'm sorry, Ziva. I didn't mean to bring up bad memories."

"It happened a long time ago," Ziva returns. "I just miss him."

"But the wound you carry still has not completely healed." Ami squeezes her friend's hand in comfort.

They enter the Great Hall and follow Titchna as she leads them to the main table so they can find a seat. Once her group is settled, Titchna takes her seat at one of the other tables.

Soon, Tovah, Frema, Chaya, and Mazal join them around the table, all wearing simple white dresses similar to the clothing of everyone else from Uthal. They talk excitedly among themselves, each describing their rooms and who shares their building with them. Gradually, the hall fills with women.

People begin to notice Calene standing behind her chair at the main table, dressed in a white dress with brightly colored embroidered birds. The room quiets and Calene claps her hands twice.

The doors to the courtyard are opened, and the men enter the Great Hall, heading to the main table where they are seated. When the men are settled and silence is restored, Calene speaks. "Men of Uthal, thank you for bringing these women safely to Arnac. Tonight, we celebrate your arrival. Women, tonight will be the last night you will see these men until the time comes to return to Uthal. Tomorrow morning will be an orientation to Arnac before lessons will commence." She claps her hands once and upbeat music of drums, rattles, whistles, and flutes begins while platters of food are brought forward and set on the tables. Conversation resumes as food is served and eaten.

The group enjoys the savory dishes of venison, squash, potatoes, and carrots along with a supply of flat bread made of corn. The men, when they are done eating, interact with the women around the room. Soon, a group of men stand around their table, some on each side, where Ami, Ziva, Tovah, Chaya, Frema, and Mazal are seated.

Noticing the men, Segara finishes what is in her mouth before introducing them to the new women. "Shapash and Koki, these are Tokal, Kish, Tovar, Limhi, Nehor, and Antion," she says pointing to each in turn as they are introduced.

As conversation among the group resumes, Kish bends down and talks in Ziva's ear. "May I speak with you?" Ziva looks up at the man, surprised he's speaking just to her.

Tokal protectively intercedes. "Why do you want to speak with Ziva?"

"That is between the two of us." Kish counters, causing Tokal to glare at him. Kish returns Tokal's dislike.

"My order from the king is to protect Ziva," Tokal returns.

"But not to control my life," Ziva interjects, glaring at Tokal.

Khatoon puts down her spoon and looks at both young men. "Ziva, go and speak with Kish, but remain where I can see you. Tokal, you will stay here."

Tokal glares at the man but nods his head toward Khatoon.

Ziva, surprised by her mother's words, looks up at Tokal and Kish and takes in their countenance. "You're both angry at each other because of me. I don't know what caused this, but it must stop," she informs them. Turning to Kish, she says, "I will go and speak with you." Ziva gets up from the table and leads the way to a side of the room where she can still be seen by her mother. Folding her arms, she turns to face Kish.

"Why are you angry with Tokal?"

"Because I want to speak with you without interruption."

Ziva takes a breath. "Why do you want to speak with me?"

"Isn't it obvious?" Kish looks in Ziva's eyes. "I want to get to know you better."

Ziva, held by his eyes, asks, "Why?"

Kish takes a step closer and leans toward her ear. "Because you're so beautiful."

Ziva's head pulls away from him, and she takes a step back. Shaking her head, she says, "I don't care about that or believe those words."

"You are beautiful," Kish steps toward her again. "Why don't you believe it?"

She shakes her head again and laughs. "I know that I'm average compared to others. Nonetheless, if that is all you have to say, this conversation is done."

"I like the way you talk." He stops her from turning away. "You state what you feel."

"Yes," she frowns, "and that hasn't served me well in the past."

Kish grins at her response. "A man knows where he stands with you."

Ziva stands there, chewing on her lip for a moment, and tilts her head. "You're here because the king has given me a guard, which is unusual, and out of curiosity you want to find out why. Let me save you some time. I'm only an ordinary girl who has no material possessions worth bothering about. My life is simple, and I want to keep it that way. I'm not interested in Joining any man at this time and that includes Tokal."

"I appreciate your honesty. Your assessment is correct that I started to get to know you better out of curiosity. Would it be possible enjoying each other's company without a goal?"

"How?" I won't see you for several months."

Kish smiles at her. "When we travel back to Uthal, I would like to spend time with you and get to know you and your mother better."

Ziva turns her head toward the man, really looking at him. He hasn't gotten upset with her words but has acknowledged them. She decides she likes him. She nods. "I can do that." She grins at him.

He reciprocates. "We still have tonight where we can talk."

She nods her head in acknowledgement, and they head back to the table to join the others.

Tokal glowers at Kish, who smugly smiles at him.

Ami brings the newcomer into the conversation. "Kish, what did Ziva and you talk about?"

Kish looks at Ziva before turning back to Ami. "We talked about getting to know one another better." Ami is surprised and looks at Ziva, who confirms it with a small nod.

Ami turns her attention back to Kish. "How long have you been in service?"

"Seven years."

"That long?"

Kish nods his head and smiles.

Mazal, hearing the conversation, asks, "How many times have you been to Arnac?"

"This is my first time," Kish takes a breath. "This is the best assignment because of you ladies."

A chorus of assent is heard around the table from the men while the young women shine.

The mothers stand to take a walk around the perimeter.

Chaya mischievously grins and asks the men, "What do the men's lodgings look like?"

Mazal turns red from her friend's words. "Chaya, that is not something to ask."

"I agree with Mazal." Tovah frowns.

"I want to know," Ami innocently returns, surprising the women. "How are your accommodations?"

"We have a place to lay our heads up in the loft of the building," Nehor returns. "It smells of animals and hay."

Kish pipes in, "Our accommodations are fine. I've slept in worse."

"So have I," Antion affirms. "They will serve us well while we are at Arnac."

"How is your housing?" Tovar asks with humor sparking his eyes.

"It is clean and nice," Ami returns, shooting Chaya a warning look.

"Our building is the nicest house I can ever recall seeing," Ziva adds.

The conversation continues around the table as the men compete for attention while the mothers listen and watch their daughters. Finally, Calene concludes the festivities, inviting the men to depart. The hall doors are closed behind them, and the women are taken back to their rooms to sleep.

THE NEXT MORNING ARRIVES WITH Titchna waking up her guests and informing them that their meal awaits them in the main room.

After quickly dressing in the clothes provided, the Uthal visitors enter, seeing a table laden with food. Six women sit and eat.

"All of us have the same color dress." Ziva states the obvious. "I wonder why?"

Khatoon scratches her head. "If I recall correctly, the dress color determines what class we are assigned."

"I think you're right," Segara recalls, and Shapash nods in agreement.

"I don't look good in yellow," Koki announces, frowning at the bright yellow dress she's wearing.

"No man will see you in it." Shapash pats her daughter's hand as she continues to eat.

Once they have finished their meal and their hands and faces have been cleaned, Titchna leads the way to the hall, orienting them to the city and how to move within it. When they arrive at the building, they again take their seats, noticing seven different colors of dresses among the women.

"We are defined by color," Ziva observes.

"I wonder what our class will be," Ami returns.

Khatoon sighs. "If we listen, we will soon find out."

Calene greets them in the Great Hall. Once everyone has arrived and is seated according to color of dress, Calene raises a hand.

When the room is quiet, she begins. "Women, today your lessons start. As you have already noticed, you are seated according to color of dress. This classification will help you identify those that can help you as well as what you will be learning. The women in multi-colored dresses are the women of Arnac, who serve as your guides. If your dress is blue, you will learn basics in the art of healing. Those in brown will learn how to keep a garden to enhance their tables. A yellow dress means you will learn womanly skills to help you attract husbands. Those in red will learn cooking skills to enhance their meals. The women dressed in orange will learn decorating skills to brighten their homes. Finally, if your dress is green, you will learn how to weave and sew to keep your family clothed. Each class will last seven days before it changes.

Once the rotation is complete and you have participated in all the classes, your assignment will change daily until your time at Arnac is done. Your class leaders, although they are dressed in many colors, have a sash the same color as your dress. Follow them and they will take you to start your education."

Once this announcement is made, the leaders of each group gather their students and leave the Great Hall, followed by others from Arnac who will help them.

The Great Hall is left with Calene and a small group of women around her. She smiles and says, "The day has started out well. Keep me informed of their progress." She nods dismissing the remainder.

As the women in yellow follow their teacher, landmarks are pointed out to them, orienting them to the Great Hall and where they are heading. They arrive at a smaller building and enter, finding several tables. Each student finds a seat. One leader stands at the front of the room and explains, "Here, you will learn how to create and do things that will make your body presentable to a man. Today, you will learn different braiding styles, which can be practiced on a daily basis. I need mother and daughter volunteers." After looking around the room, she picks two volunteers; they come to the front of the class, and the lesson begins.

"I don't need to learn this. I'm fine the way I am," Ziva mutters to her mother but is loud enough for the class to hear.

Khatoon, embarrassed by her daughter's outburst, glares at her and loudly reprimands, "While we are here in Arnac, you will learn whatever is being taught, and you will learn it well."

Ziva turns red, realizing why she's being openly chastised.

Khatoon turns to the teacher nodding. "Please continue."

Ziva, discomfited, doesn't look up, but the comments of the students around her, bring her attention into the lesson.

Before long, her mother smiles at her, approving of her positive participation even though she remains quiet.

One night, after the light is blown out, Ziva breaks the silence, stating, "Mother, when we get back to Uthal, I think I'm going to choose the Challenge. I don't want to be Joined, and I'm definitely not ready for that."

"Why don't you want to Join Tokal?" Khatoon's surprise cuts through the darkness.

"He's like my brother," she appallingly counters. A pause occurs as Ziva gathers her thoughts. "In the class, there has been talk about romantic feelings and love from several of the others.

I love Tokal, but I don't have romantic feelings for him. I'm not going to kiss him or get all mushy inside."

"Sometimes, feelings change over time Ziva," Khatoon explains from her bed.

"Sometimes, they don't!" Ziva fires back. "I prefer to take the Challenge, returning home to dwell with you. After a year it will be over, and I can do what I want and be what I want to be."

Khatoon frowns in the darkness and sighs. "What do you want to do, Ziva?"

"I definitely don't want to be forced to Join someone. I want to remain with you."

"In all actuality Ziva, I suspect that whomever you Join, will take me with you if you ask. Having a widow stay in the home of a daughter or son is quite common. Time passes and children must grow up. You must grow up. While you're here in Arnac, spend this time finding out who you are and what you would like in your life. I won't be around forever but hope to be around to see you settled and have your own children to tend." Khatoon tiredly explains, "You don't have to choose at present. When we do return to Uthal, if you choose the Joining, you'll still have a year available to you before a decision is required."

Ziva yawns. "Perhaps you're right."

EACH DAY, ANOTHER COMPONENT OF the class is taught, and by the end of seven days everyone in their group is ready for a change.

"I'm tired of wearing yellow." Koki frowns, sitting down at the table in the main room.

"So am I," Ziva acknowledges, joining her. "On the bright side, at least we're not traveling," she quips. "I haven't learned anything that I would use in everyday life. I have no need of fancy hairstyles or fragrant oils."

"I have," Ami pipes in. "I'm grateful for what has been taught."

"You already know who you're Joining. Why would you need to know this?" Ziva counters.

"I may get tired of the same hairstyle and want something different. I may have a daughter one day that will like something special in her hair. I may have occasion where one style would be better than another." Ami sniffs.

"I learned a lot as well," Koki agrees nodding. "Ami's reasoning is sound. Knowing how to style your hair is important for what you want to accomplish. You don't need to have the same braid daily. It adds variety to your life. The fragrant oils may help me attract a spouse."

"Or keep him interested afterward." Ami looks at Koki and they both giggle.

Ziva stubbornly crosses her arms. "I don't care about any of that."

"One day, Ziva, someone or something is going to happen where you will be thankful for the things that you have learned during this class," Ami reprimands. "You'll see."

Koki looks down and, seeing the yellow dress, mutters, "I'm so glad I don't have to wear this color anymore."

THE NEXT COLOR THEY ARE assigned to wear is brown. On the way to the first class, the group talks as they follow the leader to the garden area.

"I like gardening," Ziva announces to her friends.

"I don't," Ami returns. "Back home we have servants for that."

"I don't like getting dirt under my nails," Koki reveals, frowning.

"Knowing how to grow your own food is something good to know," Ziva enthusiastically emphasizes.

At the garden area, they are brought to stand in front of a woman. "Good morning. My name is Kanti. I arrived in Arnac two years ago and love working in the garden. For the next seven days, you will learn about light, water, soil, plants, and irrigation."

Ziva takes it all in, enjoying each day of the class and the work she gets to do within the garden. It makes her feel happy and that she has accomplished something useful.

On their last day of gardening class, they find they have a little time to sit and talk under a tree in front of a pool of water.

"I have so enjoyed this class," Ziva declares.

"I have learned some things, but I still don't like getting dirt under my fingernails," Koki returns.

Ami grimaces as she looks at her hands and moans. "I'm so glad a man doesn't have to see my hands and nails at this moment. They look so ugly." She shudders, shaking off her negative thoughts. "There has been a lot of information, but I prefer to eat the food than grow it. The only thing that has made this course worthwhile is the beauty of the garden. I will take the information back with me to incorporate in my home, but I won't be doing the work." She sighs. "This place is peaceful."

THEY FIND THEMSELVES FOLLOWING TITCHNA to a new area, wearing the dress color orange. They chat as they walk.

Ziva's brows furrow. "What is this next class?"

"I believe the class is decorating," Koki recalls.

"This, I think, will be my favorite course." Ami smiles. She enthusiastically sings, "I love decorating."

Bewildered as to the need for such a class, Ziva mutters, "Why do we need to decorate? Isn't having a clean house enough?"

Koki rolls her eyes, quite familiar by now with Ziva's blunt speech. "Having a clean house is not enough," she explains.

"It must also be inviting and comfortable to your family."

"Ziva, your father worked with jewelry, right?" Ami asks.

"Yes."

"Did he make a living with it?" Ami continues probing.

"Yes, he's still considered the best in the city," Ziva proudly says.

"Why is he still considered the best?" Ami eyes Ziva.

"Because he created beautiful jewelry that people wanted." Ziva thinks about what she voiced.

Koki and Ami glance her way, waiting for some comprehension.

Finally, Ziva's eyes light up. "So, learning these skills *is* important."

"Yes, for many different reasons." Ami smiles at Ziva approvingly. "Keeping a house clean is one thing, but decorating can make it a home, like the differences between our bracelets."

They enthusiastically join the class. Each day, a project is presented—painting, pottery, jewelry, or rug making. Two days are set aside for finishing projects already underway. At the end of their instruction, they admire their completed projects around the table.

"Ami, you're the best painter," Ziva informs those at the table.

"Koki, I like the colors and patterns in your rug," Ami declares, caressing one of the dark-green geometric turtle patterns contained within. "If your rug is for sale, I will buy it."

"Are you being truthful?" Koki, surprised by the compliment, looks at Ami.

"Yes, I am," Ami confirms, smiling at her friend.

"Thank you," Koki returns with gratitude shining in her eyes, "but the rug is not for sale." She looks at her pottery project and frowns. With great feeling, she informs the group, "I don't like working with pottery. I can do this, but I truly dislike clay."

The new women laugh, recalling her dislike for dirt under her nails.

Ami picks up the simple bracelet that Ziva made, examining the workmanship. "You seem quite at home with the carving tools."

"I used to help my father work." She smiles at the treasured memory before frowning, missing him.

"It shows. This is beautiful. I would buy the bracelet, if you had it for sale," Ami informs Ziva before looking up and seeing Ziva's somber face. Ami, concerned for her friend's well-being, laments, "Ziva, I'm sorry. Did making the jewelry bring back painful memories?"

"Not painful memories, but memories that make me miss my father," Ziva shares. Pulling herself from her gloomy feelings, she smiles. "I learned that my mother knows a lot about jewelry as well, but I've never seen her work on something until this class, when she shared her knowledge with me." As an afterthought while thinking about her mother, she murmurs, "Perhaps making jewelry is too painful for her, so she prefers not to do it."

"Maybe. You need to talk with her about it," Koki empathetically offers.

"Maybe." Ziva frowns.

Koki's words continue to sit in the back of Ziva's mind.

When the lights are out, she can't sleep, so she finally speaks to her mother. Breaking the silence, Ziva cautiously asks, "Mother, did making the jewelry with me make you sad?"

Ziva hears some shuffling in the dark as her mother comes and sits on the edge of her bed. Khatoon finds her daughter's hand and holds it. "Before you were born, I would sit with your father in his workshop helping him. He taught me how to do many things. This class has been bittersweet for me. I got to remember those times with him, which makes me miss him even more. I know that his absence saddens your heart as well. Remember, you're not at fault for what happened to him." Khatoon squeezes Ziva's hand affectionately. "This class has also been sweet because I got to share his knowledge with you. I want you to know that this time with you has been precious to me, especially with our shared memories of him. Remember, my daughter, you are our pearl of great price. You are our treasure, and we both love you deeply." She squeezes her daughter's hand again. Taking a deep, cleansing breath before she continues, she says, "One day, we'll be reunited with him."

A tear rolls down Ziva's cheek in the dark. "I miss him so much."

A heavy sigh is heard. "So do I."

"Do you think you'll make jewelry again?" Ziva inquires.

Khatoon laughs. "I don't have the skill that your father had in designing jewelry, but I believe that you may."

Letting her daughter's hand go, she affectionately orders, "Get some sleep, because tomorrow brings something new to learn." Getting up, she returns to her bed.

After Khatoon has settled herself, she hears, "I love you, Mother." She smiles and says, "I love you, too," before closing her eyes.

ARRAYED IN BLUE, EVERYONE MEETS around the table the following morning to eat and talk about their new class.

"Does anyone recall what blue means?" Khatoon asks.

Blank faces stare back at her. Segara looks up at Titchna, who places a pitcher of water on the table. "Titchna, what does blue represent?"

"For the next seven days, you'll be learning the art of healing. These skills will allow you to care for your family during illness without having to go to the infirmary."

"Thank you, Titchna." Turning to the table, Segara says, "Healing is an important skill."

Titchna smiles and moves away to allow her visitors to eat.

When the women are done eating, Titchna leads the group to another room near the garden. Inside they sit, ready to hear from their new teacher. She begins with, "Every person gets sick or hurt at one time or another in their life. For this class you will learn basic healing skills to care for yourself or others."

At the end of class, they walk back to their room without a guide, now knowing the layout of the city. "I am tired. Too much information given in a short amount of time." Ami groans feeling overwhelmed. "Mother, how am I to learn all of this?"

Segara puts an arm around her daughter reassuringly. "I agree the class gives a lot of information. Learn what you can. Your spouse will provide you with a comfortable home. If someone is sick, you can always send for a person from the infirmary to help."

Shapash, a quiet observant woman, feels the need to speak up. "Even though you can afford to have someone come from the infirmary, it does help knowing when to be concerned and when the illness is something that will pass with time. Another reason to know this information is so that a loved one is not poisoned if someone uses the wrong herbs."

"Poisoned?" is heard all around.

"It didn't happen to me, but I've heard of it happening," Shapash reports.

Khatoon, seeing the glare from Segara to Shapash, tries to help soothe ruffled feelings. "New women, do your best and learn what you can. You have mothers and other friends who are willing to assist should a question of health and well-being come to you, and as a last resort, the infirmary or a person from the infirmary is available. Healing will not be denied a person."

By the end of the class, the six of them feel overloaded with information. They sit around the table in the main room.

"I don't think my brain can handle any more," Ziva reveals rubbing her forehead.

"We have a different class tomorrow. I'm ready for a change. I can't do another day of this." Ami puts her head on the table.

"This healing class had a faster pace than any class I've ever had at school or any instruction we've had thus far during our stay."

"I agree with you. I'm glad that healing is over," Koki gratefully returns, propping her chin in her hands. "How long have we been at Arnac?"

"Over one moon," Khatoon answers. "New women, you have a little time before dinner, why don't you go lie down and rest if you need to, or you can go outside and find something to do to make yourselves feel better."

"I'm going to lie down," Ami quickly announces.

"Me too." Koki yawns as she gets up from the table.

Ziva, seeing her friends desert her for their beds, decides to go outside and explore. She starts to wander through the streets of the city. Women in different-colored dresses smile at her as she walks by. Eventually, she finds herself in the garden and walks toward the weeping willow tree near the pool of water to sit beneath it.

She deeply breathes in the fresh fragrant air and relaxes in the solitude this place provides.

After some time, she finds that a woman in dirty traveling clothes is sitting near her, with a sword strapped to her back and a quiver of arrows lying on the grass next to a bow. She looks up at the woman's face and finds bright blue eyes and a welcoming smile.

"I don't mean to intrude upon you, but this is my favorite place to sit as well." The blue-eyed woman smiles. "Do you mind if I sit for a time? I returned from a hunting trip and would like a moment to sit before cleaning up."

Ziva dons the "Ami" response without thinking. "Hi, I'm Ziva and I'm from Uthal." Her eyes widen and she frowns for a moment before shaking her head and grinning.

"I see that." A finger points to Ziva's clothes. "I'm Loyola. Why did you frown and shake your head?"

"Oh. Sorry about that." Ziva self-consciously laughs. "I've been practicing being friendly, and I realized my friend Ami is rubbing off on me. I don't even have to think about it anymore. You see, I'm not normally outgoing and my greeting at present was abnormal for me." She shrugs. "Perhaps the change is from being in Arnac or the fact that Ami is staying in the same building as me or the fact that I've been trying to be more like her."

"The greeting is friendly," Loyola returns, complimenting her efforts. "How did you like your healing class?"

"Too much information in too short a span of time. I tried my best to retain it all, but . . ." Ziva shrugs her shoulders.

Loyola frowns. "What are the other classes you have already completed?"

"Let's see . . ." Ziva looks up trying to recall the other classes. "I liked gardening the best. Decorating skills made me happy, and I learned why I need to know them." Ziva grins before scrunching her forehead. "Womanly skills escape me, although I've been told multiple times that I need them too." Ziva smirks. "Guess we'll see what happens."

Loyola laughs at Ziva's speech. "That's a very direct answer."

"Are you laughing at me?" Ziva frowns.

"No, Ziva. Not at all. When I ask someone about a class, I usually get very little information from them: 'The class is fine' or 'The class is all right.' I'm delighted to hear so much more than that," Loyola explains, grinning.

"Oh." Ziva digests her response. "Do you like being at Arnac?"

"Yes, I do." Loyola smiles again. "I'm lucky, though, that my aunt is here."

Ziva blurts out, "Who's your aunt?"

"Calene."

Ziva's eyes widen. "The woman in charge?"

Loyola nods, unable to contain the smile that spreads across her face. Ziva is quiet as she thinks, a puzzled expression on her face. "What brought you to Arnac?"

"I have an arranged Joining. My future husband has recently postponed it, for some reason, requiring me to take the Challenge. My brother brought me here so that I can help my aunt. At present, I . . . wait." Loyola sighs.

"Do you know how to fight?" Awed, Ziva gestures toward the weaponry.

Loyola's eyes sparkle, delighted to meet Ziva. "Yes, my father taught me," she explains. "He teaches all his children."

Ziva sits back and blinks, impressed. "Wow!" Her voice, deeper at first, continues to climb. "I thought women are not supposed to know how to fight."

Loyola chuckles. "Most women don't know how to defend themselves, but the skill is a good one to have."

"I know how to use a sling since I work with the sheep back in Uthal. I also know how to set traps to obtain food," Ziva blurts out.

Loyola smiles. "Those are good skills to have."

"The day before we arrived in Arnac, I had my first archery lesson. I learned how to hold a bow and arrow, though I still can't shoot very well."

"Who showed you how to shoot?"

"One of the guards showed me."

"He must be interested in you to spend time teaching you."

Ziva frowns and forcibly returns, "Well, I'm not interested in joining him." Catching herself, she takes a breath, explaining further. "He's more like a brother to me."

Loyola's eyes widen for a moment and her forehead crinkles.

"Why did you accept learning from him?"

Ziva shrugs. "Archery intrigued me, so I wanted to learn."

"With practice, you'll get better."

Ziva looks away, out toward the waterfall. "Except I don't have a bow and arrows nor the means for purchasing one."

Loyola, understanding her, nods. "Would you like to learn that skill while you are here in Arnac?"

Surprised, Ziva's face swivels back toward Loyola. "It would be wonderful to learn before returning to Uthal. Would you be willing to teach me?"

"Why do you want to learn?"

"Because . . . I like it. If it helps, I'm also planning to go on the Challenge. I understand such a skill is necessary to survive."

Loyola searches Ziva's face before deciding. "I will teach you, but it will have to be after your classes. Are you willing?"

Ziva excitedly punches the air. "Yes!" Turning to look at Loyola again, she says, "Tell me when and where, and I will be there."

"Follow me." Loyola gets up, gathers her gear, and starts walking.

Ziva jumps up and hurries to catch up. Before long, they arrive at a tree. "Do you know where you are?"

"Yes, I think I can find my way here. When are we to meet?"

"Meet me daily, after your last class, and I will teach you. We will begin tomorrow."

"Thank you, Loyola. This means a lot to me. See you tomorrow." Ziva smiles at Loyola one last time before she skips away.

The new class starts with red-colored dresses showing up in their room for them to wear. Taking the one that will fit her best, Ziva puts it on and passes the other dress to her mother.

"Ziva, do you recall what red stands for? What will be our class for the next seven days?"

"I don't recall, but I'm glad it's different. Healing had way too much information in it." Ziva sits down to comb out her hair. "I'm sure that Titchna will be able to tell us what we will be taught."

"Let me braid your hair before you help me with mine," Khatoon says, sitting behind her daughter.

Ziva passes the comb to Khatoon. "After practice today, I'm going to meet Loyola, to learn how to use bow and arrow. I'll be back in time for dinner."

Intrigued by this new information, Khatoon asks, "Who's Loyola?"

"Yesterday, when I went walking, I met Loyola—her aunt is Calene," Ziva excitedly chitters. "She lives here in the city, and we got to talking. Her father taught her to defend herself. I like shooting arrows, so I told her about Tokal starting to show me. She offered to teach me, which resulted in a plan to meet after class but before dinner so I can learn."

"I'm very happy that you're making more friends. If that is what you wish to do, I'll not stop you." Khatoon finishes Ziva's braids and gently tugs on the end, letting her daughter know she's finished.

Ziva jumps up and gives a grateful hug. "Thank you, Mother. My turn to do your hair." She grabs the offered comb, plops on the bed behind her mother and starts combing her hair. "We've been at Arnac for at least two moons, and I love being here. I feel . . . safe."

"I'm glad that you feel safe, Ziva, but Arnac is only temporary. We'll have to leave this place soon and return to Uthal. When that time comes, I hope you will take the things you've learned here with you."

"I will." Ziva finishes combing her mother's hair and starts braiding it.

After styling her mother's hair, both Ziva and Khatoon enter the main room to eat. Titchna greets them as they sit at the table.

"Good morning, Titchna. Thank you for the food. What will we be learning today?" Khatoon asks.

"Cooking." Titchna sets a pitcher of water on the table. "Every woman needs to know at least the basics of cooking."

"And if she already knows how to cook?" Khatoon inquires.

"The opportunity to learn more will be available, and you can share your knowledge with your daughter." Titchna smiles at Khatoon and Ziva.

When everyone is done eating, Titchna leads them to the kitchen.

This learning is very different from the other programs. In this class, Ziva and the other women are expected to complete errands that give them hands on experience. Ami and Koki have never had to build a fire, so it takes them a bit longer to be able to move on.

Ziva and Khatoon quickly show their expertise and progress to the next task of boiling water.

Their teacher finishes the first day of class by separating the students into three different groups based on skill level—beginner, intermediate, and advanced—before allowing everyone to meet their new teachers. Ami and Koki are in the beginning class with their mothers. Only a handful of students make it to the advanced class. Ziva and Khatoon are placed into the intermediate level, which is the largest group and contains the most instructors.

"Tomorrow morning, you will all meet here in your respective groups, where we will continue your education. Everyone is dismissed for the day," the primary instructor announces.

In a quick movement, Ami stops Ziva as she turns to leave. "Where are you going, Ziva?"

"I'm going to another class."

Hearing about this for the first time, Ami scoffs. "Why would you want to go to another class when we can go back to our room and talk?"

"Because I've been offered a chance to learn something I'm interested in."

"What is that?"

"How to shoot a bow and arrow." Ziva grins.

Irritated that Ziva is going to actually pursue this, Ami sniffs. "Are you sure you want to do this?"

Ziva nods her head.

"That is not a skill that a woman should know," Ami scolds, trying to inform her friend again.

Hearing the condemnation from Ami, Ziva raises her chin and stubbornly replies, "I want to learn it, so I'm going to. See you at dinner." Ziva stalks away, not listening to another word from Ami.

A very excited Ziva arrives at the appointed place to begin her class, but she finds herself alone and wonders if Loyola forgot about her. She paces for a while before finally sitting and leaning her back against the trunk. Closing her eyes, she reprimands herself.

"Hi Ziva, are you ready to learn?" Ziva's eyes fly open to see two bows and a basket containing arrows. She raises her eyes to Loyola's face, seeing her instructor smiling at her.

"Yes." Ziva jumps up. "I've been excited all day for this lesson. I thought you may have forgotten about it."

"I can see your enthusiasm." Loyola chuckles. "I didn't forget, but it took me a little longer to get here." Ziva follows Loyola as she walks to the archery court. "Let's start off by you showing me what you already know."

Ziva takes a bow and an arrow and positions herself perpendicular to the target next to Loyola. She nocks the shaft and raises it toward its destination, simultaneously exhaling as she releases the dart. The missile misses the pole but hits the fence behind it. After walking to the barrier, she pulls the barb from it before returning to Loyola.

"That is a good start. Try again and I will give you some pointers. This time, stand and aim but don't shoot."

Ziva returns to where she is to shoot from and positions herself.

"Widen your stance. Good. Raise your elbow. Stop. Perfect. Take a breath, and always remember: when you exhale, release the arrow."

Ziva takes aim and inhales. When she exhales, the arrow launches forward, nicking the pole and hitting the wood fence beyond. Ziva frowns.

"That is better, but it will take practice. Ready to try again?"

Ziva starts walking toward the fence to pull the arrow.

"Ziva, come back. We have lots of arrows. Let's shoot a few arrows and gather them afterward."

"Oh." Ziva turns, returning to Loyola's side.

"Try again." Loyola hands her another arrow before moving back a few feet to watch.

The arrow sails through the air and lands in the fence. Ziva picks up another arrow and tries again. And again.

"Stop, Ziva. Put the bow down for a minute and look at me." Ziva follows her instruction, frustrated that every subsequent arrow has missed the target worse than the one before.

"You're getting frustrated. Why?"

"Because each arrow released is worse than the one previous."

"That's because you're trying too hard," Loyola explains. "Shooting an arrow should be as easy as breathing. Don't over think it."

"How do you do that?" Ziva exhales.

Loyola shrugs her shoulder. "Aim and shoot. Let's try this. Don't look at the target. Walk up to where you will shoot from, aim, and shoot. See if that helps."

Ziva follows her instruction again and this time the arrow nicks the pole before hitting the fence.

"That is better," Loyola announces. "Let's gather the arrows and try again."

Loyola and Ziva take turns shooting until the force behind Ziva's arrows has diminished, causing a stop to practice.

"You did great for your first lesson," Loyola comments. "We need to pick up the arrows and return again tomorrow."

"I have enjoyed this." Ziva puts the last of her gathered darts into the basket. "Thank you, Loyola."

"I enjoyed it too. Before you go, let me show you where to get the bows and arrows. You can practice without me—in case I'm late." Loyola grins at her after she puts her gathered missiles into the quiver. Picking up the basket, Loyola hands it to Ziva to carry before grabbing the bows and heading toward a nearby building.

Ziva steps inside the door to find a small room with large containers full of arrows, quivers, and bows of various sizes organized around the room. "Wow!"

Loyola turns to Ziva and raises an eyebrow. "I trust you will not show another without Calene's approval?"

"It seems I'm the only one who wishes to learn, but I will get permission if that should change." She grins at Loyola. "Thank you for allowing me to practice on my own."

"Calene already knows about this, so there shouldn't be an issue with members of Arnac; however, no woman from Uthal is to be told, understood?"

"Why? What's so bad about learning to use bow and arrow?"

"Nothing is wrong with knowing how to hunt," Loyola explains, "but you are in Arnac to learn womanly skills. This is not one of them. It would not improve relations with our neighboring cities if they were to hear that we teach these skills to the women that come here, so don't mention it."

Ziva nods as Loyola takes the basket of arrows from her. Regretfully, she asks, "What if I've already mentioned it to a friend I room with?"

"What was her reaction?" Loyola queries as she puts their gear in its place.

"That a woman shouldn't be learning this skill," Ziva huffs.

"And you told her otherwise." Loyola knowingly grins at her.

Sheepishly, Ziva answers, "I told her, 'I am learning it.'"

Loyola takes a breath while she thinks. "Tell no one else."

Ziva nods in agreement.

"See you tomorrow, Ziva," Loyola concludes before departing.

Ziva smiles, calling after her, "Until tomorrow."

Several days later, as Ziva heads toward the archery course, she thinks over the cooking class. Ami came and talked with her, apologizing for being haughty, and their friendship resumed. Every day, the recipes in class are more complex than the previous day. One time, Ziva asked the instructor why she would need to know how to create complex meals. Her teacher's reply of potentially wanting to make something complicated for someone or some event never made sense to her. She mutters to herself, thinking of the incident, "Of course, I don't know what the future may bring, but why would I cook something complicated?" Later, she vents to her mother, "The only thing that makes sense to me about continuing to go to cooking class with the others is that the meals that are prepared are served at dinner."

"I understand your frustration with the class—I haven't experienced a time when I would cook the dishes either—but we will do our part and take it as a learning experience," Her mother gives her a supportive hug.

Arriving at the archery range, Ziva doesn't yet see Loyola, so she goes to the supply room, gathers the bows and quivers of arrows, and returns to the range with the gear. Daily archery practice has felt wonderful to her, a way of releasing pent up feelings. She takes a breath, aims, and slowly releases a portion of her frustration from cooking class with another dart. It strikes the target.

"You're getting better," Loyola calls out, arriving at her side. She picks up the bow that lies next to the quiver and grabs an arrow to join Ziva.

"Yes, practice helps." Ziva smiles at her before releasing another missile.

"Practice helps no matter what you're learning. Even after you learn something, if you don't use it, you can lose that skill." Loyola releases an arrow.

"I've learned I dislike cooking class. Practicing archery makes me feel so much better." Ziva grins, setting loose another missile.

"It does have a way of helping relieve stress." Loyola lowers her bow to watch Ziva. "What do you dislike about the class?"

Ziva drops her equipment to face Loyola and reveals, "I'm not one to spend a lot of time and effort cooking. The food we're making is something I don't feel I would ever use."

Loyola keeps her expression neutral. "What group do they have you in?"

"I'm in the intermediate group," Ziva returns.

Loyola nods and queries, "What do you like about the class?"

"The only thing I like about the class is that what is cooked is served for the nightly meal, so I feel I'm doing my part while here at Arnac." Ziva shrugs. "I guess someone's got to make the meal."

"That they do." Loyola grins, raises the bow, and launches her arrow. "It sounds like a good thing for you that cooking class is almost over."

Ziva brightens at her understanding. "I'm so ready for it to be over." Ziva raises her bow and the projectile flies, hitting its target. "What happens when all these classes are over?"

"You get to practice what you've learned by applying it to your life." Loyola smiles at her before returning her concentration to releasing another dart.

CLASS HAS CHANGED AGAIN. TODAY, she has a green outfit waiting for her. Quickly dressing, she arrives at the table to eat. Sitting down, she greets her companions, grabbing some sweet bread and stuffing it into her mouth. Khatoon joins her daughter and asks Titchna about today's class.

"This will be your last class before daily assignments will be made. This class will be weaving and sewing. A woman must know how to make clothing," Titchna knowingly informs them.

"I've already made my future spouse's shirt and shoes," Ami reports.

"That's good, Ami," Titchna smiles at her, "but this class goes beyond making Joining clothes. Wait and see."

"I've dealt with cloth since I was a little girl; I don't know what this class can teach me," Koki questions.

Titchna smiles patiently at Koki. "The class is similar to your cooking class: you'll start at different levels. Regardless of your level of skill or specialty, you will have the opportunity to learn something, whether it be from a teacher or from your mother, but you must be open-minded enough to listen and learn."

"Very well said, Titchna," Shapash adds. "Koki, you can always learn something new."

Titchna nods to Shapash and then turns her attention to the group. "Enjoy your meal. I will be back shortly to pick you up for class."

TITCHNA RETURNS TO THEIR BUILDING a little while later, gathering the women and leading them to a different building.

They arrive and each new woman is asked if she has completed her future spouse's Joining clothing. Based on her answer, the woman is either turned to the right or the left of the passageway with her mother by her side. In this case, Ziva is pointed down the left passageway, which leads to a room with only a few women in it.

Titchna smiles at them from the front of the room before the class starts. The teacher begins the class by saying, "Women, you have been put in this beginning class to prepare your future spouse's clothing before your Joining. The supplies are here for you to choose from. Your mother may lead you in this task, but many here in this room are available to guide you through this process. Mothers, please proceed with your daughters."

Khatoon takes her daughter's hand and squeezes it, regarding her. "At home, we didn't have the means to do this, but at present we can prepare."

"I don't want to be Joined to anyone," Ziva contradicts, confused by her mother's words. "Why do I need to prepare?"

Khatoon patiently smiles at her daughter. "Your father made the bracelet you wear before the opportunity arrived for you to have need of it. I know this bracelet is very special to you. One day, you'll want to be Joined. This is our chance to make the clothes that will be required for that. We may not have another chance, as we are too poor to make them at home. Please allow me to share this with you," Khatoon wisely pleads, encouraging her.

Ziva searches her mother's face.

Khatoon waits for her daughter's response.

Finally, Ziva nods.

Khatoon smiles, patting her daughter's hand. "Let's get to work."

The day continues as both mother and daughter discuss what needs to be done to the shirt and shoes. By the end of the day, the design and fabric cutting have been completed. Sewing has started. Before leaving, they store their supplies in a basket to continue working on later, and then they walk arm in arm back to their room.

"Mother, I enjoyed today," Ziva grins.

"What made this day so special for you?" Khatoon glances at her daughter as they continue forward.

Ziva looks at the ground, trying to put into words how she feels. "This class isn't like the other classes. I think the creative time we had together in this class is what I liked.

Khatoon looks at Ziva, meeting her eyes. "I liked it too."

After a few steps, Khatoon asks, "Are you going to continue your class tonight with Loyola?"

"Yes, I like the class." She laughs. "It helps me feel . . ." she looks down as they walk, determining what word to use, ". . . like I have some control in my life. Isn't that weird?" She laughs again. "It definitely helped get me through the cooking class."

"I don't understand, Ziva, but I'm glad." Khatoon gently hugs her daughter. "You seem a lot happier these days."

Arriving back at their room, Ziva gives Khatoon a quick hug before turning around and leaving for archery.

Khatoon smiles at her daughter's receding figure and decides to lie down for a little while before dinner.

The sewing and weaving course is pleasant for both mother and daughter; they spend each class sewing and talking. Time with Loyola on the archery range is a highlight of Ziva's day every day, and she spends as much time as she can before joining everyone for the nightly meals. Ziva seems happier than she's ever been, but Khatoon starts to worry.

After seven days, classes are finished. Following the completion of classes, a different colored dress arrives each day that indicates their assignment.

Ziva greets awakens with a smile on her face, remembering Loyola's words, "This is the time to practice what has been taught in the classes." Her decision to make an effort to practice what she's learned stays with Ziva, and she works hard to challenge herself. She likes the daily variety and enjoys finishing her days with archery before the evening meal. After dinner, she works on the Joining clothes at the table while her roommates talk with her and give her some pointers.

Many days pass when the dinner assignment is changed to being in the Great Hall, announcing the coming end to their visit. Old friendships are renewed, and new ones are created. Ziva continues to learn and grow, endeavoring to use the remaining time she has in Arnac to the best of her ability.

A couple of days before their scheduled departure from Arnac, Ziva is on the archery course with Loyola. "I'm happy being in Arnac. I almost don't want to go home, but I know that life must resume. I will miss the friends I've made here," Ziva says, releasing a projectile at the target.

"Arnac has always been a safe place for women, but eventually, most of us have to leave." Loyola releases her dart that hits its target. "You have become a confident woman compared with when I first met you."

Ziva laughs. "Thank you for the compliment. I want to make my parents proud."

"I think your parents have always been proud of their daughter," Loyola returns.

Ziva's eyes widen as her head swivels to Loyola. She spends a moment weighing her friend's words and realizes they're true. She looks down, blinking away her tears. She clears her throat, removing the emotion stuck there before she speaks. "I think you're right. I think I've been my worst enemy.  Forgiving myself for my father's death allowed me to move forward again. That happened during the journey to Arnac." She moves away and releases an arrow. Changing the subject, she asks, "Do you think you will ever leave Arnac?"

"I have to." Loyola looks sideways at Ziva, "I have an arranged marriage." She shrugs. "But whatever happens, choices are part of life's journey, and I will make it the best it can be." Loyola lets loose another dart. "Have you determined what your choice will be when you return home?"

"I don't want to be joined," Ziva returns, sighing, "but it seems a better choice than having to leave my mother. I've come to realize that if I were to take the Challenge and stay with her, my community would know, creating unpleasant feelings among its members. I've learned while here at Arnac that the whole point of the Challenge is to be away from your parents and figure things out for yourself through experience. I feel so conflicted because if I stay in my community, I would not be accomplishing its purpose. I prefer to stay with my mother, so I'll stay at Uthal and choose the Joining like she wants. We'll return to our home outside the Uthal gates together." She scoffs, "Perhaps I'll find someone that will accept not only me but my mother as well."

"But that is not what you want," Loyola interjects.

"No, I don't." Ziva shrugs. "But I don't see a way around it if I'm not going to leave my mother."

Loyola looks at Ziva and frowns. "Life will work out as it is meant to." She releases another arrow, which hits its mark, before Ziva releases one of hers. Loyola nods approvingly. "You've gotten a lot better."

Ziva laughs. "At least I can hit the target."

ZIVA ARRIVES BACK AT HER quarters smiling, ready to join her mother and the others for the walk to the hall for dinner. She enters to find her friends waiting for her at the table. Segara, seeing Ziva's cheerful countenance, grins. "You look to be in good spirits. Did your class go well?"

"Yes." Ziva smiles. "I enjoy it."

"I'm glad archery isn't a required class" Ami taunts. "I don't know why I would learn it."

"I like it and that's all that matters," Ziva confidently volleys back at Ami. Her expression changes as she realizes her mother is missing. "Is my mother still in our room?"

Segara nods once. "She has not come out. Please check to see if she is ready."

Concerned, Ziva quickly turns, entering the room to find her mother still in bed, lying on her side. Ziva feels her expression deepen, knowing this is so unlike her.

# ILLNESS

ZIVA GOES TO KHATOON'S SIDE and touches her shoulder to wake her. "Mother, time to get up for dinner," she says softly, only to have her hand scorched by Khatoon's hot body. Pulling her hand away.

"Go without me. I'm not feeling well." Khatoon remains still, but the tone of her voice echoes her discomfort.

Ziva walks to the other side of the bed to see her mother's face. Khatoon's eyes are closed, and her skin looks flushed and sweaty. Her mouth is drawn back and clamped shut. Ziva touches her mother's head, which feels the same temperature as her shoulder.

Khatoon involuntarily moans.

"Mother, you're sick."

Khatoon opens her eyes briefly and tries to reassure her daughter with a smile, but it shows as a grimace. "Go without me. I'll be fine. I only need to rest." She closes her eyes.

A stillness settles in the room, and Ziva's face crinkles as she tries to recall things she learned in healing class that could help her mother.

Another moan escapes Khatoon, which launches Ziva into action.

"Mother, get up. You need help," she loudly orders.

Within seconds, the room fills with the building's other occupants.

Segara rushes to Ziva's side. "What's wrong, Ziva?"

Ziva continues encouraging her mother to sit up.

Khatoon lies still, but a moan escapes her mouth.

The noise prompts Segara to turn her attention from Ziva to the ailing woman. Segara looks at Khatoon and touches her forehead before quickly removing her hand from the heat. She next moves the covers away from Khatoon while she barks out orders. "Ami, get Titchna. We need to get Khatoon to the infirmary. Ziva, help me get your mother up."

Ami, with her mouth open and eyes wide, nods once and disappears from the group.

Ziva, with fiery eyes that narrow and flash at Segara, is ready to retort that this is what she's trying to do. Practicing what she's learning, Ziva grits her teeth to keep from speaking and returns her attention to her mother. Segara assists her in getting Khatoon up. "She has a fever. Why?" Ziva asks Segara.

"I don't know, but she needs help. Her fever is too high."

Pulling Khatoon on her feet, they move to stand on either side of her. Segara, Khatoon, and Ziva walk back to the main room.

Titchna meets them and leads the way out the door toward the infirmary.

Khatoon's moans escape her clenched mouth.

Arriving at the infirmary, Khatoon is taken to a bed and deposited.

Segara and Ziva, struggling to recover from their efforts, fall back so that others can attend Khatoon.

When Segara's breathing has recovered, she puts an arm around Ziva as silent tears course down the girl's worried face.

It seems like an eternity as Ziva watches from a distance before someone steps toward them. "What's wrong with my mother?" asks Ziva, unable to remain silent any longer.

The woman's eyes widen for a second in surprise before she calmly replies, "We don't know yet."

Ziva looks at Segara, who reassuringly smiles back. "It will be all right, Ziva. Your mother is in good hands."

The infirmary woman asks, "Has she been complaining of not feeling well?"

"No. I found her like this." Concern and worry come out in an exasperated tone. "Will she be all right?"

"We will do everything we can for her," the woman patiently returns. "Perhaps you would like to get something to eat at the Great Hall before returning? We should know more at that time."

Ziva's flaming eyes snap to the woman at the suggestion of leaving. "I don't want to eat. I don't want to go anywhere. I want my mother better," she forcefully points out.

Segara squeezes Ziva's shoulder gently and her other hand takes hold of Ziva's. "Ziva, they need to care for your mother, and that is going to take time. We need to give them space to do what they need to do. Staying here won't shorten the wait," Segara encourages.

Ziva shakes off Segara's arm and hand, and stands at her full height. "I won't leave my mother!"

The woman acknowledges Ziva's statement, pointing to a row of stools. "You can sit here, but you must be quiet while we help her."

Ziva continues standing, giving all her concentration to her mother and what is going on. She hears her mother moaning and takes a step forward.

Segara pulls her back, wrapping her arm around Ziva's shoulder. "You must stay here, Ziva, and let them work. We must wait. Please, take a seat," she gently orders.

"I can't sit," Ziva cries, looking up at Segara with eyes filled with tears and worry. "My mother's sick."

"I know." Segara pulls Ziva into her arms, consoling the weeping girl. "It will be all right."

Ziva, struggling to regain composure, ceases her tears and dries her eyes.

An infirmary worker helps Khatoon drink from a cup.

Ziva takes a deep breath, releasing some of her concern, thankful that her mother's face contains less pain.

"Come. Let's sit," Segara says, moving Ziva toward the empty stools.

Ziva sits without word, continuing to watch her mother's care from a distance.

Time passes very slowly for Ziva, but eventually the woman returns, standing in front of them. Ziva jumps up, biting her lip, ready to hear what she has to say.

"Your mother has a bad infection. We are treating her, but she will be here some time," the woman informs them.

Segara's eyes widen. "What do you mean some time?"

"She will be in the infirmary beyond when the Uthal women will return home."

Ziva blinks several times as the information sinks in. "I will remain with her. Can I see her?"

"You may, but she will need to rest; if we tell you to move, you will need to do so."

Ziva nods in agreement before rushing to her mother's bedside and sitting on the provided stool. She carefully takes her mother's hand, watching Khatoon sleep.

Segara remains where she is and softly asks the woman, "I have never heard of someone not returning from the Journey. What does that mean for Ziva?"

The woman smiles briefly before delivering her answer. "It means the Challenge will begin for her at Arnac."

"Oh dear," Segara gasps. "I don't even think she realizes that." Segara glances at Ziva.

Ziva's face is covered with concern and worry. Her eyes are glued to her mother's face.

"I'll go to the hall and check on my daughter, and I'll return with a plate of food for Ziva." Segara takes one last look at Ziva and frowns before leaving the infirmary in search of Ami.

SEGARA VISITS ZIVA IN THE infirmary the next morning, bringing Ziva her sewing project. Segara inspects Khatoon briefly and drops the sewing basket on the chair before pulling Ziva outside the infirmary to talk.

Segara's brows are drawn together, and she frowns as she asks, "How is your mother doing?"

Ziva takes a breath before she looks up at Segara. "She's resting. They are giving her medicine every couple of hours. She seems to be doing better than before. I've heard less moaning and see more sleeping."

Segara nods and examines Ziva from head to toe, noticing her tired eyes and rumpled clothes, before she asks, "How are you doing, Ziva?"

Ziva shrugs, frowning. "Fine, I guess."

"They will help her get better. Everything will turn out as it should," Segara returns, giving Ziva a quick hug. "But we need to talk about something before I return to Uthal."

Ziva's eyebrows hike up and her wide eyes look upon Segara, wondering what she needs to talk to her about.

Segara takes a breath before jumping in. "Ziva, due to her illness, your mother will need to remain in Arnac for a time. I know you want to remain with her, but by doing that . . ." she pauses before continuing.

Ziva sees the concern in her face.

"… you will be starting the Challenge from Arnac." She takes a breath. "Last night, I went and talked with Calene and our guide from Uthal, and both confirm that this will be the case." She waits so that Ziva has time to digest that information. Segara smiles at her. "I would like to offer you another option. If you want, you could return to Uthal with Ami and me and stay at our home until such time as your mother can rejoin you. Multiple people travel to Uthal from other cities beyond Arnac. When your mother is well enough, she could return with one of them." Segara encouragingly smiles again.

Ziva pauses a moment, considering her options and how to respond carefully to such a kind offer—emulating Ami. "I thank you for the offer, but I'm not going to leave my mother, even if it means taking the Challenge."

Segara gazes at Ziva and places a hand on her arm. "It will be easier for the both of you if you come with Ami and me. Khatoon will have to concentrate on getting better, and you'll not have to worry about food or housing."

Ziva looks back at Segara and restates, "Thank you for the offer, but I'm not going to leave my mother." She moves her arm so that Segara's hand falls away.

Segara's frown deepens and concern lines her eyes. "Ziva, do you understand that you will not be able to return to, to even step foot in, Uthal for a year?"

"I understand that, but I had not stepped foot in Uthal for many years, until the day we left for Arnac. We already live outside the city walls. When my mother is well enough to travel, we will decide what to do at that time."

Segara lays a hand on Ziva's arm. "Think on my offer, Ziva. Taking the Challenge, I understand, is very difficult. I will bring you some food later today." Segara squeezes Ziva's arm gently before leaving.

THE NEXT TWO DAYS ARE broken up with friends that arrive at the infirmary to converse with Khatoon and Ziva. The visits to Khatoon are limited to a few minutes, during which Ziva talks to the visitors briefly and quietly while her mother rests. Ziva's guests are asked to converse outside the infirmary so that those within are not disturbed. Her friends bring their well wishes for her mother, their goodbyes to her, and some quiet activities, like an embroidery project, that Ziva can do to pass the time while her mother recovers.

"Please come back to Uthal with me," Ami pleads, grabbing Ziva's hands. "You can stay in my home, and we can be like sisters."

Ziva tries to smile at her friend, but it doesn't meet her eyes. "Ami, you already have sisters. I appreciate the offer, but I'm not going to leave my mother. She's all the family I have left. I hope you can understand." Ziva pulls her hands away.

Ami frowns at her. "But if you stay, you'll start the Challenge in Arnac. Haven't you heard how difficult the Challenge is?" Thinking this bit of knowledge will help sway Ziva, Ami points out, "Very few come back from the Challenge."

Ziva frowns at her friend and shrugs. "It doesn't matter. I'm not going to leave my mother."

Ami opens her mouth to speak.

"Thank you for your kind offer, Ami, but we shall be fine." She grins at Ami. "Who knows, perhaps I'll be one of the women who returns."

Ami throws her arms around Ziva. "Please be safe. When you do return to Uthal, let me know you're back. You know where to find me."

Ziva hugs her friend. "I will. Safe travels back to Uthal." Ziva releases her.

Ami turns, walking quickly away with her head bowed. She doesn't look back.

Ziva, frowning at the retreating form, takes a breath and, with sagging shoulders, returns to her vigil next to her mother's bed.

That evening, a man shows up at the infirmary and stands in the door to the courtyard, causing passersby to stop and watch him. Infirmary services are provided to all who reside at Arnac. It is rare to find a man inside the building.

Finding Ziva hunched over on the stool and looking at the ground, the man comes forward and stops at the foot of Khatoon's bed. Frowning, he looks at both mother and daughter. "How is Khatoon?" he questions softly, concern lacing his words.

Ziva jerks up with wide eyes and an open mouth. It takes her a second to recognize her visitor before her mouth closes. "She's sick."

"I see that." Tokal takes a breath, trying to control his irritation with her response. "Is she getting better?"

"Yes, but her healing is going to take time." Ziva responds automatically after fielding these questions over multiple days. She stands and stretches. "You awoke me."

He gazes at Ziva, examining her. "I came as soon as I heard. How are you doing?"

She smiles at the reoccurring question. "I'm well enough, Tokal." She yawns.

"Is there anything you need? Do you want me to stay with you?"

She frowns at him and shakes her head. What would he do once confined to the infirmary courtyard? "No, Tokal. We're fine." After a pause, Ziva continues, "You're free to return to Uthal with the others."

Tokal's eyes widen, and his mouth briefly opens. His lips thin. His eyes narrow as he takes a step forward, "I'm responsible for you. The king himself gave me this duty, and I intend to honor that."

Ziva opens her mouth to speak, but he cuts her off.

"Even if that means we take the Challenge together."

Ziva looks at his angry face and stands at her full height, eyes narrowed and jaw set, before speaking. "I don't need you, Tokal. I definitely didn't want a guard assigned to me. You are free to leave with the others and return to your life in Uthal."

One of the infirmary women touches each of them to get their attention and orders, "Both of you take this conversation outside and allow Khatoon to rest."

Tokal grinds his teeth and furrows his eyebrows, thinking of how to respond as they are ushered outside the infirmary door to the courtyard. When they stop and face one another again, his face morphs into a smirk. "Whether you like it or not, we are in this together. I'll wait until you're both ready to leave Arnac, and I'll escort *you* home." Turning on his heels, he leaves her standing in the courtyard.

Ziva, irritated at his response, stomps her foot, and her eyes spit fire at the retreating figure. She spends a few minutes calming herself before returning to her mother's bedside.

Pulling out a sewing project to take out her frustrations on, she drops to the stool and mutters under her breath about Tokal being a stubborn man.

AFTER THE UTHAL WOMEN LEAVE Arnac the next morning, Titchna and Loyola visit Khatoon and Ziva. They don't stay long, but their visit brightens both Khatoon's and Ziva's outlooks.

AS THE DAYS PASS, KHATOON is more alert. Each time she wakes, she converses with Ziva for a time before falling asleep again. The women in the infirmary take good care of both of their needs, making sure that mother and daughter eat and sleep. By the seventh day in the infirmary, Khatoon is up and moving around by herself.

Loyola visits Khatoon and Ziva, who are conversing quietly as they walk the floor.

Loyola clears her throat.

Khatoon and Ziva look up to find her smiling.

"Khatoon, you look so much better than a couple of days ago."

"I feel so much better than I did a couple of days ago," Khatoon returns with a cheerful countenance. "Is the city quiet since the women of Uthal have departed?" Even though she's on the mend, Khatoon knows that her daughter would like to be outside but doesn't want to leave her.

Loyola chuckles. "Yes, the city is quieter for the moment, until the next city of women shows up."

"How many cities come to Arnac?" Ziva probes, curious about the workings of the city of women.

"Two cities visit, taking their allotted turns," Loyola says. "The Journey is a good thing."

"Why? Because it keeps you busy?" Ziva scratches her head, wanting to know.

"It does keep us busy, but it also helps the women of this city to look beyond themselves by serving others," Loyola answers.

"Why is that important?"

"Most of the women at Arnac are here for a specific reason, including me. Being here helps us to look beyond our problems— helping others helps us."

"Arnac sounds like it benefits all the women that are privileged to be here. I've seen much growth in Ziva since arriving. Arnac is a good place," Khatoon adds. "So, with another group arriving soon, will Ziva and I be in the way?"

"We expect them anytime, but you will not be in the way," Loyola returns. "Khatoon and Ziva, you are currently a part of Arnac."

"That is good to hear." Changing the subject, Khatoon asks, "Before anyone else shows up, please take Ziva out to shoot some arrows and get some fresh air. Being cooped up inside with an ailing mother isn't good for one so young. With all the projects that have been given to Ziva, there is plenty available to keep me busy while she's gone," Khatoon takes a breath, repositioning herself in the bed.

"I'm not leaving you, Mother." Ziva frowns.

Khatoon pats her daughter's hand and smiles. "And I'll be here when you get back." Turning to Loyola she orders, "Take her, Loyola."

Between the both of them, Ziva submits and follows Loyola.

"I'm happy to see your mother doing better," Loyola mentions as they walk together.

"Me too. I worry so much about her. She's never been sick before." Ziva frowns but doesn't look at Loyola as her mixed emotions threaten to erupt.

"If something happened to my mother, I would be concerned too," Loyola says with empathy. "I completely understand why you wanted to stay with her."

Reaching the archery range, they grab their gear and start shooting arrows at the target.

"Seven days have passed since Uthal left Arnac; you should officially be starting the Challenge today," Loyola informs as she releases an arrow.

Pent up emotions roll off Ziva as she forcefully spits out, "Does it matter?" Ziva concentrates, releasing her arrow.

"It does if you're keeping track of time," Loyola counters, noticing her friend's inner struggle. She calmly takes aim and shoots, hoping that Ziva can work through her issues.

"I never wanted to go on the Journey, the Joining, the Challenge—any of this. Look what's happened," Ziva mutters, putting all her anger into releasing another dart.

Loyola stops and watches Ziva, seeing the internal turmoil trying to escape. She takes a breath, proceeding carefully. "I've heard many wise women say that life never goes as one plans it. We need to live in the moment and find joy in the journey," Loyola calmly returns before releasing another arrow.

Ziva stops and stares at Loyola, not fully understanding her words. She sighs and nocks another projectile. "Change has been the story of my life, which I've always hated." She aims and discharges her weapon. "I have learned much while being here," she breathes, "but I still don't like change."

Loyola looks at her and grins. "I wish I knew how to teach living in the moment, but everyone must find it for themselves."

Ziva nods. "Ami has. She's a good friend who enjoys life and all that it includes." Ziva and Loyola go get their arrows from the target. When they return to the line, they drop their darts in their quiver. Ziva looks at Loyola and smiles at her friend. "You have it too."

"Have what?" Loyola nocks a shaft.

"The ability to live in the moment," Ziva returns.

Loyola releases her projectile. "Thank you for the compliment," shrugging the praise off her back. "I try to live each day as best I can."

A pause occurs as Ziva releases an arrow before she looks at Loyola. "Perhaps, that is where I should start."

Ziva and Loyola enjoy their time together. After a little while, Ziva feels she needs to get back to her mother, so they put away their gear, and Loyola walks with her back to the infirmary.

"Khatoon and you are currently part of the city of women. When you are out of the infirmary, you'll wear the style of Arnac women until you decide to leave the city." Loyola smiles. "As always, archery is available to you anytime you would like."

"Thank you, Loyola," Ziva looks her way. "You're a true friend."

"As are you." Loyola smiles back. "Please, give Khatoon my best wishes for her continued recovery. You are both in good hands."

"Will do." Ziva nods to Loyola. Feeling so much better, she turns, leaving her friend in front of the infirmary.

Inside the building, Ziva returns to her mother's side to find her asleep. She smiles, sets herself on the stool, and picks up her sewing, continuing to work on the Joining shirt. Late in the afternoon, word comes to the infirmary that another group of women have arrived at Arnac and are settling in. For a moment, she wonders about their belongings left behind at their quarters. She realizes that Titchna would have made sure everything has been accounted for.

THE WOMAN IN CHARGE ARRIVES at the bedside. "Khatoon, you have three days left of medicine to take, and when your strength has returned, you will be released from the infirmary."

Khatoon's countenance brightens after hearing this information. "I would like to get outside and walk around. Is this possible?" she asks her caretaker.

"Yes, but someone needs to accompany you."

"I have my daughter. She can go with me."

"It's fine that Ziva is with you, but an infirmary woman will join for your first couple of outings to make sure that you don't overdo it."

"After I eat, may we venture out?"

"Of course," the woman returns smiling. "Is there anything else you desire?"

Ziva looks to her mother and bites her lip, waiting for her response.

Khatoon smiles and returns, "I don't need anything. Thank you."

The woman nods and departs.

Khatoon and Ziva silently consume their food together, allowing others to continue resting. After eating, they get up and leave.

An infirmary woman follows them outside with a collapsible stool made of durable cloth and three sturdy branches that are tied together in the middle. "Khatoon walk slowly and only go to the stool that is placed."

Khatoon reaches the stool and realizes how tired she is, despite covering only a small distance. She sits, breathing in the fresh, clean air that is so different from the air inside the infirmary. After a few minutes in silence, she smiles. "The day is beautiful. I'm happy to be outside again."

Ziva smiles back at her mother. "The outside air is very refreshing. Would you like to remain here in the shade, or would you like to walk again?"

"This is her limit for today," the infirmary woman interrupts. "Maybe in a few days she will be ready to walk further. Please let me know when you're ready to return to your bed."

Khatoon nods in acknowledgement and the woman leaves, returning to the infirmary.

The pair sit in companionable silence, enjoying the fresh warm air, with Ziva at her mother's feet.

After some time has passed, Khatoon looks at Ziva. "I'm ready to return to bed."

Ziva nods and gets to her feet. She leaves for a moment before reappearing with the woman from the infirmary.

Once the woman is watching, Khatoon, not waiting for assistance, stands up and returns to her bed with Ziva following.

Khatoon settles, quickly falling fast asleep.

The infirmary woman touches Ziva's arm, seeing her concern. "She will get stronger over time. She did well for her first walk."

Ziva nods, realizing she didn't know the severity of her mother's illness. "Did you ever figure out what caused her illness?" Ziva asks the woman.

"As near as we can figure, she had an infection of some kind. The medicine is resolving it, but it will take time for her to fully recover her strength."

Daily, Khatoon practices short distance trips outside, and she naps often. Several days later Khatoon stands up, excited that her strength is returning, and wants to be released from the confinement. "Let's see if I can walk to the Great Hall and back."

The woman from the infirmary adjusts Khatoon's goal. "I think that will be too far for today. How about we set that goal for next time and walk half that distance today. Remember, you have a return trip back."

At the noon meal, Khatoon says, "Ziva, I'm getting better and will soon be released from the infirmary; however, I will not live forever. Have you thought about life without me?"

Ziva cringes and reprimands her mother. "How can you say something like that, Mother?"

Khatoon sighs and looks at her daughter. "Life happens, Ziva. This illness has reminded me of that fact. I'm getting old and one day, I will die."

Ziva shakes her head frowning. "I don't want to think of such things, much less hear of them."

Khatoon takes a breath, patting the side of the bed next to her. "Sit down."

Ziva complies, frowning at her mother.

"Ziva, I don't mention this to upset you, but to prepare you for what will eventually happen. Death is a part of life as much as birth or breathing. Death is a happy time, for I will be with your father again. I hope to be around to see you have children of your own, but you must understand that when my time comes to leave, you will have to accept it and know that my death isn't your fault no matter what happens." Khatoon sighs, dropping the conversation as she sees Ziva's eyes cloud over.

Ziva's not yet willing to discuss it.

Khatoon will try again later. "I love you, daughter, but whether or not you or I are ready, my time will come." She squeezes Ziva's hand.

Titchna shows up, interrupting the conversation. "How are you feeling, Khatoon?"

Ziva gets up with her back turned toward Titchna and quickly wipes her eyes before turning to greet their guest.

Titchna, upon looking at Khatoon, exclaims, "You look so much better."

"I'm doing much better and am glad that my time in the infirmary has come to an end." Khatoon smiles at Titchna. "Your face is always good to see."

Ziva masking her feelings, smiles. "Hi, Titchna."

Titchna sees Ziva's sadness and looks from one to the other. "I wonder if the both of you would be interested in bathing before I take you to your quarters to continue your recovery?"

"A bath would be wonderful!" Khatoon enthusiastically returns.

"Very well." Titchna turns to Ziva. "Is everything packed?"

Ziva nods pointing to a sack on the floor.

"May I carry your pack?"

"No." Ziva turns to pick up the sack. "We are sisters. Not visitors."

Titchna nods, taking Khatoon's arm and leading the way.

The next few weeks pass by as Ziva and Khatoon are assimilated into Arnac. Khatoon continues to regain her strength as she participates in tasks she can do while she recovers. Ziva finishes her sewing on the Joining clothes and, after her mother has reviewed it, packs it away, not looking forward to pulling it out—ever.


ZIVA'S DAYS ARE SPENT BY Khatoon's side, serving her mother, except during the late afternoon when her mother takes Ziva to Loyola to practice archery while she watches.

At the end of one such exercise, Khatoon makes her feelings known. "Loyola, thank you for being a true friend to Ziva. She has grown much in Arnac, and I think a lot of that is because of you. Tomorrow will be our last day here. Our time is ended; we need return home."

Ziva's eyes pop open in surprise, and she looks at Khatoon. "Mother, are you sure?"

"Yes." Khatoon nods. "In the morning, you will need to let Tokal know."

Ziva looks to Loyola. "How do I find him?"

Loyola frowns examining the both of them. "You will find him in the courtyard in the building on the right. Do not enter the building but remain outside where you can be seen, and have someone send him out. I recommend you have someone accompany you."

"Tokal will not harm me," Ziva informs Loyola.

Loyola nods to Ziva. "I'm glad that you trust your guardian; however, other men besides Tokal reside in the courtyard."

Turning her attention toward Ziva's mother, she says, "Khatoon, I don't think leaving Arnac without a traveling group is advisable. Wait for a group of merchants traveling in that direction. It will be much safer than traveling by yourselves."

Khatoon hears her concern but continues to explain her rationale. "If my daughter is participating in the Challenge, she will be expelled from Uthal with only her guardian. I would like to be home before winter is upon us, and I fear my pace may be slower than a traveling group. We will survive outside the gates of Uthal in our home during the winter season. All will be well."

Ziva, excited to be going home, adds, "Titchna can accompany me to visit Tokal." Taking a breath, she looks at Loyola and smiles. "Thank you for sharing archery with me."

Loyola frowns but accepts their decision. "We can still meet tomorrow, one last time."

Ziva smiles. "I would like that."

ZIVA STRIDES TO THE KITCHEN to get the morning meal for her mother and herself. She finds Titchna there gathering food and joins her. "Titchna, I'm wondering if you would be available to accompany me to the courtyard to talk with Tokal."

Titchna nods at Ziva's request. "After I deliver this, I can go with you."

"I will help you," Ziva picks up a tray.

They gather the food.

Titchna leads the way back to a building.

Once the food items have been placed on the table and the platter removed, Ziva and Titchna leave. They head first to Ziva's building to deposit a meal for Khatoon before turning to the courtyard to see Tokal.

Titchna and Ziva are walking together toward the courtyard when Titchna breaks the silence between them. "Khatoon seems restored to health. Does this mean you're leaving Arnac?"

"Yes. She feels strong enough to return to Uthal." Ziva takes a breath and blows it out before continuing. "Loyola mentioned traveling alone outside Arnac isn't wise, which didn't bother me until this morning."

"Gadianton are outside Arnac, and rumors have reached the city that traveling parties have been attacked by them. Loyola speaks the truth that it would be better to travel in a large group."

"When I mentioned my unease, Mother wouldn't listen." Ziva takes another breath, frowning. "She's more interested in returning home before winter."

They walk in silence for a time, not knowing what to say.

Ziva sighs. "I will miss Arnac."

Titchna briefly glances at Ziva's face. "As you should. Arnac helps many women."

"I will miss the people most of all." Ziva smiles at her friend. "Titchna, do you mind if I ask you what brought you to Arnac?"

"Why do you ask?" Titchna carefully volleys back.

Ziva shrugs. "Curious, I guess."

Titchna's mouth drops at the corners, recalling her history before she masks her expression. "My past is not important."

Ziva frowns, wondering what happened to her friend. "Will you ever leave Arnac?"

Titchna is quiet for a moment and takes a breath before responding, "Where would I go? I have no one else. Arnac has become my home."

Ziva's mind suggests the possible difficulties Titchna endured, but Ziva shrugs them off.

They arrive in the courtyard, and Titchna points the way to the building where the men reside.

Men are already up and about outside the building. The men, noticing the two women in colorful dress, send a man to get their leader while the others walk toward them.

When the women get close enough to the men, Titchna drops a few steps behind Ziva.

"Good morning," a man says. "What brings two Arnac women this way?"

Ziva scrutinizes the men before talking to the one who greeted her. "I'm here to speak with Tokal."

"How about you speak with us," another man demands.

"We would all like to hear the words of a woman."

"I have no dealings with you. Only with Tokal. Please get him."

"Enough!" bellows a man standing a few steps from the group walking toward them.

Startled, Ziva turns her attention toward the leader who has joined the group. He glares at the man who last spoke. "Go get Tokal," he orders.

The man frowns but turns away, jogging into the building.

The leader turns his head toward the women. "He will be here in a little while. You must be Ziva."

Her eyes widen, surprised that he knows her name. "I am."

He nods. "How is your mother?"

Ziva grins, hearing the all too familiar question. "She is recovered."

"That makes me happy."

Tokal comes out of the building, which catches Ziva's attention. The leader follows Ziva's gaze to see Tokal quickly approach. "Here he comes." Turning to the other men, he says, "Give them some space so they can speak."

The men return to the exterior of the building where they are housed, leaving Ziva, Tokal, and Titchna in a small group.

Puzzled, Tokal asks, "What brings you here, Ziva?"

"Mother is better, and she would like to leave for Uthal in the morning."

Tokal smiles. "I'm glad to hear that she's better. I'm ready to return to Uthal myself." Tokal's excitement changes to authoritarian. "But I will be staying with you."

"As my guardian." Ziva scowls at him. "Nothing more."

A pregnant pause occurs between them as they warily watch each other.

Ziva turns to Titchna giving her a brief smile. "Would you wait for me by the infirmary?"

Titchna frowns, looking from Tokal to Ziva, before excusing herself to begin the short return trip.

Ziva's attention returns to Tokal. "Walk with me."

As they walk the perimeter of the courtyard, she gathers her thoughts while Tokal silently walks beside her.

"Tokal," she begins, "you're a wonderful friend, but I'm not the little girl who arrived here. I've changed. There will be no talk of Joining on this return trip to Uthal. Nor throughout the Challenge. Is that understood?"

Tokal perplexed, stops. "Why are you so against us Joining?" He catches up to Ziva who continued walking.

"Because I'm currently on the Challenge. I don't want to be badgered by you throughout this. If you cannot keep that to yourself, I release you to return to Uthal without us."

"You can't be serious," Tokal fumes.

Ziva turns on him, stopping him in his tracks. Flames lick her narrowed eyes, and her set jaw tells him he'd better listen as she grinds out, "I'm very serious. Get it through your head, we shall not be discussing this."

He stands for a minute blinking, his brain digesting her words before he speaks again. "You haven't answered my question. Why are you so against us Joining?"

"I've told you before, you're like my brother."

"I'm not your brother."

Ziva sighs. "No, you're *not* my brother but you are *like* a brother. I've heard plenty about love for the past few months from the other women. I only feel for you as a sister does her brother. Nothing more.

Mother's health is my primary concern right now. I want to get her safely home. Can you help me in that endeavor?"

He turns and starts walking, and she falls in step beside him. After a time, Tokal breaks the silence, sullenly stating, "I can do that."

A wave of relief washes over Ziva and she smiles. "Thank you, Tokal. It means a lot. We'll be ready after the morning meal."

Resigned to his fate, Tokal takes a deep breath. "I will meet you at the gate."

When they pass by the infirmary, Ziva veers off toward Titchna, who has watched them as they walked the perimeter.

Tokal continues back toward the men's housing.

THE LAST DAY IS SPENT gathering supplies for their trip back home. That evening at archery practice, Ziva puts a lot of effort in her shooting and Loyola feels it.

"What's bothering you, Ziva?" Loyola asks as she releases her arrow.

Not looking up, Ziva releases another dart. She glances over at Loyola before her thoughts pour out of her. "Tokal, my guardian, is like a brother to me. He's a good man. He wants to be my husband. It would make my mother happy, and he would care for my mother . . ."

Loyola looks at Ziva's frowning face. "But . . .?"

"But he feels like a brother. I've heard the others talk about men and how they have feelings for them. I don't have any of that. I love him as a family member, but that is it." Ziva stands there, looking at Loyola for answers.

Loyola nods at her, nocks a projectile, and releases it, taking her time to formulate her words. Once she's ready, she looks at Ziva, who stands ready to hear her wisdom. Loyola gazes at Ziva and in a serious tone says, "I don't have an answer for you and I'm not the one with the knowledge." She breaks into a grin.

"Remember, I'm the one with the arranged Joining to a man I have yet to meet." She takes a breath. "Have you talked with your mother?"

A forceful "no" falls from Ziva's mouth.

Loyola cocks an eyebrow. "As close as the both of you are, I would think she would provide you with the wisdom you desire."

Ziva takes a frustrated breath. "Thank you, Loyola." Ziva nocks a dart and shoots. Their practice goes a little longer than usual before they part company.

For their last night in Arnac, Ziva takes her mother to the tree by the pool, and they sit there for a time before going in search of dinner in the kitchen. Khatoon feels something is bothering her daughter but waits until Ziva's ready to tell her.

That night, after the light has been extinguished, Ziva speaks. "Mother, how did you and father meet?"

"I wonder what, or rather who, might be on your mind to prompt such a question?" Khatoon returns in the dark.

"Well, I'm not thinking about Tokal." Ziva grimaces in the dark. "I wondered about how you met."

"Oh, that occurred so long ago."

Ziva thinks her mother isn't going to share it with her.

Khatoon breaks the silence. "He looked so handsome and was already quite talented with jewelry. My heart would pound when he looked at me, even when I didn't know why."

Ziva could hear the smile in her mother's voice.

"After the Journey, he and his parents visited my home. I walked with him, chaperoned by our mothers. He came to eat with my family, and we would talk. I liked being in his presence. He made me feel . . . special. He always made me feel loved. I think that's what I miss the most about him."

"Me too," Ziva whispers in the darkness.


MOTHER AND DAUGHTER DRESS IN their travel clothing, eat their morning meal, and gather their gear. They walk to the courtyard, where they find Titchna, Loyola, and—to their surprise—Calene.

"We could not let you leave Arnac without saying goodbye." Loyola greets them.

"What a surprise to see you here. It makes us feel special," Khatoon delightedly informs them. "You make it difficult to leave."

Calene smiles. "That is because you have been happy here. Your time at Arnac has ended, allowing you to continue your journey through life."

"Thank you, Calene, for taking such good care of us," Khatoon says, bowing.

Calene touches Khatoon's shoulder and smiles again "We enjoyed having you at Arnac."

"I shall miss you, Titchna. If you ever make it to Uthal, please find me." Ziva touches her friend's arm before embracing her.

"I will do so." Titchna and Ziva giggle, both knowing Titchna will probably never leave Arnac.

"Loyola, I will miss you the most. Thank you for being such a wonderful friend. I hope our paths will cross again." Ziva sniffs.

"I hope so too."

The two share a meaningful embrace.

When everyone has said their farewells, Ziva and Khatoon pick up their packs and take them over to where Tokal waits for them by the gate. The packs are tied on the horse, and the three walk outside the safety of Arnac's door. They head for home, hoping to avoid an encounter with Gadianton.

Finding themselves outside Arnac is like being in another world. Ziva is touched for the first time by the raw beauty of the forest. She quirks her head, wondering what has changed within her. The intoxicating scent of fresh, clean air mixed with flowers, firs, and ferns hits her nostrils. The visual grandeur of tall trees in differing varieties, interspersed with flowers and ferns along the side of the road and revealed by the light-tipped fingers of the sun, touches Ziva's heart. The auditory stimulation of the distant waterfall, interrupted by birds chirping and animals scampering about in the branches above, completes the landscape. She knows she'll never see anything like it again and works to capture the memory.

They walk down the mountain, conversing among themselves as they watch for Gadianton. Ziva has the reigns of Tokal's horse and Khatoon walks closely next to Ziva. Tokal has his hands free to defend them, if necessary, or to help Khatoon if she needs assistance.

After a long walk, they reach the camping area, where Ziva waters the horse. Khatoon gathers wood and starts to fix dinner.

Ziva returns taking over the dinner preparation, allowing her mother to rest. Tokal puts up the tent for the night. When the chores are done, they gather around the fire to eat.

"The meal is good," Tokal says in between bites.

"That's because we have some herbs," Khatoon returns when her mouth is empty.

"We'll need to extinguish the fire soon, in order to not give ourselves away to Gadianton during the night," Tokal says.

"Will we get home safely?" Khatoon asks.

"I think we will, if we hide our position and if Gadianton miss our trail," Tokal answers, smiling confidently.

"We'll do what we can to help, but you will need to tell us what to do," Ziva returns. In between bites and the silence between them, Ziva speaks again. "I have set the fish trap, so hopefully, we'll have meat in the morning."

After he's done eating, Tokal gets up and extinguishes the flames. "Time to sleep."

Ziva and Khatoon look at each other.

"I'll sleep outside the tent door. Ziva, since you wake up with the dawn, try to be quiet when you wake me up."

Ziva nods, gathering Tokal's bowl and spoon.

Mother and daughter wash the dishes and put them away. They head to the tent. Khatoon falls quickly to sleep, but Ziva is restless. She steps outside the tent door and sits with Tokal, who's watching their surroundings. "Are you going to stay up all night?" she whispers to him.

He nods.

Her face scrunches up in the twilight. "That's not a good idea. You'll tire quickly and put your health at risk."

Hearing her concern, he grins. "Better that than our lives."

"I agree, but you cannot keep us safe alone." she frowns at him. "I can keep watch so you can sleep."

Tokal cocks an eyebrow and frowns at her. "Do you know what to look for?"

"No, but you can teach me."

After some silence, Tokal responds. "Very well. Close your eyes." When Ziva does what he asks, he continues. "Sit still and listen with your body. Open your senses to hear movement, such as a stick breaking, a change in the air, a whisper in the wind, or bird calls when there shouldn't be. Let's see if you know where I am."

Tokal leaves, giving her an opportunity to practice while he returns. At first, he makes it easy for her. With each subsequent attempt, he makes it more difficult.

By the fifth time, Ziva hears next to her ear, "You do not want Gadianton to show up unannounced." She startles, and he rests his hand on her shoulder to calm her. After some silence and her frowning at him, she responds, "I get what you mean."

"Get some sleep, Ziva," he orders. "I'll wake you when it is time to guard."

She nods and goes inside the tent, placing her head near the door so that Tokal can wake her when the time comes for her to watch.

A HAND ON ZIVA'S SHOULDER wakes her. She blinks several times before crawling out the tent door to where Tokal sits. She feels rather than sees a finger to his lips in the moonlight and nods, sitting next to him in the darkness. He situates his sword across his lap and then rests his hands, one on the handle and the other on his thigh.

"You know you can lie down," she whispers as she grins at him.

"I'm good. Remember to wake me."

The words were so soft she almost thinks her mind is playing tricks. She shakes her head.

Determining he did speak, she whispers, "I will." Ziva spends her first night of guard duty looking at the stars. So many ancestors dot the sky in this clearing. She wonders what her ancestors are telling her. She thinks about her father, knowing he is watching her. Absently, she reaches for the bracelet at her wrist, playing with it. Her eyes close as the soothing sound of the water becomes foremost in her mind.

A bird whistles.

Immediately awake, Ziva opens her eyes wide and looks about. Her heart races. Another bird chirps. Light bleeds into the sky. She realizes she must have fallen asleep. While her heartbeat slows, she listens, not recognizing anything out of the ordinary.

Tokal is still and quiet next to her.

She touches his shoulder.

He opens his eyes.

"I'm going to the river to see if we have fish." The sooner our meal is done, the sooner they can leave.

Tokal nods and stands. He helps her get up.

Ziva walks to the river, leaving him to take care of his needs. She checks the trap and finds two plump fish—enough for their meal. She pulls the trap out, puts the fish in a small sack, and smacks them hard against a tree to put them out of their misery. With fish in one hand and trap in the other, she turns back to their little camp.

Tokal is surrounded by four loinclothed men with shaved heads and red and black marks on their bodies. He raises his sword, fighting them off as they attack with what looks to be arrow points around the edge of a long, thick board.

Ziva drops what's in her hands as she screams.

# CHANGE

Something purely instinctual compels her forward toward Tokal and her mother. She feels someone throw her to the ground, but all her attention is on Tokal.

Tokal is struck with one of their weapons. He doesn't make a sound. The sword is pulled away in a sickly sucking sound. Blood gushes forth from the gaping wound. A metallic smell reaches her nostrils, calling her to action.

She struggles against the force holding her down.

"Be still," is hissed at her and a knife comes into her view as a warning.

She stops struggling, watching Tokal as he continues to defend the door of the tent from the intruders.

A loud, revolting thump rings out as Tokal is struck in the base of the skull, causing him to fall to the earth.

Ziva struggles, but is unable to escape. She cries out in horror and frustration.

The man whose weapon is currently stuck in Tokal's head puts one foot on Tokal's shoulder blades, and pulls his blade from the skull, lifting Tokal's head in an obscene manner before releasing the death kiss.

Using all her strength she tries again. She's able to stand, only to realize her hands are locked behind her. It doesn't matter because she must get to her mother.

Khatoon is roughly pulled out and thrown at the feet of the man who just killed Tokal.

As Ziva stumbles forward, she's pushed to her knees. She watches in horror as the man raises his sword against her mother. Ziva's eyes widen, but narrowing them a split second later, she bellows, "You will not touch her!"

Surprised, the man looks at Ziva as she is knocked in the head and falls over. When she's pulled up, she tastes her blood and struggles to resolutely stand in front of the leader. With head held high, firm jaw, and eyes blazing from their narrowed orifices, she firmly decrees, "You will not touch her!"

"No one tells me what I can or cannot do." The man sneers at her. He raises his club to strike the belligerent girl.

Ziva faces him without fear. She lifts her chin, pointedly stares in his eyes as fire blazes in hers. With an ominous tone maintains, "You and your men will not touch my mother or me if you desire to reach your home."

The man swings his sword, bringing it down.

Ziva doesn't blink or move from staring at the warrior. The sword hits Tokal's dead body with a sickening sound. Ziva doesn't flinch.

"No one else is out here to save you, woman. How can you say such a thing?"

She takes another step, coming nose-to-nose with the man. "Because what I say is true," Ziva whispers to him. "If you desire to reach your home, you will not harm us."

The man stares at her for a moment and blinks.

Another notices the bracelet on her wrist. "She's not joined."

"She'll be trouble," a second man says.

"She will make a good breeder," another chimes in as he walks around her. "She is strong and brave. Her mother will make a good servant."

"If what she says comes true, that will help us."

"I don't believe her words. She's nothing but a troublesome woman."

"We need women to breed."

"She's known no man. Let us take her."

"Kill the old woman, she's of little worth."

The leader listens as they speak about both women as though they are fodder under their feet.

Ziva stands, watching the leader.

The chief rakes each woman from her head to toe, determining her worth. When he stops his perusal, he turns his attention back to Ziva.

"Who is he to you?" he asks, cocking his head toward Tokal's body, which still contains his sword.

Ziva doesn't look but keeps her eye on the commander. "My brother."

"Where were you going?"

"To Uthal."

"You're a long way from Uthal." Taking another walk around the women, the leader asks, "What's in Uthal?"

"Nothing of consequence."

"That's good to hear." The commander pulls his weapon from Tokal's body. "You will join us."

"What if we don't want to join you?" Ziva challenges.

The commander marches toward her, stopping inches away. "You have no choice," he sneers in her face.

Ziva smells the malodorous breath and wrinkles her nose.

"You will join us anyway."

The packs are dumped out and rummaged by the men, who take what they want. One of the men brings the bag of fish and gives it to their chief.

The leader looks at the contents before tossing the bag toward Khatoon. "Old woman, prepare food so we may eat."

Khatoon gets up, takes the fish, and retrieves the contents she needs that are scattered on the ground. She looks to her daughter.

Ziva understands that she's missing a knife.

"My mother is a good cook, but she will need a knife to clean the fish."

The commander regards Ziva and Khatoon, evaluating them. Turning to the man who gave the bag of fish, he orders, "No knife is to be given to the women. If you want your fish cleaned, you do it yourselves."

The man stomps to Khatoon and opens his hand for the bag.

She hands it over without question and goes to work on the fire.

"You've seen our belongings; can I pack them back up to take with us?" Ziva asks.

The commander haughtily stares at her.

Ziva returns his stare and interrupts the silence with, "Keeping my hands tied will not help anything. Let me assist my mother."

"Do you ever keep quiet?" the commander mocks.

"Yes, when I don't need to say anything."

He stares at her and sneers. "You will keep quiet unless I speak to you. Follow your mother's example."

Ziva laughs at his ignorance. "That's impossible." She looks at the man. "I speak when moved upon."

His eyes widen then narrow.

Ziva sees danger there.

"The consequence of such action will be the punishing of you or your mother according to my desires."

"If my mother or I am—"

A robber hits her hard in the face with the blunt side of his weapon.

Ziva falls to the ground. It takes her a moment for the ringing in her head to subside. The metallic taste in her mouth makes her spit, and she sees crimson in the spittle. She struggles to stand with her arms tied behind her, blood running from her nose and mouth. She looks at the man who hit her, turns to the commander, and succinctly predicts, "He will die before seeing your home."

"She's a witch." The robber retorts. "Don't let her say anything more."

"If my mother or I am harmed in any way, you will not return home alive," Ziva reinforces.

The robber pulls out his knife, stepping forward to cut Ziva's throat.

"Laman!" the commander warns.

The robber, with his hands on Ziva's hair pulling her head back, stops.

"Let her go," the leader orders.

Laman stares at his commander, evaluating whether to obey, before roughly releasing the woman he would like to kill.

Ziva topples forward.

The commander catches her in his arms, keeping her from a hard fall, before setting her upright and turning her away from him. The chief, with knife drawn, watches Laman for an attack.

Laman backs away a few steps, muttering to himself.

The leader keeps Laman within eyesight as he calmly cuts the young woman's bonds.

Ziva moves her hands in front of her, picking off the remains of the rope and rubbing her wrists. Speaking soft so no one else can her, "For your kindness, I will give you this warning. One of your men will attempt to kill you before you return home."

"She's a witch. Quick. Kill her!" Laman bellows.

The commander, knife still in hand, glares at Laman. Without breaking eye contact with the man, he marches right up to him.

Laman falls back in retreat.

The commander grinds out, "You will not touch her or her mother."

Laman nods, submitting to his commander's authority, and withdraws from the campsite.

"Woman, pack your things. We leave after we eat," the chief bellows before walking away.

Ziva wipes the blood from her mouth. She doesn't say a word while she packs up their belongings.

Khatoon fixes the fish and vegetables they brought, watching as her daughter stands against the robbers. She is amazed at Ziva's courage and doesn't know where it came from. Once the food is prepared, she dishes a portion into bowls for the robbers.

Khatoon takes a bowl to the commander.

A warrior stops Khatoon. "That woman, take to chief."

Khatoon redirects herself. She grabs her hand in silent support. "You're to take this to him." She indicates with her head where Ziva needs to take the food.

Ziva inwardly cringes but keeps the mask in place; it has thus far kept them alive. She looks at the commander, who is watching them. Ziva takes the bowl of food, and presents it to the commander.

Their leader reaches for the bowl and wraps his hands over the young woman.

Ziva's skin crawls. She swallows before looking up at the commander's face, which reveals his plans for her. She jerks her hands away as her stomach twists, ready to give up its contents.

"Sit."

Ziva complies, trying to mask her emotions.

"Open your mouth."

The first bite of food is inserted into Ziva's mouth, and she carefully chews the hot morsels.

"If your mother has poisoned the food, you will also share in the consequence." The man watches her for a response.

When Ziva's mouth is empty, she replies, "Not poisoned." Even if her mother did poison the food, she isn't going to tell him.

The commander sits down next to her and begins to eat. "What are you called?"

"Ziva."

Khatoon feeds two other guards with the available residual bowls.

The remaining two get mad at Khatoon when they aren't given food.

Laman is one of the men who hasn't yet been served. "Old woman, where is our food?" he vehemently roars.

"Give us food," another orders.

Ziva, seeing the men's intent to harm her mother, jumps up and stomps toward them, yelling, "Leave her alone. We don't have any more bowls. You'll have to wait your turn."

Laman shoves Khatoon out of the way.

The other grabs the pot and moves it further from the ash.

Both warriors fight over the remaining contents.

Ziva reaches her mother and helps her up. With her eyes she asks if she is all right.

Khatoon nods.

"Is there a potato left?" Ziva asks.

Khatoon brushes herself off. She points to the bag near the fire.

Ziva pulls a potato from the sack and hands a potato to her mother. "Eat mother. I will pack the remaining supplies and put out the fire."

When the commander is done eating, he calls, "Ziva."

She goes to him, and he hands the empty bowl and spoon to her. "Your mother's food is good. I will let her live."

Ziva takes the bowl and spoon.

He doesn't release them.

Ziva looks at him.

"My name is Pahoran."

Ziva nods in acknowledgement, keeping her face bland.

Pahoran releases his hold on the container and utensil.

Ziva washes the dirty dishes, then returns them to one of the two packs.

Pahoran watches her the whole time.

Those with the remaining bowls and spoons drop them at old woman's feet.

Khatoon gathers and washes them.

The last two who fought over the food, scrape out the last of morsel. They arrive at their commander's side, indicating they are ready.

Ziva doesn't like any of them, especially the two that ate from the pot. She bites her lips, refusing to speak more, and concentrates on helping her mother with their supplies.

Tokal's horse, the only thing left of her friend's, is brought forward to join them on their journey as a prize.

Khatoon places a repacked bag on the horse to be tied down.

The pack is tossed away.

Pahoran directs, "You carry what we tell you."

Ziva bites her tongue. She retrieves the bag, helping her mother to put on the lighter pack.

Situated between the four guards, Ziva and Khatoon follow.

Pahoran leads the way.

Ziva helps her mother, but the pair travel slower than the men would like.

"Old woman, you slow us down," the commander complains.

Ziva steps between them. "Remember what I said." She looks directly at him. "She is a good cook. You need to go slower for us to stay with you."

The chief sends two scouts ahead. Pahoran walks at a slower pace.

Khatoon and her daughter follow the robbers deeper into the forest.

"Ziva, we cannot follow them," Khatoon whispers to her daughter. "We must escape."

"To go where, Mother?" she returns frowning.

"Anywhere is better than being at a Gadianton compound," Khatoon fires back.

The side of Ziva's mouth quirks up, and she gently squeezes Khatoon's hand as she whispers back, "Give me time to think."


KHATOON IS GIVEN A DRESSED porcupine to cook for dinner. "Can you cut it into pieces?"

"No.'"

Khatoon changes tactics and roasts the animal over the fire.

Pahoran wants his meat delivered to him.

When the meat is cooked, Ziva gathers the meat into a bowl and carries it, keeping her face devoid of emotion.

"Sit, Ziva."

Ziva obeys, sitting next to the chief. The first bite is fed to her.

After Pahoran is satisfied that the food isn't poisoned, he eats.

The robbers use leaves to grab their meat off the spit and sit in various areas around camp away from the women.

After the men have eaten their fill, Khatoon and Ziva sit together, eating the remains from the carcass while cautiously watching their captors.

"Why did you tell Pahoran that they would die if they touched us?" Khatoon whispers between bites of food. She keeps the food level with her mouth to mask her words.

Ziva, emptying her mouth, responds using the same technique. "If something were to happen to you, there would be nothing left for me." She takes a bite and swallows before continuing, "I would fight to the death, taking as many of them with me. As long as they don't hurt us, I won't hurt them."

"They killed Tokal," Khatoon says from behind the cooked meat.

Ziva frowns and her head dips, looking at the ground. "I know. I couldn't do anything to prevent it."

That night, mother and daughter are tied to a tree to sleep sitting up. They are close enough to each other to clasp hands, infusing strength and love in one another.

In the morning, a warrior kicks their legs, waking them up. He unties them from their bands. "Food, old woman."

Khatoon nods, moving toward the fire.

Ziva follows her mother, where they work creating a meal to break their fast. She brings a bowl to Pahoran and again is ordered to sit at his feet, taking the first bite of food from her captor.

When Pahoran's satisfied, Ziva is ignored.

The last two men that didn't get a bowl push Khatoon out of the way, fighting for the food in the pot.

An empty bowl and spoon are dropped into Ziva's lap.

Khatoon and she feed themselves with what little is left before heading to the river to clean the dishes and refill the waterskins.

"Go, Ziva. Swim to the other side and escape from here," Khatoon whispers as they clean each dish.

"I will not leave you mother," Ziva returns.

"You must leave. I will slow you down. The longer we're with them, the closer we are to their home. Only a few of them are here. There will be many more at their camp. We must *not* reach it."

"I will *not* leave you," Ziva hisses back, her brows pulled together and down as sharp, fiery eyes dance.

When they are done with the chore at the river, Ziva starts to stand, only to find herself knocked into the cold, swift current that drags her away from her mother.

# TIES

ZIVA OPENS HER MOUTH TO scream, but it fills with water, and she coughs. She reaches for the air and, finding some, takes a deep breath. A moment afterward, her back hits something solid, forcing the air out of her lungs.

Trying to keep her wits about her, she moves her arms, working to bring her body toward the surface of the water. Her head breaks the barrier, and she inhales deeply, realizing that she must do something or be taken by the current to her death.

She struggles, reaching for shore with everything she's worth. Coming close to land, she grasps for a limb but misses a secure hold. The current continues pulling her through low-hanging branches that inflict damage to her skin. She slams into another rock. It holds her there. She succeeds getting a good hold on a branch.

Ziva pulls herself to the surface, breathing in once more. *Move.* She pulls and breathes until she is fully out of the water. She collapses on the earth. Struggling for breath, her body shivers uncontrollably.

Time stops as she lies in the mud.

ZIVA GATHERS HER WITS ABOUT her and rolls onto her back, opening her eyes. She doesn't even know what side of the river she's on, but she recognizes she must move.

Slowly, Ziva pulls her bruised and scratched body up and stands. She decides to continue walking downstream as best she can and starts off slowly, stumbling forward, determined to go as far as her body can carry her. The further away she gets from her mother, the worse she feels. She stops and sits down, wondering what she needs to do. Ziva rests her head upon her hands and thinks.

"I must find out what happened to my mother. I can't leave her there," she mutters, getting to her feet again. She retraces her steps upstream. Ziva hears the swift movement of several creatures coming her way. She hides under a tree and closes her eyes, willing herself to remain completely still, waiting for them to pass.

Hearing their departure, she opens her eyes to see a robber disappear into the brush. Ziva waits until she feels it's safe before continuing her search for her mother. Traveling quicker, she feels the day pass. Her stomach growls, but she doesn't dare stop. Concern for her mother drives her forward.

Thirst makes her stop.

Ziva spends time trying to find something to use to gather water from the river to drink. Finding a sharp rock to use as a tool, she uses the implement to dig a hole adjacent to the river, which fills up with water. Ziva drinks her fill, relieving her incessant thirst. Grabbing her tool, she hikes upstream, pondering on the tool's possible further uses.

Pahoran has left a couple of warriors at the camp to watch the old woman as he continues downstream with the rest of his men to find the woman named Ziva. She is pleasant to look at, and he doesn't want to lose his prize. An old woman is good for work, but a young, strong woman will give him many children.

Finding the evidence where Ziva pulled herself to shore and lay, he begins to trail her. He uses her footprints as a guide.

Pahoran stops seeing two sets of footprints. Based on the patterns, it appears Ziva went downstream first before turning back. Now, she's headed upstream. He smiles, feeling this is a good omen. She's coming back to him.

The robbers move quickly toward camp, while continuing to use her trail as a guide.

Pahoran indicates with his hands for the men to continue following behind her while he moves ahead of her to intercept her. He disappears into the brush.

The men continue their pursuit.

Ziva stops, making another watering hole. After quenching her thirst, she looks around. How far down the river did she travel? Did she pass her mother?

"Keep on moving, Ziva. You must be close," she tells herself. "Keep moving."

A bird calls up ahead.

By pure will, she treks onward, despite how tired he is. "Keep moving forward."

An answering birdcall comes from behind her.

The hair on the back of her neck raises, notifying her that something's not right. She stops. She examines the area. A movement catches her eye.

A whitetail buck, interrupted in drinking, stares at her. He starts grunting and moving forward with his antlers pointed at her.

Ziva steps back a few paces. She runs.

The buck's instinct kicks in, lunging toward her.

Glancing back, the stag is gaining ground. She wants to scream, but all she can do is breathe. Something whizzes through the air passing her. Ziva looks up to see a robber with a bow still aimed in her direction.

The deer grunts in pain behind her.

The robber drops his bow and pulls out a large knife, charging toward her.

Ziva changes direction, away from both threats, leaving behind the combat between man and beast. It doesn't last long.

Fear keeps her moving without looking back.

Something catches Ziva's leg. She falls hard.

Something heavy lands on her.

She pushes with all her might, struggling to get free.

The force continues up her body, pinning her to the ground. It stops on her chest. Her arms are pinned down above her head.

Ziva lies on her back struggling for breath with her eyes closed, waiting for her death blow.

"Open your eyes, Ziva."

Pahoran is sitting on her, covered in blood.

She realizes it must be his hands pinning her arms above her head.

"You're safe from the deer. We'll eat well tonight," Pahoran eyes move to her heaving chest. "You must be tired from today. I will take you back to camp where your mother waits."

Ziva's chest rises and falls with each breath. She stares at the man above her.

Pahoran, waits.

Her breathing slows. Fear subsides.

Pahoran leans down and places his lips on hers in a bruising kiss.

The punishment is over before Ziva can respond.

He lifts his head, raking her body with his eyes. His eyes meet hers. "You're mine, Ziva. Don't run from me again." He pulls her to her feet and into his arms. "You're mine to do with as I please."

Too tired to resist, Ziva follows him back to cam. His warriors carry his kill behind her.

Khatoon runs to Ziva when she sees her.

Pahoran pushes the old woman away. He glares. "You let your daughter be taken by the river. You're lucky to be alive. Cook the meal, old woman. Tonight, she stays with me."

Ziva searches her mother's face, too tired to do anything other than shake her head.

Khatoon frowns. She turns away, heading back to the fire to prepare the meal.

After food has been eaten, Pahoran sits close to Ziva. "You stay with me tonight."

Ziva, exhausted from the day's events, has very little energy but doesn't like the implication. She turns to face Pahoran. "You cannot trust me. I will sleep with my mother."

Pahoran laughs at Ziva. "I saved your life." He places a hand on the back of Ziva's neck. "You're mine."

The kiss is painful. It's meant to punish her.

When their lips part, Pahoran meets her eyes. He grins. "When you see that, your life will be better."

Ziva's anger ignites. "I will sleep with my mother."

Pahoran's temper flares at her tone. He grabs Ziva's arm, pulling her toward the tree.

Ziva struggles to get to her feet under her.

Pahoran forces her down at the base of a tree. "Making me angry is not wise. Much can be done to you that is unpleasant." He lashes her to the sturdy vertical wood.

Ziva locks eyes with him. "Remember what I said."

Pahoran stands up. "Tie up the old woman." He stomps back to his seat near the fire.

His men carry out his order.

In the dark, Ziva and Khatoon grasp hands before succumbing to sleep.

KHATOON AND ZIVA WAKE WITH one guard watching them. They look at each other, not knowing how to react.

Releasing them from the tree, the robber says, "Get your packs. We go."

Ziva's movements are slow as she deals with her bruised and battered body.

The warrior pushes her to move faster.

While traveling, Khatoon whispers to her, "Ziva, you can't allow them to take us back to their camp. We'll never escape if we make it there."

"I know, Mother."

When they make it to the top of the ridge, they hear a baby's wail. They look to where the noise is coming from and find a road scattered with the remains of supplies and bodies. A baby sits howling next to a dead woman. Ziva and Khatoon frown as they realize the robbers have attacked another traveling band.

The guard pushes them forward.

Khatoon leads the way.

Ziva follows.

Finding Khatoon nearing him, Pahoran turns to her. "Old woman, make food."

Khatoon removes her pack and starts gathering wood for a fire.

The commander examines Ziva. "Woman, quiet the child."

Surprised at the order, Ziva doesn't know how to proceed. She has never touched a baby in her life. Her only experiences with babies have been with lambs. "I've never held a baby."

"Pick up the child, or it dies."

Ziva stares at him, shocked by his words. She recalls who he is. Turning her face toward the child, she contemplates the choice.

She sighs, dropping her pack. Ziva quickens her pace, figuring out what to do. She picks the baby up by the chest and hugs it to her body.

The baby instinctively grabs her, looking for comfort, and cries into her shoulder.

Ziva starts rocking the child, making soothing sounds. Before long, quiet returns. Frowning, Ziva walks to Khatoon. "What do I do with a wet baby?"

Khatoon inspects the youngster, seeing a bright and observant countenance. "Continue holding the child and watch the food while

I search for the babe's belongings. I will also see what I can find for the mush," she whispers to her daughter.

Khatoon returns a little while later with several bags. She lays out a cloth on the dirt and takes the child, showing Ziva how to change a soiled cloth.

During the process, one of the guards looks and announces, "A man-child."

When the infant is done being changed, Khatoon pulls out a large piece of cloth and ties the infant to Ziva's chest so that her daughter can use her arms. "You can bind the boy to your front or back so that your arms are free." Changing the subject, Khatoon says, "I've found more bowls and spoons. The child will be fed from your bowl." Lowering her voice, she whispers, "The one named Laman is among the dead."

Ziva masks her delight. With a slight nod, she returns to stir the morning meal.

Khatoon, frowning, delivers a bowl filled with mush and a spoon to her daughter. "Pahoran has made it clear that you are his. You must take him his food. He will not accept it from me."

Ziva eyes her mother, wondering how to avoid the man, but concludes she is unable to evade him. She takes the offered bowl.

"What's this?" the commander asks staring at the bowl containing his food as though it's something poisonous.

"Mush, made from corn. The food is good, especially with dried nuts and fruit," Ziva informs him.

"Sit."

Ziva sits next to him.

"Open your mouth."

Ziva complies, receiving some hot mush.

Seeing this, the baby wails his complaint that he's not being fed.

Ziva takes some of the mush from her mouth and gives it to the infant, who sucks it off her finger.

Pahoran after watching the exchange between Ziva and the infant, sniffs the bowl and takes a tentative bite. He takes another.

Seeing that the chief is content with his food, Ziva moves to get up.

Pahoran notices her movements. "Sit, woman. You haven't been dismissed."

"The baby needs to be fed. I need to help my mother."

"You will stay here."

Ziva frowns but settles.

Watching Pahoran as he eats, the baby boy gnaws on his fist. Saliva dribbles from his mouth.

Khatoon gives the remaining three guards bowls of food. Returning to the fire, Khatoon scoops out another bowl and sets it to the side. She fills the last bowl. She sits back and eats.

The hungry baby wails as Pahoran takes another bite without feeding him.

Ziva automatically tries to soothe the child with no luck.

"Quiet the child so I can eat."

"I'm trying!"

Khatoon arrives next to Ziva with a bowl. "The baby is hungry and the only way he will stop crying is with food. Let my daughter feed him."

"If it stops this noise, do so."

Khatoon gives Ziva the bowl of mush.

Ziva scoops up some food transferring it into infant's mouth.

The wailing stops. Sounds of contentment are heard from the baby's lips.

Every time the little mouth opens, Ziva inserts another spoonful.

Eventually, the child doesn't open his mouth anymore and turns his head away.

Khatoon wipes the boy's mouth. "He's full." She offers a cup of water.

The boy drinks a bit of it. His eyelids begin drooping. "He will sleep soon."

Ziva eats what's left in her bowl and drinks from the waterskin. Once finished, she gets up, gathering the dishes from Pahoran. She cleans the dishes and packs them away, feeling the men's eyes on her.

Warriors gather dousing the fire with their urine and dirt, saving the water for later.

Since Ziva still carries the sleeping child, Khatoon helps her get her pack on. Travel continues at a slower pace. Most of the time, at least one guard is behind them while the others lead the way.

The child wakes up and smiles at Ziva. A few minutes later, a stench comes from Ziva's front.

"What is that?" Ziva asks. "It stinks."

"The baby has released its waste," Khatoon informs her. "We'll need to clean him." Khatoon stops. "Untie the knot that holds the boy."

Ziva follows the instructions.

Khatoon pulls out a piece of cloth. The rope holding the cloth around the child's waist is loosened. She instructs Ziva how to clean the infant.

Ziva's nose crinkles up, and she clenches her jaw, trying not to gag.

The baby smiles, grabbing for a braid that Ziva tries to keep away.

The guard stands upwind from them, observing the process.

Once the child has been cleaned and bound to Ziva's chest, the child starts fussing.

Ziva gazes at her mother with a what-do-I-do-now look.

Khatoon pulls out the cup and waterskin to give the boy a drink.

When the child is satisfied, they resume walking.

They come to an opening and find two Gadianton robbers standing there with a couple of dressed squirrels.

"Time to eat," Pahoran informs them. "Water exists here. We'll stay until morning." The squirrels are tossed at Khatoon's feet."

"Where is Moron?" their Gadianton guard asks looking for his friend.

"Dead." The warrior turns and walks away.

Their guard follows the man to get the details.

Pahoran takes his place under the shade of a tree and watches everyone.

"Ziva, untie the boy from your chest and lay the cloth out on the ground for the baby to sit upon. I will gather wood to make a fire," Khatoon whispers as she helps her remove her pack.

Ziva follows her mother's words and places the infant upon the cloth.

Khatoon brings back some pine cones and hands them to the child to play with. "Watch the boy while I start the fire." She turns her attention to preparing the meal.

Ziva intrigued by her young charge watches as he clumsily picks up and drops the pine cones, trying to get them to his mouth. She brings her head to his view.

He starts smiling, reaching toward her.

"You're cute," she chuckles.

He smiles back at her and babbles his delight.

Pahoran comes to stand next to her and squats down, letting the infant grasp his finger and try to take it to his mouth. "You're good with the boy." He wiggles his finger. "Tonight, protect yourselves." He places a knife next to next to her skirt, without the other guards seeing it.

Ziva gazes at him, wondering why he would do such a thing, but carefully hides the knife in her pocket.


THAT NIGHT, THE STEW FEEDS the group. Some broth feeds the baby.

Pahoran announces, "The women will not be tied anymore because they will stay with the child. The boy will slow them down so much, they will be easy to catch."

No word is spoken by the remaining guards.

Ziva and Khatoon look at one another but don't say a word, feeling the underlying tension between the remaining two robbers and their leader.

Ziva knows they want to kill her. Pahoran is keeping them from accomplishing that.

Both women continue their chores, since there isn't much else they can do. The dirty cloth soiled by the child earlier in the day is washed. Dishes are cleaned and packed. Waterskins are refilled.

When the baby is tired and fussy, Ziva walks with him tied to her chest until the infant settles and sleeps. Ziva unties the boy from her and places him next to her mother. She settles beside them, hoping she can protect them both.

ZIVA STARTLES AWAKE. SHE LOOKS up to find a robber looming over her with a raised hatchet over his head and an arrow sticking out of his chest. She kicks at him as he continues forward.

Another arrow hits the assailant, and teeters back a pace but gathers his strength pushing forward again.

There is a bloodcurdling scream.

Glancing that way, her mother scurries away with the baby. Ziva rolls to the side, standing up with the knife in her hand.

The robber falls on her.

Ziva loses her footing with the attacker's weight and momentum, tumbling to the ground. She slashes and kicks her way from him. When she stands up, the knife is missing.

She breathes hard.

The attacker lies motionless on the ground.

A movement in her periphery catches her attention. Her head swivels in time to see her mother step in front of her.

Khatoon is propelled into Ziva.

They fall to the ground.

Ziva pushes her mother's body off her and scrambles to her knees, rolling her mother over so she can see.

Khatoon's face is white, but a determined look is present, "Get the knife. You must protect us."

Ziva nods. She throws herself on the dead robber lying nearby, searching for a knife. Finding a weapon, she pulls it from his body.

When she looks up, one of the guards has an arrow aimed at her. Pahoran raise his knife behind the man.

She's frozen to the spot as the scene unfolds.

Pahoran disrupts the guard's aim before the arrow is loosed, and his knife slices the guard's throat.

Ziva registers a child screaming and glances in the direction of the sound. Seeing the boy, she scoops him up, and dumps him with her mother. She turns her attention back to Pahoran.

Two bodies are lying on the ground.

Her cautious steps bring her to the bodies.

Pahoran has blood streaming from multiple wounds. He glares at her and vehemently howls, "I should have killed you both at the beginning like my men wanted. Your words have killed us all."

"You have killed yourselves," Ziva returns, frowning. "Since you spared us, I will bury your body."

Pahoran coughs. He gurgles. He looks at her one final time and stills.

After his final breath, Ziva returns her mother. Her mother's arm is around him.

The child is quiet.

Arriving at her side, Ziva realizes an arrow is lodged in her mother's chest. Horrified, Ziva drops to her knees.

# ALONE

"ARE THEY DEAD?" KHATOON INQUIRES.

"Yes." Concern laces Ziva's words. "We need to get this arrow out of you."

"Leave the arrow where it lies." Khatoon breaths. "It will give me time with you." She smiles, trying to reassure her. "If you pull it out, I'll die quicker."

Her words reach Ziva's core, as though someone has stabbed her heart. A sob escapes. Tears course down her cheeks. She realizes she doesn't have the skill necessary to help her mother. "Why did you run in front of me?" she wails.

"To save your life, dearest." Khatoon smiles. "I'm happy with my decision."

"I'm not!" Ziva wipes her leaky nose with her sleeve. "What am I to do without you? What are we going to do without you? I don't know how to take care of an infant. I don't know how to get us home." Her voice climbs with her anxiety.

Khatoon interrupts Ziva's rant. "Breathe, Ziva. Everything happens for a reason."

Ziva stares in disbelief. "How can you be so calm at a time like this?"

"I have to be calm in order to maximize the time I have left with you," Khatoon closes her eyes for a moment. "Calm yourself so we can get to work."

Ziva stares. Her words sink in even more. She takes a couple deep breaths and closes her eyes. Her shoulders sag. She wipes away her tears. "I will do what you tell me."

"That's better." Khatoon takes a breath. "Break the shaft so I don't hit it on anything." She steadies the wood.

Ziva places both hands on the arrow. "Ready?" She glances at her mother.

"Yes."

Ziva breaks the stick.

Khatoon is pale. Her color slowly returns as she relaxes. She coughs. "We're fine where we are, under the shade. Take care of the bodies so that predators don't come this way. Keep some of their weapons as you will need them in the forest. Get rid of the horse. Work quickly. I have much to tell you before my time ends."

Ziva, filled with sadness, squeezes her mother's hand. She strokes the boy's head. Standing, she decides where to start. Wiping her leaking eyes, she takes a final cleansing breath.

Ziva drags the first two bodies to the river to be taken downstream. The horse is released. She hopes it will find its way to safety. She gathers up the weapons, deciding which ones to keep.

Pahoran's body takes more time since she stated it will be buried. Finding a place that has soft dirt, she takes a sharp rock and uses it to dig the hole. The discarded weapons are tossed in the grave.

Hearing the child cry, Ziva returns to camp.

Khatoon is cooking mush.

Ziva rushes to Khatoon's side. "Mother, let me do that."

As Ziva takes over, Khatoon explains, "He's hungry and won't wait any longer."

"I have the hole dug for Pahoran."

Khatoon's eyes widen in disbelief. "You're going to bury him even after he killed Tokal?"

Ziva moves the pot from the embers before picking up the infant and placing him on her hip. "Yes, he saved me multiple times. I don't know why."

"He liked you."

Ziva looks at her mother with thinned lips and one raised eyebrow.

Khatoon fills the bowls and juts her chin toward the boy. "You're doing well with him."

"He's easy to care for."

"Not all children are that easy." Khatoon smiles, joining Ziva where their gear sits. Ziva's eyes rivet toward her mother.

With a loving smile, Khatoon sets the bowls down, getting herself situated against a tree. "Yes, you were one such child, but I so enjoyed raising you. He may not always be easy. Will you keep him should he become difficult?"

"I cannot abandon him," Ziva cools the food.

The infant reaches for the bowl.

Ziva moves it out of his reach.

He fusses.

"That's good, because he will be yours." Khatoon adds some dried fruit and nuts to her bowl. "Don't you think he needs a name?"

"I guess so." Ziva crinkles her forehead as she settles the boy beside her and spoons food into the drooling mouth. "How do you choose a name?"

"You pick one. A name is not something difficult to give." Khatoon watches her daughter as she pours some water into a cup and hands it to Ziva.

The child empties the offered cup.

"Pahoran took away Tokal's life, but he also gave this life to you. Would you like to name him Tokalihah?"

Ziva's mouth turns down at the corners. She shovels another spoonful into the child's mouth. Her attention turns to her mother. "I never was going to be Joined to Tokal, even though you had hoped it would happen. He still feels like my brother." Ziva thinks over the name. "I don't think Tokalihah is appropriate."

Khatoon frowns at her daughter's response. "It can be whatever you would like."

At the sight of the bowl and Ziva's slow response in feeding him, the baby drops the spoon he holds, reaching for the bowl in an effort to feed himself.

Ziva holds him back as she keeps it out of his reach. She shovels in more food.

A little clumsy hand grabs the spoon she holds. The contents fall off the spoon and on a chubby thigh, hand, and forearm. A fist rushes to an open mouth.

"It will be easier to feed him and less mess if you put him in your lap and control his arms. Put one of his arms behind your back." Khatoon passes Ziva a cloth.

Ziva cleans the food off of the child.

The boy wails.

Ziva places the child in her lap. She retrieves the spoon and feeds him again. This time, she's able to keep the mess to a minimum.

After the boy is full of mush and water, Ziva changes his cloth and lays him on the blanket on his stomach while she eats. "I think I'm going to call him Tokal as a reminder of a good man, but not as the man's child."

"That's good." Khatoon finishes feeding herself. "Since you are his new mother and in dangerous territory, I advise you to change your bracelet to your right wrist so that you will not be displaying yourself as single."

"But I will be displaying myself as a widow and available."

"Yes, but a man will choose to Join a single woman over a widow who has a child." Khatoon shrugs and grins. "But that depends on the man." The smile disappears. "Having the bracelet on your right wrist will protect you."

"I don't see how, but I will do as you ask." Ziva takes her last bite.

"Give me your wrist."

Ziva complies.

Khatoon switches Ziva's bracelet to her right wrist. "That is better." She smiles and nods. "Leave Tokal here with me for his nap while you clean dishes and finish with the robber. We'll be fine."

AFTER BURYING PAHORAN AND THE unwanted weapons, Ziva cleans up at the river before returning to camp.

Khatoon has Tokal occupied with a bowl and spoon as well as some pinecones as he plays on the blanket next to her.

"I have completed the task."

"Good," Khatoon nods. "Much needs to be done during these next few days I have with you. Tokal will be hungry soon. Can you cook some food?"

Ziva nods, dropping a wooden bow decorated in rattlesnake skin, a woven quiver with turquoise embellishments on the edge of the rim, three knives, and a spear next to Khatoon.

She smiles apologetically for noise her quick release of the weapons made, then gathers supplies to cook some more mush for them.

When the food is cooked and Tokal is done eating and cleaned, Khatoon speaks again. "You will need to make traps and set them so we can have food in the morning. Meat will need to be quickly dried and supplies gathered so you can travel. When you come to a road, someone will be at the end of it." Khatoon coughs, lasting longer. "One more thing, you will need to prepare my grave."

"Mother!" Ziva gasps before frowning, realizing again what her mother says is true.

"Don't be sad for me," Khatoon soothes. "I'm grateful to have this time with my daughter and grandson. Soon, I'll be reunited with your father and Tokal. I'm happy." She smiles. "What saddens me will be leaving you here. You need people, Ziva, in order to survive. A mother out here on her own won't last long. Promise me you'll search for good people." Holding up her hand to stop her daughter's response, she continues. "When you find good people, promise me you'll stay with them." Khatoon drops her hand.

Ziva considers her mother's words, not fully understanding, but she trusts her mother's wisdom. "I promise."

"Good." Khatoon pats her daughter's hand. "I'll care for Tokal while you work."

Ziva spends the rest of the day preparing. Once the traps are made, she takes the knowledge that the shepherds taught her over the years and sets the traps. She returns with juniper to dry what meat is obtained. She checks on Khatoon and Tokal before turning her attention toward digging another grave. They are comfortably resting in the shade.

This time, she cries as she prepares the hole, allowing her heart to unburden itself of the pain and loss of the last few days. With the grave dug, she washes and returns to camp with wood for the fire, anticipating Tokal to soon to be hungry. At camp, Ziva builds a fire closer to her mother.

Khatoon watches as Ziva fixes the meal.

When the mush is fixed, Ziva brings both bowls under the shade tree where they eat.

"Ziva, douse the fire before it gets dark. I don't want to attract Gadianton our way. Tomorrow, I'll teach you how to diffuse fire and smoke so that it will be harder to find us."

Ziva changes Tokal's cloth before extinguishing the fire with a waterskin.

In the twilight, Ziva walks to the river, taking care of the final chores before returning to camp. She finds a very awake and playful Tokal. Her mother looks tired, leaning up against the tree.

"Mother, how are you?" Ziva asks.

"Well enough, dear." She grins at Ziva. "Although, I recommend avoiding being hit by an arrow." Khatoon coughs.

Ziva leans down and kisses her mother's head. "You look tired."

"So do you. Meanwhile, our little friend is wide awake."

Khatoon pats Tokal's foot, while he endeavors to capture one of his toys.

"Sleep, Mother. I'll stay up with him." Ziva sits down next to Tokal, and he smiles at her.

"I'm almost afraid to sleep. I'm not ready to leave you." Khatoon closes her eyes. "Do you have the weapons with us?"

"Yes, they're right here."

Khatoon looks directly at her daughter. "Do not be afraid to use them."

Darkness descends.

Khatoon sleeps, sitting up.

Ziva keeps her hand around Tokal's leg so he doesn't get lost.

Tokal starts fussing.

Ziva moves him next to her for the night. Crickets chirp and frogs croak in the distance. Ziva's eyes grow heavy as dreams of better days dance upon her mind and exhaustion sinks her into slumber.

Ziva wakes with a start.

Tokal and Khatoon are sleeping.

Ziva with quiet steps moves away. Taking some weapons with her, she searches the traps, hoping to be back before Tokal stirs.

Ziva's happy that she now has some meat. She prepares some mush knowing that Tokal will wake soon. While it cools, her attention turns to drying the food. She sews thin pieces of meat on thread and hangs them in the full sun.

Tokal's head pops up. He looks around and starts babbling.

Khatoon opens her eyes.

Ziva brings the cooling bowls of mush. She sits down, handing a bowl to her mother. Filling cups with water, she hands one to Khatoon and places the other one next to her.

Tokal smiles at her with a loaded cloth.

"I smell your morning gift." She lays him down to change his cloth. She cleans her hands using the waterskin. The child is set in her lap.

Khatoon coughs. "You're doing well with him."

"I'm glad you're still alive." She feeds her young charge. "I'm not ready to say goodbye."

"I can't leave until more is done. I hope you know that my spirit will remain with you even though my body will go the way of the earth. What have you completed, and what still needs to be done?"

"Of the traps, a couple had game, which I have drying. I'll need to search for some food and see what other supplies can be found."

"Ziva, listen carefully to what I tell you. To keep a fire hidden from others, dig a hole for the fire under some nearby branches. Create a smaller hole next to the first hole and connect the two with a tunnel. In the larger hole"—Khatoon coughs—"build your fire. It will be hotter, there will be less smoke, and the branches overhead will diffuse the rest." Khatoon coughs again and takes a breath. "Do what you can today to get as much accomplished. My strength wanes."

Ziva frowns. "Do I need to take Tokal with me?"

"At this time, leave him." Khatoon coughs again as her breathing becomes a little more labored. Fine drops of blood show up, spattering the dirt, and are quickly erased by Khatoon's hand before her daughter can see them.

Ziva completes her food before leaving Tokal in Khatoon's care.

ONCE FINISHED GATHERING WHAT SHE can find, she returns to camp.

Tokal sleeps in Khatoon's arms.

Ziva not wanting to wake the sleeping forms, checks the drying meat. Fish is found in the river trap. She retrieves them for their midday food.

When the noon meal is prepared, Ziva brings a bowl to her mother.

Khatoon leans against the tree. Her eyes are still closed, but one hand is fastened on Tokal's leg while he plays.

After getting her mother to release her hold, Ziva changes Tokal's cloth and feeds him. When he's done, she places him on the blanket to play.

"Mother, I have fish to eat. Would you like some?"

Khatoon's eyes flutter open and fasten her. She slightly smiles and shakes her head no. "Water."

Ziva takes the cup and presses it to her mother's lips.

Khatoon drinks. With a firm grip she grabs her daughter's hand and squeezes. She coughs again and struggles for breath. "I fear, I can no longer watch Tokal."

Ziva exhales and her body sags with it. "I'm not able to find any herbs to ease your pain. Is there something else I can do to relieve your suffering?"

"It will pass soon." She coughs again. Khatoon peers at her daughter. "Take Tokal and finish your tasks. I'll be here when you return."

Ziva grasps her mother's hand as her fear spills out her mouth. "I don't want to leave you."

"I will still be here," Khatoon squeezes her daughter's hand to reassure her. A coughing fit takes over. She releases her hold. When she's able to breath again, she stills. Her eyes still closed. "My time is not yet. When it does come, you and Tokal will be fine." She examines her daughter's face. "Remember your promise to find good people and stay with them. Press forward, Ziva. Don't give up."

Ziva smiles and nods to reassure her mother, but it doesn't reach her eyes. Inside she feels a jumbled mess of emotions. She gently hugs her mother before tying Tokal on her back.

She takes one last look at Khatoon. "I love you, Mother."

Her mother gives a weak smile. "I love you, Ziva. Remember, you're a pearl of great price."

Ziva nods before gathering the dishes.


SHE RETURNS TO CAMP AND finds Khatoon with her eyes closed. Her skin is dusky. Her breathing rattles in an irregular pattern.

There is nothing is nothing left to be done but wait. Her emotions rise up clawing its way out. She takes a deep breath to steady herself, pushing it away. She leaves camp to finish the last task she's been putting off—her mother's grave.

After an afternoon of digging, Ziva returns.

Khatoon's skin is now very pale. There's a stillness in her body.

Ziva falls to her knees next to her mother, afraid that she may already be dead. Her breath hitches. She's scared to touch her. What if she's already dead? She looks for signs of life.

Khatoon takes a shallow breath.

Ziva exhales a sigh of relief. Picking up the flowers she dropped, she prepares a small amount of tea. She found the flowers on her way back.

"Mother, I'm here." Ziva blows on the tea. "I found some purple coneflowers, which will help relieve your pain. You continue to rest." Ziva sits herself next Khatoon. "Please drink the coneflower tea so you may rest easier."

Khatoon's eyelids flutter. When the cup is pressed to her lips, she drinks. Most of the medicine dribbles out her mouth.

Ziva blinks back the tears that threaten to fall. She fixes dinner for Tokal, while he babbles and practices pushing himself up onto his knees, making Ziva smile. The fire in the pit she built gives off heat and very little light. She feeds Tokal. Taking a deep breath, she settles herself between Tokal and Khatoon. She will watch both as the profound sadness grows within her.

Tokal relaxes and sleeps.

Khatoon is no longer conscience.

Ziva listens to Khatoon's irregular breathing that waxes and wanes, knowing that death will come soon.

Silent ears begin coursing down her cheeks. She lays Khatoon down. "You can leave, mother. We will be all right. Go to father." She sniffs. "I will continue to move forward with Tokal back toward civilization, as I promised." Ziva holds onto her mother's hand, dreading the moment that is coming.

The night passes slowly for Ziva as she listens and waits with dread.

Khatoon exhales her last.

Quiet fills the air.

Ziva blinks back her tears, trying to look through the darkness at her mother's face. She presses a hand to Tokal's sleeping form, feeling his rhythmic breathing and beating heart, reminding her that she's not alone.

Ziva closes her eyes, succumbing to the uncontrollable outpouring of tears. There is nothing else she can do in the dark. "Goodbye, Mother."

When light dispels the darkness, Ziva kisses her mother's forehead and begins the process of dragging her to her grave. Not being able to carry both, she leaves a sleeping Tokal behind.

After depositing the body in the hole, she quickly washes before returning to find the still-sleeping form.

Tokal is strapped to her back after his morning meal. She packs her supplies and places them near her mother's grave. All remains of their stay are obliterated.

The final task she must do before moving on looms over her with a heavy weight.

Khatoon is laid out in the grave.

Taking a breath and squaring her shoulders, the dirt is pushed over her mother as tears stain her cheeks. When the task is finished, she sits there catching her breath.

Ziva stands up. She sings the Song of the Dead to her mother, which is joined by Tokal's babbling.

Loved ones you leave, Will miss you so.
Remembered in our hearts, Through life we go.
Life does not end, Life does go on.
Follow the path, To return to the Son.
Loved ones you greet, That have gone before.
With open arms, To return once more.
One day we too, Will take this path.
To return to your arms, At long last.

She stands there, staring at the mound.

Shaking her head to clear it and wiping away her tears, she forces herself from her grief and pulls on her pack. Looking down at the soft head that is babbling in front of her, she says, "We have only each other." She takes one final look at the burial mound before heading back the way she traveled, on her search for civilization.

# WILDERNESS

Tired, Ziva can go no further. She makes camp near the river under a tree. The air smells fresh and clean here. The nearby waterfall hides Tokal's sounds, which she hopes will keep them safe throughout the night. She feeds Tokal, who continues to practice push-ups, while she cleans the dishes. She feels heartbroken and alone.

The surface of the river is smooth as she watches leaves and sticks being pushed toward the cliff and disappearing. Ziva's mind wanders as she watches.

Her mother pushed her into the water so she could escape from the robbers. Treading water in the river had taken her somewhere, but not where she had wanted to go. Not making a choice was a choice; making that choice is what had slammed her into a rock. If she had gone with the current, she would most certainly be dead at present. She made a decision and moved, which brought her to shore.

Thinking of her choice to not leave her mother with those men, only to see her mother die, overwhelms her. She swallows her sorrow and blinks. "There has been enough of tears," she tells herself.

It would be so easy to walk over the edge of the waterfall into oblivion and join your family. It would be so easy.

Something touches her, catching her attention.

Tokal managed to push himself next to Ziva. He endeavors to climb over Ziva's leg.

"How did you get over here?" Ziva asks him, which is drowned out by the waterfall. She picks him up and hugs him.

He wraps his arms around her neck, seeming to know of her misery, and he settles.

Tears escape Ziva's eyes. As she speaks to him, he comforts her. "I almost gave up, but you've reminded me of my promise to my mother." She squeezes him tight, savoring his little body as he holds her neck. "I must continue forward with you and hope for better things to come." She caresses the little head. "You'll need to remind me periodically." She picks up the cloth, tying Tokal to her. "Let's get some sleep."

She's awakened by a moving form on her chest. Her eyes open to find Tokal crying, but she can only hear the sound of the waterfall. She caresses the little head, realizing that she overslept and Tokal is hungry. An odor hits her nose, notifying her of Tokal's other problem. She sits up, detaches him from her chest, and rolls him over to change him. Grabbing a large strip of jerky, she hands it to him to gnaw on. "I'm sorry I overslept. Here's some dried meat to chew while I get you changed before working on your food." Her stomach growls since she didn't eat the night before. "Our food," she corrects herself.

Still feeling depressed, she thinks about Ami's positivity. Ami always looked at the bright side of things. She recalls Ami stating that when she has a rough day, she counts her blessings. Ziva starts by being thankful for Tokal.

Ziva takes care of their needs and gathers her supplies. The both of them travel upstream. She breathes easier when Tokal stops babbling and falls asleep. "I'm thankful Tokal sleeps," she mutters to herself. When the sun is high in the sky, she stops. She prepares what she pulled from the trap that morning. Tokal will awake soon for some food. "I'm thankful for this meal to fill our belly." Their meal ends with her resuming the journey, hoping to find their way back to civilization.

She settles into a daily routine of caring for Tokal, gathering supplies, and evading other Gadianton warriors who are traveling the area. Over time, her depression disappears as she concentrates on being thankful for the things she has, consciously choosing to move forward and to serve Tokal.

To keep Tokal's babbling to a minimum, she learns giving him something to chew on keeps him entertained. Along the way, she finds the remains of travelers who met Gadianton, salvaging what she can use to replace their dwindling supplies before moving on.

Her thoughts turn to her parents, who protected her and helped her as she struggled with people and how they reacted to her. "I'm so thankful for my parents. For their patience with me."

One day, she stops and looks at the pearl, smiling as she recalls her parent's words: "Ziva, you are of great worth. A pearl of great price." As she continues traveling, she remembers her community with the shepherds, especially the old shepherd. He sat with her many times, overlooking the sheep. They would talk about life and people. The shepherds taught her so much. "I'm thankful for community."

When she's ready to give up, the promise to her mother pokes her mind on occasion and prods her forward. In these moments, Ziva takes a deep breath before moving again in an unfamiliar forest. She hopes that she is on the right path to find good people and civilization.

One evening, on a hill overlooking a valley, Ziva sits resting against a tree.

Tokal sings himself asleep.

Ziva smiles, resting a gentle hand on his side. She has grown to love this little person who has been her only companion since her mother's death. She examines the sky to find the new moon, the third one they've seen while on their own. She sighs and her attention returns to the sleeping form against her. Because of him, she will keep her promise—to find people. She knows she would have quit long before if it weren't for him and the things she learned from Ami.

Closing her eyes, she rests with her spear and knife within easy reach as they shelter for the night. In the dark, she whispers to Tokal's sleeping form, "We need to find people soon, Tokal. My strength is waning. Our supplies are dwindling. The weather is changing, and soon it will be very cold. Know that I will still do what is necessary to keep you safe."

ZIVA'S EYES FLY OPEN AS her hand reaches for the spear. She searches the forest for what woke her. A fire in the near distance—a campfire by the looks of it catches her attention. She ties Tokal's sleeping form to her chest. Gathering her pack, Ziva travels in the dark to discover whether the people are Gadianton. Without a sound she treads with caution toward the fire. Every now and again she stops and crouches until she can hear their words. She hides herself.

"I would give anything to have a woman's cooking. They know what they're doing when they cook."

"At least we have food while we complete our schooling."

"If any of us could cook, we wouldn't have to eat burned meat with little variation. I'm tired of it."

"How many more moons do we have left before we can return to Zarahemla for the winter?"

"Quit whining. This is good for you and will help you understand what will be required of you as an astronomer. In the spring, you'll be finished with your schooling and can return to your families."

"I've felt the change in the season. Winter is coming."

"There'll be times when you will need to be able to care for yourself as you converse with the sky. This is part of your training."

"Yes, Nephi."

"Your city and family have sent you to Zarahemla to learn astronomy. It doesn't matter if you're a Nephite or a Lamanite, your city will need your expertise to know when to plant and when to harvest. If you pay attention and learn what I teach you, knowing the signs in the sky will help your city prosper. If you don't learn well, you could read the sign incorrectly and cause your city and family harm."

Ziva listens intently to the conversation, feeling that they will be safe within this group until they return to their city. Tomorrow morning she'll show herself and hope the group will let her stay with them until she can get back to civilization. She can cook for them.

"Finish eating so we can begin tonight's lesson."

Ziva makes her way back to a secure and hidden area. Ziva's stomach clenches announcing her hunger. She breaks off a piece of her leftover meat and pops it in her mouth. Her eyes close and her hand drops to Tokal's back as sleep takes over.

A SOUND WAKES HER. SHE looks down.

Tokal wails loud and strong.

Something in her periphery catches her attention. A spear is descending toward the two of them. She rolls to the side, protecting Tokal. The point pierces the dirt, missing her back. Grabbing hers, she launches to her feet, ready to defend herself. Once she's upright, a wolf-like animal jumps in the air. Jaws clamp down on the neck of her attacker. Screams and growls pierce the air.

Ziva steps back against the tree, frightened by the gruesome scene unfolding in front of her. As quick as it came, it ends.

Tokal cries.

Ziva searches the area, anticipating something else will attack. One hand pats Tokal's back, trying to comfort him. As the child settles, she hears screams of pain from others in the distance.

The night is silent.

She continues her soothing dance for Tokal as her ears probe, listening for any sounds.

Torches move through the dark not far away.

Ziva presses herself to the tree trunk with her spear in hand. As long as Tokal is quiet they may be able to disappear into the night. She rests her arm against Tokal's back to reassure him, hoping he'll remain that way. Ziva barely breaths as the torches come her way. Her heart pounds in her ears like a strong beating drum.

Tokal babbles.

Ziva cringes. She covers his mouth with her hand.

Startled Tokal, stops his utterance.

She feels her heart in her throat choking her as the lights get closer and closer.

Tokal, not liking her hand on his mouth, shakes his head to remove it.

The torches near and her heart drops. She stands immobile with nowhere to hide.

Tokal wails, expressing his complaint loud and strong.

They've been found!

# ASTRONOMY

THE TORCH LIGHT FINDS HER pressed to the tree, eyes wide, brows drawn, and lips pulled back. She's ready to fight. The baby at her chest, unhappy with the hand that is covering his lips, attempts to push it away. Ziva blinks, to clear her vision, finding seven men of varying ages staring at her. One looks older than the others.

"You're safe." The older man motions to the baby "It looks like he would appreciate it if you would remove your hand from his mouth."

Ziva blinks.

"We're from Zarahemla. Thanks to the child's cry, we were able to save you." He looks at her and steps forward.

Ziva removes her hand from Tokal's mouth, raising her spear.

Tokal's anger pierces the night air.

The old man raises his hands. "I have no weapons. You're safe." The man grins at her. "The baby has a good set of lungs. What's its name?"

Ziva blinks twice, trying to comprehend. Finally, she swallows and answers. "Tokal."

"How long have you been out here on your own?"

"I . . . I don't know," Ziva stammers, still skittish.

The older man juts his head toward the spear. "You can lower your weapon. You're safe."

Ziva's mind understands the word safe. She glances at the javelin, that she's ready to use, before returning her gaze to the man. Realizing the men are not there to harm her and Tokal, she slowly lowers it.

"You are lucky to find us. It looks like you were being pursued by robbers. Fortunately, Kelev stopped the one who attacked you."

"Kelev? Robbers?" Ziva's eyebrows come together, trying to understand all that happened.

"You and your baby are safe. Come to the fire and tell us your story," the older man suggests, stepping back and raising his arm toward the fire that still can be seen in the distance.

"Safe." Ziva comprehends, crumpling to the dirt.


ZIVA AWAKENS, FINDING HERSELF lying on a blanket near a fire. Absently she reaches for Tokal, but he's not there. Memories flood back, causing her to bolt upright to search for him. Immediately, stars and blackness cover her field of vision. She lies back down. "Tokal! Where's Tokal?" she hollers. Forcing herself to sit again, she battles back her dizziness with clenched teeth.

Surprised, the older man dashes to her side. He presses his hand on her shoulder to keep her down. "Easy there. You've been out for a while. After feeding and changing the young'un, he settled right back down to sleep. Lie still and we'll place him in your arms."

Ziva stops fighting. She breathes. A wrapped bundle is placed in her arms, and the firelight reveals it to be Tokal.

He sleeps.

With a light touch, her hand rests upon his chest.

Tokal's breathing is even, verifying his unconscious state.

Ziva covers him up from the cool air and exhales a sigh of relief.

"You look like you could use a drink," the older man grins. "Are you thirsty?"

She nods.

"Let one of my students help you sit up before you drink."

"I can sit up." She lays Tokal down next to her. She pushes herself up. From behind, strong hands are placed under her shoulders, lifting her to a sitting position. She feels something firm at her back and leans against it for support. She blinks her eyes, trying to clear them.

"Easy there, boys. We need to be gentle with her and the babe. They've been through a lot."

She realizes she's leaning against someone's chest as a cup with something warm is handed to her. She gulps down the heavenly liquid. It warms her insides. The cup in her hands is pulled back from her lips.

"Easy there. If you drink too fast, you're going to make yourself sick," the older man warns. "You can have as much as you want, but you need to slow down."

Ziva nods. The hand on the cup disappears, allowing her to drink again. She drinks slower this time, emptying the cup.

Another mug, as if by magic, replaces the empty one.

Feeling somewhat better, she inspects the group of men surrounding her. The older man faces her. Muscular young men possibly in their twenties down to the age of twelve or thirteen years are eager to help. From what she can see in the firelight, they all have black or dark-brown hair, but she is unable to determine their eye color. They are clothed with shirts and skirts similar to those in Uthal. Something stirs her memory of a city named Zarahemla and an attack. She takes another drink. "What happened?"

"From our point of view, Kelev growled to warn us before she ran into the forest. We retrieved our weapons, following after. A baby hollers. We found multiple Gadianton and stopped them."

"Kelev?" Ziva's brows scrunch together, looking to Nephi for answers.

Nephi laughs, leaning his head toward the man on his left. "Lib's beast of a dog."

"Dog?" Ziva's eyes widen as her mind snaps the missing puzzle in place as to what happened at the tree.

The man on the older man's left, whistles.

A large furry animal appears, panting. The dog lies down next to Tokal, sniffing the infant."

Ziva's eyes the beast, concerned for Tokal. "He's not going to hurt us, is he?" She doesn't move even though she wants to push the animal away.

"Kelev is actually a girl and is very fond of infants. She kept both of you safe," the owner reassures. He has dark-brown hair. She still can't see the color of his eyes, but they belong to a friendly face, which sits atop a well-defined torso.

"Oh." Ziva stares at the large animal, not sure she can put her trust in it.

"Have you ever met a dog before?" Nephi gently probes.

"The shepherds in Uthal have dogs. Kelev looks more like a wolf."

"Perhaps she does have some wolf in her." Lib chuckles, petting the beast's head. "She's very smart and keeps us all safe."

Nephi clears his throat, taking control of the conversation. "Were Gadianton following you?"

Ziva sips the warm liquid. She realizes it's broth. "I didn't know they were following me. They could've seen your fire. That's what attracted me."

The older man peers at Ziva. "Gadianton are usually not this close to the city. Something or someone brought them here." He watches her.

Ziva drinks, starting to feel better. She doesn't know what to say to his accusation, but she better explain.

"I'm Nephi and these are my astronomy students. What's your name?"

"Ziva." She takes another sip. "I'm blessed to be with people again."

"Where are you from Ziva?"

"I'm from Uthal." Finishing what is in her cup, she sets it on her lap, hands grasping the warm mug.

"Lib is from Uthal," Nephi nods toward the man sitting on his left, next to Tokal and Kelev. "You're a long way from Uthal."

Ziva glances at Lib again, but she doesn't know him. Their eyes meet. She turns her attention back to Nephi. Lib's inquisitive, intelligent gaze unsettles her. It wasn't negative-just, searching. She swallows. "Gadianton attacked my group while we were traveling back to Uthal, and I became their prisoner."

Ziva's eyes drop. She swallows. "A fight broke out among them, and they killed each other." Ziva touches Tokal, taking comfort from him. "We've since been trying to find our way back to civilization." She trades her empty one for the new one offered to her. She closes her eyes, taking a drink.

"What city were you traveling from before you were taken?"

"Arnac." Ziva frowns, looking at the empty cup.

"And that is when your trouble started?" Nephi coaxes.

Ziva nods but doesn't look up.

"You're husband?" Nephi inquires.

Ziva closes her eyes and swallows as memories flash to the forefront of her mind. She remembers her mother's words. "Everyone is dead."

With compassion, Nephi nods. "I'm sorry for your grief."

"If only . . . if only . . ." Ziva stammers as tears come to her eyes. She blinks them away.

Nephi takes her hand and squeezes it as he continues in his soothing tone. "If, would have, and should have only canker the mind. They won't change the past. Let the past go and use it as a learning experience for the future." He pats her hand. "You've been through a lot, and these students of mine have a lesson that needs to be given. Get some rest, and we'll talk more in the morning."

"What about Gadianton? You said they are out there."

Nephi takes a breath and reassures her with a smile. "They were out there, but they're now food for beasts. Kelev will inform us if any more are in the area. You look tired, Ziva. Rest. We'll talk more in the morning. May I have the cup?"

Surprised that she's still holding the cup, Ziva glances at the empty mug. The dish is passed to Nephi.

Nephi turns his attention to the group at large, "Time for your lesson."

Ziva feels strong hands on her shoulders push her forward so she's not leaning. With a slow movement, the unseen hands help her lie down. Another blanket is settled over her and Tokal, wrapping their bodies in warmth. The fire is doused, and the men move to the smoldering wood. Nephi starts talking to his students, pointing up at the sky. Although she doesn't understand what's being said, Nephi's voice is soothing. She puts an arm over Tokal, tucking him closer, and for the first time in a long time, they sleep with blankets.

ZIVA STRETCHES. TOKAL ISN'T NEXT to her. She bolts upright, looking around.

Tokal crawls in the dirt toward Kelev.

A man stands nearby watching over him—she vaguely recalls Lib being his name.

The dog, Kelev licks Tokal when he arrives. It nudges him back toward Lib. She trots back to the man, lying down.

When the dog settles, Tokal smiles at the animal before crawling in her direction.

Lib picks up Tokal when he reaches him, puts his face on his belly, and blows.

Tokal smiles and laughs.

Lib sets Tokal back on all fours.

Kelev gets up and trots away, putting space between the child and where it settles.

Tokal crawls back to Kelev, where the game starts again.

Ziva smiles, watching the dog and man be so gentle and kind with Tokal. She looks at the others who sit nearby, ignoring the man and child while working on various things. She gets up, wrapping a blanket around her shoulders before walking over to where Lib sits on the ground.

"Good morning, Lib," she sits next to him.

Tokal sees her and makes a beeline to her, with an overjoyed expression on his face.

"Good morning, Ziva." Lib grins at her, watching Tokal crawl to her.

She picks him up, and they hug each other.

"Your son loves his mother very much."

She sets him in her lap. A smile on her lips. "I love him too." Changing the subject, she asks, "He doesn't seem hungry. Has he eaten?"

"Kelev notified me when Tokal awoke, bright and early this morning. I thought it best to let you sleep. I hope you don't mind. Nephi fed him some mush and changed him before we started this game."

Ziva is glad that Lib doesn't look at her while he tells her this. Mixed emotions of gratitude and embarrassment war within her. "I'm sorry. I overslept."

Lib notices the frown on her face. "You needed a good night's sleep." Lib reaches over, protecting Tokal's head before it hits the dirt as he slides over Ziva's leg, starting another adventure.

"Now that he knows how to crawl, I don't know what to do." She takes a breath. "How do you know so much about children?"

Lib grins. "I have an older sister who has two children of her own. They spend a lot of time at my home. When I'm not in school, I help watch them."

Reluctantly, but needing to know, their eyes meet. "So, what do I do with him?"

Lib's eyes open wide for a second before his mouth quirks up on one side as he looks at her. "Same thing you've been doing." He shrugs.

Tokal reaches Kelev where he is kissed again and turned to head back to Lib.

"Are you hungry?"

It takes a second for Ziva to respond. "Yes."

"Food is by the fire. Help yourself. I'll watch Tokal while you eat," Lib keeps his eyes on the little dirty boy crawling his way.

Ziva watches Tokal as he crawls toward them. "Thank you." She glances from Tokal to Lib and back again. She heads to the fire to fix a bowl to eat.

Tokal whines.

She turns back to him evaluating his safety. "You're quite well where you are, little man. I'll be back before you reach him." She smiles at him before realizing there are others around now. Her face turns red. Her eyes drop as her face fills with heat.

Tokal smiles at her.

Ziva misses it. Without looking at the others, she returns to Lib's side with a filled dish, cup and a spoon.

Lib keeps his attention on Tokal. "You're safe here, even to speak."

Ziva glances at him. She nods a silent thank you. The water is refreshing.

Tokal arrives reaching for the cup.

She gives him a drink.

He tries to pour it on himself.

Stopping the mug from emptying out, she pulls it away from his mouth.

Tokal takes a few breaths before reaching for the cup again.

Ziva returns it to his mouth.

Tokal takes a few more swigs. He climbs out of her lap, returning to Kelev, who seems to be waiting to continue the game. "He's going to take an early nap with all this exercise. I better hurry and eat before bathing him." Ziva takes a bite of the mush. She chokes on it and nearly spits it out. The spoon is set in her bowl.

Lib, watching Tokal, informs her, "I can't cook. None of us can—except Nephi."

"Tokal ate this?" Ziva asks in disbelief.

Lib looks at her and grins. "He did at first, and then refused. I gave him a piece of fruit, which he enjoyed."

"You all eat this?"

Lib chuckles. "As best we can."

She can't believe they would consume such food. Perhaps their supplies are limited. "What supplies do you have?"

Lib shrugs and leans his head in a direction. "They're under the tree."

Ziva gets up and takes her meal. She rummages through the supplies. A few are pulled out. A small amount from each sack is added to her bowl. She takes a bite, closing her eyes and dropping her shoulders. She savors the taste with a contented smile on her lips. The sound of feet causes her to divert her gaze.

Five men, bowls in hand, stand around camp, staring as if she's their deliverer.

Ziva laughs. "Bring your bowls and I'll help make it more palatable."

The men swarm.

Ziva adds dried fruit and nuts to their bowls. She sends the men back to the fire to eat.

After closing the bags. Ziva finishes what's in her bowl. Grabbing the bags, she adds some missing ingredients to what is left in the tightly weaved basket and mixes the remaining mush. She refills her empty bowl, returns the supplies, then returns to Lib's side. "Thank you, Lib. I'll take Tokal."

Lib exchanges the whiny infant for the filled container.

Tokal wipes his face on her shirt.

She glances at Lib.

Lib set the bowl down.

She wonders why. "That bowl is for you." Her attention turns to her pack where she pulls out some cloths. She grabs Tokal's blanket and heads for the river.

Tokal hollers at the indignity of a cold bath.

By the time Ziva returns to camp, Tokal is asleep. She lays him down wrapped in a blanket.

Ziva gathers the dirty supplies. "Lib, may I have your dishes?"

Lib looks up from his book, surprised to see her there. As he hands her the empty bowl and spoon, he grins. "Thank you for the food. It tasted much better." His attention reverts to the open book.

"Um," Ziva starts, unsure of herself as she adds the tableware to the others in the empty pot.

Lib peers at her, waiting for her to continue.

"Would you be willing to watch Tokal while I clean?" She raises the pot. "He's sleeping so he won't be much trouble at present."

"I can do that," Lib gazes back at her.

Curious, Ziva asks, "What are you doing?"

Lib's brow's draw together.

Ziva juts her chin toward the book.

Lib looks down, seeing what she's asking about and grins at her. "I'm reading."

"What's that?"

"Words . . ." he thinks to himself how best to explain, "that you speak written down."

Ziva cocks her head, trying to understand. "I don't believe you."

Lib chuckles. "When you're done, we'll continue this." Turning his eyes away from her, he remarks, "You may want to spend some time getting cleaned up while you're there before coming back to camp. I'll watch Tokal."

She turns away as heat fills her face again. She's sure she's red.

"By the way . . ."

She stops not turning back.

"I'm sending Kelev with you as a precaution so no one can sneak up on you."

After the shock of being told she needs to bathe passes, she's not too sure about the privacy and protection given by Kelev. "Thank you," she breathes, feeling her way. She walks away.

Lib calls Kelev and speaks to his dog.

Kelev follows Ziva.

Ziva picks up her pack in her other hand before heading to the river. She glances back.

Lib moved himself near Tokal. "Nephi, tell me again about the bear constellation. You said last night that it's in the Northern sky?"

The other men gather around Nephi to participate in the discussion brought on by their teacher's answer. A multitude of eyes Before disappearing from view, she glances back one last time.

All eyes are on her. Some students start to walk her way.

Nephi clears his throat. Men. All of you stay here."

Ziva disappears from view.

"Sit."

Students settle while their attention still remains on the forest.

"How do you find the bear constellation? Anyone?"

Silence.

"All right. We will have a pop quiz."

Tokal is placed in Lib's lap, though the infant wants to explore. Every time he is pulled back to Lib's lap, he howls his complaint.

"Lib, let him crawl so we can have some peace," Nephi scratches his cheek.

Tokal, free to explore, is quiet.

"Students, I saw all your eyes follow her," Nephi's eyes warn of his displeasure. "You're all confined to camp until she returns."

"She's not safe out there by herself," Paanchi returns. The other students agree with his statement.

"Kelev is with her," Lib redirects Tokal from the fire. "She's safe."

Nephi's students start walking around camp, trying to figure out what to do next. After a few minutes, Jashon picks up his hunting gear and a few others join him. "We're going hunting so we can eat."

"Me too," Melek, the youngest, begins searching to find his gear.

"She's been gone a long time," Zeram interjects as he rubs his chin, searching the forest where Ziva disappeared.

"And yet, all of you will remain in camp," Nephi orders. "Any man caught missing from camp will return home without recommendation from me. If I catch any man alone with Ziva, the consequences will be that the both of you will be Joined." Nephi stares pointedly at each of his students in front of him, letting them know he's serious.

One by one, they put their gear away, except for young Melek, who shows up. "Found my gear!".

"We can't leave camp," Paanchi informs him.

"Oh." Confused, Melek asks those around him, "So we're not going hunting?"

"No." Nephi takes a deep breath, trying to control his temper. "You're not going hunting at this moment. I'm going to say it again in case someone wasn't listening. Any man caught missing from camp will return home without recommendation from me. If I catch any man alone with Ziva, the both of you will be Joined. Understand?" He eyes each in turn, ending with Lib.

Lib smiles at his teacher. "You're all welcome to help me in watching Tokal." He redirects the crawling form away from the fire again.

"It looks like you've got it covered," Zeram yawns.

"I'm going to study," Amnor heads to his pack looking dejected.

"I think I'm going to do the same," Jashon stretches, following the others.

"That sounds like a great thing to do," Paanchi sits, pulling out some reading material.

"Me too," Melek drops his hunting supplies. "First, I must find my book."

Lib frowns at the response from the other students. He catches his teacher's attention, hoping for some help.

Nephi joins Lib in keeping Tokal occupied. His gaze rests on his other students. "Am I going to have a problem with you?"

Lib searches his instructor's irritated face. "Me? A problem student? Not if I can help it." He grins at Nephi. "Your newest student," he redirects Tokal's activity, "may be a different story."

Nephi grins at Lib before preparing to deflect the crawling infant.

Someone walks their way within the forest. The men scatter to grab their spears.

Kelev barks, announcing herself as she leads Ziva back to camp.

A neat braid falls down Ziva's back, confining damp hair. Her pack is slung over one arm. Her hand holds a washed pot with clean dishes. A blanket is wrapped around her shoulders and held by the other hand. Underneath, if someone were looking, is a damp dress still releasing water drops from its hem. A smile radiates from her face. Two squirrels hang from her belt. She heads toward the fire.

Black-haired Jashon blocks her path, revealing a beautiful smile that spreads to his black eyes and enhances his handsome features. "May I take the pot from you?"

"Uh, sure." Ziva examines his face. "Who are you?"

"I'm Jashon, but you can call me Jash." A confident smile graces his face. His fingers linger on hers as he takes the pot.

Ziva, not recognizing the gesture, strides toward the fire. It beckons to her cold body. She shivers.

Paanchi, a brown-haired Nephite with blue eyes, swaggers in front of her. "I see you've been hunting." He nods toward the catch at her waist. "Can I clean them for you?"

"You are?" Ziva smiles, while her eyes are set upon the fire.

"Paanchi. At your service." He gives her his best greeting.

She reads his face before responding, "Thank you, Paanchi, but they've already been gutted. I kept the skin on to keep them clean and fresh until I can cook them." Ziva sidesteps him to reach her destination.

Three more men crowd around her.

Nephi pushes the men away. "For goodness' sake, men, if you'd had any sense, you would have noticed how cold she is. Get out of her way." He takes her arm and moves her toward the fire so she can warm up.

A relieved smile crosses her face, aimed toward Nephi.

Under his breath, he whispers as his eyebrows waggle, "Warm up, my dear, while I keep the wolves at bay."

She grins.

Turning to the men that hover, he frowns. "Back away and give her some space. Time for introductions will come when she's warm and dry."

The men step away, grumbling as they return to their books. "In fact, Paanchi, Amnor, Zeram, Melek and Jashon, gather up your gear and get us enough meat for the rest of today."

"But what about meeting Ziva?" Melek whines.

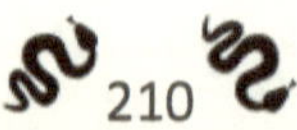

"The sooner you finish, the sooner you can be introduced." Nephi frowns at the boy.

"What about Lib?" Zeram points to him.

"What about him?" Nephi returns, blank faced, knowing full well what Zeram's response will be.

"You didn't mention Lib in this hunting party."

"Ah, you noticed that?" Nephi grins at Zeram and chuckles. Nephi's gaze at Zeram takes on a hard edge as his lips thin. "That is because I heard it said earlier that it is Lib's responsibility to care for Tokal. According to you all, 'he's got that covered,' so he gets to remain in camp." Nephi glares at the young buck who feels he's been mistreated. "On your way, Zeram."

Ziva warms her hands and body at the fire, keeping the blanket on her back. She looks around for Tokal and finds him being held in Lib's arms on the other side of the fire across from her.

She smiles at the both of them, nodding a silent thank you to Lib for understanding her need to see him.

Lib turns, taking Tokal away to occupy him further while Ziva's clothes dry.

Nephi stands guard, watching the rest of his students leave camp. "This is going to be harder than I thought." When the last one has disappeared, he gets another blanket and returns to Ziva's side.

"Why did you wear a wet dress? You could have asked for something to change into while your clothes dry," Nephi wraps the dry blanket around her.

Ziva's face turns red before she answers. "I wanted to get clean and that included cleaning what I own."

"The last thing we need is for you to get sick."

"I didn't wash with my dress on. I took it off and wrapped myself in the blanket while I cleaned it. I hoped it would dry quicker than it did. But it didn't. I returned, afraid that Tokal would wake up." Ziva realizes what she's blurted out. She gets even redder. She turns away from Nephi.

Nephi turns his attention to Lib.

He's overseeing Tokal climb on Kelev.

Nephi wonders if Lib can hear them. "He did wake up, but Lib is good with him."

Ziva's eyes follow Nephi's, resting upon Lib as he occupies her son. She smiles. "I'm grateful that he was willing to watch Tokal so I could clean up. I feel a lot better. Safer, too."

Nephi frowns as she dries herself at the fire. "Don't feel too safe, Ziva. Those young bucks are interested in you."

Ziva's eyes widen in surprise. Her gaze reaches the older man intent to find out if he's telling the truth.

"Sit down. We need to talk."

Ziva sits down in front of the fire.

Nephi sits down a little way from her. He takes a deep breath determining the best way to proceed. He scratches his chin. "What are your plans, Ziva?"

Her brows come together and her eyes narrow. "What do you mean?"

Nephi sighs. "What do you want to do?"

Ziva doesn't understand why he's so serious. "I want to go home to Uthal." She briefly smiles. "With Tokal, of course."

"A simple request, but a not-so-simple answer." He scratches his chin. "You don't seem to be a widow looking for another husband. What happened to your husband's necklace?"

Ziva's eyes drop, and she plays with the bracelet on her wrist.

Someone clears his.

Ziva's and Nephi's attention is redirected.

Lib stands next to them holding the infant.

Tokal is reaching for Ziva.

"He saw you, and if I keep him away any longer, he's going to start fussing."

She let's go of the blankets and reaches for her child.

Tokal gets excited as he's dropped in her lap.

Lib places the blankets back on her shoulders as she hugs the little boy. He sits next to her. "I couldn't help but overhear the conversation." Lib watches Nephi. "Nephi, I don't think Tokal is her natural son. He became hers during her captivity."

Ziva's face confirms what Lib deduced.

"That explains the Joining clothes in your pack."

"Ziva, in order to help you the best we know how, it would be good to share the whole story with us."

"When did you search my pack?" Ziva feels insecure. Are they going to let her stay?

Nephi scratches his chin. "When you were unconscious, I searched your pack for clues as to who you were. I found the clothes."

"Please share the real story, Ziva."

Ziva sits with Tokal standing in her lap. "Would you mind if I turn around, away from the fire? The heat is too warm for Tokal, and my back needs to dry."

"Let me take Tokal while you position yourself." Lib offers his arms.

She hands a not-too-happy Tokal back to Lib.

Lib bounces him.

Ziva repositions herself.

Tokal is placed in his mother's lap. He stands holding her neck.

Ziva feels as though he's supporting her.

Lib and Nephi wait.

Ziva takes a breath and releases it. "Lib is right, Tokal's care became my responsibility while I traveled with them."

Nephi clears his throat as if some emotion was lodged there. "I'm sorry that all of this has happened to you, Ziva." Taking a breath and pausing a moment, he scratches his chin. "Without a necklace, you announce yourself as available. Do you trust me?"

Ziva, not sure what to do, glimpses at both men.

Lib nods.

She understands that he's telling her to trust Nephi. She doesn't know why she knows that, but she does. Ziva glances at Tokal, who has found her braid and is content pulling on it while he sits in her lap.

Tokal pulls on the braid.

She winces, removing her hair from his grasp. The trade is completed with a small cloth thrust into his hands to play with.

"I will do what must be done to protect Tokal and myself."

"I have an idea, Ziva." Nephi picks up the cloth Tokal has dropped and hands it back to him. "Lib can take you back to Uthal, but you will need to remain in Zarahemla with my wife and I throughout the winter."

Ziva's shoulders sag. "I have nothing to offer in return other than my ability to work." She takes a breath. "Will you please tell me about the city you call Zarahemla?"

"The plan is set. Zarahemla was founded by King Zedekiah's son, Mulek. When Jerusalem was attacked by the Babylonians long ago, Mulek escaped on a Phoenician ship and ended up in this new land, where they settled and named the city Zarahemla. It is now the Nephite capital." Changing the subject, scratches his chin. "In the meantime, while you are under my support, you are not to be alone with any of my young men. If you are found alone with one of them, the consequence will be that you will be Joined with that man. Is that understood?"

Ziva is *not* looking for a husband. She nods.

"Good." Nephi pats Ziva's back and stands up. "I think we have an understanding."

Ziva joins him, meeting their eyes. "While I'm here, I'll cook and clean." The least she can do is earn her keep. She gathers Tokal in her arms. "I need to fix the meal. Everyone will be hungry when they return."

Ziva ties Tokal on her back. Recovering the blankets, she hangs them over a branch to air out and dry before she prepares the meat for a stew.

Lib and Nephi take a couple of the waterskins to the river to refill.

Kelev lies near Ziva, enjoying the squirrel remains she tosses her way.

Nephi and Lib return placing several waterskins next to her. They take their conversation to the other side of the fire.

Ziva concentrates on preparing the meal.

Kelev barks.

Ziva jumps while cutting some meat. She's grateful that she didn't cut a finger. She prepares herself for an attack.

Students return from their hunting with a mink and porcupine.

She sets down the knife. She watches the five men.

The group walks to her.

Ziva stands.

The scholars stop, standing around Ziva.

Nephi arrives at Ziva's side, glaring at his students. Reminding them with one look to use their manners.

"Thank you for the meat." Ziva smiles, ready to receive their catch.

"We got it for you," Melek informs her.

"It didn't take us long," Jashon replies, flaunting his hunting skill.

"They will taste good with some of the wine I've brought from my father's vineyard," Paanchi suggests.

"At least the food will taste better than what you cooked," Amnor quips, teasing Paanchi.

"If what we tasted this morning is any indication, everything she cooks will taste better than what we can do," Zeram slaps Paanchi on the back in good fun.

"Ziva, these are my fellow students," Jashon interjects in upper-class civility. Pointing to each one as he names them, he says, "This is Paanchi, Amnor, Zeram, and Melek. You seem to already know Lib, who has been helping with Tokal's care. We apologize if we overwhelmed you earlier."

Ziva endeavors to match faces and names. "I'm happy to meet all of you. While I'm here, I will cook and launder your clothes if you have any that need cleaned. Melek, is it?"

Melek nods.

"May I please have the mink and porcupine so I can get back to work?"

"Uh. Sure." Melek hands over the animals.

"Would you like some help with the meal? I would like to learn so that I can do better at this when I'm on my own," Amnor asks, wanting time with Ziva.

"I would like to help as well." Jashon grins, not wanting to miss his chance with Ziva. Raising his eyebrows, he boasts to her, "I'll probably do a better job of it too."

Ziva chuckles at his lighthearted bragging.

"I will help too," Melek interjects, wanting to be included.

"I didn't have to cook at home, and I'm not going to learn." Zeram touches his chest. "I will hire someone to cook for me." He bows. "Nice to meet you, Ziva. Perhaps we can talk more later?"

Ziva accepts his invitation.

Zeram leaves, returning to his books.

"I'll supply the wine, but I'm not going to cook." Leaning closer to Ziva, Paanchi purrs, "Save me a seat for dinner." He winks, then grins before walking away.

Ziva is left with three. "Jashon and Amnor, would you please clean and pike the meat so it can be roasted over the fire for dinner?

"Call me Jash." He holds out a hand for one of the animals.

"I can't believe you. Jash? Do all the women call you that?" Amnor scoffs, trying to look better than Jashon.

Ziva hands over an animal to each of them. "Thank you, Jash and Amnor. I will show you how to season it when you get back."

"What is Melek going to do?" Jashon grumbles.

"He's going to help me chop some more vegetables for the stew so we can have a hardy meal."

"Want to trade, Melek?" Jashon holds out the dead animal to Melek.

"Nope." Melek triumphantly smirks, not taking it.

Amnor and Jashon walk off, grumbling as they work on their task.

Nephi nods to himself. "This may be easier than I thought." He returns to his spot by the fire.

"Melek, do you have a cutting knife?" Ziva asks.

Melek pulls out a large knife that hangs from his belt. "Will this do?"

"Is that all you have?"

Unsure what the problem is, Melek's happiness turns into a frown. He nods.

"It will have to do." Ziva pats his shoulder. "These potatoes and carrots need to be chopped up and added to the stew. Do you think you can do that?"

"How do you chop them?"

"Any way you'd like as long as they are in small pieces this size." She points to the potato she's finishing. Melek looks at the chopped potato, not sure he can cut them like that.

"I thought we were doing this together?"

"I think you can handle it." She finishes cubing the last of the meat. She drops it into the pot. "I'll I bake some bread," Ziva soothes. "When you're done chopping them, toss them into the pot."

"Bread?" Melek perks up, and his black eyes dance as he thinks about how good it will taste. "I can do that."

Ziva grins.

Nephi settles near Lib, watching and listening for trouble. "Point goes to Ziva this round."

Lib chuckles, returning to his book. He studies Ziva from under his lashes. She expertly goes about making the dough, with Tokal enjoying the ride on her back.

When Amnor and Jashon return with their cleaned meat on pikes, Ziva cleans her hands and grabs the seasonings, explaining what they are. "Hold out your meat." She rubs on the herbs and continues talking about what to do and how to cook it.

When she is done seasoning the meat, Amnor and Jashon follow her to the fire.

Ziva continues their education. When the meat is cooking, Ziva smiles and takes a breath. "You need to turn it every so often so that the food cooks evenly." She returns to preparing the bread.

Lib chuckles. He leans over to Nephi. "She won that round too. I don't think she even realizes what she's doing."

"You're probably right," Nephi snickers. "I see that you're interested in her."

Lib hides his feelings well. "We'll see what happens." He ends the conversation by leaving Nephi's side. Walking around camp, Lib finds a good-sized piece of wood, and returns to his spot by the fire. He begins to carve the wood.

The aroma of freshly baked corn bread wafts through the camp. The men gather around the fire, stirring the stew and eyeing the bread.

Tokal starts drooling and gnawing on his fingers.

Ziva smiles at the hungry group and doesn't say a word. She dishes out a bowl for Tokal and cuts the contents into small pieces placing the bowl on her blanket to cool. Returning to the fire, she removes the stew from the hot ash.

Ziva checks on the bread again and pulls it from the stones, setting it on a clean cloth to cool. She tears off a piece of bread and backs away. "The food is ready."

Men swarm between the bread and stew.

She removes Tokal from her back and sets him on her lap. One of his arms is behind her while she manages the other arm as she feeds him.

Tokal happy to be fed, opens his mouth like a baby bird as each spoonful is sent his way. He hollers when she's not quick enough to refill it.

Around camp "mmm" and "so good" from the men are chorused between bites. Many of them go for seconds.

When Tokal is full, Ziva cleans his face and changes him. She sets him on the blanket with some toys. Keeping one eye on him, she turns the pike of meat that will be their dinner. She arrives at the weaved pot for some food.

The food is gone.

Ziva frowns, wondering what to eat. Her stomach rumbles. She surveys Tokal, making sure he's not getting into mischief.

Lib is seated next to Tokal. He raises a bowl her way, beckoning to her.

Hoping the bowl contains food, Ziva walks his way.

Lib motions to a spot that keeps Tokal between them. "Sit down and eat. I saved you a bowl of food and a piece of bread."

Grateful, she drops to the blanket.

He passes over the meal.

She digs in. After a few bites of food, she looks up at Lib and smiles. "Thank you. I didn't realize how hungry I was."

Tokal starts to fuss, ready for a nap.

Lib reaches over and grabs Tokal. "I've got him. Finish eating."

Awed by this man's continued service to Tokal and herself, Ziva chews her food while watching him with her son.

Lib moves around camp while he pats Tokal's back. She notices no ulterior motive—just kindness. By the time she has finished her meal, Tokal is asleep on the blanket where Lib has placed him.

There is more to do. She takes a breath and gathers up the dirty dishes into the empty pot to earn her keep.

Stopping by Lib, she asks, "Can you watch him while I work?"

Lib looks at her full arms.

"I won't be long this time."

He nods his head.

Ziva hurries to the river, followed by Kelev.

Amnor grabs a waterskin, following her. The other students see this, and, grabbing waterskins, race to catch up to her.

Nephi gets to his feet, following the men to make sure they mind their manners while in her company.

"May I carry the pot for you?" Amnor asks sweetly as he reaches Ziva's side.

"Oh!" Ziva yelps, surprised to see the men. She passes the pot to Amnor.

"We need to fill the waterskins after eating," Melek announces, stumbling to her other side.

"You're quite pretty," Amnor purrs, beaming at Ziva.

"That was a wonderful meal," Zeram pats his full abdomen. "You're a great cook."

"Best meal I've had while being out here," Jashon informs her. "I'm looking forward to dinner."

"Wine will make it even better," Paanchi smacks his lips at the thought.

"How many wine skins do you have?" Jashon pulls on Paanchi's shoulder.

"Two left."

"Are we here for three more days?" Melek trots beside them.

"Yes, Melek," Amnor gives a long-suffering sigh. "You need to keep up with what's going on."

Arriving at the river, Ziva, bites her lip, hiding a grin. She fenagles the pot from Amnor. "Thank you, Amnor." She cleans the dishes.

The men continue their conversation, traveling upstream to fill the waterskins.

"You're in my way, Jashon," Paanchi complains.

"Go up river," Jashon returns. "I've got this spot."

"Move out of my way, Melek," Amnor pushes the young man.

Melek keeps himself from falling. "I arrived here first."

"You guys are pathetic," Zeram announces, reaching Ziva's side first. Turning to Ziva, he smiles and purrs, "May I carry the dishes back for you?"

Ziva smiles and hands over the pot of clean dishes to him. She strides back to camp with the other hurrying to catch up.

Nephi watches from a distance with a frown on his face.

"What city are you from, Ziva?" Zeram inquires.

"I'm from Uthal," Ziva answers. Uncomfortable with all the men crowding her in an effort to get her attention, she frowns. She picks up the pace, trying to distance herself from them.

"I haven't heard of it. Is it a Nephite or a Lamanite city?" Paanchi asks.

Ziva glances at Paanchi before watching her step. "Uthal is a Lamanite city."

"Jashon, Lib, and I are Lamanites," Melek's exuberance ends with him stepping on her heel.

"Ow," explodes from Ziva's mouth. Her foot stays where it was stopped. She nearly falls.

Jashon catches her.

Ziva steps away from them.

"Sorry," Melek stammers, mortified that he hurt Ziva. "I didn't mean to."

"I'm not hurt, Melek," Ziva mollifies, taking some breaths and rubbing her throbbing heel. She tries to smile at the men around her. "If you could all back up so I can have some space, it would help."

"Yeah, Melek. Move back," Paanchi shoves Melek further back.

"Way to go, Melek," Jashon does the same.

Ziva stands up straighter, frowning at what she sees. "I'm talking to all of you—not just Melek." She glares at them.

"Men."

All eyes turn to Nephi who stands nearby with his arms crossed.

"Head back to camp. I'll walk with Ziva."

The students grumble.

Melek, happy to follow Nephi's orders, tries to move past the older men.

The other students knock Melek on the shoulder as they brush past him, returning to camp.

Melek left behind, bows his head. "I'm sorry, Ziva."

Ziva smiles at him, letting him know that she doesn't harbor any ill will. "I know you didn't do it on purpose. I'm well."

Melek trudges behind the others.

When Melek is out of earshot, Ziva glances at Nephi. "They're not very nice to Melek."

Nephi sighs. "They tolerate him, but he has a lot of growing up to do."

"How long have you been teaching?" Ziva ambles forward.

Nephi scratches his chin, "I think about twenty years at present." He chuckles. "But this is the first time a woman has shown up at one of my classes."

"I'm sorry if I've interrupted your teaching."

"They'll learn what they need to know before heading home." Nephi considers where his students' knowledge levels are before continuing. "I'm not concerned." Nephi glances at Ziva. "What I'm concerned about is you."

"Me?" Ziva stops, perplexed.

"You're not thinking clearly. I need to lay down some ground rules for you. The first one being to not go to the river by yourself."

"I had Kelev. Most of the men were with me."

"And you experienced that they couldn't hold themselves back from wanting your attention." Nephi takes a calming breath. "My advice is to have me accompany you to the river and back."

"I don't see why you would waste your time coming with me." Ziva frowns, brows draw together. She contemplates, still trying to understand his reasoning. "I don't understand why they are following me. I didn't ask them to go with me. I'm just trying to take care of the chores."

"I know you are." Nephi pats her hand. "If you were truly a widow, you would understand better. My wife is not here to guide you." He takes a breath and continues. "I will be as clear as I can be so you understand. I've mentioned this to you before. If I find you alone with one of the young men, you will force my hand. You will be required to Join him. Understand?"

"I don't want to Join any of them.," Ziva takes a breath, controlling her anger. "I only want to return home."

"Like we talked about . . ." Nephi scratches his chin. "Your best bet will be to work with Lib, since he is also from Uthal."

"Paanchi asked me questions about Uthal like he didn't know it."

Nephi chuckles. "Like I said, the men will say and do anything to be near you."

"Do they know of these rules?"

"Of course they do, but they are hoping for your attention without getting caught." Nephi swipes a hand over his face." Do you understand the consequences of being found alone with one of them?"

"Yes, but I still don't see the reason these rules are in place." she wraps her arms around herself. "I need to clean laundry this afternoon. How am I to do that?"

"I will go with you," Nephi informs her. "I can give them an assignment that will keep them occupied while we're gone. We have two more days out here. Don't worry. I'll take you with us to Zarahemla and place you in my wife's care for the winter."

Ziva nods.

The pair walk in silence the rest of the way.

Ziva checks on Tokal.

He still naps.

Going to each of the men, she asks, "Do you have any dirty clothes you would like washed?"

Several give her some clothing.

She turns the meat on the spit.

Toka's head pops up, looking around. Finding the pretty dancing flame, he gets on his knees and heads that way.

"No, you don't," Ziva intercepts him, picking him up mid-crawl. She hugs him to her.

He wraps his arms around her neck.

"I need to wash some clothes to earn our keep. Time for you to be on my back." She grabs the cloth and moves him behind her, tying him to her back.

She takes another cloth and wraps it around the dirty clothes dropped near her blanket. Once she has the laundry tied in the cloth she walks to where their instructor sits.

Nephi looks at her bundle and nods. "Men."

The students stop what they're doing and look at Nephi.

"Your assignment this afternoon is to create the she-bear constellation. When I get back, each of you will have to show me your project and name each of the stars associated." He leaves camp with Ziva and Kelev.

Melek kicks the dirt but gets to work on his project.

The rest of the students see Melek's reaction. No one speaks to him.

Sometime later, Ziva returns with Nephi and Kelev. Ziva checks the food, turning the meat. She removes Tokal from her back.

Zeram walks up to her. "Where are our clothes?"

"They are clean and drying on some bushes. I had to come back to check our meal."

"When are you bringing our clothes back?"

Ziva frowns. "Before dinner. At present, I need to let Tokal play."

She puts Tokal on the ground, and he takes off, crawling toward Kelev.

When Tokal arrives, Kelev gets up and licks him before trotting toward Lib, who sits nearby.

"Zeram, it looks like you're done with your project. Are you ready for me to check it?"

"Sorry, sir. I got sidetracked."

"You best get back to work." Nephi eyes the young man in front of Ziva.

Zeram frowns and retreats to where he is working on his project.

Tokal, free to roam, finds Kelev sitting near Lib. He smiles at the dog and crawls as fast as he can to her.

When he gets close, Kelev finds another place to lie.

Tokal blinks and looks around him. He sees something intriguing. He speeds toward it A hand clamps on it.

"Noooo," falls out of Lib's mouth. He reaches for the little dirty boy, scooping him up as his mother arrives.

Ziva helps remove Tokal's hands from Lib's model. It falls to the ground in pieces.

Tokal smiles at Lib, happy he's in someone's arms. He babbles to him.

Lib laughs at the little boy, giving him a quick hug before depositing him in Ziva's care.

"I'm sorry, Lib. Can you fix it?"

"I'm at fault for not watching." Lib laments as he tries to smile at her. "I'll figure something out."

"Don't bring him over here," several of the other men state as they stretch their arms out to protect their models of the she-bear constellation.

Ziva moves to another area of camp, and the rest of the students act in the same manner.

Finding that they are not wanted, Ziva grabs some cloths and leaves camp. She heads to the river with Tokal.

"It looks like we've worn out our welcome."

The afternoon sun has dipped below the tree line, and a gentle breeze blows. Arriving at her destination, she checks how the clothes are drying. She sits down and plays with Tokal. She bathes him. She ties him to her back. Folds the dried clothes with a tied cloth.

Upon her arrival, she drops the bundle, untying it for the men. They can retrieve their own items.

Checking the contents on the spit, she finds the meat almost ready. Sliced pumpkin is placed on a heated stone. When the pumpkin pieces are cooked, she drops one in a bowl for Tokal and removes the meat from the fire. Gathering a little bit of the meat and adding it to Tokal's bowl, she mixes and smooshes the contents contained therein.

When she moves away, the men swarm around the food. She walks to her blanket and feeds him before he's released to play with his toys. Too tired to do anything else, she sits there with tears in her eyes.

Lib sits down next to her and gives her a bowl of food. Accepting the offering, she blinks away her tears before looking up at him. "Thank you."

"Ziva, Tokal didn't destroy my project."

She frowns at Lib, not willing to accept that. She saw that his project was destroyed.

"Well, he did," Lib grins at her, "but I passed my test." He takes a breath. "Don't be sad." he quietly counters for only her to hear.

His words were meant just for her ears. Ziva looks down at the bowl of food in her hands.

"The food is good. You need to eat."

She stares at the food, trying to control her emotions. What bothers her the most is that she doesn't know why she feels overwhelmed. She feels . . . exhausted.

Lib touches her arm.

Tears pool in her eyes. She can't look up.

"What can I do for you?"

"I don't know." Ziva sniffs. Tears slide down her cheeks.

The pronounced silence is broken by Lib. "Do what you need to do, Ziva. I'll watch Tokal tonight." He picks up Tokal and his toys, going back to the students as they gather around the fire for another lesson, leaving Ziva to herself.

Ziva places the bowl of food away from her. She wraps herself in a blanket, crying herself to sleep.

# MEN

LIB AND TOKAL ARE OVER by the fire. Tokal has a blanket under him, playing with some toys. Lib sits next to the little boy, chuckling at his antics.

The men are also awake, doing various things around camp. One man looks to be cutting the remains of yesterday's meal. Two have just arrived at camp with what look like clean dishes and filled waterskins on their back, and two others are absent. They are taking instruction from Nephi.

Ziva sits. The air is crisp. She wraps the blanket more securely around herself.

Nephi noticing her, comes to her side. "If you would like, grab your blanket and come to the fire. We have food for you."

Ziva stands up, readjusting the blanket around her.

"Tokal has been well cared for. Come by the fire," he encourages. Nephi takes her elbow, guiding her there.

Ziva settles.

Tokal's smile shines.

 She gathers her son and hugs the little boy.

He hugs her back, babbling about what is going on in his world.

She hugs him again.

He gives her a wet kiss before wriggling out of her arms to play. Tokal returns to play with his toys.

A cleared throat, causes Ziva to look.

Nephi handing her a bowl of steaming mush. "Don't fret, it tastes decent."

Ziva grins, wondering why everyone is catering to her. She still feels puny. She takes a breath, taking the bowl of mush from him. "Thank you."

Nephi drops a waterskin next to her and steps back, allowing her some space to eat.

Tokal, seeing the bowl, reaches out for it while she drinks.

In a flash, Lib stops Tokal's hand. He removes the empty bowl from Tokal's iron-clasped grasp.

Ziva picks up a small cloth, that's with his toys. She shakes it several times, making it move.

Tokal's fit ends. He plays with the new toy.

"I'm sorry I overslept," Ziva utters to Nephi. "Why didn't you wake me?"

Nephi smiles at her. "You needed to rest."

Lib picks up Tokal, sitting next to Ziva. "How do you feel today?"

"I'm well enough." Ziva juts her chin to Melek. "What's Melek doing?"

"He's chopping up the leftover meat from yesterday for the midday meal." Lib puts the cloth on Tokal's head.

Tokal pulls it off, revealing a smile. "He may need your help with what to do with it."

"Where's Paanchi and Jashon?"

"They're out hunting for our last day here," Nephi informs her from her other side. "Tomorrow, we'll return to Zarahemla."

"Where is Uthal compared to Zarahemla?"

"Zarahemla sits along the river Sidon," Lib tells her as he drops the cloth on Tokal's head again.

Tokal pulls it off, smiling at Lib.

"Uthal is several rivers away to the southeast."

"Will you help me get back to Uthal?"

Lib's gaze meets hers. "I will take you back to Uthal, Ziva."

Unable to pull her eyes away from his, she simply nods.

Lib breaks the eye contact. He's grateful that winter is coming to add a few pounds to her before they travel back to Uthal; she needs to recover.

"Is Zarahemla a large city?"

"Compared to Uthal, Zarahemla is a very large city."

Ziva frowns, not sure how to take this. To her Uthal is a very large city.

"All will be well, Ziva. You won't be alone."

Lib's words sink deep into her heart, wrapping her in a warm blanket and settling her fears about how to survive the winter in Zarahemla. At the same time, it also disquiets her to trust in another and lose everything again. Her mouth thins, and she doesn't look at him as she ends their conversation. "I better get up and start earning my keep." She steadies herself to begin the day. "Thank you for watching Tokal."

"I like watching Tokal." Lib notices her change in mood and touches her wrist, stopping her as she tries to stand.

Ziva closes her eyes, not understanding the mixed emotions she's feeling. If only he would let her go.

"Are you feeling better today?" he questions, searching her face.

She wants him to hold her, but at the same time she doesn't want him—afraid of another loss. She nods, turning away from him.

"Take it easy," he warns.

Her head whips around to his, surprised by his warning.

Her dark-brown eyes betray her feelings, revealing to Lib the war within. They drop to the wrist he holds and returns to his face. Unvoiced words are clear as though she uttered them. He realizes that he doesn't want to let her go. Nevertheless, he will for now. Removing his hand from her, she's free to stand.

Ziva moves away. Finding the cloth to tie Tokal to her, she returns and reaches for her son, who is still in Lib's arms.

"Turn around and I'll place him on your back."

Ziva, at a loss for words, does what he asks.

She feels the warm heavy bundle deposited behind her. The cloth in her hand disappears.

Tokal starts babbling.

Ziva reaches for the cloth ends, adjusting it before tying it at her waist. She turns.

Lib stands in front of her.

The closeness to his body jars her. Something electric passes between the two of them. Something she has never felt before. She wants to flee. She wants to stay. "Thank you."

Lib clears his throat and takes a step back, breaking the tension.

Ziva retreats to where Melek is working on the meat, determined to ignore what just occurred. "Good morning," she sings as though all is right in her world.

"I . . . I'm truly sorry about yesterday." Melek feeling dejected tries to explain. "My father, a military man, doesn't like how unobservant I am. I didn't mean to step on your heel."

"I'm not hurt. I've forgotten all about it," Ziva soothes. She smiles at him. "Thank you for chopping up the leftovers." Ziva takes a breath. "I need to apologize for oversleeping."

"Last night, we heard you crying. I don't want to make you cry."

Ziva cringes. She thought she was quiet.

"We didn't know what to do. Lib said you were overly tired and needed to rest. Nephi chewed us out, stating we needed to be more helpful and observant of your needs. I'm not very good at being observant."

"Forget it happened, Melek." Ziva places a hand on his shoulder. "You've helped me today." She removes her hand, grasping them together. "What can we make with the meat that would be warm and tasty?"

Melek's eyes meet hers. "You could make that delicious stew again. We still have a few potatoes and carrots left. I would rather not have to carry it back." His mouth waters in anticipation of more of her good food. He swallows. "Your bread tasted delicious with it, and that would help use some of the corn."

"The same thing twice?" Ziva gazes at him, her brows creased.

"Yes," Melek returns. "We don't care what we eat, as long as it tastes good and fills our bellies."

Ziva chuckles. "If that's what you think they'll want. But . . . we'll change it up a little bit."

"I'll grab the vegetables." Melek smiles, dashing away to their supplies.

Ziva smiles at the retreating back. "Grab an onion as well."

Melek stops. He turns back to her and nods. A short time later, he returns with his arms full and excitement on his face. Melek sets the supplies down near a flat stone.

Ziva picks up the waterskin and hands it over to him. "Here, Melek."

A puzzled look crosses his face, but he takes the waterskin from her.

"I'm confident that you can make the stew today."

Melek frowns, not liking this idea.

"Don't worry, I'll be with you every step of the way."

Her reassuring smile changes Melek's frown to a grin.

"This" she says, holding up the small onion, "is a great seasoning for many things. You don't need a lot of it, but it makes a big difference. For the stew we'll need it all chopped up.

When you cut it, make sure you're up wind from it, otherwise your eyes will sting."

Melek nods in understanding. She peels the onion before passing it to him.

"When you're done with the onion, chop up the potatoes and carrots and add all of it to the pot."

He nods again.

"I'll be back soon with some more items."

Melek starts on his tasks.

Ziva walks to their stock of supplies and rummages through the seasonings until she finds the one she wants. She fills a bag with some corn. Melek is still chopping when she returns to his side. She waits, patient with him while he works.

"Very good. Here's some corn to add to the stew." She hands over a small bag. He takes it and dumps the contents into the pot.

"The last thing we need to add is sage." She hands him the bag.

Melek opens it up and smells it. He looks up at her. "It smells strong and slightly sweet."

She chuckles. "Yes, it does. Put three leaves into the pot. Fill the pot with water so the vegetables are almost covered.

Good. Time to stir it."

He completes the tasks.

"Bring the pot and you can place it in the hot ash."

Melek follows her, carrying the heavy pot.

When they get to the fire, Ziva stirs some of the embers.

Melek places the filled pot.

"Stir the pot every few minutes and soon we'll have some food to eat."

Amnor and Zeram drop some wood by the fire.

"What are you doing, Melek?" Amnor asks.

Melek's delight fades to misery.

"Melek is making our meal. The food is going to be delicious."

Amnor and Zeram look in the pot.

Zeram sniffs the air. "Doesn't smell that great."

"Give it time." Ziva beams.

Amnor pats Melek's back. "Good job."

The men walk away.

Melek's eyes flit between his belongings and the stew.

Ziva smiles, understanding that whatever is contained in those things called books is something he greatly desires. "If you like, you can get your book and bring it back. You only need to stir the stew every few minutes."

Melek's eyes light up. He retrieves his book, returning to his spot near the stew.

Ziva stirs the pot before turning her attention to their teacher. "Nephi, I need to go to the river and get clean. Are you available?"

Nephi stops his packing. He nods.

Ziva gathers the dirty cloths and her pack. She slings the pack over a shoulder.

"Let me hold that for you," Nephi stops her, taking the pack. "This pack is loaded down. Are you sure you need everything in it?" They stride, heading to the river.

Kelev follows.

"The pack contains everything I own."

"Carrying the pack and a baby is not an easy task. You're a strong woman, Ziva. Very few women would have made it this far on their own—and even less with a child."

"I'm grateful to you and your students for taking me in." Ziva glances at him. "I don't want to be a burden."

Nephi chuckles. "I think my students are glad to have you as well." He grins at her. "Their food tastes better."

Ziva giggles.

At the river, Ziva hands Tokal to Nephi. Nephi keeps Tokal nearby but remains out of site.

Ziva continues to the river's edge making sure she's alone. Kelev sits nearby. She washes the cloths. While alone she makes herself presentable. Her hair now fresh and braided, she returns to Nephi.

Tokal sleeps in Nephi's arms.

"He's a good child. Heavy, but good." Nephi smiles at her. "Where is the laundry?"

"It's hanging. I'll come back later and get them. If you place him on my back, I'll wrap him up and we can return to camp."

Following Ziva's instructions, Nephi loads Tokal on her back.

Tokal stirs, getting himself comfortable. His settles, becoming dead weight.


Back at camp, Nephi drops her pack near her blanket. He visits with Paanchi and Jashon, who've returned to camp.

Ziva returns to Melek's side.

Melek stirs the stew.

"How's it going, Melek?"

"Fine, I think."

"It smells wonderful," she compliments with a smile.

"Paanchi and Jashon couldn't find any meat."

"Oh?" Ziva frowns. "I could make some fish traps."

"What about the bread?"

"You like bread, don't you."

"Bread tastes good," a sheepish grin crosses Melek's face.

"I'll start on the bread. I'll make some fish traps afterward."

Ziva kneads the dough.

Toka's head pops up. He looks around. He's quiet.

Ziva knows that Tokal will want food soon, but she needs to first finish her task. She works the dough, hoping to be done before Tokal starts crying.

Lib leaves the group of men and moves to the pot. He grabs a bowl and scoops out some stew, cutting it into small pieces and blowing on it to cool it off. He sets the bowl down near his things.

A pair of feet get Ziva's attention. Her hands are covered in dough. She looks up.

Lib stands there. "Tokal's hungry. Let me take him from you. I have a bowl of food ready for him."

"I expected him to wake up soon but hoped he'd wait until I had the bread baking."

Lib smiles at her. "He doesn't need to wait. I have stew ready for him. How do I get him off your back?"

On cue, Tokal fusses for food.

Ziva stands up.

Lib helps her, steadying her.

She points to her middle where a knot of cloth resides. "Um, the ends are tied here, but I can't untie them at this moment." She raises her hands, showing that they're covered in dough.

Lib nods. "Hold still and I will remove him."

Ziva stands with her hands in the air.

Lib unties the knot at her waist.

His touch makes her stomach flutter.

He takes hold of the bundle behind her, bringing their bodies within a hairbreadth of each other for a few seconds.

Her heart speeds up, making her short of breath, and she feels butterflies in her stomach. She takes a few breaths to steady herself and looks up, frowning.

Tokal in Lib's arms. Tokal is quiet, distracted by the cloth which held him seconds before.

Lib nods to Ziva. He turns away, taking Tokal with him.

Ziva stands there watching him with her son.

Lib sits Tokal on his lap.

Returning to the job at hand, Ziva finishes kneading the dough in the basket, covering it with a cloth. Tokal is still quiet. She glances in the direction she last saw her son.

Tokal has stew smeared on his hands, hair, front, and Lib's shirt.

Lib, careful of the grabbing hands, shoves another spoonful into the open mouth.

Ziva tries not laugh.

Lib new to infant feeding, finds the endeavor dangerous, especially with stew. He catches Ziva's eye. He grins and shrugs.

Ziva gets the bread baking on some hot stone and cleans her hands. She wets several rags and wrings them out.

More food seems to be on Lib and Tokal than what seems to have been consumed, but Tokal is content sucking on his hands, which indicates a full, content belly. Finding stew remains in Lib's hair, she can't help but laugh. She picks off the chunks.

Her laughter sets off a chain reaction as other students look up, seeing stew covering Lib.

Lib glances at her. "Feeding a baby is harder than it looks."

She wipes the tears from her eyes, becoming serious again. "Let me get him cleaned up and changed before I wash your shirt." She hands a wet cloths to Lib. "By the way, you have food in your hair. I picked out what I could."

Bending down, she cleans Tokal.

Tokal protests the wet cloth taking the food from hands, front, and face.

Ziva drops the rag. She picks up the little boy, taking him to her blanket. A clean cloth is pulled from her pack. After Tokal is clean and dry, she wraps him onto her back. She searches for Lib to get his dirty shirt.

Lib is nowhere to be seen.

Ziva checks on the bread. Finding it ready, she removes it from the stone. "Food is ready. Melek prepared the wonderful stew, and the bread is here."

The men, awaiting her announcement, come like bees to honey, scooping stew into their bowls and breaking apart pieces of bread.

"Where's Lib?"

"He went to the river . . ." Nephi answers grinning.

Ziva doesn't wait to hear more. Feeling responsible for the shirt that Tokal dirtied and wanting to clean it, to remedy the situation, she leaves camp.

On her way, she scoops up the remaining dirty cloths left earlier.

Nephi's command to stop falls on deaf ears.

Kelev follows quietly behind.

When she reaches her destination, she stops dead in her tracks. Lib is climbing out of the river, shirtless. Water cascading off his body.

He's the most beautiful man she's ever seen. She doesn't know why. Her eyes widen. Her mouth drops open. Her breath catches., Her heartbeat races all at once. She stares at the defined chest. Her fingers itch with want, filled with a hunger to touch him, a hunger she's never known before.

Kelev announces their arrival with a friendly bark, and Lib looks directly at her.

The realization that she's staring at him and he knows it, causes heat to climb up her neck and cover her. Her eyes drop. She doesn't know what to say.

Without missing a beat, Lib frowns at her. He grabs his clean shirt, tugging it on. "What are you doing here, Ziva? If someone sees you here . . . turn around and head back to camp."

"But your shirt? I came to clean it." She holds up the dirty laundry in her hands. "These need to be cleaned too."

"As you can see, I've already cleaned my shirt," Lib returns in warning. "Return to camp, Ziva."

She stands there, unable to make her legs move. He looks . . . beautiful.

He moves toward her, still frowning.

Her heart beats faster. She swallows.

When he reaches her, he whispers, "Go, Ziva." With a soft but firm touch on the shoulders, he turns her back toward camp.

# JOINING

"LIB AND ZIVA, I HAVE warned you both about the consequences of being found alone together."

They look up to find Nephi frowning at them. The rest of the students are gathered behind him, watching to see how this plays out. "You leave me no choice," Nephi huffs, displeased.

"Nothing happened," Lib and Ziva say at the same time.

"I went to wash Lib's dirty shirt as well as these cloths. The responsibility is mine."

"I understand that you've taken it upon yourself to do the laundry, but I've warned my students and I have specifically warned you about not being alone with a single man. You've failed to listen to me."

"I only went to clean the shirt."

Nephi shakes his head. He sighs. "Lib, give Ziva your necklace."

Without saying a word, Lib removes his necklace and places it around Ziva's neck as she stands there stunned at what is occurring still holding the dirty linens.

"I only went to clean the shirt." she whispers in disbelief.

"When we get back to Zarahemla, you will be Joined," Nephi says. "Lib, she's presently your responsibility." He turns and leaves with the entourage of students following behind, leaving Lib and Ziva alone.

After the others disappear, Lib and Ziva stand there stunned.

Lib takes a breath. "Give me the cloths, Ziva, and I will clean them."

"They're dirty." Ziva reminds him in her tone that this is her responsibility. His words launch her into action. "I'll clean them."

He watches her. When she's done wringing out the water from the clean cloths, helping her stand.

Ziva struggles to her feet with the weight of on her back. She's grateful for Lib's help.

Lib jerks the drying shirt from the branch. "Let's go back to camp. They can dry on a bush or branch there." They walk back to camp together, not sure what to say to the other, so remain quiet.

Arriving at camp, everyone is eating as though nothing occurred. Lib tosses the drying shirt on a branch. Ziva lays out the wet cloths next to it before straightening Lib's carelessly placed garment.

When she turns from that task, Lib's walking her way with two bowls and bread in his hands.

Lib hands her a filled bowl and bread, which she takes. She heads to her blanket to eat.

Lib follows, sitting next to her. He starts eating.

"I . . . I . . . I'm sorry." Ziva breaks the silence, stirring the food in her bowl. "I wasn't thinking. I'm at fault. Nephi did inform me of the consequences." Ziva swallows.

"All will turn out as it should."

"How can you be so calm about this?"

"I like you and Tokal," he takes a bite of food. When his mouth is empty, he continues, "You need someone to care for you."

From under her lashes Ziva watches Lib. She takes another bite.

When everyone is done eating, Ziva gathers up the dishes. Lib walks beside her as she takes them to the river to wash. She doesn't say a word.

Lib carries the clean dishes back and returns them.

Ziva removes Tokal from her back. She watches as he crawls and climbs, standing himself up for a few seconds before plopping down on his bottom.

Ziva thinks about Lib's words, "All will turn out as it should." What does that mean? She looks at her charge.

Tokal chews on something.

Ziva catches up to Tokal and squats down. She forces her fingers into his mouth, scooping out pieces of a beetle. "Oh, disgusting, Tokal! You can't eat that." She scoops out the contents from his mouth, avoiding his sharp little teeth as she shudders at the body parts.

He howls at her interference in his snack.

She confirms his mouth is empty. She picks him up, taking him to the remains of the stew.

Tokal receives a cooled potato chunk to chew on. He eats it.

Ziva lets him loose. This time keeping a better eye on her charge.

Tokal stops and crinkles a dead leaf. A piece of it heads to his mouth.

Ziva dives to stop him from inserting it into his mouth, hoping not to find another bug.

Nephi, chuckles at Tokal's antics. "Before long, he'll be walking. You're going to have fun with that stage."

"What do I do?"

"Exactly what you're doing." Nephi laughs, which only enhances the frown on Ziva's face as she deters her boy again.

Off he crawls, leaving her behind. He stops and sits, looking down with a funny look on his face.

"I know that face," Ziva groans, heading to her pack for some clean cloths.

A stench surrounds Tokal as he continues on his adventure.

"He stinks," Zeram informs the group, plugging his nose and steering Tokal with a foot in a safer direction. "Children look to be a lot of work."

Ziva gets some cloths wet from a waterskin and wrings them out. She scoops up the active boy, taking him to her blanket to change him.

Tokal, more interested in exploring, squirms to get away, making it difficult for Ziva to clean him.

Lib drops a wooden rattle in the child's pudgy hands. He gnaws on it and looks at it while babbling.

Ziva finishes the task and sets him free.

"They are a lot of work," Nephi says, laughing as he gets up. "Ziva, grab the dirty cloths, and I'll go with you to the river while Lib watches Tokal."

Ziva looks to Lib, confirming he's willing to watch the little boy.

He gives a quick nod.

She gathers things up, leaving Tokal in Lib's care.

The walk to the river starts off awkward for both Nephi and Ziva.

Nephi chuckles and starts the conversation. "That is one ripe load. You're a good mother, Ziva."

Ziva remains silent.

"Lib will make a good father for Tokal and will make a good husband for you."

Ziva continues walking forward without comment.

She arrives at the river and washes the cloths. When the task is complete, she stands up and faces Nephi, prepared with a reply. "If you care for Lib, you'll relieve him of this obligation. I'm not a good match."

"I believe you and Lib to be a good for each other. Because of your actions, you have made a choice and have to live with the consequence."

The frown on her face only deepens, and the damp cloths in her hand drip water as she tightens her fist, trying to control her tongue. She stomps back to camp.

Nephi follows her.

When she arrives, she adds the clean linen to the branches.

Ziva finds Tokal tiring, so she picks him up and starts soothing him until he's asleep. She straps Tokal to her chest and takes the blanket, placing it on the ground under some low hanging branches that provide the both of them some privacy away from the prying eyes of the men. After they settle, she begins to think of her options, falling asleep before reaching a resolution.

When Tokal starts moving, Ziva rouses from her nap. To occupy him while she thinks, as she chews on her lip, she gives him a chunk of wood she finds nearby.

Tokal gets bored with the wood. He starts fussing.

She needs to feed him before night falls. Ziva takes a breath. She climbs out from under the branches, pulling the blanket with her. She shakes the bedding free of forest, then returns it to her spot near the campfire. Stirring the embers, she places the leftovers from the midday meal on the ash to heat up.

Tokal likes the ride. He looks around and enjoys being bounced.

Ziva touches the cloths hanging from branches. Finding them dry, she pulls them down and shakes them. After depositing the folded, dried linens in her pack, she returns to the fire and stirs the leftovers. She dishes some stew out into a bowl and prepares it for Tokal. She still doesn't say a word as she feeds her son.

Tokal plays with his mother until he tires.

Ziva walks him with a rocking motion until Tokal sleeps. She lays him down for the night.

Lib hands her a bowl of food.

Ziva eats in silence. When she's done with the food, she settles next to Tokal ignoring the men.

She can't sleep. She ponders her options.


Near sunrise, she moves. Making sure that Tokal is covered. She kisses the sleeping form before removing Lib's necklace. She places it on the blanket covering her little boy. She grabs the weapons she came with and heads out of camp, blinking back the tears that threaten to fall. "It will be better this way," she tells herself.

Keeping her head facing forward, Ziva moves from camp.

Kelev stands before her, stopping her in her path.

Ziva tries to go around the animal.

The dog in front of her is no longer the friendly but a growling fiend, intent on stopping her progress. Kelev barks, informing every one of her betrayal.

Ziva cringes inside. She takes a step forward, hoping to disappear into the forest.

Kelev growls and snaps at her.

Ziva takes a few steps back. She raises her spear. "Kelev, I don't want to hurt you, but I must leave."

Kelev woofs. He snarls at her.

"Please move. I don't want to hurt you."

"Don't!" Lib's voice interrupts, with a discernable undercurrent of anger. "Put down your weapon, Ziva."

Ziva turns to see six students with spears facing her.

Nephi brings up the rear, holding a crying, blanket-wrapped Tokal.

The cool air envelopes her. She shivers. Ziva lowers her spear in defeat.

Lib pierces the dirt next to him with his spear. He takes the squalling infant covered in the blanket.

Nephi marches forward and confronts Ziva. "Why were you leaving, Ziva?"

"I had to," Ziva answers, focusing on the ground.

Tokal homes in on the sound and looks her way. Seeing his mother, he cries even harder, reaching toward her with his small hands.

Nephi huffs. "You will need to do better than—"

"Stop, Nephi." Lib strides to Ziva. "Tokal needs to be cared for first." When he reaches her, Lib dumps the little form in her arms.

Tokal grabs her neck and cries and babbles at the same time.

Ziva hugs the small, warm body and her heart melts. She starts crying in turn. Something warm envelopes her body. It feels nice. She feels safe. Her eyes open.

Lib stands behind Tokal holding a blanket that surrounds Ziva and Tokal. His mouth is flattened into a thin line. His beautiful brown eyes full of fire. They bore into her.

A chill slides down her spine.

With controlled anger, he orders, "Leave us."

No one moves, surprised at this new side of Lib.

"I said, all of you go back to camp," he yells.

Ziva and Tokal jump.

Ziva steps backward. The blanket holds her in place. She turns away to protect Tokal from Lib's anger. She's held in place. She does her best to soothe Tokal as he continues to wail.

Nephi sets a hand on Lib's shoulder to help him calm down.

Lib doesn't break eye contact with Ziva. He lets her see the storm in his eyes. "We will all return shortly."

Nephi nods. He leaves with the rest, leaving the threesome to the dawn.

Lib and Ziva stare at each other.

Tokal begins to soothe and settle in Ziva's arms.

When Tokal is quiet, Lib takes a breath, breaking the silence. "Why were you leaving, Ziva?"

"I am freeing you."

The fire in his eyes intensifies. "From whom?"

Ziva blinks back tears and armors her heart.

"From whom, Ziva?"

She peers at Lib showing him all the pain she has inside. "From me."

The fire within his eyes doesn't diminish. "You were leaving without Tokal? Why?"

She has to make him understand. "So, he can have a family with you."

"He has a family with us," Lib rumbles. "Did you even consider his feelings? He's bonded with you. You, out of all of us, know what losing a parent feels like. Why would you put him through another heartache? Feel how fiercely he clings on to you."

Ziva does feel how tight he clings to her. Her heart aches with what she must do. "My only thoughts were for Tokal and you. It doesn't matter what happens to me. You both have a chance for a happy life without me."

Lib's eyes widen in surprise at her words. He tightens his hold on the blanket. His anger burns brighter. "You will have to do better than that, Ziva. Explain it to me."

"What's there to explain?" Ziva takes a breath when he doesn't respond. "You won't be forced to join with me, and Tokal, I know, will be well taken care of by you."

A taut silence punctuates the air until Lib breaks it. "Make no mistake, Ziva, you and Tokal are linked together."

"You must let me go, Lib," Ziva implores. "I must leave so that Tokal can live."

"Where did this thought come from?" Lib shakes his head. "Explain it to me."

"Can't you accept that it must be?" Ziva implores him to see common sense.

He stares at her in disbelief. "No. I don't see." He puts his forehead on hers.

She removes her head from his, trying to step away.

He tightens his hold on the blanket, not allowing an inch of space between them. "Your family is here, Ziva."

"I can't stay," she whimpers.

"Why?" his voice caresses as his arms wrap around her, holding them close together. For a long time, they stand there without words.

"Everyone I have ever loved has died." She closes her eyes. "I don't want to be responsible for another death."

He stands there holding her while he thinks. He takes one of his hands and caresses her face. With a gentle touch he cups her chin, pressing upward until their eyes meet. Tears sparkle in her eyes. A brief smile touches his face. "You are your own worst enemy."

She's heard that before. She's even said it. A tear slides down her face. She stares back at him, trying to fortify herself against him.

"You need someone to watch your back. Be on your side. Remind you that you're not alone."

She drops her eyes as the memory of her time with only Tokal for company flashes through her brain, reminding her how difficult it was alone. How adrift she felt. Another tear escapes, sliding down her face.

He pauses and takes a breath. "Do you love me, Ziva?"

Her eyes widen at his ridiculous question. "How can I? We've only recently met."

He grins at her. "Then you have nothing to worry about, since you don't love me."

Ziva opens her mouth to speak.

He interrupts her. "Between the both of us, we'll keep Tokal safe. Have faith, Ziva."

She opens her mouth again.

He cuts her off. "Before you speak, one more question must be considered."

In a very soft, firm voice, he asks, "Would you rather try to survive the winter alone with Tokal? This is a package deal. Tokal will be my son, but not without you as his mother. Do you understand that? There will be no running away. Whatever happens, we'll face it together. Understand?"

Her jaw clenches, and her lips disappear from the force as her eyebrows drop a fraction and slam together. "How dare you do that to Tokal."

"How dare I? How dare you do that to your son."

Ziva's mouth drops open at his response. He has a point. Her eyes fall to the ground, and her anger dissipates.

Softly, he continues, "If we do this"—he waits until she looks at him again— "we do this together. Make your choice."

Ziva nods and looks away as her mind whirls into activity. Without the blanket around her this morning, she felt how cold the air is getting and knows it will only get worse before spring arrives. How Lib can stand here keeping her and Tokal warm within the blanket—she doesn't know, but is grateful for it. He's so gentle and kind to Tokal. Tokal's weight and silence tells her he has fallen back asleep on her shoulder.

She isn't planning on surviving the winter. Without Tokal, there wouldn't be a reason to. If she had Tokal with her, there would be an even lower chance of surviving with very little to no supplies. Of course, she could make that choice, but does she want to fight daily for survival? This man, whom she doesn't know, is offering to keep Tokal safe. He doesn't care that they don't know each other. Doesn't seem to care that she doesn't love him. Will raise Tokal as his son, but . . . *only* if she Joins him.

He has been kind to her. He has looked out for her. Has made sure she has food and her needs are taken care of. Is she willing to Join a stranger?

She is willing to sacrifice herself and walk away from Tokal to keep him safe. This man says that if she were to Join him, she wouldn't have to leave Tokal. She wouldn't have to deal with another loss. Could it be possible that she could remain with Tokal and he be safe? She bites her lower lip as her mind runs through the scenarios, trying to pick the best option.

"In the spring, we will return to Uthal if that's still where you wish to go," he whispers, adding more bait to the trap, hoping to tip the scale.

She looks up into the face of this man she barely knows. "I will Join you for Tokal's sake."

Lib kisses her forehead. "Let's get back to camp, where you can warm yourself by the fire." He readjusts the blanket around her and grabs both spears, allowing her to lead the way.

Kelev brings up the rear.

Ziva returns to camp, stopping near the fire.

Lib steps in front of her. "Let me have him."

She passes Tokal over to him with the blanket, readjusting it around the sleeping form before backing away.

With gentle care, Lib places Tokal a safe distance from the fire, within the confines of the blanket.

He motions for Kelev to lie next to the sleeping boy.

Picking up his necklace off the dirt, he wipes it clean and steps behind Ziva.

Ziva stiffens as her heart begins to race.

Lib whispers in her ear, "I'm going to place my necklace on you again. Are we still in agreement?"

She nods, not trusting her voice.

"Good." He sets the necklace around her throat as the rest of the party watches the spectacle. "Nephi, will you Join us before we head to Zarahemla?"

"If that is what you wish." Nephi scratches his chin. "Melek, get in Ziva's pack. At the bottom, a set of Joining clothes is stored. Grab it and bring them here."

Melek retrieves the Joining clothes, while Lib guides Ziva to stand in front of Nephi.

Her body betrays her nervousness. Her legs and hands shake. She grasps her hands together, clamping them to the blanket around her shoulders, trying to keep them still. She hopes the others will think she's cold.

Melek returns with the shirt and shoes, presenting them to her.

Ziva stares at them for a second and swallows. Looking at Melek, she swallows again and tries to smile at him. "Will you help me do this?"

Melek's face scrunches, confused. "Isn't this something a female friend is to perform?"

"I'm the only woman here and I consider you a friend," Ziva shifts her weight back and forth, trying to keep her knees from knocking together. "Will you help me?"

Melek positions himself on her right side.

Standing on her left, Lib reaches under the blanket. He finds her trembling hand. He peels one away from the blanket and squeezes it, hoping to transmit some comfort and support in what's about to take place.

Nephi clears his throat, scratching his chin. "I haven't done this before, so bear with me. Uh, Lib do you take Ziva as your wife?"

"Yes."

"Good. Ziva, do you take Lib as your husband?"

Ziva doesn't answer.

Lib squeezes her hand.

Ziva glances his way.

Lib juts his chin toward Nephi, prompting her response.

She turns her attention to Nephi. "Yes."

"You may dress your husband."

Ziva examines the clothes that Melek holds. She looks at Nephi for an answer. "What do I do?"

"Er." He scratches his chin. "Put the Joining shirt on Lib before moving to the Joining shoes. Lib, it will help if you kneel."

"Oh." Lib kneels.

Ziva takes the Joining shirt from Melek. Her shaking arms put his hands through the arm holes.

Nephi chuckles. "Ziva, you have to take the other shirt off first before you put the new one on."

Ziva stops what she's doing and pulls the shirt to her. *I have to replace his shirt?* She stares at the garment in her hands, feeling uncomfortable. She spent a lot of hours making it with her mother. *I miss her. I can do this for Tokal.* She takes a deep breath. *I've seen his chest. Don't look at it. Treat this like changing Tokal.*

She drops the Joining shirt on her shoulder. Taking another breath, she reaches down, grabs the bottom of the material, and whisks it up over Lib's head. She drops the garment on her other shoulder. She grabs the Joining shirt and pulls it over the offered arms. Tugging his hands through their proper holes. She finishes with his head popping through.

"One task down and one more to go," she mumbles under her breath. Hands shaking, Ziva retrieves the shoes without looking at Melek or anyone else. She kneels down for this next task, attempting to figure out which shoe fits which foot. Determining the solution, she grabs the offered limb that Lib lifts. She removes the shoe on his foot and replaces it with the new one. Ziva does the same with the other. She smiles to herself at her accomplishment.

As she stands, she realizes a looming unknown exists beyond the present. Her face falls as her fear threatens to overwhelm her. *I'm doing this for Tokal.* She swallows her fear. She pulls her hands together again, clasping the blanket to her chest. Her limbs shake.

"Lib, you may stand and take your wife's hand," Nephi solemnly instructs.

Lib, once again on his feet, reaches for Ziva's hand under the blanket.

Ziva gives her hand this time.

Lib feels the tremors within Ziva's small, slender fingers. He squeezes, trying to reassure her.

"You're Joined," Nephi declares. "Let's have some food and head back to Zarahemla."

# ZARAHEMLA

THE MEN COME FORWARD AND congratulate them. Leaving Ziva and Lib staring at each other, the rest work on their meal and the remaining packing.

Lib takes Ziva's hand, inviting her to sit by the fire. He sits next to her. Holding both her hands in his, he gazes into her eyes. "I promise, I will be a good husband for you. Your needs will always come before my own. Our children's needs will come before my own."

"There will be no children. I won't mate with you," Ziva informs him.

"I won't force you. How do you know about . . .?"

Her face burns. She won't look at him. "I was raised with shepherds and helped watch the sheep." She pauses. "I don't know how to be a wife."

"I don't either," he chuckles. "We'll figure it out together."

The warmth of the fire starts seeping into Ziva, though her hands still shake.

Lib takes a breath. "The Joining is done." He examines her face. "Breathe."

Ziva's eyes move to his face.

The fear in her eyes screams at him. Lib takes a breath, trying to exude calm assurance. "Everything will be well. I will be by your side always." He squeezes her hands one last time before letting go. He pulls the blanket back around her shoulder, leaving her there while he gets their food.

Ziva hugs herself, feeling that her world has spun into something unknown. Besides mating, what does having a husband entail? She has no clue—it's a foreign concept that others around her seem to accept and expect from her. She's joined to a virtual stranger on an unknown path. She swallows the fear rising in her throat. She agreed to this for Tokal's sake. She will follow through.

When Lib returns, he hands Ziva a bowl of mush.

Ziva takes it even though she has no appetite. With the trip in front of them, she eats the food without tasting. When the meal is gone, her bowl is whisked away.

Lib helps her to her feet.

Ziva blinks and looks at him as she's pulled from her inner thoughts.

"Time to go." Lib places Tokal into her arms.

Tokal blinks and smiles at her.

She hugs his little body, gaining strength and reminding herself that she's doing this for him.

The little boy urinates.

Ziva launches into action. She retrieves a clean changing cloth and drapes it on the ground.

Lib holds Tokal down, while Ziva makes him ready for travel.

After completing the change, she wraps him to her front. Ziva slings her pack over her shoulders and looks up.

Everyone, except Lib, is standing around, waiting.

"Where's Lib?"

Nephi scratches his whiskers. "He went to clean the cloth and will be back soon."

As Nephi finishes the statement, Lib jogs into camp, sporting his brightly colored Joining clothes. Pinched between his fingers is a wet cloth, fluttering behind him. He grabs his bag, pulls something out, and tosses it Ziva's way.

She catches it.

Lib shrugs into his pack and nods to Nephi.

When she looks up, Nephi's back disappears into the forest with several of the students following behind.

Lib speaks behind her. "For Tokal. Hurry, we need to catch up with the others."

Ziva dashes, persimmon in hand, to reach the others. Getting her bearings, she follows three students on a path. Lib is behind her. Three others trail him.

Tokal smacks his lips and starts whining.

Ziva takes a bite out of the fruit. She gives the rest to Tokal as they continue at a brisk pace.

Tokal slurps and gnaws on the fruit.

In the late afternoon, they stop for the night. A stream, shaded by trees, is nearby. A fish splashes the surface of the water as it eats a bug. Transparent water reveals places for fish to hide.

Tired, Ziva watches as the men place fish traps and set up camp. She takes a breath, deciding she better join them with the work. With one hand wrapped protectively around Tokal's sleeping form, she uses the other to wash the soiled cloth. Cold water kisses her hand, and she shivers.

Ziva rings out the cleaned cloth, dropping them on branches to dry. She grabs the tie at the end of her disordered ponytail and removes it. Her hair cascades around her. Ziva combs her hair. She wants to create a neat braid before cooking dinner.

Tokal stretches.

She looks down, finding brown eyes looking up at her.

Tokal breaks into a happy smile, greeting her.

She smiles back.

Realizing that a curtain of hair surrounds him, Tokal's small, sticky hands grab on tight.

"Let go, Tokal. That hurts."

Tokal, delighted to get her attention and thinking this is a new game, laughs.

Ziva works fast to free the hair from a small fist.

Tokal releases one grubby fist.

Ziva works on the next one.

Tokal's free hand clamps onto her silky strands. He tugs and cackles.

Ziva cringes. A hand stops his yanking.

"It may be easier for you to do your hair if I hold him," an amused voice beside her says.

Ziva distracted my Lib's voice, tries to look at him through her brown tresses.

Tokal reclaims a good grip on her hair and tugs, thinking this is great fun.

Ziva winces, reaching to stop him.

"Let me help you with him—before he pulls your hair from your head." Lib moves close, without waiting for permission, and removes Ziva's hair from Tokal's strong grasp. "Hold your hair back from him."

Six pairs of eyes watch the new family as Ziva follows Lib's instructions.

"Good." Lib holds each little fist in his palm.

Ziva holds her hair back.

"I'll take him so you can do what you need to do."

Ziva tries with one hand to untie the knot under Tokal's bottom without letting her hair loose with the other. Frustration bubbles out of her. "I can't undo it with one hand."

"Let me." Lib pushes her hand away from the knot. "Continue holding your hair back so he doesn't get it again."

Tokal's little form is boosted higher in the front of her while his hands grab at her face. She kisses the sticky hands in an effort to keep him occupied and away from her hair.

Lib uses both hands to untie the knot. He pulls the active boy from her chest.

Exhaling a sigh of relief, she whispers, "Thank you."

Lib holds Tokal in his arms.

Tokal smiles, reaching for the man's nose and mouth with his outstretched fingers.

"You're one sticky, strong, happy little boy." Lib sits down with Tokal and keeps him occupied.

Ziva takes one of the clean cloths and dunks it in the water, wringing it out. She tosses it Lib's way so he can wipe Tokal's sticky hands and face. After combing out the knots in her hair, she braids it into a single rope behind her back. She hopes she'll get a chance to bathe when they reach the city. After ringing out a cloth, she turns away from everyone, wiping away the sweat and dirt from her face, arms, and dress front.

Tokal wails, not appreciating the cold cloth that's being wiped over him.

Not expecting Tokal's attack on his ears, Lib cringes. A moment later warm liquid soaks into Lib's Joining shirt. Lib pulls Tokal away from him, laying him down. "Be still, little man. She's right here, but you need changed first."

Tokal reaches out his hands to be picked up, only to have his bottom wiped with the cold wet rag. He cries at this abuse as a fresh cloth is placed.

When finished, Ziva picks up Tokal to comfort him.

Lib stops her. Concern laces his words. "Your front is wet. Your dress needs changed."

Tired and embarrassed, Ziva says, "I don't have anything else, Lib, and even if I did have something, I'm not going to change with a bunch of men around. Tokal needs consoled. I can use him to cover me and stand by the fire until it dries. We'll be fine." She pulls Tokal to her and ties him to her chest. "*Your* shirt needs changed."

Lib sees exhaustion and irritation dance in her face. He nods. Without a word, he pulls off his shirt and goes to the stream to clean it. After ringing it out, he puts it back on.

Ziva watches in disbelief. "You *do* have another shirt. You *don't* need to wear a wet one."

"Yes, but you *don't* have any other clothes and wear a wet dress."

"The air is warm enough," Ziva mutters, wishing for this conversation to be over. "I'll be just fine."

"Let's move to the fire and dry our clothes." Lib grabs the dirty cloths and, muttering under his breath, cleans them, forcefully wringing out the material as though it was something else. Grabbing the other clean linens from the branches, he wads them in his hands and follows her to the fire.

"Feel better?" she snips when he catches up with her.

"I'll feel better when you're dry."

"I'll feel better when you're dry." After a charged silence, Ziva changes the subject. "How many more days of traveling?"

"We'll arrive in Zarahemla tomorrow." he returns through clenched teeth. He moves her closer to the fire.

Standing her ground, she says, "I need to make sure that the heat doesn't hurt Tokal. That's why I'm not too close."

Lib steps close to her. "Put him on your hip that is away from the fire so you can get dry. Once the fish are obtained, they'll need cooked." In a deft motion, he loosens the knot, repositions Tokal, then tightens it again with a jerk.

Ziva glares at him, stamping out the strange feelings low in her stomach trying to flutter to life.

They stand there fuming at each other. Lib wiggles his fingers in front of Tokal, keeping him occupied while their shirts dry.

"Ooooooowwwww," Lib shrieks, pulling his hand away from Tokal. He sticks a finger in his mouth.

Startled, Tokal howls.

Ziva jumps away from Lib, confused as to what's going on. She gathers Tokal closer in her arms, soothing her son.

The men, hearing the commotion, gather round.

She looks at Lib with concern and spits out, "What happened?"

Lib takes his finger out of his mouth and looks at it. Four little teeth marks, two on each side, indent his finger. He looks up in disbelief, uttering, "He bit me."

The men roar with laughter as Lib shows his injury to the others.

She looks at the finger, finding no broken skin. She glares at him. "Keep your fingers out of his mouth." Dispensing common sense.

Nephi slaps his hand on Lib's shoulder. "You're fine. I would follow Ziva's advice." He grins, wiping the tears from his eyes. "If you have to stick your fingers in a child's mouth, be smart about it."

Nephi scratches his chin. "Ziva, I'll take Tokal and keep him occupied so you can make dinner. It seems this little one isn't going to wait much longer for something to eat."

Nephi's attention sharpens on the men standing about. "Check the fish traps. If you find fish, bring it. If not, we'll try again in the morning."

"Melek lost his knife," Zeram reports.

Melek's mouth drops open before his brows draw together, and he whines, "Why did you have to say that?"

Nephi sighs. "When and where did you lose it?"

"He lost it making the fish trap, because he was too busy watching Ziva and Lib." Jashon gins.

Taking another breath and blowing it out, trying to control his own temper, Nephi says, "Melek, find your knife. The rest of you, check the traps."

The men turn, wandering off to do what they're told.

Nephi turns back to Ziva, suggesting, "Make a simple meal."

Ziva nods not looking at Nephi. She lifts Tokal, revealing her front.

Lib interrupts the exchange. "Ziva, is your dress dry?"

She glares at Lib. She feels the heat in her face raise. "It's dry enough." Turning to Nephi with a masked facial expression, she says, in a sweet tone, "Here's Tokal. I'll start working on a meal."

Nephi takes Tokal from her and starts bouncing him while he uses the carrying cloth to play peekaboo with the boy.

With her arms crossed over her front, Ziva walks over to the supplies to decide what to cook.

Lib stands by the fire in a damp shirt, fuming.

When Ziva's out of earshot, Nephi addresses a haggard Lib. "Tough time today?"

Lib takes a deep breath. His eyes remain locked on Ziva. "A Joining is harder than it looks."

When Tokal pulls the cloth from Nephi's head and laughs, Nephi grins back at Lib. "You're both new to this. A Joining takes time to adjust to."

"I don't know what to do." He sighs, glancing at his teacher. "She's tired so I try to help, but it seems to be the wrong thing."

Nephi nods with understanding. "I've got this little guy. Why don't you see if you can help her with dinner?"

Lib's eyes narrow and the corners of his mouth turn down. "I don't think she wants me around her at this moment."

Tokal pulls the cloth from Nephi's head again, laughing at the funny faced man.

Nephi glances at Lib before he turns his attention back to Tokal. "Offer and follow her lead." Nephi tosses the cloth on his head again. "The men will report to Ziva. See what you can do to help."

Lib eyes his teacher wondering about his wisdom.

Nephi makes a funny face for Tokal.

Lib smiles. He looks at the angry woman across camp. He takes a calming breath before walking over.

Nephi and Tokal continue their game.

When he reaches Ziva, Lib asks, "Are there any fish?"

Ziva looks up from what she's doing, emitting a "be careful" warning. "No." She stands, looking around her. "I think we're going to have mush tonight."

Concern touches Lib's face. "What are you looking for?"

"A waterskin to fill the pot."

"I'll find one for you."

Ziva nods, dismissing him. She turns her attention toward this campsite's grinding stone. After cleaning it off, she crushes the corn.

Lib stands behind her for a minute, watching her take some anger out on the corn seed. He sighs, going in search of a filled waterskin.

It doesn't take him long to find a waterskin, but the container is almost empty. Looking around, he finds a few more with no more water than the first. He gazes at the sky and sees that he must hurry before darkness falls. Taking them to the stream, he fills them up and returns to her side. "I have three filled waterskins. What else can I do to help with our food?"

Ziva glances up from the grinding stone as though he were a small child that isn't using common sense.

Lib feels like one.

"Fill the pot and place it in the ash." She continues taking out her anger on the corn. He tosses all but one waterskin and grabs the pot, taking it close to the fire.

Zeram and Jashon walk up while he's working. "I've enjoyed watching your family this evening. I've never laughed this much in my life," Zeram pats his shoulder.

"Neither have I," Jashon concurs. "Glad I'm not stuck with a woman or child."

"I'm happy to make your day," Lib mutters, placing the pot in the hot ash. "I'd like to chat, but I need to find what else I can do to help with dinner." He walks away from them, returning to Ziva's side. "The filled pot is in the ash."

"Good." She gathers the cornmeal into a bag, taking it to the fire. She stirs the meal into the pot. "Lib." She calls over her shoulder without anger.

Lib moves to her side.

"Can you stir this for me while I get a few more items?"

Lib takes the spoon from her. Happy to help if it keeps her happy.

Ziva dashes to the supplies. She grabs different bags, returning to the pot.

The last moments of daylight fade away into night. As the heat from the day dissipates, more people gather around the fire. The fire crackles and the pot boils.

While Lib stirs the contents, Ziva drops a few handfuls from several different small bags she has with her.

The air becomes sweet and fragrant with their dinner. Stars blink in the dark blue tapestry above them. Crickets chirp in the distance.

A loud wail from Tokal disturbs the air.

"I forgot to get the bowls before nightfall," Ziva exclaims to herself.

Handing the stirring implement to Ziva, Lib stands. "I'll get them." He grabs a stick from the fire to light his way. He brings Melek with him. Lib searches for the bowls.

The other students join him.

Nephi is left soothing Tokal.

Tokal informs them all that he's not waiting anymore for some food.

As quick as he can, Lib returns with the other students and hands bowls to Ziva.

Ziva fills a bowl for Tokal and cools it. She heads toward Nephi.

Lib follows, trying to give her a spoon.

Now that both Ziva and Lib have moved from the pot, the students fill their bowls with their meal.

Ziva sits on her blanket, settling to receive Tokal. The bowl is removed from her hand. She looks up to see what happened.

Lib blows and stirs the food.

Nephi dumps the crying boy in her lap. She positions him for feeding. The food magically appears at her side.

"Be careful. The food is still a bit hot."

Ziva scoops up some food and blows on it.

Tokal sees the food. He stops hollering. When the food doesn't come fast enough, he wails again. Angry that people aren't moving fast enough.

By this time, the food has cooled enough to be inserted in the open mouth.

Ziva turns the spoon over, dumping its contents on Tokal's tongue.

Tokal stops crying. He blinks a few times. He swallows.

Ziva spoons another. When Tokal's mouth pops open, she inserts some more.

Everyone breaths easier now that Tokal's quiet.

Lib joins Nephi at the pot. Lib fills some bowls for Ziva and himself.

After everyone has eaten, they sit around the fire.

Tokal falls asleep in Ziva's arms. She lays him down on the blanket next to her and covers him up.

"Everyone." Nephi waits until all eyes are on him. "What will tomorrow's weather be?"

Ziva peers at the night sky trying to comprehend. "What do you see?"

Lib, sitting next to her, points to the moon. "A ring around the moon, and the sky devoid of stars, means a storm is coming."

"It will be colder too." Paanchi says.

Amnor scratches his head. "When will the storm hit?"

"Mmmm . . . late morning sometime." Nephi rubs his chin.

Jashon grabs his pack and looks through it. "We won't make it back before the storm hits. I'm going to lighten my pack."

"It looks like a bad one. We have no shelter here." Paanchi retrieves his own pack.

Zeram follows. "I don't want to be in it."

"None of us wants to be in it," Lib returns. "What are we going to do?"

"That's what I'm deciding." Nephi scratches his cheek. "We need to leave earlier to at least get to Zarahemla before the downpour."

"What about Ziva and Tokal?" Lib asks.

"What about them? They'll have to endure it like the rest of us. We'll all help where we can." Nephi strokes his chin. "Men, clean the dishes tonight and remove the fish traps from the stream. Release any fish. They will take too long to cook. How much jerky and how many persimmons do we have left?"

"We have two persimmons and a small bag of jerky left. I saw them before cooking."

"The rest of the supplies will be destroyed with the rain," Melek grimaces.

"Yes. We'll leave them here." Nephi turns to the young man. Melek, did you find your knife?"

Melek looks at his feet. "No."

Nephi nods, feeling for the young man. "We'll make do without it." Turning to the group, Nephi sighs. "Everyone, get to work."

The group rises to finish what needs done.

"Ziva and Lib, not you."

The other students' glance at them, wondering why Lib and Ziva are kept back. They're not going to ask Nephi. They split up, each taking a task.

Jashon and Zeram head for the fish traps.

Paanchi, Melek and Amnor gather up the dishes, heading to the edge of camp to clean them.

Nephi waits until all are out of earshot before speaking to Lib and Ziva. "Tomorrow is going to be harder for you, Ziva, than today. Get some sleep the both of you. Stay close together."

Nephi grabs a torch and makes sure the other students are done with their tasks.

Lib leaves the fire. He returns with their packs. Going through his pack with the help of firelight, he pulls out some more clothes. "Put these on Ziva."

"If tomorrow is going to be cold and rainy, what are you going to wear?"

Lib doesn't answer.

"These are your clothes. You wear them. I will use the blanket to cover Tokal and me from the storm."

Lib frowns and starts to open his mouth.

Ziva stops his reply, as she looks him in the eye. "If tomorrow is going to be worse than today, I'm going to need your help. By having the mobility your clothes will provide, you will be able to help me more than if you used a blanket or, even worse, nothing."

Lib frowns at her thinking it through. He nods, putting on the extra clothing. Bringing his blanket next to Tokal, he places it before lying down. "Time to sleep."

Ziva settles down under her blanket.

With Tokal between them, Lib and Ziva examine the other for a moment. Not a word is spoken.

Ziva closes her eyes.

SOMEONE SHAKES HER SHOULDER. ZIVA'S eyes meet Lib's in the darkness.

"We need to get moving."

Getting out of the blanket, her body shivers from the sudden cold.

Lib doesn't wait. He picks up Tokal, who's wrapped in a blanket, and passes him to Ziva to hold. The cloth is wrapped around Tokal and Ziva. He ties the knot at her front. After shaking the blanket out, he wraps it around her shoulders.

"My pack!"

"Everything has been loaded in mine." He makes sure she has a grasp on the edge of the blanket. "Your job is to take care of Tokal."

She nods.

"Let's go." Lib's arm encourages her forward.

Ziva falls in line behind Jashon.

Lib follows.

The leave camp a little before sunrise at a rapid pace, moving as fast as Ziva's feet.

When daylight arrives, looming dark clouds lower the canopy above. Thunder is heard in the distance. The smell of rain thick in the air.

As they hurry, Jashon and Lib help Ziva, keep her feet under her.

Tokal fusses. He's handed a persimmon to eat.

The rest of the group consume jerky continuing their brisk pace, trying to beat the storm. They stop when Tokal loads his cloth, requiring a change.

Ziva is winded and tired. She pushes forward with the blanket wrapped around her, keeping Tokal warm. She feels she didn't move this fast even when pursued by the Gadianton. She's not going to complain.

Ziva's stopped by her guardians. Unable to speak, she looks up. A very large river in front of her. On both sides of the river are many different types of canoes. On the other side of the river is a fenced city. Two rows of vertical timbers have been lined closely together with dirt between, creating a solid wall similar to Uthal's. Animal and family carvings on the outside of the city decorate the walls. Many people travel to and from the mouth of the city.

A hand on her back pushes her forward. Her attention diverts to Jashon. He's moving forward.

At the edge of the river, she's put inside of a long canoe.

The group join her.

She sits.

The men paddle.

While in the canoe, she checks on her son.

Tokal peeks out of the blanket up at her, showing rosy cheeks.

Ziva's legs and arms shake with the exertion of the day. She repositions the blanket so that it will remain closed even with the wind. Wrapping her arms around Tokal, she closes her eyes.


PEOPLE PULL HER TO HER feet. Ziva moves forward. The blanket slips from her shoulders. It feels like a bucket of cold water has been thrown on her. She shivers.

"Take the blanket," Lib says throwing it around her shoulders. Wide awake now, she grabs the ends, holding it around herself and Tokal.

They're on shore again.

"Move, Ziva," Lib encourages behind her. "We're almost to Zarahemla."

Her body cramps. Somehow, she's trotting. She hikes up the road toward the city.

It starts sprinkling. By the time they reach the gates, she feels she's under a waterfall. With head down against the elements, she pushes forward.

The blanket around her shoulders is soaked as they rush through the streets. Her body shakes.

Tokal howls.

Ziva has no idea where their destination is, but hopes they'll get there soon. Her nose runs. Her teeth hurt as she grinds them together to keep from chattering. She can smell the oncoming snow in the air. She stumbles unable to keep her feet under her any longer. They feel like limp yarn. She's so tired. She floats. Her vision goes dark.

# HEALING

FEELING WARM, ZIVA BURROWS FURTHER under the blanket's warmth. She opens her eyes and blinks. A dry blanket covers her. She peeks out of it. Lined timbers above her come into view. Where is the sky? She blinks again, trying to recall. She starts looking around her. On one side of her, the warm embers of a fire glow in a fire pit. It feels wonderful being comfortable again. It hits her—Tokal is gone!

She sits up as panic sets in. Her head feels like a large rock has struck her. The blood rings in her ears as dizziness overtakes her. Her vision blurs around the edges. She grinds her teeth, trying to keep herself from passing out. She closes her eyes, willing herself to stay awake. "Tokal!" she screams.

"Lie back." A hand pushes her back down.

Ziva collapses back on the bed.

A woman's voice breaks through the ringing in her ears. "Lie there and be still. Tokal is with Lib."

Ziva relaxes by degrees as she comprehends the woman's words. The last of the ringing in her ears dissipates. "Your husband is most concerned about you. During the day, I watch after you, and he spends his time caring for Tokal, knowing that is where you want him. At night, while I sleep, he tends to your needs."

Ziva opens her eyes again, looking toward the source of the voice. A woman comes into view. She has light-brown hair, streaked with gray. It's tied in a braid down her back. Her chestnut-colored eyes smile. Laugh lines run around the perimeter of her eyes. She reminds Ziva of her own mother.

"I'm glad you're awake." The woman smiles at her. "My name is Sariah. I am named after our first mother that traveled to this land so long ago." She smiles to herself as if recalling what she has been told all her life. Sariah takes a breath. "Now that you're awake, let's try to sit you up without you passing out. You need to drink."

Ziva sits up slower this time.

"That's it," Sariah encourages, placing a warm wooden cup in Ziva's hand. Sariah squeezes Ziva's forearm, reassuring her. "The cup contains broth. Drink it slowly."

Ziva takes a sip. The warm, savory liquid is delicious. She drinks more. Soon the cup is empty.

Sariah chuckles. "You must be hungry. No matter. We will wait a little bit to see if you can keep that down." Sariah reaches for the empty container.

Ziva passes it over. "Where am I?"

Sariah sits next to Ziva. "I would probably be asking those same questions." Sariah sets the empty cup down next to her and decides to start from the beginning. "I'm Sariah. I'm married to Nephi. You're in our home in Zarahemla. The men brought you here. From what I understand"—she scratches her head—"when you collapsed, Lib carried you and Tokal the rest of the way. Your arrival here prompted me to give Tokal to Nephi. The child needed changed and warmed up. Lib helped me get you out of your wet clothes and dried. Lib is so worried about you."

At Sariah's words, a realization hits Ziva. She examines herself. "I'm naked."

Sariah chuckles again. "No man, besides Lib, saw you."

"Where are my clothes?" Ziva's voice goes up an octave. She's doesn't hear Sariah's response.

"They've been washed and are drying," Sariah is confused by Ziva's agitation.

Ziva's voice rises. She stands, holding the blanket around her. "I need my clothes."

"If you must. But stay where you are." Sariah exits the building. She returns with the damp clothes. "I don't understand why you need them at this moment."

Ziva grabs them from her, searching the pockets. "No. No. No." Her voice gets higher as her anxiety grows.

"What's wrong?"

Ziva's countenance falls. Tears cascade from her eyes, "I can't find it. It can't be gone. Where did you take off my clothes?"

"Right here." Sariah's concern grows. She doesn't know how to calm the girl.

Ziva searches the floor to see if she can find what she's looking for. "It must be around here somewhere."

With careful regard, she searches the bedding. She examines the mat for holes.

"What are you looking for?" Sariah asks, wanting to help.

"A black cloth."

"Any black cloth?"

"No! My black cloth." Ziva's voice rises again as she continues her hunt. She starts at one end of the room, searching everything again. She concentrates on finding her father's pearl.

Sariah, not knowing how to help her, leaves her home. She returns with Lib.

Ziva wrapped in a blanket is on all fours with her head close to the ground.

"What are you doing, Ziva?" Lib comes to her side.

"I can't find it. I had it in my pocket. She washed my clothes, and my father's gift is gone."

"Ziva, stop." He pulls out a black cloth from his pocket.

Ziva doesn't hear as she continues her frantic search. The blanket slips from her body.

Lib grits his teeth. He pulls Ziva into his arms. With a shake he says, "Stop this, Ziva." He turns her so that her back touches his front and his arm is wrapped around her, pinning her to him. He speaks in her ear. "Look at my hand, Ziva."

With her arms pinned to her sides, Ziva hears his words and looks at his fist.

In slow motion his hand opens, revealing the small black cloth. She stills and his arms loosen. Her hands break free of their restraints. She cups the outstretched hand, protecting the prize inside. With careful fingers she opens the dark cloth. The exquisite pearl blinks at her. She breathes. Her legs give out.

Lib pulls her to him, holding her within his arms.

"The pearl!"

"I still have it in my hand." He picks her up, carrying her a few steps where he sets her down on the floor next to the crumpled bedding. "See?" He shows the pearl to her again.

Ziva oblivious to anything but the pearl, peers up at him Gratitude shines in her eyes. She sighs. "Thank you."

Without looking at her, Lib folds the fabric around the pearl. "I will keep it safe and return it to you when you're well." He puts it in his pocket. He fixes the blankets and deposits her on the makeshift bed. "You need to rest." Lib retrieves the blanket that clothed her from the floor. Shakes it out, then covers her body from the neck down. Lib turns away, trying to stop his body's response.

Ziva realizes that Lib saw her naked. She's covered in the flames of embarrassment. She looks at anything but Lib. Her arms pull the blanket closer, securing it around her. She feels mortified. As her discomfort dies, she changes the subject. "Where's Tokal?"

Lib clears his throat. "He's staying with Sariah's daughter, who is across the way. I take care of him during the day and return after he falls asleep to care for . . .so Sariah can rest. Would you like some water?"

"Yes."

Lib hands a filled cup to her.

Ziva takes a few drinks and shivers.

"Are you going to be calm?"

She takes another sip of water and peers at him under her lashes. He stands as if everything is normal. "Yes."

"Concentrate on your recovery, Ziva. I will be back tonight. I need to get back to Tokal. Are you good with that?"

Ziva nods, feeling childish and self-conscious. She still can't look him in the eye.

He leaves the house.

Sariah returns to Ziva's side. "You had me worried, so I sent Lib while I watched Tokal. He's such a good child and so smart. What did you lose?"

"I apologize for my behavior. I lost something important to me." Ziva takes a breath before she explains. "I didn't know Lib was holding my father's gift while I recover."

"I'm glad you have your senses back." Sariah picks up the empty cup and fills it. She places it in the girl's hands.

The coolness of the water slides down Ziva's throat, refreshing her. Trying to organize Lib's words in her mind, she takes another drink before speaking. "So, Tokal is at your daughter's home at night. Lib takes care of him during the day. He's been here during the night to care for me?" Her face heats up.

"Yes."

Ziva has to know. "How long have I been sick?"

"Two days. The fever broke last night. Lib insists he care for you himself so I can rest. He must be very tired."

Ziva grimaces, not liking her condition. She takes another drink and mutters to herself. "I've never been sick—that I can recall."

Sariah chuckles again. "Everyone gets sick at one time or another. Illness is part of the natural experience."

Ziva finishes what's in the cup and passes it to Sariah.

"Thank you for the water and broth. I'm tired." Ziva lies back down and buries herself more under the blanket. She yawns. "Tell Lib I'm fine. He doesn't need to care for me."

Sariah watches, surprised at how quick the girl falls asleep.

ZIVA BLINKS A FEW TIMES, getting her eyes to focus. She sits, looking at the fire as it licks the bark in the fire pit. Sap pops, spraying brightly colored light that fades moments later.

The warmth that was there is gone. She shivers. She looks down as something touches her. A hand reaches from behind, pulling the blanket to her shoulders.

Is she dreaming? She blinks.

"Tokal's safe, Ziva. Lean back on me."

She jumps, not expecting anyone. Her mind recognizes the tired, groggy voice as Lib's. She feels his hand settle on her shoulder, guiding her back. A strong warm chest supports her. A protective arm wraps under her breast, holding her in place.

"You've been sick for several days."

She shivers at this new experience. She's never been in a man's arms. Her heart races. Her stomach flips.

Lib's arm tightens.

"Your fever broke last night. Do you remember being up earlier today?"

Ashamed at her performance, she rasps, "Yes."

"Tokal is well. Your pearl is in my pocket. You need to drink to recover your strength. I'm going to hand you some broth. Drink it slow so it doesn't come back up." He places a warm wooden vessel in her hands.

"I kept it down earlier without issue," she mutters.

"Tokal's at Sariah's daughter's home. With you being so sick, Tokal needed to be removed until you recover. He has other children to play with during the day and is learning to walk. At night, I hold him as he cries for you. He misses you very much. I can't bring him back to you until you're well enough."

Ziva is quiet. She misses her active son.

"Ziva, are you still awake?"

One side of her mouth curves up. "Yes. Thinking about what you told me."

She feels the smile on his face.

"Do you want or need anything?"

"I need Tokal."

Lib repositions himself. He looks Ziva over, evaluating her health. "When you're stronger, I will bring him to you."

She frowns. "I'll recover faster by seeing him."

She feels a chuckle reverberate in his chest. "I'll take that under advisement and will think about it. Here's some water."

A cup comes into view in the dim firelight. She drinks, thankful that the water is room temperature. "What happened?"

Lib takes a breath and blows it out. "What do you remember?"

"We made it to a city, and it started raining hard. It felt like I . . . floated."

"You passed out while you were walking." Silence echoes between them before he continues. "Why didn't you speak up before that happened?"

She shrugs. "I focused only on reaching our destination so we could get out of the rain."

His arm around her middle adjusts. He chuckles. "You need to concentrate on getting your strength back. I will bring Tokal when you're a little stronger."

She doesn't like his words, but she can't prevent the yawn.

"Sleep. When you're feeling better there will be more time to talk." He takes the cup that rests in her hand. "Know that Tokal is well."

She feels something like a kiss pressed to the side of her head.

Lib keeps her in his arms as he lies down.

It feels good to be warm and safe. Knowledge hits her that she's naked and a man holds her. She tenses.

"Easy, Ziva. A blanket resides between us. Your health and wellbeing are my primary concerns. Even though we are Joined, I do this only to keep you warm. Nothing more." Under his breath he whispers, "For today."

Ziva remains still.

Even breathing reaches her ears. *The man fell asleep!* She frowns. She closes her eyes. She wriggles deeper into the warmth, getting comfortable.

Lib's arm tightens around her.

She stills. Something comes alive low in her abdomen.

Lib's grip relaxes. His breathing a steady cadence.

She wonders at the sensation as her mind drifts to dreams.


LIB IS NO LONGER NEXT to her. She stretches. Her stomach growls. She sits up, pulling the hair away from her face.

"Good morning." Sariah smiles. "I bet you're ready to do something other than sleep. First things first, let me help you get cleaned up."

When she's clean, Ziva, holding a blanket around her shivering frame, asks, "Where are my clothes?"

"Hold on dearie, and let's get you seated before we move forward with getting dressed."

Ziva sits on the nearest stool and waits.

Satisfied, Sariah disappears from Ziva's view. She returns with a stack of items. "Lib bought you these for a start. When you get better you can purchase your own clothes."

Ziva opens her mouth.

"Before you speak, these are much warmer than your old clothes and will do well throughout the winter."

Ziva forgot what she was going to say. She closes her mouth.

Sariah drops the clothes near her. "I will be in the other room, getting your food. If you need me, call me."

Ziva nods and watches as Sariah disappears around the corner. The cream-colored shirt is soft to the touch and looks to be lined with another layer of some sort of warm fabric. She touches the red embroidery on the shirt that has been left. It's beautiful. A skirt that matches is folded in the pile. New stockings and boots finish the outfit. These are all nicer than anything she recalls ever wearing. Her heart softens toward Lib. Taking breath she gets to work, dressing herself. When she's done, she feels wrapped in warmth. She summons her caretaker.

Sariah examines the outfit Ziva wears. She smiles in approval. "You look lovely in those clothes. Are you ready to go into the other room?"

Ziva, not knowing how to respond to her compliment, gives an awkward smile. She decides to let it pass and just follow Sariah into the main room. She settles her trembling body on the first chair she sees at the table. Broth and bread rest on the surface.

"When you're done with your food, I will do your hair and we'll see how you're feeling." A cup of water is placed on the table. "We don't want you to overdo it, you know."

Ziva, unsure of herself, thinks of Ami and how she would act. "Thank you."

"I'll be back soon." Sariah exits the house.

Ziva sips the hot broth to avoid burning her tongue. The fresh bread melts in her mouth. She stares at the empty cup in her hand and wonders when she will get to see Tokal.

Thirsty, Ziva searches for some water. She discovers that a clay pot on the table is filled with water. She pours herself another, drinking her fill.

Ziva sits holding a full mug feeling weary. She yawns. She leans against the wall, debating whether to return to bed.

When Sariah enters, Ziva says, "When you're done with my hair, I want to see Tokal."

"You look tired. Are you sure?"

"Yes."

Sariah combs Ziva's hair and braids it. "I will let Lib know your request."

Ziva closes her eyes, feeling exhausted but not willing to lie down until she sees Tokal. The sound of the door causes her eyes to fly open.

Lib enters the home holding a filled blanket.

When the door is shut, he uncovers Tokal.

A little head pops out.

Lib looks for Ziva by the fire, not finding her.

Tokal, however, finds his mother. His little arms and legs race through the air as he tries to get to her. He squealing his delight.

Lib's attention turns to the squirming infant, who nearly jumps out of his arms. He readjusts his hold so he doesn't drop him.

Tokal fusses in frustration. He can't seem to reach his mother.

Lib spots Ziva leaning against the wall, smiling at Tokal. He comes to her side.

Tokal escapes, jumping into his mother's awaiting arms. He begins to tell her everything as he holds tightly to her neck.

Ziva, overjoyed at the little body that hugs her, begins to cry, relieved to have him in her arms again.

Lib settles himself next to them and places a hand over her hand that supports Tokal's back.

She raises her eyes to Lib in gratitude. "Thank you."

They huddle as a family, not speaking.

Tokal's wet kisses on Ziva's face breaks the moment.

Ziva laughs. She wipes away her tears and kisses the child's sweet little face.

Tokal, feeling safe in Ziva's arms, grows bored. He explores, grabbing whatever is within reach.

Lib pulls Tokal into his arms. "You look spent, Ziva."

Her tired eyes meet his. Ziva smiles. "I feel a lot better seeing him."

"Nevertheless, you need to rest." Lib gives Tokal a cloth to play with. "Let me help you to bed."

Ziva nods. She pushes herself to her feet.

Lib moves Tokal to one hip and wraps his other arm around her. He helps hold her up as he guides her back to her bed by the fire.

Ziva slides out of Lib's arm settling on the mat.

"Sleep. I will bring Tokal back this afternoon for another visit."

She pulls the blanket to her and lies down.

Lib retrieves Tokal's blanket and covers him.

When the door closes, she welcomes sleep once more.

LIB ARRIVES AROUND MEALTIME WITH Tokal.

Sariah greets them at the door. "I'm happy to see the both of you. Ziva took a long nap. I've been keeping her still and occupied with some mending." Sariah moves to the doorway. "I'll be back with your meal." She disappears outside.

Lib walks over to where Ziva sits by the fire.

Ziva's face lights up at seeing Tokal. She drops the sewing in a basket, moving it away.

Lib deposits the child in her lap and sits beside them.

Tokal and Ziva are overjoyed and greet each other with hugs and kisses.

Sariah returns, leaving a tray of carrots, potatoes, flat bread, and venison for the family. The different aromas spread through the room.

A pitcher of water and cups are left near Lib.

Before leaving, Sariah says, "If you need more food, I'll be outside."

Tokal, seeing and smelling the food, begins drooling and starts moving toward the offered feast.

Lib grabs the escaping infant, picking him up. "No, you don't, little man. Sit here, and I'll bring you some food."

Tokal looks up at Lib and blinks but sits where he's placed and watches Lib dish up a small plate of food.

Ziva is ready to stop the hungry boy should he move.

A dish is delivered between Tokal's legs, and his pudgy hands bring handfuls of food to his mouth.

"You know he's going to make a mess," Ziva informs Lib.

"Let him. I'll clean it up," Lib returns, dishing up a plate for her. She takes the dish and waits until Lib has served himself.

For a time, the only sounds are happy mouth noises coming from Tokal as he sucks, bites, and gums his way through the food.

Lib is the first to break the silence. "How are you feeling this afternoon?" He asks between bites. Without looking at Ziva, he offers Tokal a drink of water.

The child wraps his hands around the cup.

Lib continues to hold the mug steady, to keep Tokal from pouring water all over himself.

Ziva watches, grinning at his efforts.

Once Tokal is done drinking, Lib removes the container from Tokal's sight.

Ziva glances at Lib. "I feel better after sleeping. He seems like he's grown up a lot while I've been sick."

"Once here, Inna's children have kept him busy. You'll need to take it slowly for a few days as you recover your strength."

Ziva nods. "Tell me about your family."

Lib examines Ziva for a moment before his attention returns to Tokal.

The boy eats another potato slice.

"I'll be back in a minute."

Tokal's and Ziva's eyes follow Lib until he disappears around the corner.

Lib shortly reappears with several damp rags.

Tokal watches Lib sit. He places a messy hand on Lib's thigh and smiles at him. He grabs a carrot and stuffs that into his mouth.

"What would you like to know?"

"Nothing specific." Ziva glances at Lib under her lashes. "My parents are dead. What of yours?"

Lib stops eating. He gazes at Ziva with a frown on his face. "I'm sorry to hear that. My parents are alive. My father is a carver. He works hard, and the king likes his work. My mother works hard maintaining the home. They're going to like you, Ziva, and are going to dote on Tokal."

Ziva frowns, not sure about that. "Are they going to be upset that they weren't there for your Joining?"

Lib looks away, hiding his concern that they indeed won't be happy, especially his mother. "They aren't going to be happy about that."

"Did you have an arranged Joining?"

Lib looks back at her, surprised by her question, but feels that she has the right to know. "They did have someone in mind that they liked for me, but nothing was arranged."

Concerned, Ziva stops eating, staring at him. "How can you say that they are going to like me when I have upset your family's plans for you?"

"I didn't offer for her." He didn't want the girl his parents picked for his wife. He's not sure how to explain that to Ziva.

At that moment, Tokal leans forward to crawl away. Their attention is pulled to him.

Lib grabs Tokal.

Ziva, using the damp cloths, removes the food remains from his person and the floor.

Once Tokal's cleaned, Lib offers water.

Tokal drinks.

Moving the cup out of sight, Lib pulls out a sack of toys he brought for Tokal to play with. When Tokal is settled, Lib's gaze meets Ziva's. "They will get past it. They will like you."

Ziva closes her eyes. She organizes her thoughts, and makes a decision before she looks at Lib again. "When we get back to Uthal, no one need ever know we were Joined. You can return to your family with Tokal and your necklace and tell them your wife died. I will not be the cause of conflict in your family."

The shock and hurt on his face stab her heart. His brown eyes grow darker. Ziva wants to look away but stubbornly continues her stance.

Lib's voice is filled with a mixture of anger and pain. "You and Tokal are my family. Remember? We are in this together."

Startled by the forcefulness in Lib's tone, Tokal starts crying. Lib picks up the little boy and stands up, soothing him. He grabs the blanket and covers Tokal, leaving the home without a backward glance.

Ziva feels deserted and even more alone. Her appetite is gone. She gathers the plates and cups together, taking them to the kitchen. She returns to the fire and picks up the tray of food to join the dishes. Sniffling, Ziva jams Tokal's toys into their bag. She grabs the mending that Sariah gave her. *This is what you wanted, isn't it?*

She stabs the fabric, but after one stitch, she can't lie to herself any longer. She throws the mending back in the basket, acknowledging she has grown attached to the man. Scared that something might happen to him if she opens her heart.

# RECOVERY

ZIVA FEELS ALMOST BACK TO normal.

"Good morning, Ziva," Sariah greets her. "How are you feeling today?"

"Better. Thank you." Ziva smiles at Sariah. "I'll be back." She gets up and goes to the bath house. She returns looking fresh and clean. "What can I help with today?"

Sariah examines her. She frowns. "You, my girl, are still recuperating. You must take it easy." She wipes her hands on a rag. "If you would like a change of scenery, you're welcome to join everyone outside for the morning meal. I know many would like to see you again, and others—my family members—would like to meet you."

"I would like that." Ziva's countenance brightens.

"Good. The air is cold. Gather up the blanket and wrap it around yourself."

Ziva follows her instructions and meets Sariah by the front door.

The courtyard contains several buildings nearby and a great yard surrounded by a tall vertical fence of posts. A tent is in the process of being erected on the far side of the courtyard. An open fire pit resides in the middle of the courtyard with several logs nearby to sit upon. Many people are gathered there, doing different things. Varying-sized children run about, darting in and out, playing a game of some sort. When everyone sees Ziva standing next to Sariah, wrapped in a blanket, the scene freezes.

"Everyone, this is Ziva. Lib's wife." She ushers Ziva to sit on a log by the fire.

A bowl of mush is placed in Ziva's hands. The men she camped with smile at her. Others, whom she hasn't met, look her way with curious eyes. Self-conscious, Ziva returns the stares with a tremulous smile.

"Ziva, eat your food while the meal is hot. You can talk with everyone later." Sariah pats her shoulder.

Ziva concentrates on the contents in the bowl in front of her.

Sariah walks away.

When Ziva finishes her food, a woman stands before her. Ziva looks up. The woman is some years older than her, with black hair and hazel eyes, similar to Sariah's.

"I'm Inna, Sariah's daughter. May blessings come to your Joining. Would you like some more?"

Ziva feels heat rise to her face. "Thank you, Inna. The food is filling. I don't need anymore." Ziva hands the bowl her way.

Inna takes the empty bowl.

Ziva watches as she walks away.

Someone clears their throat next to her.

Ziva turns her head.

The students Ziva camped with stand there grinning.

"Hello," she cheerfully chimes, recognizing them.

"How are you feeling, Ziva?" Melek asks.

"Much better. Thank you." She grins.

Melek mirrors her expression.

"We've missed your smiling face." Jashon bumps her on the shoulder in a teasing gesture.

She chuckles. "I've missed seeing you too."

"You still look tired." Zeram frowns.

Her eyes widen a bit. *He's probably right*. Ziva grins. "But I feel a lot better."

Concern fills Panchi's face. "Can I get you a drink?"

Ziva smiles at the man and nods. "A cup of water would be wonderful."

"We were all worried about you." Melek sits next to her. "Especially Lib."

Overhearing Melek's words, Nephi reiterates, "Especially Lib." Nephi grins at Ziva. "I'm happy to see you outdoors again."

"I'm happy to be outdoors again." Ziva beams at Nephi. She searches the area but can't find what she's looking for. Her brows furrow and a frown invade her face. "Where are Lib and Tokal?"

Paanchi offers Ziva a filled cup of water.

Ziva takes it. "Thank you, Paanchi."

Nephi scratches his chin. "Lib is chopping some wood for the fire. Tokal is playing with one of the older children."

Ziva now understands the sounds that come from the other side of the house.

Noticing Ziva's concern, Nephi examines the area for the little boy. "Perhaps he's inside Inna's home. I'll find him."

As the men wander off, Melek lingers. "Um, I'm glad you're feeling better. Lib's been hard to be around. He's been very short with everyone, especially yesterday afternoon. Now that you're better, I hope his mood improves."

Ziva inwardly cringes, knowing she's the one who hurt him. She needs to make it better but isn't sure how to proceed. She swallows and smiles at Melek. "I'm sure it will."

A squeal, from a child, floats through the air.

Ziva turns her head toward it. She reaches for her son.

Nephi dumps Tokal into Ziva's lap.

Ziva hugs her little boy.

Tokal plants a wet kiss on her face. He squirms out of her arms to crawl around.

Ziva struggles to keep Tokal with her. She notices the warm clothes on him. Warmth fills her breast as she silently thanks Lib for caring for him. She realizes she can't wait any longer to talk with Lib about yesterday. She needs to smooth things over.

Tokal fusses.

She stands.

A firm hand stops her.

Ziva looks over her shoulder. Lib is behind her.

Tokal squirms and fusses.

Lib stops in front of Ziva. "Let me have him."

Ziva passes Tokal to Lib.

Lib passes Tokal to Inna. She takes him to go play with the other children. Lib scrutinizes her. "Ready to go inside?"

Ziva opens her mouth to refuse. She closes it, realizing she's tired from this morning's activities. She nods instead.

Lib helps her stand.

They stroll to Nephi's and Sariah's home, away from the others.

Inside the house, discomfort permeates the room as they try to figure out how to proceed.

"I need to apologize," Ziva blurts out as she gazes at the ground. "I didn't mean to upset you." She glances his way. "We know very little about each other, and presently . . . we're Joined because of my mistake. I don't want to ruin your life or make things difficult for you." Gaining confidence she meets his gaze. "You've been so good to me . . . to us. I am . . ." Her eyes falter. "I'm giving you a way out."

A pregnant pause becomes pronounced.

Ziva can't stand it any longer. She looks at Lib.

With a soft caress, Lib cups Ziva's face.

Her eyes link with his. A storm brews within his brown eyes. She gulps, not meaning to hurt him more.

"I recall, before we were Joined, that we agreed to raise Tokal together."

Ziva recalls her words.

"Do you remember?"

She tries to nod, but with his hands cupping her face, she can't. Unable to look away from his tumultuous gaze, she breathes out. "Yes."

"Did you agree to this?" There's a hard undercurrent in his soft baritone.

Ziva's eyes are fastened to his. She can't pull away. "Yes."

Warmth transmitted from his eyes invades her core and emanates outward. He strokes her face and whispers, "I intend to keep our agreement. Do you?"

"I want you to be happy." She takes a shuttering breath. "If I'm the problem, let me go."

His thumb caresses her cheek. "You are the problem."

She feels as though he slapped her. She pulls away.

Lib holds her there with his hands still cupping her face. "Letting you go won't solve it."

Frowning, Ziva shakes her head, and her eyes escape his.

His hands hold her face still.

"I . . . I . . . I don't understand."

"Understand this, Ziva. I want your happiness."

Her eyes go to his, seeing a mighty storm within.

"Letting you disappear from our lives will only destroy all of us. When you're sick, I worry about you. When you're unhappy, I want to fix it so you're happy again. Being Joined will not be easy for us, but by working together through the challenges that come, whether it be the journey back to Uthal or my parents, or anything else —the only way we'll find happiness is together . . . as a family. I want you as my wife. Nobody else. I want you, Ziva."

# TRANSITION

THE STONY EXTERIOR OF ZIVA'S heart cracks open. He wants and accepts her for who she is.

Before she can think any further, Lib tips her head. He kisses her, showing how much she matters to him.

With a will of their own, Ziva's arms reach around his neck.

Lib's hands slide from her face to her back, pulling her closer.

The kiss deepens, blocking out everything as Ziva's heart sings. All of a sudden, she stiffens as clarity hits her like a lightning bolt.

Lib lets her pull away with a question in his eyes.

Shocked and amazed at the same time, with the realization that comes to her, she stares at him. "I have feelings for you." She pushes him back, shaking her head. "Oh no. Oh no." The words fall from her lips as she moves distances herself from him.

"You make no sense, Ziva. Why is it bad to have feelings for me?"

Ziva trembles. Tears trickle down.

"What is it, Ziva?"

"I don't want to lose you. I don't want you to die." She wails. A snort erupts from her as she takes a breath.

Lib has no idea what just occurred. He walks toward her.

She retreats.

"How does having feelings for me cause my death?"

My . . . my parents," she sobs. "I loved them. Everyone I've ever loved is dead. They're all dead."

Grasping Ziva's arm, he tows her to him, wrapping his arms around her while she cries.

Exhausted, Ziva quiets. She leans on Lib.

Lib pulls her into his arms and sits. Taking a corner of the blanket, he wipes her eyes while he holds her.

"Do you love Tokal?"

"You know I do."

"Is he dead?"

"No."

"Are you worried about him dying?"

"Yes."

"Are you worried about him this instant?"

"No."

"Why do you think that is?"

Ziva is quiet for a moment as she thinks. "Because he has good people around him."

"Good people make a difference. That's true. You have faith in these people that they'll treat Tokal well."

She cocks her head to one side, considering his words. "Yes. Meeting up with all of you made a difference in our survival."

"We have challenges in front of us. In order to survive, *we* must work together. Have faith in each other. How am I different from that?" Lib strokes Ziva's back.

Ziva leaning against Lib's chest hears the steady cadence within him. It lulls her. She can't think.

Lib waiting patiently for a response, realizes her breathing has become rhythmic. He looks down at her on his chest.

Ziva fell asleep.

As skillfully as he can, he lies down with her in his arms. His mind begins to wander, thinking about how to help her past her demons. How will he deal with his parents when they return to Uthal. He puts an arm over his eyes.

Someone opens the door.

Lib removes the arm that covers his face.

Sariah stands in the doorway.

Lib puts a finger to his lips.

She nods, exiting from the house.

SOMETIME LATER, ZIVA STIRS. SHE'S still gathered in Lib's arms. She feels safe here and wants to remain in his cocoon. Unfortunately, nature calls. "I'll be back," she informs him as she scoots away.

Lib's perplexed, but lets her go. He sits up and rubs the sleep from his eyes.

Ziva opens the door and moves to his side. "I'm sorry to have woken you." She avoids looking at him embarrassed for several different reasons. She sits at his side.

He takes her hand and holds it.

"I didn't mean to . . . to fall asleep on you or . . . to run off." Warmth creeps up her neck as she tries to explain. "Nature called."

Lib kisses her hand. "I would rather walk with you even if it means waiting."

Ziva gives a slight smile, glancing at him under her lashes. "You asked if you were different than Tokal. You are different than Tokal." She takes a breath. "If I lost either of you, it would be very difficult to continue. I suppose what you're trying to say is that because I trust those here, I'm able to let go of my fear, which allows me to let Tokal out of my sight."

"Yes." He grins at her. "When you focus on what is and not what if, you can move forward and count your blessings. You and Tokal are blessings in my life. I will stand by you both, and together, we'll make a happy home." He takes a breath, kissing her hand again. "I need to apologize to you." He gazes at her. "I'm sorry I walked out with Tokal and didn't return and talk with you sooner." He shakes his head. "I don't know what my parents are going to say or how they will react. While chopping logs, it came to me to focus on what I can do and not the things I can't. When Nephi came and let me know you were asking about me, I decided that we needed to talk. That is something we can always do. This winter, we can work to know one another better. By working together, we can create that happy home."

Her eyes meet his. "I'm scared."

He sighs. "So am I, but . . . I'm willing to walk with you, one day at a time. I believe that if we do it together, we will succeed."

Ziva's eyes falter as ponders his words. *Focus on what is and not what if. Focus on what I can do. Walk together, one day at a time.* She looks at him. "I will walk with you."

He smiles and cocks an eyebrow. "Just confirming, are you willing to do this with me?"

She smiles back. "Yes."

Without breaking eye contact with her, Lib kisses her palm.

Warmth heats Ziva's core.

"You make me a very happy man." His face morphs into a grin. "Shall we see what our son is up to?"

They gaze at each other and laugh. They get to their feet.

Lib wraps the blanket around Ziva's shoulders before heading outdoors in search of Tokal.

The large tent is erected. Ziva wonders about it.

Lib walks Ziva to the log next to the fire. "Stay here and I'll find our son."

Ziva watches the children, who are delighted to be running in and out of the tent while the men and Kelev watch.

Lib returns with a young woman and Tokal. He places their son in Ziva's arms.

"He's had a nap and has been changed. This is Tanna, Inna's oldest daughter, who is helping care for Tokal while you recover." His eyes get serious. "Don't let him wear you out." He kisses her on the forehead. "I'm going to help the men."

"Thank you for caring for Tokal. I know he's very active and can be a handful." Ziva lowers herself from the log to the ground and leans back against it. She has a full view of the tent that the men are working on.

Tokal squirms to be free. She lets him go in front of her.

Tanna sits down next to Ziva and shrugs. She drops a few toys in front of Tokal. "He's no worse than my younger siblings or my cousins."

In the distance, men talk together while children continue to scamper. "Is that them, playing in the tent?"

"Those that can walk," Tanna informs Ziva. "My other cousin is inside with the babes. We help our mothers so the work can get done."

"You're a good daughter to help your mother and aunt. You will be experienced when you become a mother. It will make things a lot easier for you." Ziva takes a breath, recalling her own experience. "I'm not as fortunate, being an only child. I didn't know what to do."

Tanna's eyes widen. "How can that be? You must have been asked to help with other children."

Ziva chuckles while Tokal plays with the toys in front of him. "I never asked to help with other children, nor was I asked. When Tokal came into my life, we both had to learn." She ruffles the little boy's hair.

Tokal looks up at who touched him. He smiles at his mother. His attention returns to his toys.

The men finish talking.

The children are sent away from the teepee.

Some of the men work inside the tent while others bring heavy furs or rocks to be placed inside.

"What are they doing?"

"They are setting up the tent for the winter," Tanna says matter-of-factly.

"Why?"

Tanna confused, examines Ziva, wondering why she doesn't know. "When we run out of room for guests, the tent is placed."

"Are more guests coming?"

Tanna scratches her head. "The tent is for you and your family."

Ziva's eyes widen as her head swivels to Tanna. "For us?"

"Yes. My grandfather would like to be with my grandmother." After a moment's silence, Tanna asks, "How is it that you have a baby before a Joining?"

Ziva glances at the girl.

Tanna won't meet her eyes.

"Tokal's parents were killed. He came to be left in my care."

Tanna gazes at Ziva, "Why not left to a family member?"

"That is a very good question for a smart girl," Ziva smiles at her. "We were in the forest. The few people that were with me placed Tokal under my care."

"How sad for his family." Tanna thinks about it. "I'm happy he currently has a family."

Tokal, tired of his toys, spots Kelev. He crawls toward the dog.

Kelev, seeing Tokal, trots over and sniffs the child.

Tokal giggles.

Kelev licks the little head. She cantors away. She turns, facing Tokal. After lying down, she waits for Tokal to follow her.

Tokal charges forward, crawling as fast as he can.

When Tokal almost reaches her side, Kelev moves.

Tokal squeals his delight as he continues the game.

"I'd never seen a dog before Lib arrived." Tanna grins at the urchin crawling on the ground. "I like her."

"She's a very good dog." Ziva smiles. "I like her too. She saved our lives."

"She saved your lives? What happened?"

Men leave the tent. Women carry things inside.

Lib picks Tokal up. He tosses the toddler in the air, catching him.

Tokal cackles.

Lib catches the child again. He hugs Tokal.

Ziva smiles at her family. "Kelev stopped a bad man from hurting us before your grandfather showed up."

AT DUSK THE CHILDREN ARE moved inside with some of the women.

Lifting two wineskins above his head Paanchi shows up. "Cups all around. Now that Ziva is better, we can celebrate Lib's and Ziva's Joining."

Vessels are passed.

Paanchi and Jashon fill them.

When everyone has some wine, Paanchi raises his. "We've gained a sister, whereas she's gained five brothers. I don't know how she puts up with us. To Ziva and Lib."

"To Ziva and Lib," the group around the fire cheers.

Ziva takes a sip of the wine. This is her first time. It tastes fruity and warms her insides. She notices the undercurrent around the fire but doesn't say anything.

"I don't know how my wife puts up with you rambunctious brats," Nephi teases.

"To Sariah," Paanchi salutes.

"To good cooking," Jashon throws in.

"To good women," Nephi asserts.

"Here, here," is heard around the campfire.

"Paanchi, this is good wine. Where did you get it?" Nephi asks.

"I ran into my father today, who provided me with some skins." Paanchi takes another drink. "He wanted me to thank you for taking me as a student."

"Your father's gift is so Nephi will keep you," Zeram interjects.

Laughter is heard around the fire.

Zeram takes another drink from his cup. "This is good wine. Thanks for sharing, Paanchi." He raises his cup to Paanchi. "My cup needs refilled."

Jashon lights up his carved tobacco pipe. It's passed around the group. Those that want a puff, smoke it. Those that don't pass it on.

When it comes to Ziva, she marvels at the intricate carved bone that looks like a beaver. She doesn't like the smell and passes to Lib.

Lib gives the pipe to the person on his left.

Amnor examines the sky, studying the stars. "It looks like this will be a cold winter."

Everyone joins him.

Nephi looks back at those around the fire. "It does look that way." He scratches his chin.

"Do we have enough wood gathered for the winter?" Inna asks.

Nephi wipes a hand over his face. "I will take the men with me tomorrow. We will get the last of the supplies."

Inna gazes at her father. "If you're going to the market, I think some of us would like to go with you before snow sets in,"

Nephi scratches his chin. "I think we can manage that."

"Ziva needs a coat and a change of clothes," Sariah sits next to Nephi. "I don't think she's strong enough for the market. Inna, would you help Lib in making sure his family has what it needs for the winter?"

"Yes, mother."

"Thank you, daughter."

Laughter is heard around the fire.

Lib stands. "The air is getting colder out here. Even with a blanket. I'm taking Ziva inside."

Nephi scans the sky. "A storm is coming our way. I think it's a good idea for everyone to prepare for the night."

Paanchi tosses a skin to Lib. "Enjoy."

Lib catches it. "Thanks."

Ziva strides to the bath house to prepare for the night. When she exits, Lib waiting for her. She walks toward Nephi's home.

Lib takes her elbow and guides her toward the tent. "You're well enough that you've been moved to the tent."

"Why didn't anyone tell me?"

"Didn't Tanna tell you while you were watching it being set up?"

"Yes. But it would have been nice to hear it from Sariah, Nephi, or you, rather than from a child."

Lib takes a breath. "An oversight on my part. There has been a lot going on today. Everyone has been busy."

An uncomfortable feeling follows Ziva as they stroll. She feels that all eyes are on them. She doesn't hear anyone talking around the fire. "Why is everyone watching us so closely?"

They arrive at the tent door. Lib pulls back the flap so she can enter. "Because tonight will be the first night we will sleep under the same roof together. Tomorrow, Tokal will be returned to us."

Ziva stops. Her head swivels up. Their eyes meet in the dark. Embarrassed, she looks back to the people around the fire. It increases her discomfort. She peers at the entryway not willing to take another step.

"We are Joined, Ziva."

Ziva stands where she is.

"Please."

*He won't force me.* Would he? With everything she knows about Lib, she doesn't think so. Nephi can return to his wife She takes a breath and with brisk steps disappears into the tent. Her anxiety builds over what will occur during the night.

The warm glow of the embers surrounded by rocks greet her. They provide enough light in the darkness for her to find her way deeper into the room toward the fire pit. It radiates heat. The floor is covered with fur. She settles in front of the fire, raising her hands toward the heat. She moves her stiff fingers, hoping to warm them up.

Lib follows. He closes the tent door, moving to a dark area of the room. He retrieves some logs and places them in the fire pit. He sits down next to her, bringing his hands closer to the fire to warm them.

Outside, a lively tune from those around the fire makes its way into the tent.

Two are now joined,

Making life together, Joined as one.

Man serving woman,

Woman serving man,

Making life together, Joined as one.

Ziva's eyes open wide, hiking into her hairline. Her eyes dart to Lib's face. Her mouth drops to an open frown.

Lib stares back at her. His mouth thins.

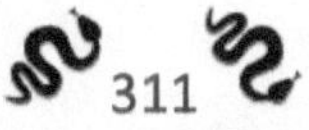

Embarrassed heat covers her. She wants to run from the tent. Where would she go? What about Tokal? It doesn't matter; she must escape. She stumbles to her feet.

The wood in the fire pit catches fire. The electricity in the room increases.

"I won't touch you, Ziva." Lib sighs. "Not until you ask me to."

Ziva stops her retreat. She doesn't turn back to him.

"I didn't touch you yesterday or before that. I won't touch you at present. When you're ready, you will tell me. Agreed?"

Slowly, Ziva turns and looks at him. "I don't know if I'll ever agree."

He takes a breath and blows it out. "Sit down, Ziva, and warm yourself. We're both tired."

With cautious steps she sits on the other side of the fire, separating them.

He takes the wine and pours a cupful, swallowing the contents. He pours another cup. "I'm going to bring this cup to you. The wine will help warm you. Once I give this to you, I'm going to find the other blankets so we may rest." Lib delivers the beverage. Lib feels Ziva's on him as he searches the shadows.

Ziva takes a drink. The liquid seems to seep from her core outward. She takes another drink and sighs.

Lib returns with several blankets and skins. He places one around the one that she already holds.

Ziva's cup is empty. She sets it down. A burp escapes her mouth. She peers at Lib with a frown on her face. What will he do?

Lib chuckles. "Wine will do that." He stops in front of the closed door with the remaining skin and blanket. The woodpile is nearby. "Do you have everything you need?"

She looks around the room before nodding.

"Let's take it one day at a time. Like we agreed." Lib settles for the night between the door and the fire. He covers himself. "See you in the morning." He closes his eyes.

The new logs in the fire brighten the room, sending shadows dancing on the wall. Some bags are near the wall as well as what looks to be a pot. Her eyes droop. She yawns. Pulling the covers around her, she lies down.

SHE WAKES UP SHIVERING. FIRE embers barely glow. A storm howls outside. She trembles again. With the blankets fastened around her, she navigates the dark in an effort to feed the fire. She stubs her toe. Bending to rub it, she falls down.

"What are you doing?" a groggy voice sounds in the dark.

Her teeth chatter as she breathes out, "The tent is cold." She shivers again.

"It is." Several logs are placed on the embers.

Ziva watches with bated breath until it glows to life.

"Come here." Lib holds out a hand to her.

Shivering, Ziva moves to the fire and sits.

He scoots so he's behind her. "We need to warm you up. The last thing we need is for you to get sick again."

"I don't know why I'm so cold." Her teeth chatter.

"Your recent illness may be causing this." He scans the room for the wineskin. He can't find it.

"Do you trust me?"

"Your words have always proved honest."

He realizes her trust is a fragile thing and hopes he can keep it. "I'm going to pull you close against me, and we are going to layer the blankets from two for each of us to four."

"If you think it will help."

"I do." Lib pulls her close to his body, laying her down next to him. He arranges the four blankets to cover their bodies. He feels her tremble next to him.

Lib isn't prepared when her ice-cold limbs touch him. His body recoils. "You are cold! Let me have your hands." He puts his arms around her and pulls her even closer. One big hand covers both of hers. "Put your feet between my legs. My body heat will warm you." He braces himself as her cold, stocking-covered feet are moved between his thighs. He hugs them.

She snuggles into him.

"Tomorrow, I think we'll need to get more than coats for this winter."

"Hats and mittens." Ziva's shivering subsides as Lib's heat radiates to her. She closes her eyes and relaxes into a blissful slumber.

Lib lies there in the darkness, listening to her even breathing. He experiences a sweet torture. Now that she's well, the soft body tucked next to him is all he can think about. He wants to share his affection for her. If he does move, he will scare her way. The effect her body has on him makes it difficult to keep still. He doesn't rest for a long time.

# WINTER

The noise of morning activity awakens them.

Lib reaches over, grabs another piece of wood, and tosses it into the fire.

Ziva moves away.

After putting on his shoes, Lib grabs the pot, and yawns. Over his shoulder he says, "I'll be back with some water." He disappears from the tent.

Ziva folds the blankets and furs they used during the night. She inspects the different supplies left for them within the tent. Hearing the door flap, Ziva turns.

Lib steps in with a pot of water.

Ziva offers a tentative smile in greeting.

Lib places the pot within the embers to boil the water. Catching her with an open sack, he explains, "The supplies are in case we get snowed in. Even though the air is cold, we'll eat with the family around the main fire pit as long as we aren't snowed in. It shouldn't be too long before the water is heated. You can use it to ready yourself before going out to see everyone. In one of the bags over there"—he indicates by moving his head—"are some rags. I'm going to fetch Tokal so that you can bathe him while I get the rest of his things. Your cloth to wrap him to you is on the hook." He steps outside not giving her a chance to reply.

Ziva ties the bag of grain and places it back with the other food stuff. Ziva frowns, seeing that there isn't a jar in which she can store food. Jars are a necessary protection against insects and the elements. She moves to the area of the tent that Lib had indicated. She finds a pack containing everything she owns. She searches for what she needs.

After washing, she feels rejuvenated. She braids her hair, expecting Lib to return soon.

A male voice says, "May I enter?"

Recognizes Lib, Ziva feels awkward, but is grateful that Lib gave her some privacy says, "Yes, I'm done."

Lib enters holding a wide-awake boy.

Tokal searches the tent. When his eyes home in on Ziva, he squeals in delight.

Ziva and Lib smile.

Lib drops Tokal into Ziva's arms.

Ziva presses Tokal to her breast in a warm hug.

"Food will soon be ready. Would you like me to wait?"

"Yes. It shouldn't take too long," Ziva returns, peeling Tokal out of the warm clothes while he tries to escape and explore.

Lib holds him down.

Ziva cleans every nook and cranny.

Tokal hollers at the injustice. Once cleaned, Tokal is redressed in some warm clothes.

Lib holds the child.

Ziva covers Tokal with a blanket. "I need some time. I'll come get him when I'm done."

Lib nods, taking Tokal outside to the main fire.

Ziva finishes her preparations. She wraps a blanket around her shoulders and joins the group.

AFTER THE MEAL, THE MEN and a few women prepare to leave. Tokal is attached to Ziva's front, watching everything. Sariah converses with Ziva.

Lib joins them, asking, "Is there anything you would like me to get?"

"Yes. Tokal needs more warm clothing. He's growing so fast. We also need a clay pot to protect the food."

"I have a clay pot you can use. No need to purchase one," Sariah interjects. "I guess it got missed in yesterday's activities."

"Thank you, Sariah," Ziva smiles, grateful for the woman.

Lib takes Ziva's hand and puts something in it.

Ziva recognizes the feel of cloth holding a sphere pressed between their hands. It's her father's pearl wrapped in fabric. Her eyes meet his, understanding passes between them.

Lib nods, touching Tokal's head before turning away. He leaves with the group headed to the market.

Turning to Sariah, Ziva tucks the pearl into her pocket. "I've been meaning to ask more about your name. You mentioned you were named after a woman named Sariah. Who was she?"

"A family left Jerusalem around 575 years ago, a few years before Babylonians attacked the people in Jerusalem. The mother's name was Sariah. They traveled to this new land. We're their descendants."

Ziva scratches her head. "I've never heard of that. How do you know that really happened?"

"They kept records on plates, and we can read them."

Ziva recalls the scrolls that the students looked at over and over again. They kept them in a tube of sorts that had a strap. It could be carried. She's curious to know more. "I would like to learn how to read."

"Lib can teach you while you're here." Standing up, Sariah stretches and sighs. "I need to get to work."

"What can I do to help?"

"Follow me." Sariah takes her to the other women. She assigns tasks that deal with cleaning, storing, weaving, sewing, feeding, gathering, cooking, and caring for children. Time passes as they work to accomplish everything. In the late afternoon, the men return with the other women, loaded with their purchases.

Ziva's blanket is taken from her shoulders and replaced with a warm fur coat with a hat and mittens stored in the pockets. She saw other things delivered to their tent. Lib will show her later. The family eats before the children are released to play. Like every previous night, Jashon's beaver pipe is lit and passed around. Paanchi drinks some wine from the wineskin.

Tokal fusses, showing he's tired from the day's activities.

Ziva ties him to her chest.

Lib and Ziva sit together around the fire enjoying the conversations.

"The market was busy today," Nephi says.

"The weather grows cold," Jashon explains.

"People are trying to get the last supplies they need before snow gathers on the ground," Inna clarifies for Ziva.

"I have a few more wineskins from my father." Paanchi holds up some wineskins.

"Don't you think you drink a little too much wine?" Amnor shakes his head.

"I don't think so. I only have it at night after day's work is done," Paanchi justifies, a little offended.

Amnor clears his throat and speaks. "We stopped to hear some Lamanites telling news. They stated they were from the land of Nephi. They told of two missionaries who traveled there. They were cast into prison. One missionary was actually named Nephi, which I find amusing, and I can't remember the other name."

"Lehi." Melek offers, already knowing the story. "They arrived at the city and were thrown into prison. After many days, they were going to kill them."

"When the people went in to kill them, the missionaries were encircled by fire, but weren't burned." Amnor lays a hand on Melek's shoulder, suggesting to Melek to be quiet and let him tell the story.

Melek glances at Amnor.

Amnor shakes his head. "These men, Nephi and Lehi, when they spoke, the ground shook. The Lamanites said that Nephi and Lehi taught everyone in the prison about the Great Spirit, and the prisoners were converted."

Not hearing the story before now, Lib asks, "What happened to this Nephi and Lehi?"

"Whatever did happen in the city of Nephi, my father doesn't know, but he told the same story when he traveled there and found the people within the city . . . different," Melek interjects. "In the story my father told, after everyone in the prison converted, they released Nephi and Lehi. They were revered as prophets of the Great Spirit. After setting up a church in the city and teaching many others, they left the Nephi to continue their preaching. My father said those that lived there were a happier and kinder people. That their perspective on life changed. I think because the transformation in the people occurred in such a short time span, making it unusual, he brought it back home and shared it with us. He wondered at how a whole city could be so . . . changed."

Amnor glares at Melek.

"What did these Lamanites want?" Sariah asks, spellbound.

Melek stays quiet.

Amnor turns to the group. "That is the interesting part. They said they traveled to Zarahemla by order of the Great Spirit to testify of what had occurred and to share the same message that Nephi and Lehi delivered to them, which is that the people need to change."

Melek grins at Amnor, "They did say that if the people in Zarahemla didn't change from setting their heart upon their riches to helping the poor and needy, telling the truth, being honest in their dealings, and being kinder to others, bad things were going to happen in the city."

Nephi scratches his chin. "What kind of things?"

Amnor speaks before Melek can answer. "They didn't know. Because they wouldn't say, the people in the market got angry and drove them out."

"Sounds like a bunch of manure to me," Zeram says. "Only people trying to cause mischief in Zarahemla."

"That's what the people said too," Amnor returns.

"How can being kinder to others be a bad thing?" Sariah asks.

Lib tucks the blanket more securely around Tokal, who fell asleep. "Or helping others."

"Or being truthful and honest," Melek interjects.

"I like my family's riches. They allow me to have the finer things in life." Zeram dismisses. "I'm not giving that up."

"Can you live the other things?" Nephi's son-in-law prods.

"Being truthful, honest, and kind?" Zeram questions.

The man nods back.

"I believe that I have learned this from Nephi and Sariah while here under their roof."

"That's a start." The man grins at Zeram.

Nephi stands and stretches.

The conversation stops.

"That's a very interesting experience, Amnor and Melek. The story is definitely something to think about." Nephi reaches for his wife's hand. "Come, Sariah. Time to go inside."

Sariah gets up, grasping the offered palm as they stroll toward their home, leaving the rest around the fire.

Ziva yawns. She heads for the water room, followed by several other women. When she's done, she heads toward the tent. By the time she reaches the door, Lib is at her side.

Lib pulls back the door.

Kelev lays nearby.

Smiling, Ziva says, "You don't have to go to bed on my account. You can stay with your friends."

"I know." Lib shrugs, and one side of his mouth curves up, "I want to show you what I bought."

Ziva enters the tent and grabs a log for the fire.

Lib steps in behind her and grabs two more.

Before long, the tent is warm and bright. Ziva takes off her new coat, hat, and gloves. She hangs them on a hook.

Lib does the same.

Ziva settles the sleeping child on the furs before sitting down.

Lib presents her with a stack of goods. He sits down next to her, grinning. He watches her.

Ziva investigates each item. Two new warm outfits for Tokal and her are contained in the stack. A small coat with two different colored hats and a pair of mittens for Tokal accompanies the new clothes. A larger hat in bright, vibrant colors is the last item she pulls out to study. She places the hat on her head. "How does it look?"

Lib adjusts how the hat is placed on her head. "It looks beautiful on you."

Ziva captures his gaze. "These are beautiful, Lib." She smiles at him. "Thank you for taking care of us."

The pair sit in comfortable silence, eyes locked on each other.

The light in Lib's eye's changes to affection.

Ziva's gaze breaks from Lib's. She coughs and starts folding the clothes in her lap. "I'm worried about Tokal waking up and finding the fire.

Lib goes to the fire feeling dejected. He pokes at it with a stick. "I am too." He hoped for something more from Ziva. He admonishes himself. He tosses the stick in the flames, returning to her side.

Ziva moves the clothing stack to her pack.

Lib takes her new jacket, placing it between Tokal and the wall to the tent.

"There. That should help keep him warm." Lib glances at Ziva. "Perhaps if you lie down nearest the fire, I think he will climb over rather than go around."

"I think you're right." Ziva settles herself.

Lib covers her and Tokal with two blankets. He lies near the door, away from them.

Ziva watches him. "Why do you sleep near the door?"

He glances at her while he breathes. "If anyone tries to come in that is not wanted, I will be able to better protect you both."

Realizing the logic in his decision, Ziva smiles at him. She doesn't understand why it's needed here with Nephi and his family. "You're a good man, Lib."


ZIVA WORKS WITH THE WOMEN while Lib and the others around the main fire play with Tokal. With the proper clothes, Ziva feels warm.

Once Tokal is napping under Tanna's care, Lib brings out a bow and arrows. "Ziva, show me what you know." He passes the weapon to her.

Other men gather.

Ziva shoots, hitting the target.

"Let me try," from the men morphs into a silent competition between the students and Ziva.

"Hitting a moving target is different." Melek takes the bow.

"I suspect. I haven't had much opportunity to learn that," Ziva moves out of the way.

"Where did you learn to shoot?" Zeram asks.

"When I traveled to Arnac for the Journey, a friend started teaching me. While at Arnac, I practiced. It became my favorite thing to do while I lived there."

"The Journey?" Paanchi asks.

"In Uthal, when a girl is in her sixteenth year, she takes a trip with her mother and the others her age to Arnac. The city of women provides a final time for a daughter and her mother before the daughter takes the Challenge or chooses the Joining."

"What's the Challenge?" Zeram pulls out an arrow.

"If a woman returns from the Journey and doesn't want to be Joined to a man within a year, she takes the Challenge instead. It takes her outside of the city. She isn't able to enter Uthal until the new women return from their Journey the following year."

Zeram shoots. He turns to Ziva, passing the bow to someone else. "She lives by herself?"

"Not by herself." Ziva licks her lips. "She has a guardian who accompanies her."

"The guardian is a man who spends his year protecting her and is usually a family member," Lib takes his turn, then hands Ziva the bow.

"What did you choose?" Melek asks.

"I took the Challenge." Ziva shoots hitting the bulls-eye.

Jashon scratches his head. "Why would you do that?"

"I didn't want to be Joined. Besides, my mother's illness kept us at Arnac, which forced me to take the Challenge."

Paanchi frowns at Ziva. "All that time you survived on your own?"

Lib throws bow and quiver on a shoulder. He grabs Ziva's hand. "Yes, she did."

Ziva is pulled away. She notices his glare and doesn't say anything.

"We'll see you later."

Perplexed by his actions, Ziva follows, pulling her to the tent.

"Why are we going to the tent?" Her feet falter, knowing it's something she said, but doesn't know what or why.

"Because after that bit of exercise, you look tired. I think it would be good to rest for a little while before continuing your day."

"I am tired, but that's no reason for cutting me off from correcting you by stating that I'm still on the Challenge."

Pulling her into the tent, Lib turns and catches her. "When you joined me, your Challenge ended." He kisses her nose. "Take a nap so you feel better."

"It hasn't been a year, and I haven't returned to Uthal."

He takes a breath. "Did your Challenge start at Uthal?" he volleys back.

"Well . . ." she exhales, realizing where he is going. "No."

He steps closer. He brushes away an escaped tendril from her face, placing it behind her ear. Looking into her eyes that seem to hold his own, he whispers, "So, your Challenge can end without returning to Uthal."

"It still feels like a challenge to me." She breathes, feeling short of breath. Butterflies seem to dance inside her.

"Why?" he murmurs, caressing her chin.

"Because . . . this is only a stopping place." she whispers, "Not our home."

His shoulders deflate. He takes a breath, exhaling slowly.

He steps back. "Sleep, Ziva, so you can remain well." He leaves the tent without another word.

Standing there alone, she feels frustrated. By what? She doesn't know. She huffs. She shakes her head, trying to clear her mind and the feelings that accompany it. She lies down on the fur rug, pulling the blankets over her.

THE WEATHER OUTSIDE DOESN'T PERMIT being around the fire in the courtyard. Chores are done in the morning, and everyone returns to their dwelling place to ride out the weather.

On days like this, Kelev joins them in the tent. While Lib studies his books, Ziva occupies Tokal. One day while Lib is studying, Ziva asks, "Will you teach me to read?"

Lib waits until Ziva looks at him. He smiles. "I would like nothing better." From that day on, any time they are confined to their tent and Tokal is taking his nap, Ziva learns a whole new world of letters and words.

When the days are good to be outside, everyone takes advantage of it. The students' fascination that started with Ziva's ability with the bow, leads to them including her as they practice their fighting skills. During these days, while Tokal naps under someone's care, the men teach her ways to defend herself from an attack.

At first the other women watch, surprised that Ziva is participating in such an activity with men who are not her husband. The women change tactics by not being in the same area where the practice takes place.

Despite Sariah's persistence that "fighting skills aren't appropriate for a woman to learn" Nephi watches and coaches Ziva on what to do

Sariah, combatting her husband's deaf ears, assigns more chores for the girl to complete, causing Lib's distress. One night, Lib brings it up to Nephi as they talk about it in hushed tones near the fire. "Nephi, Sariah has again added additional chores for Ziva to do."

"Ziva has complained to you?"

"She hasn't complained." Lib sighs. "But she's so busy that she can't get everything done if she joins us with our exercise."

Nephi scratches his cheek. "My wife worries that she may be with child and the exercise will injure the babe."

"She's not with child." Lib frowns.

"How can you be so sure?"

Lib is silent as he debates within himself. He sighs. "I haven't shared my seed with her."

Nephi's eyes widen, and inspects Lib's face to make sure he's serious.

Lib stares at the dirt. "Why not?"

Lib rubs the back of his neck at this awkward conversation. Is he telling too much? "She's not ready."

Lib scratches his chin. "So, she doesn't trust you yet?"

"Not yet." Lib sighs. "We talk about things and work well together, but she won't let me get close to her. She uses Tokal as a shield.

Nephi takes this added information, figuring out how to proceed. He breathes before speaking. "I cannot take away the added chores that my wife assigned, because it helps another who is having difficulty carrying a babe. I can speak to my wife about not assigning more chores to Ziva."

"Thank you."

"Lib." Nephi waits until Lib meets his gaze. "You're a good man. She'll come to trust you. Be patient."

Lib nods in the light of the fire.

Nephi returns to his wife's side.

Lib watches the group around the fire.

Ziva joins him with Tokal tied to her chest. "What is troubling you Lib?" she asks so no one else can hear.

He smiles at her and squeezes her hand. "How to lighten your load."

"What do you mean?"

"The added chores you've been assigned have bothered me, but I now know why."

"Why?"

"One of the women is with child and is having problems."

Ziva doesn't say anything.

Lib searches her face. "Does that bother you?"

"No." Ziva chuckles. "I'm trying to figure out whom."

He chuckles at her awkward delivery. "That is a good question. I'm sure we'll know eventually."

They sit, listening to all the conversation around them.

Lib holds her hand.

When Lib caresses her palm, her breath catches.

"Would you mind if I help you with the chores? With two of us, it will go much faster."

She doesn't believe her ears.

He gazes at her.

"You would help me with the chores?"

"Yes."

Ziva blinks a few times, trying to get her emotions under control. She squeezes his hand in thanks.

"Are you all right?"

In a voice heavy with emotion, she chokes out, "I'm grateful you are part of my life."

He squeezes her hand back, pulling her closer to him.

A PATTERN EMERGES DURING THE winter as Lib helps Ziva. When the weather is nice, she exercises with the men. During the days when they are tent bound, Lib shares his knowledge with her, spending this precious time teaching her how to read and write. They use the dirt under a fur to write with a stick. She learns to read from the scrolls he has with him.

If Lib becomes affectionate, wanting more than hand-holding or kisses, Ziva distances herself from him.

Much of the time is spent in caring for Tokal, who learns to walk to the delight of his parents.

"What do we do now?" Lib asks.

"I don't know." Ziva admits, catching Tokal in her arms and hugging him. She turns him to walk back toward his father. "I will have to ask Sariah when I next see her."

Tokal toddles to Lib.

Lib catches Tokal, pumping him up in the air.

Tokal squeals and laughs, loving every moment.

Ziva smiles at the two men in her life. Fear of the unknown and what ifs rapidly fill her mind, threatening to strangle her. Will they be safe? Will her happiness be taken from her again?

Lib, seeing the concern in her face, sits next to her with Tokal in his arms. "What is it?"

"What we have is temporary."

Lib frowns, grabbing some toys and placing both Tokal and the baubles between them. "What do you mean, Ziva?"

"I've realized I'm happy, but afterward, the thought came that this is only temporary." Fear laces her words as she explains.

"This family isn't temporary."

She shakes her head. "Not that. This." She waves her hand around the tent. "In the spring, life will change again. I'm scared that by the time I return to Uthal, one or both of you may no longer be with me."

Lib moves closer to her and places Tokal in her lap.

The little boy climbs onto his feet and places a wet kiss on her cheek. He reaches for a toy.

Lib and Ziva, both catch him before he tumbles headfirst and adjust him again to sit satisfied with his toys.

"I cannot comprehend what you went through, Ziva. We can't change the past, but we can learn from it, not dwell on it." Lib picks up another toy and shakes it.

The string of beads clanks together.

Tokal looks at it. A little hand grabs it.

"The future is in front of us, and we can prepare for it, whatever it will be. Tokal's success today makes me happy. His progress is a step in the right direction." Lib grins at his own joke and takes her hand. He holds it in his strong one, gently caressing it with a finger. "That you've let your fears overtake you again makes me sad. You must let them go so you can be happy, no matter what the future will bring our way." He smiles at her.

"What will happen if I can't let it go?"

He releases her hand. "You'll miss out on so much, Ziva." He takes a breath. "Remember the joy you just felt? Is it worth missing out on that again? I want to give you so much joy, but you have to trust me."

The warmth she felt moments ago is gone. Ziva watches as Lib removes himself to sit with his books. As Ziva watches Tokal, she contemplates his words.

Days pass slowly inside the tent. Lib's words follow her, repeating themselves in her mind. Ziva practices concentrating on the present and what she can do within it.

The next time Ziva sees Sariah, she asks, "Do you have some fabric? I would like to make a shirt for Lib."

Sariah brings her into her home and shows her what material and thread she has.

The two of them decide on the fabric and cut it.

Ziva sneaks the project to her tent that's nestled within a basket.

Soon afterward, another snowstorm arrives, keeping most by their fires.

Tokal rouses from a nap but isn't the happy child he normally is.

Ziva picks him up, and he feels hot to the touch.

His nose is both stopped up and runny at the same time, making it difficult for Tokal to breathe. He whines in distress and coughs into his mother's shoulder.

Ziva and Lib look at one another after exhausting their medical knowledge.

Lib stands up, grabs his winter gear, and puts it on. "Keep him here, and I will return with Sariah."

"The storm."

"I'll be back soon," Lib reassures before stepping out of the tent into the white. The door is fastened.

Ziva does what she can for Tokal while waiting for Lib. What seems like an eternity, holding a sick Tokal, ends when Lib arrives with Sariah and Nephi. Ziva dissolves into tears, blubbering out her concern for her son.

Sariah takes Tokal from Ziva. She examines the boy. "Everything will be all right, Ziva," she soothes. "Children get sick. He will most likely get better." The congestion disrupts the child's breathing. Placing her ear on his chest she listens.

Tokal coughs. He breathes. Congestion builds up. He whines, then coughs again.

"What can we do?" Ziva asks, overwrought with concern.

Sariah places Tokal on her shoulder. She pounds on his back with a cupped hand. "This will help break up the congestion in his chest. Lib, fill the pot with snow and set it in the hot ash." She beats a steady rhythm on Tokal's back. "Nephi, get the medicine. They will need some too."

The men rush to action.

Ziva cries, "What do you mean, 'too?'"

"Tokal isn't the only one sick at present. Others are too."

Ziva watches. She feels helpless as the others work.

After Lib places the pot of water in the ash, he sits by Ziva, tucking her into his arm.

Sariah peers at them. Tears streak Ziva's distraught face. Lib's concern for his family shows on his face. "Tokal is a strong boy, but he'll need both of you to get through this." Turning to Lib, she instructs, "I need some snow in a bowl. We need to bring the fever down." Lib scoots away.

Sariah removes Tokal's remaining clothing.

Lib enters, setting the bowl of snow next to Sariah.

Sariah creates a ball with the snow. She wipes it over Tokal's head and torso.

Tokal wails in protest.

Ziva bites her nails as she weeps.

Nephi arrives with a covered cup in one hand and two small sacks in the other. He hands the cup to Sariah when she's ready.

Sariah brings the cup to Tokal's lips. "Drink, Tokal," she encourages.

A thirsty Tokal drinks.

After a good swallow, Sariah removes the beverage. She dips another cup into the pot of melted snow.

This cool drink is pressed to Tokal's mouth. He drinks.

Sariah holds the cup for the child until he pushes it away.

Tokal settles in Sariah's arms, struggling to breathe through his nose.

Sariah touches his forehead. "Already, he feels better. Not as hot. Keep the pot of water in the hot ash. Make sure it stays filled with water or it will burn." Sariah places Tokal in Ziva's arms. She reaches out her hand for Nephi to give her the bags. She opens each bag and drops the herbs in the water. The room soon smells of garlic and mint. "In the morning, get a fresh pot of snow and add some of the herbs to the pot, like I just showed you. When Tokal is hungry, give him a swallow from this cup." She touches the covered cup. "The boiled herbs will help his symptoms. He doesn't need a lot, and too much is harmful. Do you have another pot here?"

"No."

Sariah nods to Nephi.

Nephi departs.

"Keep his head higher than the rest of his body so he can breathe easier. Offer him cool water often. If his head is hot, wipe him down with snow. When one of you is caring for Tokal, the other person needs to rest. It will take both of you to get him through this."

Nephi closes the door behind him.

Ziva pats Toka's back like Sariah did. "Who else is sick?"

"Everyone in our daughter's family." Nephi sets the pot next to his wife. It contains a large bone in it with a bunch of snow.

Sariah sets this pot in the ash. She adds some herbs to it. "Each of you is to drink one cup of broth daily. This will supply your body with strength. I will return tomorrow with food."

Without stopping her pounding on Tokal's back, Ziva peers at Sariah. "How can we help your family?"

"They have what they need. You need to now care for your family." With a reassuring smile on her face, Sariah touches Ziva's forearm and squeezes. "All will be well, Ziva—with time."

Ziva nods her head, trusting in Sariah's words. She watches her guests leave. She peers at Tokal, who sounds horrible but is no longer whining. She gazes at Lib, seeking strength and comfort.

Lib sits next to her. He wraps his arm around her, pulling her to him. In varying degrees, the pounding subsides. Feeling Ziva struggle with the dead weight of a sleeping child, he gets up. After rearranging things around the room and putting things behind her, he takes Tokal. "Lie back on our gear I've placed behind you."

Ziva glances back seeing the incline of things the own. She follows his instructions without word.

Lib places Tokal on her chest. He reassures her with a smile and a gentle touch on her head. "Rest. I'll trade places with you later."

FEELING FIRE ON HER CHEST, Ziva stirs. She realizes the heat radiates from Tokal's body. "He's hot again."

Lib rubs down a screaming Tokal with a snowball. Tokal swallows some medicine. He drinks some cooled medicine and some water.

When he will no longer drink, Lib takes Tokal from her. "Time to eat. I have him." Nodding across the way, he says, "A bowl of stew sits there."

She smiles at Lib as they trade places. She drinks the broth first. It tastes different but is good. She drinks some water and eats the provided stew.

Lib's eyes are closed while Tokal lies on his chest. She listens to Tokal's breathing. Already, he seems to be breathing easier. She's grateful for Sariah's knowledge. Her concern for Tokal erased what she learned at Arnac.

Ziva puts on her coat and hat and steps outside into the night with a bag of dirty dishes. The snowflakes glide on the wind. She breathes in the fresh air, only to start hacking as her lung's spasm from the cold. *That was a bad idea.* She rushes to the bath house with Kelev next to her. On the way back, she cleans the dishes and fills the bowls with snow. Inside the tent, her fingers ache. She dumps the snow from the bowls into the pots. Rubbing her palms together, she warms them up.

"You know, you do have mittens," Lib reminds her.

She turns, meeting his eyes.

Lib's smile at her.

"So, I do." She forgot about that. Ziva pulls on her mittens before exiting their home with two empty bowls. She fills the containers with clean snow. When she returns, they are added to the pots. She removes the broth from the hot ash.

Her winter gear stored, she asks, "Do I add another log to the fire?"

"Leave it off and see how we do."

Ziva nods. "How does he feel?"

"Like a fire. Do you mind getting some snow?"

Ziva rushes outside in the cold, gathering up a snowball. Stepping inside, she stops for a moment. The coldness in her hands hurts. She rushes forward, rubbing down Tokal again.

Tokal screams.

Lib shivers as the cold infant is placed back on his bare chest. He offers Tokal some water.

Tokal drinks until he realizes the water is cold.

Lib holds him close, patting his back like Sariah.

Tokal returns to his fitful sleep, struggling to breathe.

Each day, Nephi and Sariah visit, dropping off supplies and support as Lib and Ziva care for their son. They encourage Tokal to drink the broth, medicine, and water provided, which continue to sustain him despite very little sleep. Due to their efforts, after a few days, the fever breaks. Tokal starts to recover.

Ziva sits up and checks on Tokal.

He's draped over Lib's bare chest in peaceful slumber.

She observes her sleeping men. Tears prick her eyes. Tokal has wormed his way into her heart, and his illness scared her. She was frightened that she would again be saying goodbye to a loved one. Would she rather have not known him? *No.* Would she want to change anything that happened to her? It surprises her that her answer is no. Everything that has occurred has brought her to the present. Would she have been able to care for him alone? *Not at all.*

She realizes that life is uncertain for everyone, not only for her. She recalls Lib's words to live in the present. These past few days, she's had no choice but to do so. Even though she worried about Tokal, caring for both her men made her, somehow, content. Seeing them happy makes her . . . joyful.

She's thankful for everyone who helped in Tokal's recovery. Gratitude fills her heart for Nephi and Sariah as well as the many others of their family who did her chores, releasing her to care for her son. "Thank you," spills forth from her lips.

Lib's eyes open. His perceptiveness gazes at her in the dark. "What's bothering you?"

She shakes her head and smiles at him. "Nothing. I'm just thankful."

He peers at her for a moment, reading her face. "Come. Let me hold you."

"I'd like that." She moves over to lie next to his inclined form while he still holds Tokal on his chest.

His arm curves around Ziva's body. A hand rests on her hip.

SNOW TURNS TO RAIN, ANNOUNCING the advent of spring. With the storm outside, they still are confined to the tent.

One day, Ziva and Lib play with Tokal.

He giggles. "Rawr!" He tries to imitate Kelev's bark as Lib brings him close to his mother.

Ziva reacts with a yelp.

Tokal laughs even more.

Ziva catches the toddler and falls backward onto the furs. "He's got me. He's got me."

More giggling fills the tent as Tokal makes his growling sound again.

"Help, Dada. Tokal's got me," Ziva exclaims as she twists and turns, holding the little boy to her.

Tokal laughs.

Lib picks up Tokal and looks at him. "How about we tickle Mommy?"

The little boy nods, grinning. Tokal swoops down again.

"Rawr!" He lands on his mother's stomach and tries to tickle her.

"Noooo," she cries out through her laughter.

Tokal squeals and laughs.

Lib reaches out a hand and tickles Ziva's side.

Ziva squirms away, laughing and holding Tokal.

Lib tickles her other side, and she squirms the opposite direction.

Peals of laughter erupt from Tokal.

When the next tickle occurs, Ziva laughs and wriggles away right into Lib's arms. In that moment, her eyes lock with Lib's. Her breath catches.

Tokal looks at them both, wondering what is going on.

The air inside the tent feels hot. Ziva forgets to breathe. Lib's face moves closer to her. Slow enough for a retreat. She stays where she is, living in the moment.

Tokal kisses Lib's cheek and squeals in delight. "Rawr."

Lib grins at her.

She grins back. The space disappears. His gentle kiss catapults Ziva into another plane—one she hasn't felt before. One where she's enveloped in . . . love. Without a word, the kiss deepens, full of promise, safety, hope, and joy. She yearns for Lib.

Tokal whines that something is amiss.

Both of them jump away, realizing that Tokal is squished between their bodies.

The side of Lib's mouth turns up.

She offers a radiant smile.

Lib picks up Tokal. He tosses him in the air as their attention reverts back to their son.

Ziva, feeling self-conscious at being so attracted to him, moves away from Lib. She sits on the other side of the fire to concentrate on the mending. She reprimands herself for getting "lost in the moment" and forgetting to protect her family.

Lib notices her retreat. He frowns for a moment.

Tokal calls for more playing.

Lib's attention reverts to his son.


LIB CARRIES A STACK OF wood into the tent. "Tomorrow, we're going to go to the market. The weather is such that it will be open again. I would like you with me. Tokal will stay here with Tanna. We need to prepare to leave."

Ziva's eyes meet Lib's. "To Uthal?"

He smiles at her. "To Uthal."


THE AIR IS FULL OF EXCITEMENT as chores are done and the morning meal is eaten around the main fire. Conversation around the fire consists of the market and the things that need purchased. The women and men put together their lists while they eat. Children run around, glad to be outdoors again. Tanna arrives.

"Hi, Tanna." Ziva greets her. "It makes me happy being outside again."

"I agree." Tanna smiles back. "I've come to get Tokal. I understand I'm watching him today."

"That is my understanding as well. He's finished eating and probably would like to run around with the other children for a time. This bag contains some clean cloths, clothes, and toys." Lib hands it over to Tanna.

The girl bends down to Tokal's level. "Would you like to go play?"

Tokal nods his head, squirming off his mother's lap.

Ziva sets him down on the ground.

Tokal takes Tanna's hand as they walk away.

Lib and Ziva watch.

Lib clears his throat. "Come, Ziva. Let's gather some bags to hold our supplies." They stroll to their tent.

Ziva hands the bags she prepared last night to Lib

Lib places them in his pack and straps it to his shoulders.

Ziva heads to the door.

Lib places a hand on Ziva's arm.

She stops and looks back with an eyebrow raised in question.

Lib doesn't say a word. Instead, he pulls her to him and wraps his arms around her.

She examines his face, wondering what this is all about. A fire lights Lib's eyes. A mischievous smile crosses his face.

"You're beautiful, Ziva." Lib's mouth covers hers in a gentle kiss.

Ziva kisses him back. Heat radiates low in her abdomen, spreading outward. The kiss ends too soon—leaving her breathless. Wanting more.

Ziva has a question in her eyes. "You are of infinite worth to me. For your safety, stay close while we're in the market. I don't want to lose you."

Unable to speak, she nods.

His arms move from her shoulders, sliding up her neck to cup her face. He kisses her again.

This time radiating heat fills her. Her legs become weak. Her arms hang on his neck, holding her upright.

He pulls her closer, molding her body to his.

New tantalizing feelings spread through her.

Abruptly, Lib pulls away.

Irregular breathing assaults her ears.

Lib examines her with hawklike eyes. "Stay close."

She gazes back, trying to read his face. She endeavors to catch her breath.

"Time to go" is heard outside from Nephi.

After Ziva is able to stand, Lib lets her go. He pauses at the door until his breathing is under control. He leaves the tent.

Left by herself, she stands there trembling, still affected by all the new feelings. She exhales to calm her beating heart. Taking a cleansing breath, she follows him.

Outside, Nephi stands near the gate. Once everyone is gathered, they enter the street on their way to the market. The roads of Zarahemla are bustling with activity.

Sariah sees friends and calls them over. Their neighbors join the group, catching up through conversation.

When they reach their destination, the plan to meet back at the food stalls is accepted. Smaller groups depart. Ziva and Lib are left behind.

Lib takes her hand. "I know you haven't been in a market since your father's death." He caresses the back of her hand with a finger. "We will be well if we remain together." They walk hand in hand among the stalls.

Ziva is fascinated as she watches a demonstration of how a shiny black rock cuts things. In another stall, different-colored stones are available for purchase. Memories of her father working with stones, pearls, and shells to make jewelry fill her mind, and she absently touches her bracelet.

Lib notices the movement. "I hope they are good memories."

Ziva smiles up at him. "They are."

"Ready?"

"For what?"

"We have so much more to see, and we still need to get our supplies."

She nods, but worry covers her face.

Lib reassures her by squeezing her hand. He pulls her deeper into the market to a clothing area.

"You and our growing son need travel clothes. Pick out what you want."

"I don't need anything. I have more clothes than I've ever had before."

"Two winter outfits and an old worn-out summer ensemble isn't sufficient. Get yourself something for our trip back to Uthal." He pulls her to a stall. "Here." He picks up a skirt that is colored a bright yellow. "This is a beautiful color that will look good on you."

"The skirt is so bright." she laughs at his fashion sense. "If you insist on me getting another outfit, I will pick something a little less colorful."

"Very well." Lib waits, keeping his eyes on her.

Ziva finds a top and skirt weaved with muted colors. The material is sturdy, which will work well for travel. She turns to Lib.

Lib moves forward. "Is that what you want?"

"Yes." She shows him her choices. "It will be good for traveling and will last a long time."

"As you wish." Lib completes the transaction.

Ziva adds it to the pack.

When she's finished, Lib leads the way to another stall. "Tokal needs an outfit or two. I think we can find it here." He pushes her to the table front.

Lib stands behind Ziva.

Ziva appreciates his presence, but also that he lets her choose. She sorts through the available children's wear. Finding something with the right thickness, durability and size, Ziva holds it up for Lib to see.

Lib moves forward and haggles. The price agreed upon, he pays for it. "Since Tokal has an outfit, he's going to need some leggings and shoes." They stroll down the aisle until they find a stall that will work. When that business is completed, they move to another area in the market that contains legumes, grains, tubers, spices; and dried fruit, meat and vegetables.

"How long will our journey take?"

"Don't know. I haven't found a merchant heading to Uthal."

She looks at Lib. "Why are we buying supplies today?"

"There may be something here that you would like to eat or introduce to Tokal. See the large variety of foods brought by the merchants?"

"I don't care for trying something new. Let's get the supplies we need in our tent. The ones we discussed last night."

Once their food supplies have been placed in Lib's pack, they go to another area. This one contains weapons.

Ziva walks beside Lib as he peruses the different stalls. She points out a stall that contains something she's interested in.

Lib leads the way to that table.

A merchant waits on them. "This bow is made from a ram's horn. We soften the horn and unravel it, turning it into a bow. If treated well, the bow will last a long time."

"How do you soften the horn?" Ziva asks.

"The horn is bathed in warm water."

Ziva touches the bow. "The ram's horn makes a beautiful bow."

"A ram's horn bow fires an arrow faster than other bows do," the merchant entices.

Lib looks at the bow again then inspects the merchant. "That is a bold claim."

"Yes. It responds faster than a wooden bow made from maple, oak, ash, or even elm wood."

Lib nods. "Thank you for showing us."

"If you're interested in the bow, an archery range is here in the market. You can see it in action."

Ziva gazes at Lib. "I would like to see that."

Lib nods. Turning, he inquires, "Where is the archery range?"

The merchant gives directions.

Lib nods. "Thank you."

Together Lib and Ziva stroll down the road hand-in-hand.

Ziva says, "We need to finish our shopping first. If we have any time left, we can go."

"Agreed." Lib guides the way to the remaining stores.

When the last item is stored in the pack, Lib examines the sky. "We have some time left before we need to meet the others. Would you like to see the bow in action?"

Ziva smiles and nods.

Lib guides their way, striding to their destination. He stops in front of a long area that ends in the city wall.

Ziva watches the archers while listening to a merchant explain the differences in bows.

Patrons ask questions.

The seller answers.

The ram's horn bow and a wood bow are matched up and fired at the same time. The arrow from the ram's horn bow hits the target at the end, faster than arrow from the wood bow, surprising both Ziva and Lib. They look at each other.

"How does it handle?" Lib asks.

"How about you try it for yourself?"

Lib looks at her.

Ziva nods.

Lib joins the demonstrator.

Ziva backs away, positioning herself to get a better view.

After receiving instruction, Lib releases an arrow. The first misses the target. The two men talk again. Lib notches another arrow. Behind her, a conversation interrupts her concentration.

"You better know what you're doing," a man argues. "If this isn't done correctly, we'll all be caught."

"Relax," another voice soothes. "All will go according to plan."

"Is everything in place?"

"Yes."

"It had better be," the first man sneers.

"I'll focus on killing our beloved chief judge, Cezoram. You concentrate on getting the women out of the city tonight."

Curiosity gets the better of her. She turns not believing her ears. Two well-dressed men stand not far away. One looks to be the captain of an army. Their eyes meet.

Before she can say or do anything, a sharp pain slices her head.

"What's one more woman? Even though she's Joined, she looks young like the others. Hurry!"

It's the last thing Ziva hears.

# CAPTIVITY

HER HEAD FEELS LIKE IT has been bashed in. Upon investigation, her fingers find a tender bump. The pain causes her breath to catch. Stink hits her nostrils, making her gag. She hears someone moaning in the distance. Ziva opens her eyes. She's in a semi-dark room with oil lamps lit in the distance.

A female face blocks her view. It whispers, "Be quiet or they'll know you're awake. You don't want that."

Ziva realizes the moaning is from her. She shakes her head, trying to clear her fogginess. Instead, she becomes dizzy. She stops and grinds her teeth. "Where am I?"

"We're in prison."

"We're what?" Ziva sits up and blinks.

"Shhh. They'll hear you," the woman warns.

Ziva puts a hand back to her head, gingerly touching around the knot. Is she bleeding?

"You were probably stolen. Like the rest of us."

"Last thing I remember is being in the market with my—"

"Same with us." the woman interjects. "I've lost track of the time I've been here. I'm sure my parents are worried sick. Occasionally, another woman is added."

"What's your name?" Ziva holds her head, piecing things together.

"Alissah."

Ziva glances at her. She is young and fair haired with lighter eyes. Ziva can't tell the eye color in the darkened room. "How many years are you, Alissah?"

Alissah's fearful face answers without question. "This is my sixteenth year."

Ziva examines her surroundings. She's in a cage with a sticky floor that's rank. She stands, wiping whatever is on her hands on her skirt.

The other women gather round her, shielding her from something unknown near a fire.

"How are you feeling?" Alissah asks.

"All right considering," Ziva stands, but the world sways back and forth. She grabs a bar of her cage to steady her.

"Good." Alissah takes her arm. "We don't have much time before he comes again. If you fight, he will hit you."

"Clear away from the new birdie," a male voice declares.

With bowed heads, the prisoners move away from Ziva, trying to disappear from his view.

A man walks toward her. He stops on the other side of the cage. He scrutinizes her from the top of her head down to her feet and back up.

Ziva stares, undaunted.

The large, bald, and flabby man in dirty clothes mocks. "Another pretty birdie in a cage."

His foul breath reaches Ziva's nostrils making them curl.

A nasty, degrading laugh issues from his mouth. "Tho, I'm beneath you, am I? You'll thoon learn your plathe."

"I've just met you, and the only thing odious thus far is your breath," Ziva stands firm. "Where am I? Why am I here?"

A vicious, degrading laugh escapes again. "You're here, pretty birdie, in my care because I am told to keep you here."

"I want to go home." Ziva motions to the others. "We all do."

He laughs again. "You're getting a new home far from here." He points to himself. "I'm getting well paid for it."

"Where are you taking us?"

He quirks an eyebrow at her. "Doeth it matter?"

Ziva stares at the man and smirks. "So, you don't know." She takes a shallow breath of stale air.

"I do know," he roars at her. In a sing song voice he continues, "But you're not going to like it."

Ziva glares at him. "You don't know."

"The Gadianton like beautiful birdies. Thelling beautiful birdieth returns big dividendssss. However, I think out of all the other birdieth, you're the uglietht in appearance, though you're the only one who hathn't whined and cried." He walks away. "I hate whining." When he's back near the fire, he shouts, "No way to get out of here, ugly birdie—and if by some miracle you do escape, the guardth will only bring you back to me before you'll be thold anyway." He cackles.

Ziva watches him as she mulls over her situation.

Alissah comes to her side, and the other inmates follow. "How did you do that?" she says with awe. "When I got here, he beat me until I didn't make a sound. He did that with each of us."

Ziva wraps her arms around herself, trying to think. She fingers her bracelet discovering it's gone. She touches her neck. Lib's necklace missing. Turning to Alissah, she inquires, "Did I arrive with any jewelry?"

"No." Alissah shakes her head in the dark. "Our bracelets were gone as well."

Ziva shivers as ice-cold fear slices down her back. She swallows, tamping it down.

"What does he mean by Gadianton?" Alissah whispers.

"Stop crowding me," Ziva snaps at them.

Hurt wells in their eyes. The occupants move away.

Hearing the tone of her voice, Ziva cringes. She tries a soothing tone this time. "I'm sorry. I didn't mean to bark at you. Give me some time to think before I talk." She tries to smile at them.

They huddle in a corner away from her.

Ziva leans against the bars, not wanting to return to the filthy floor. She takes a shallow breath, trying not to gag from the stench within this dark room. What about Lib and Tokal? How is Lib ever going to find her? *They're not.*

*I'm alone!* An open chasm overwhelms her. Fear suffocates her. *Why try anymore?* She feels like she's in the river again, being tugged by a sweeping current. Being drowned. *Give up.* She struggles to breathe as blackness edges into her vision—oblivion.

If she wants to live, she's going to have to do something. Deciding to act, she swallows her fear and gasps for air, immediately coughing from the miasma.

*How to get out?* When her coughing spasm subsides, Ziva looks around her. No tools inside the cage, only a small rug which holds the huddling mass—young women, like her. The only difference is that they haven't had the experiences she's had. *Mother helped me with Gadianton the first time.* These women don't have their mothers with them. *They only have me.*

Over the winter, she learned to read and write. She learned some fighting skills. If she gets to know them and helps them, one of them may die. *It will break my heart.* If she doesn't help them, they will disappear, never to be heard of again. *Guilt will overwhelm me.*

The group's escape is going to be more difficult than leaving on her own. *Alone or together?* She continues to mull the arguments and ideas in her head. Her hands find their way into her pocket. She feels the scrap of material. She pulls it into her palm, feeling the pearl within. It reminds her of who she is.

Making a decision, she walks over to the huddled mass and motions for them to stand.

They comply, watching her carefully.

Gathering them around her, she smiles. "My name's Ziva. I know Alissah. She gazes at the two other inmates. "What are your names?"

"Anath."

"Didi."

"How old are you?"

"Sixteen," they say in unison.

They are all the same age. "How many days have you been here?"

"Don't know. I came after Alissah," Anath says.

"I came after Anath. You followed," Didi informs her.

"I'm happy to meet you. Although, I wish it were on better terms." Ziva grins, trying to lessen their fear. "Alissah asked some questions which I'm going to answer."

The three women look to their savior to help them. Ziva swallows hoping she can. "It sounds like they are going to sell us as slaves to Gadianton robbers."

A gasp is shared by the little group.

"I have met them. You don't want to be under their power. They are a people that take what they want. Don't show fear. Don't reveal weakness of any kind. If you show weakness, they will delight in it and use it against you." Ziva frowns, examining the man by the light. "I would lump our captor with them, but he doesn't seem to be in his right mind. Before I blacked out, I overheard a conversation that makes me think someone in the government may be involved."

Another collective gasp is heard from the prisoners.

"But I'm not sure. No one is going to find us. The only way out of this is by escaping together. We must do it outside the city but before we reach Gadianton. We must work together to accomplish this. Are you with me?"

The women glance at one another. They nod their heads.

They hear someone footsteps and look up.

In the dimness, the visitor is hard to make out. "Ready the women."

Their captor calls several minions. He opens the cage. "Here, birdie, birdie." As he gets closer, the other women mass behind Ziva.

Ziva glances at them.

They quiver, trying to get away from the man.

Greasy meat hooks grab Ziva's hair. She's moved to the cage door where one of his minions lewdly grins at her. Her hands are tied together.

The bald, fat man places a noose loosely around her neck. "Be a good birdie, and it won't tighten."

Their captor goes after the next woman, who cowers away from him, causing him to chase after her. He catches them one by one. Their hands are bound. They are tied behind Ziva. When all the women are lined up, the visitor takes the end of the rope wrapped around Ziva's neck and pulls.

She must follow or choke.

THEY TRAVEL INTO THE COOL, fresh night air, leaving the other prison patrons behind. Ziva is thankful she still has her coat around her. She takes a deep breath, clearing her lungs of the vile stale air. By the torchlight she examines her new captor. It's the merchant from the weapons table.

The merchant grins her way. "Make one sound, and I will kill all of you. Starting with you." He points at Ziva.

*That's one way to get out of this situation.* However, Ziva wants to live. She swallows her fear as he pulls them forward.

They walk through the city at a brisk pace. The few people they see ignore them, even when they pass through Zarahemla's gate. At the river Sidon, the women are set in a canoe and couriered to the other side.

Ziva is amazed at the people's reaction. These are citizens of Zarahemla. She wonders at their apathy. She doesn't understand why no one says a word or even questions that this is out of the ordinary. Is seeing four women being led out of the city by rope an ordinary occurrence? Why has no one stopped what this evil man is doing?

Ziva looks back across the river at the enormous city, Zarahemla. She hopes that somehow, she'll find her way back to Lib and Tokal. *At least Tokal has Lib.*

When the canoe reaches the shore, the merchant gets out of the canoe. He pays a man. The workers pull the tied women from the boat and set them on dry ground. Their imprisoner is handed the rope end.

Pulled by the cord around her neck, Ziva scurries to keep the rope slack. When she starts down a trail, her mind searches for a way to escape. She stumbles and falls. The rope around her neck tightens, obstructing her breathing.

Those behind her nearly fall on her.

The man transporting her grabs her by the hair and loosens the cord at her throat. "Get up."

Without the use of her hands, standing is difficult.

He grabs her by the arm, wrenching her up.

Ziva stands.

The cord pulls her neck.

Ziva lurches forward, trying to keep her feet under her.

They travel deeper in the forest.

When morning light is sufficient to see, the merchant extinguishes his torch.

It seems like an eternity before the man stops.

The women drop to the ground.

"Rest yourselves. When the others get here, we will travel on" Their assailant ties them to a tree.

After catching her breath, Ziva examines the area. Food stuff left behind is piled together. It looks to be the astronomy group's residual before that dreadful storm. Knowing where she's located settles her. She leans against the tree in deep thought—*time to put together an escape plan. One man with four women. We can do this. The only question is how.*

Her gaze follows the merchant.

He walks away toward another tree.

"Are you going to feed us, or are we to starve?"

He turns and glares at her. He stomps back. "I told you to be quiet." He kicks her.

Ziva winces. She glares at him. "We were quiet throughout the city to wherever this is. We haven't slept all night. Nor have we eaten. If you want top price for us, you need to keep your stock healthy and strong."

"Do you think I'm some imbecile?"

She raises an eyebrow at him. "I have done this before. You're not the first nor the last."

"If you have food, I'm more than willing to cook while you rest."

Surprise covers his face. "You do realize that I'm selling you."

"Yes." Ziva stares at him, trying to keep her wits about her.

"But we still need cared for if you want a healthy return."

They stare at each other.

He breaks the silence. "You're very different from the others."

"Been told that my whole life."

His eyes widen. He roars with laughter. After wiping his eyes, he comes to the tree where she's tied.

"Let us clean up first so we can look our best."

He laughs at her suggestion. He unties them from the tree. "Best watch yourself. If you try anything, I will not hesitate to kill all of you."

"And lose all profit?" She smiles at him. "I'm trying to make sure your stock stays in good condition."

In response, he jerks the cord around her neck.

She quickens her pace.

Those behind stumble along.

When they arrive at the stream, he stops. "Have at it. Clean yourselves up."

Ziva looks at him in disbelief. She holds out her arms. "How are we to do that with our hands tied?"

"Don't know. Don't care." Nodding toward the stream, he grunts. "You best hurry before I change my mind."

Ziva glares at him, trying to contain her anger.

Those behind her don't wait. The hurry into the water.

Ziva is pulled in their direction. When the cold water hits her, she realizes the others are correct. She does what she can to clean herself off and drink before he pulls them away.

Their captor laughs at them as they struggle. Tired of waiting, he stomps into the stream and pulls each of them to their feet. Taking the cord, he leads them back to the tree and binds them to it.

"What about food?"

He turns back to Ziva. "What about it?"

"Would you like me to fix it?"

"You have a temper that I worry about."

She keeps a bland expression on her face while a storm rages inside. "I'm trying to get food in our bellies."

He evaluates her. He sighs and stomps back. He unties her and pulls her away from the others. He marches her to some bushes, pulling them back. Some clay pots are exposed. "Everything is there."

Ziva nods, acknowledging the supplies.

He heads to the tree to rest.

"Well?"

He stops and turns back.

"Are you going to untie me? I can't cook if I'm tied up." Ziva raises her arms to show him her wrists.

"In a minute." He stomps to his pack, grumbling the whole way. Looking through it, he finds a long piece of leather. He marches to Ziva. "Sit down,"

Ziva does the best she can while being tied.

He pushes her down, finishing the process.

She falls to her side.

As she lies there, her abductor grabs her ankle and grumbles, "I should have done this before releasing you from the tree."

After tying each ankle to the cord, leaving enough length between to allow her to walk. He pulls out his knife. He pushes the sharp implement close to Ziva's face to see how she responds.

She watches the blade but doesn't move.

"Humph. You may survive after all." The knife is pulled away. "The others—not so much. But I will get my money." He cuts the excess cord from her ankle. He pulls Ziva to her feet. "Hear me. I'm going to release your hands, but if I find you untying the leather at your ankles, you will lose a hand. Understand me?"

Ziva nods, trying her best to look innocent.

"One more thing."

Her gaze meets his.

"You will feed me first." He removes the rope from her neck.

Ziva nods again.

When her wrists are freed, Ziva rubs at their soreness. "What would you like me to cook?"

"I don't know. See what's there and make yourself useful." He walks to his pack.

"How long will we be here?"

"We leave in the morning."

"I'd better get to work." In perusing the hidden canisters, Ziva finds an assortment of basic supplies as well as some dried meat in the containers. She doesn't find a cooking pot. She recalls what was left at the campground the last time she was here. She heads in that direction, hindered by the cord at her ankles. She changes her walking style, using minced steps which help her not to trip or fall.

"What are you doing?" her captor shouts from under a shaded tree.

"I don't see a pot to cook in. Others have camped here. Let me see if I can find something else that could work."

He nods.

She searches the pile of bags. "Somewhere around this place is Melek's knife," she mutters under her breath. She examines the ground and spots the weaved pot filled with dishes. Ziva smiles at her little victory. *Fish traps.* She hunts in the bushes near the stream. She finds them. Holding up one of the water cages for her abductor, she hollers, "I found fish traps. Would you like me to set them? We may be able to have fish later."

The merchant sits straighter from where he rests. He shouts back, "Do it!"

"I will be back after I set the traps unless you would you like to help me?"

"I'm tired," He relaxes against the tree. A hand waves her off. "You set them."

"As you wish."

Taking a cage one by one, she minces her way along the bank, finding a good place to drop the trap. While doing this she scans the ground for the lost weapon. When she places the last trap in the water, Ziva turns toward the campground. Something catches her attention—Melek's knife.

When she gets near it, she takes a big step, purposefully losing her balance. She falls next to the sheathed knife. "I'm all right," she calls. Ziva grabs the knife and dumps it in her pocket. "I forgot myself and took too big of a step." She stands and with careful steps picks up the cooking pot filled with dishes and sets it near the merchant. "Found a pot. May I take it to the stream to fill?"

He scans her, looking for deceit. "Be quick about it. My stomach's growling."

Ziva turns away so he can't see her reaction. She bites her lips shut, wanting so much to respond but knowing that her response is not going to help them. She dumps the bowls, spoons, and cups near the fire he created before mincing her way to fill the pot.

Back at the fire, she adds more wood. While she waits for hot ash, Ziva fills two cups, setting them aside.

She dumps some dried jerky, beans, and corn to start into the pot. The hot ash glows. She stirs it, placing the pot. Turning to her captor, she raises a cup and offers the water to him. "Would you like some water?"

He startles awake. "No. I don't want some water. I've already drunk out of the waterskin."

"The food is cooking. Would you mind if I give the others some water?"

"Water them. Feed them. Only, be quiet."

"As you wish."

He glares at her.

She picks up the filled cups and takes them to the women. With Ziva's back toward the merchant, she helps the women relieve their thirst. "You're all doing well. Remember to be brave. Don't cower. Be observant of what is going on. You need to rest. Sleep if you can. I will watch out for you and will bring food as soon as possible."

Ziva returns to the fire, checking on the food. She collects the waterskin without disturbing her captor. With the skin, the captives drink their fill.

She feels her abductor's eyes on her back. She stirs the stew. *How will I season it?* She wonders if any of theirs survived throughout the winter. Going to the remains of their fall supplies, she rummages through it. *They're ruined.*

*What can she use for seasoning?* Her mind recalls that she saw what looked like onion or garlic near one of the fish traps. She stirs the stew again.

She raises the empty container. "I'm refilling the waterskin."

His hand dismisses her.

Ziva fills the waterskin near the herbs. Using a stone, she retrieves some wild garlic. She washes it off in the stream. Returning to the fire, she smashes it and adds it to the stew.

Her assailant examines her. "You've been gone a long time. Why?"

"Sorry. I filled your waterskin, then found some wild garlic. I added it to the stew to make it taste better."

"Is the food about ready?"

Ziva stirs the stews contents. "A little bit longer. Do you mind if I take the women to relieve themselves?"

"They stay where they are."

"As you say." Ziva bites her lips to keep quiet. She sits and thinks. After some time has passed, Ziva uses a cup to dish stew into a bowl. Taking one of the spoons, she mixes the stew in the bowl while she blows on it. When it has cooled some, she presents the dish to the merchant.

"About time." he grumbles. "Take a bite."

Ziva looks at him wide eyed.

"Take a bite so I know you haven't poisoned me."

Ziva can't hide her offended glare. She takes a big bite of stew, savoring every morsel.

The bowl is pulled from her hands. Her captor stirs the food, and takes a bite. His eyes widen in surprise, then crinkles into a smile. "It'll do." He returns to his seat.

"How many are coming? So, I know if I need to restock the stew."

While still chewing, he grumbles, "However many they send me."

Ziva nods and moves away to the fire. She dishes out another bowl for the women.

He holds his bowl out to her in one hand. "More."

She takes the bowl from him. "As you wish." She fills container, then hands it his way.

"You didn't cool it off for me."

A frown crosses Ziva's lips. She removes it, hoping he didn't see. Taking the filled bowl, she cools it like she did the first.

He grabs the cooled offering and shovels it in, ignoring her.

Ziva removes the pot from the hot ash. She picks up the other bowl mincing her way to the women. "I can't get him to release you from the tree, but I do have food for you." She feeds them, sharing the bowl among the three.

With careful steps she returns to the fire. She glances at her abductor.

He holds an empty bowl in his lap.

"Would you like some more stew?"

The bowl is handed to her.

Ziva fills it and repeats the process. She places it in his hands.

She fills up the other bowl for herself. While she eats, she thinks about the best time to escape. More men are coming. From where, she doesn't know. If the men come from the city, the group of women could end up running into them, putting the women back into this position, except she would then be without the knife . . . or a hand.

The merchant snorts, waking himself up.

Ziva looks up.

He wipes his face. "Time for you to be tied up with your sisters." He stands.

"What about cleaning the bowls?"

"Did you hear me? Move."

Ziva sets down her bowl of stew. She minces her way to the tree where the others are tied.

He follows her. When he stops, he lashes her hands. He pushing her down, tying her to the women. Just to make sure she doesn't have any plan other plans, he returns the rope to her neck and ties it to the tree. Satisfied, he marches back to the tree, settles himself, and closes his eyes.

Ziva doesn't look at the others. "Go back to sleep. I need to think."

Didi, sitting next to her, leans over. "You've already helped us. You need to keep up your strength so we can get out of this. We can see how tired you are. I will stay awake this time. Sleep, Ziva, while you can."

Realizing the logic in Didi's words, Ziva nods in agreement as much as the rope will let her.

"Rest your head on my shoulder so the rope doesn't tighten around your neck."

Ziva complies and closes her eyes as her mind searches for a solution.

"WAKE UP, ZIVA," DIDI WHISPERS. She wiggles her shoulder.

Ziva lifts her head and looks around. Dusk is approaching. Their eyes meet. She hears footsteps. Her head swivels to her assailant.

He snores under the shadow of a tree.

She glances at the women. "Be brave and use your head." All her attention turns toward the noise.

Six soldiers walk into the clearing, not at all surprised to see women tied to a tree. The men stop several feet away appraising their victims. One covers his nose and mouth. "They stink with filth."

"So would you if you were confined in a prison and tied to a tree." A man says. He walks to the snoring man, peering down at him.

He doesn't stir.

He kicks the merchant's foot. "Wake up, you sorry excuse for a man."

The merchant snorts and wipes the drool off his face. He jumps to his feet. "Good of you to *finally* show up. How many of you did he send to protect me this time?"

"Six . . ." the leader throws back. "And you best be grateful." Eyeing the leftovers in the pot, the man sniffs. "You cook this?"

"No. One of the women cooked it." the merchant waves a hand toward the captives. He stretches as the other soldiers gather around the pot filling the bowls. They sit down to eat.

"Which woman?"

"I'll be back," the merchant throws over his shoulder as he steps toward the bushes near the stream.

"Which woman?" the captain yells at the retreating man.

"Can it wait until I'm done?" the merchant yells back.

The captain makes a face.

Finishing his business, the merchant strides back.

"Which woman?"

The merchant stops in front of the leader and folds his arms. "The one with the rope around her neck. She's different."

"How so?"

"She's not frightened." He moves his hand in a circle trying to explain. "She is the first woman, ever, who has offered to cook."

"Is the stew good?" the leader asks the soldiers.

A round of "mmm" is chorused.

The chief goes to the pot of stew.

A soldier hands him a filled bowl. He takes the vessel and smells the contents, looking for anything out of the ordinary, but all he smells is a pleasing aroma. He takes a tentative bite. The simply seasoned stew makes his taste buds smile. He settles where the merchant previously sat, concentrating on filling his empty stomach.

The merchant parks himself next to him.

"You couldn't have at least cleaned the women before our arrival?" he asks in between bites.

"With only myself here? I am not about to let them loose."

"And yet you did let one of them loose to feed you."

The dangerous tone of the leader has the merchant glancing at him. "I made provision for it and watched her the whole time."

The leader doesn't respond.

The merchant waves a hand at the women. "She's still tied to the tree, isn't she?"

The captain takes another bite.

"She found some fish traps and set them. Perhaps we'll have fish in the morning."

The leader snaps his fingers.

One guard stands in front of the leader.

"Take three with you and secure the perimeter. Let me know if you find anything peculiar. We'll leave with the women in the morning."

The soldier nods. He calls three others and they carry out their orders.

The captain finishes the stew and tosses the bowl and spoon to the side. It lands where the remaining soldiers sit. He wipes his mouth as he stands. He prowls around the women, undressing them with his eyes. He ends with the brown-haired beauty with a noose. The one that the merchant said was "not afraid."

# WARRIOR

THE CAPTAIN STANDS CLOSE TO the woman. "Knowing what is going to happen to you, what made you want to cook?"

Ziva is pinned by the ropes. She can't move away from him.

"You do know you're being sold to Gadianton, don't you?"

Ziva's jaw firms. "I'm already among Gadianton."

A hard look embraces captain's features.

*My mouth has done it again.* Ziva sighs. "We all needed food. Someone had to prepare it."

"You made it taste good. Why?"

Ziva shrugs. "Should I not have? We all need to eat."

"Why do you call us Gadianton?"

Ziva meets his gaze. "Isn't that what you are?" spills from her mouth.

The captain pulls out his knife and brings it to the captive's throat.

The merchant races to women, concerned about his profits.

The leader leans closer to the noosed woman's ear and whispers, "Not a lot of people know that." His face moves mere inches from the woman's, gazing into her eyes. He searches for any deception. "How do you know? Who told you?"

Ziva's mouth goes dry. She dares not swallow. She dares not blink. Her words got her in trouble again. Her legs shake under her skirt. She stiffens, but they only shake worse. Her palms sweat. She clutches her skirt, hiding her terror.

The merchant pleads. "Captain, don't hurt her. She will bring a lower price if you hurt her."

He ignores the merchant. His eyes locked on Ziva's. "Who told you?" He yells. "Tell me quick or I cut your throat."

"Your actions!" Spills from Ziva's lips.

"What?" The captain grasps her forehead in a firm grip. Ready to slice her neck.

Mustering up all her courage, her legs still shaking, she yells loud for all to hear. "Your actions told me. Not a person."

The knife remains at her throat as he gazes into her face. "You're right. I am part of Gadianton. Many reside in the city who are part of Gadianton. The people of Zarahemla won't know until the city is captured." A malevolent grin crosses his face. "Similar to you."

In slow motion, the blade leaves Ziva's throat. She feels warm heat travel down her throat.

The leader steps back from the noosed woman. He watches the tiny red bead cascade down the woman's throat.

The merchant pulls out a cloth and presses it to the injury. "You damaged her."

"She'll live." He strides back to the tree, taking the same previous seat.

The merchant checks to make sure the injury stopped bleeding. He follows the commander voicing his complaint.

Ziva is unable to move. She sits there for a long time, shaking, as the tears roll down her cheeks in the dark.

"He's gone," Didi whispers, trying to comfort her.

*I'm still alive. My son and Lib are still alive.* Ziva opens her eyes. *Faith over fear* she repeats to herself over and over again. *We must escape.*

The men around the fire bed down for the night.

Ziva's shaking subsides. "We must escape tomorrow. Tonight, we need to rest—to prepare. I don't know how it will be accomplished, but be ready," she whispers.

The women take turns watching over each other.

Ziva is woken by Didi late in the night. She thinks about Lib and her son. Tokal has a good father to teach him. Lib is so kind and patient. She hasn't given her body to him. She was trying to protect their little family; afraid he'd disappear from their life if she did. All she wants now is to be back in his strong, safe arms. To feel his tender kisses upon her lips and his affectionate hands holding her body.

Life happened anyway.

She snickers. Look where she is now—alone again. An internal shift occurs, like lighting a torch. *My thinking was skewed.* Life still happens whether you want it to or not. It's time to live in the moment, like Lib always tells her. *Figure a way out of this nightmare.* Ziva chews on her lip, trying to work out how.

The other women awake around dawn.

Ziva whispers to Didi. "See the ram's horn bow that the captain has? When we're free, we need it as well as the arrows to protect us. We will have to work together to make sure we leave with them."

The message is relayed. The women look at each other, wondering why the need a weapon.

"I don't know how to use a bow and arrow. Do any of you?" Anath asks.

Ziva sighs. "I know how to use it. When we leave, we need to remember it if we're to have a chance."

The merchant saunters over and unties the noosed-woman. "Time to collect the fish."

Ziva nods as he holds the end of the rope around her neck. "Do you have a bag to store them?"

"You think you're so smart." He pulls her back over to their supplies and pulls out a bag. When she falls to her knees, he realizes that he has again cut off her air. He rushes over to loosen the rope around her neck. She lies there, catching her breath.

He barely lets her have some time to breathe. "I'm getting hungry." He pulls her to her feet and says, "Get yourself up and collect the fish."

She minces toward the first of the fish traps, thinking as she goes. When she arrives at the edge of the stream, she stops.

The merchant can see the trap under the water. "Go get it."

Ziva spreads her fingers, palms out, indicating that she can't because her hands and feet are tied.

"Must I do everything?" The merchant grumbles under his breath. He frees her hands and feet.

Ziva rubs her swollen wrists.

"Well? Hurry up and get it!" he points to the trap.

"Before I pull up the trap, I need the bag and a rock to kill the fish."

He thrusts the bag Ziva's way.

She takes it. She finds a good-sized rock that fits her hand. She opens the sack. Ziva leans down and pulls up the heavy trap. Four good-sized fish are in it.

The merchant's mouth waters.

Ziva pulls out the first fish. She kills it and drops it in the bag. Soon, the bag contains the four fish. Taking the fish trap, that rests on the shore, and the filled bag, she moves to the next. She realizes her hands and feet are free.

Ziva prepares herself for an escape. She sets up the bag and the rock just as before. She pulls up the trap.

The captain arrives standing next to the merchant. He watches Ziva work.

*No!* Her plan is squashed before it starts. Ziva does her job without looking at the men. She picks up the traps, rock, and bag containing the fish, ready to move to the last.

The captain stops her. He holds out his hand.

Ziva hands over the bag of fish.

He hands the sack to the merchant. "Take the fish back to the fire so cooking can start. Bring me back another bag."

The merchant, surprised by the bag thrust in his hands, doesn't say a word. He passes over the rope and departs.

Ziva feels like something is wrong. She watches the captain.

He rakes her over with his eyes.

Ziva feels more uncomfortable.

The merchant returns, handing her a sack.

"Take the traps back with you." The captain keeps his attention locked on the noosed woman.

Ziva feels like she's being hunted, about to be a beast's prey.

"She'll bring a higher price if untouched."

The captain's attention doesn't change. Danger emanates from him. "I didn't ask for your opinion."

Ziva knows something is coming but doesn't know what.

The merchant grumbles, grabs the traps out of her hands, and stomps off.

The captain raises an eyebrow. One arm is outstretched for her to lead the way. "The fish?"

Ziva walks to the next trap. Her body tense as warning bells go off in her head.

The captain follows holding the end of the rope.

Finding the cage, she sets up the bag and rock and kneels down to pull up the last trap.

Before she knows it, the captain is on her.

He throws her to ground. He climbs on her.

Ziva fights him.

An acrid smell comes off the malevolent man. He hits her.

Her vision goes black. The cool air licks her thighs. Where's her skirt? Without thinking, she reaches in her pocket. She pulls the knife from its sheath.

The captain's hands tighten around her neck and squeeze.

Her vision blurs.

Recalling her combat training from her astronomy brothers, she reacts.

He grunts.

When Ziva's vision returns, she's lying on her back, staring up at the morning sky. Something heavy lies still on her. She pushes it away, but a bloody knife is in her hand. She drops it. Horrified, she scrambles away from the bloody body on her. With shaking hands, she removes the rope from her throat. She pulls her knees up to her chest and breaths.

Gaining some perspective, she glances at the dead leader next to her.

*The others!* shouts in her mind. She cleans off the knife, shoving it back in its sheath. She thinks about their next step toward freedom. She must release the others. *Faith over fear. No time to think of anything else.*

The only way to succeed is to get the bow and arrows before they depart. Behind a bush she searches for the weapons. The merchant deposited the fish traps next to the weapons.

She releases the fish. She cleans the blood from her. Adding several rocks to the sack, she's ready. She lifts the trap and freezes. The rope is not around her neck. The soldiers are guaranteed to think that something is amiss. She drops her gear. She gathers the rope and shudders. She has to talk herself into it. "For the others," she whispers. Taking a breath, she returns the noose. It weighs on her shoulders. Biting her lip, she forces herself to coil up its length. Picking up the fish trap and the bag of rocks, she takes a deep breath. She stumbles toward the fish traps like she's been beaten and disgraced.

She hides her actions, putting as many arrows as she can into one quiver before dropping the trap. With the other hand Ziva grabs the bow and quiver, heading toward the women.

She drops the weapon behind the women. She sits as if tied to the tree. "Quickly, Didi. Move this way so I can release your hands. You can release the others."

The men by the fire are occupied by the fish for their morning meal. They ignore their captives.

The women rearrange themselves, moving in front of Didi to cover her actions as she cuts their ropes. They hear someone coming their way. They huddle close together and remain still.

Ziva hides the knife carefully behind her back as the merchant kicks her foot. "Where's the captain?"

Ziva looks up at him, showing him her swollen and injured face. Her eyes drop.

The merchant, seeing her injured body, curses in outrage that he will receive less revenue. He storms off toward the stream in search of the captain, muttering under his breath.

Ziva glances at the soldiers. Their attention is on the mad merchant.

Ziva returns the knife to its home in her pocket. "Go. We must leave." They grab the quiver and bow, handing it to Ziva as they retreat into the forest at a run.

The soldiers follow.

Ziva rips off the rope at her neck. After the quiver is situated on her shoulder, Ziva nocks an arrow as she follows the others as they run on the path leading back to Zarahemla.

Ziva glances at the first man behind her. Each step he takes shortens the distance between them. With a momentary stop, she releases her arrow.

The arrow pierces the man's chest.

Ziva doesn't wait to see what happens but takes off again.

He runs a little more before falling.

His companions jump over him, continuing to shorten the distance between them and the fleeing women.

Ziva pulls out another arrow and nocks it. Her lungs feel on fire. Fear of being caught nips at her heels. She pushes forward while glancing back.

Two men are gaining on her. One man has an arrow drawn. He shoots.

An arrow whizzes by Ziva's ear, hitting a tree. She doesn't slow down but grabs another arrow. She whirls around, releasing both arrows in rapid succession. One arrow pierces a soldier's neck and he collapses to the ground. The other arrow hits the man's shoulder. It doesn't slow his progression.

Ziva takes off again as fast as she can, reaching for another arrow.

The women stopped, breathing hard. She doesn't know why. She looks behind.

Four more men are gaining on them.

She screams at the women to move, but no sound comes out of her mouth. She grabs two arrows from her quiver, deciding to take a stand with the others. Preparing the bow for another rapid-fire succession.

Ziva plants her feet, facing the enemy. She fires two arrows at the closest soldiers.

Four men drop which confuses her.

She turns to the women.

New men race toward them.

Women scream.

Determined to fight to the death, Ziva drops her bow and pulls out her knife.

Something brushes Ziva's leg.

A dog rushes by.

A hand touches her shoulder.

Ziva spins away to face this foe.

# TRAVEL

"Ziva, I've found you." The rich baritone announces, as a man stops her knife's descent with a hand clamped on her injured wrist. He holds her. "I'm here. You're safe."

A cry escapes Ziva's throat as she collapses into Lib's arms. He cradles her abused body, speaking soothing words in her ear.

Ziva sobs.

When their position is secure, Nephi speaks. "I'm Nephi. We're Ziva's friends. We want to get you back to your family.

The women huddle together near Ziva.

"I need your names and where you live so we can notify your parents and reunite you with them."

The women remain silent.

Nephi tries again, but gets no response.

Lib whispers into her ear. "Ziva, the women need you."

Ziva's head pops up. She examines her surroundings, seeing only those she knows. She takes a shuddering breath. "They are good. We are safe."

After Ziva dries her tears and joins the women, do they give Nephi their names.

Nephi writes the information down. When he's finished, he walks it to Paanchi and Zeram who stand at a distance.

The three of them talk.

Paanchi and Zeram nod, acknowledging their instructions.

Paanchi takes the paper, placing it in a bag.

Both men run down the path toward Zarahemla.

Seeing their condition, Nephi doesn't want to push the women any further for the day. He sends some of his students to dispose of the bodies. The others set up camp off the trail among the trees. There is no fire to draw attention. Few words are said.

The women stay huddled as a group around Ziva. They're alert to anyone who approaches.

Supplies are left for the women.

The men keep their distance. They guard the area, keeping the women safe.

The women set up camp with the supplies that are left.

Kelev remains next to Ziva.

Ziva sits, petting the big dog. She knows Lib sent Kelev to protect and reassure her.

Nephi walks toward the women to deliver a message.

Seeing him, the women stop setting up camp. They rush to huddle around Ziva.

Nephi stops. He hollers, "Eat, drink, and rest yourselves. We will travel to Zarahemla in the morning. The men will keep their distance. You are safe."

ZIVA ROLLS AWAY TO A crouch. Her knife is drawn, ready to defend herself.

The other women, seeing Ziva, jump away, ready to run.

Lib stops. He frowns at her actions. He hollers, "Ziva. We need to talk."

Ziva blinks several times before recognizing him. She nods and stands. Her body's muscles scream at her. She winces. Dropping the knife and curling into a ball.

Lib rushes to her side.

Women scatter.

Ziva forces herself to a sitting position.

"Are you well?" Deep concern overtakes Lib's face as he visually combs her body for injury without touching her.

"My body's sore. That's all." She pushes his hands away. "I need to stand and move."

Lib tries to help her to her feet.

Ziva pushes him away.

Without help getting upright, Ziva steps away from him.

Lib frowns at her. Picking up the knife on the ground, he hands the knife's handle to her.

She grabs it, keeping the knife in her hand.

He turns to the women pointing and informs them, "If you're hungry, there is some dried food in bags there. The waterskins are filled. Take care of your needs. We'll leave for Zarahemla as soon as everyone is ready." The women move as a tightknit group to the food and drink left by Lib, leaving Ziva and Lib alone.

Ziva sheathes her knife and returning it to her pocket. "Who has Tokal?"

*Ziva sounds more like herself.* "Sariah," Lib takes a step.

Ziva stiffens.

Lib stops. "Although, I suspect she has help from Inna and Tanna."

Ziva steps back.

Pain covers Lib's face.

She regrets her choice, but she isn't ready for anyone to touch her. Ziva swallows and tries to smile. "I don't ever want to be separated from Tokal and you again, but I need some time."

"You don't?" Surprise rings his words. disgusted with himself, he asks, "Even when I couldn't protect you in the market?"

Ziva's eyes meet his. "Yes."

Lib blinks several times. "I want you by my side as well."

Her eyes drop, hiding her relief after all that has happened. She can add loyal to his characteristics.

Lib waits until Ziva looks at him. "Are you well?"

She sees the concern in his eyes. Ziva blinks her tears away, bites her lip, and nods.

"Before we travel today, I need you to sit and let me check your injuries . . . and mend your clothing. Do you trust me?"

She doesn't look down, not wanting to see the damage to her body or her clothing. She swallows and nods. She sits careful of her injuries. Her body starts shaking.

"Ziva, I need to get close to you. Are you good with that?"

She swallows her fear and nods.

In a light and soothing voice, Lib talks of Tokal, taking slow steps. Between anecdotes about Tokal, which cause her to chuckle, he explains what he's doing while he dresses her injuries. With a needle and thread, he mends her tattered outfit. *If only it was just as easy to mend their relationship.*

When Lib's done with the task, he searches her face. "Are you well enough to travel?"

Ziva's eyes meet his, finding strength, kindness, and support within them. She gives him a tentative smile. "Yes." Her voice shakes.

His hand moves to a bag at his waist. He pulls out the lost necklace and bracelet and places them on his outstretched hand for her to see.

Recognizing the items, her mouth drops open. She thought she would never see them again. She never thought she'd see Lib or Tokal again. She peers at him with a question in her eyes.

He shakes his head. "Later. I just wanted you to know that I have these."

Tears come to her eyes. Her gaze falters. "I can't. I can't at this moment."

"I understand," he soothes. "I'll hold them until you're ready." The necklace and bracelet are returned to the sack. When he's done, he holds out a hand, palm up, and waits.

Ziva's hand trembles as she moves to place her hand in his.

He doesn't dare move his fingers. Grateful that she trusts him enough to touch him. Lib looks at her. "Let's go home."

Close to tears, she swallows and nods.

Lib reassures her with a smile, giving strength to her battered soul. "Let me help you stand."

She allows him.

Without word, he walks away.

She takes a shaky breath before heading to the others, not saying more about the exchange that just occurred.

Ziva stands guard for the women.

The men pack everything up. They head out.

The women follow.

Ziva and Lib bring up the rear.

Like before, the sun is passed its zenith, when they reach the Sidon River.

Paanchi and Zeram greet them at the mouth of the path.

Nephi talks in private with Paanchi and Zeram. He turns to the men with him, motioning them on.

The women reach Nephi and stop.

Nephi smiles and motions them closer. "Be very quiet. Follow us as we move down the bank of the river to where your parents wait for you."

The women's faces light up with smiles. Hands clamp over their mouths to contain their excitement.

Nodding approval at their quiet response, Nephi turns and follows Paanchi and Zeram, who lead the way.

After a short walk down the bank of the river, a group of people gather. They look to be merchants getting ready to travel. The women's steps slow.

Ziva shies away.

Lib stops her. "It's good Ziva. The women need your strength.

Ziva glances at her husband. She pushes forward.

The women follow.

Parents' faces come into view, searching the people walking down the bank for their child.

One by one, a breath catches then a woman scurries into the arms of their parents.

Ziva stops to watch them. She smiles at the reunion she's so fortunate to see.

Lib stands behind her.

Once all women are in the care of their parents, Nephi and the other students join Ziva and Lib.

When Nephi reaches her side, he watches the reunion taking place. "This is your doing, Ziva."

Ziva peers at all of the men around her. She chokes out, "I couldn't have gotten them here without all of you. Thank you."

Nephi nods in acknowledgement. "There is someone that wants to see you."

Ziva's eyebrows scrunch together.

Nephi chuckles at her questioning gaze. "Come." He doesn't touch her but leads her forward.

Lib and the others following behind her. They pass the reunion taking place, moving further South into the group of merchants.

Ziva stops. She can't believe her eyes. She blinks a few times and looks again.

Sitting on the ground near a tree are Sariah and a small boy. They toss a rag ball back and forth.

Ziva shoots forward, despite her injured state. She falls to her knees a few feet away, waiting for the boy to see her.

Hearing some noise, Tokal's head swivels up and recognition comes to his face. His toy is forgotten. He cries out in delight, running into his mother's outstretched arms as fast as his little legs can carry him.

Ziva falls to her side with the force of the impact as they hug each other.

He complains about her absence.

She soothes him.

Lib helps her sit with him.

Tears stream down her face.

When Ziva and Tokal settle, she glances at Sariah and Nephi, thanking them for everything with a single nod.

They smile at her.

She realizes that something isn't right, and her brows crash together, her eyes dart to Nephi. "What's happening?"

"Cezoram, Chief Judge of Zarahemla, has been murdered. Because of this, Lamanite's are no longer allowed in the city. They haven't found who did it, but the city is in chaos," Nephi informs her. "Paanchi and Zeram, with the help of their parents, have spent the night arranging travel plans for all those that need to return home, which includes you. Sit and rest yourselves while the other families leave before we say our final goodbyes."

Ziva's eyes meet Lib's. "What's a chief judge?"

"Chief judges are like kings; except they are put in office by the voice of the people."

"They think a Lamanite had something to do with it, so all Lamanites are expelled from the city. If any are found inside the city, they'll be arrested, no matter how long they've lived there," Paanchi says.

"I don't think it was a Lamanite," Zeram shakes his head, "but have no way to prove it."

Compassion for those expelled from the city make Ziva speak. "It wasn't Lamanites. I overheard a merchant and a military leader talking about it. That was when I was taken."

"What did they say?"

"They were talking about the plan." Ziva breathes, wishing she could have helped prevent it. "The plan to kill the chief judge. I'm sorry that it was carried out."

"I have some food for all of you," Sariah informs them, changing the subject.

Nephi touches Lib's arm, and they nod to one another, parting ways.

Nephi, Paanchi, and Zeram leave the group.

Lib sits down at Ziva's side.

Tokal throws himself from his mother's lap into his father's arms, making them chuckle.

Sariah smiles to the small family. "Rest yourselves. I'll be back with some food." Turning to the other men around her, she instructs, "Follow me and I will take you to get some food."

While Sariah and the astronomers are gone, Ziva, Lib, and Tokal sit together as a family, sharing a waterskin.

Ziva looks up to see Alissah, Anath, and Didi, followed by their parents.

Ziva and Lib stand to receive them.

When Alissah reaches her, she asks, "You're Joined?"

Ziva smiles. "Yes. This is my husband Lib, and this is Tokal."

At that moment, Tokal throws himself at Ziva.

Ziva's breath catches as pain shoots through her body. She catches her little boy, bringing him to her chest.

Lib makes sure Ziva has Tokal before letting him go.

Tokal's little arms wrap around her neck. He plants an open-mouthed kiss on her cheek.

"He's cute." Didi touches Tokal's hand.

Tokal smiles at her.

Ziva smiles at Tokal's antics and grins at the young women. "I think so."

"We wanted to say thank you for taking care of us through . . . all of this," Anath stammers.

Ziva pauses as a quick recollection takes place in her mind. She swallows, pushing her feelings away. "We took care of each other."

Didi's parents speak. "Thank you for taking care of our Didi, and for bringing her back to us."

"We did it together." Ziva gives a glimpse of a smile. "I'm glad she's back in your care."

Didi's father touches his daughter's arm.

"Bye, Ziva."

Ziva nods, watching Didi and her family depart.

"Bye, Ziva," Alissah gives her a swift, gentle hug.

"Thank you." Alissah's parents convey their heartfelt gratitude before parting with their daughter.

"Anath," the mother calls to her daughter.

"Bye, Ziva." Anath nods in unspoken appreciation.

"Thank you for bringing my baby home," Anath's mother contributes, blinking back her tears.

"Thank you," Anath's father finishes, smiling and nodding to Ziva and Lib.

Both nod their acknowledgement. Anath's family turns and leaves.

The astronomy students return.

Sariah carries two bowls of food

Nephi follows. He stops, keeping his distance. "Ziva, let me have Tokal while the two of you eat."

Lib takes Tokal from Ziva.

Nephi receives him. He tosses Tokal in the air.

The child squeals his delight.

"Be careful, Nephi." Sariah touches her husband's shoulder. "Tokal finished eating a few minutes before you all showed up. You don't want it all over you." She hands the filled bowls to Ziva and Lib. "Sit, everyone, and talk. No one is leaving until they're ready." They sit in a circle.

Lib examines his astronomy brothers. "Why aren't you all eating?"

"We already ate while you were saying farewell to the women." Paanchi grins. "Eat."

Ziva and Lib glance at the other.

Lib shrugs.

They take a bite of the delicious venison and legumes.

Small talk starts around the group while Ziva and Lib eat.

When they finish the contents of their bowls, Paanchi begins again. "As we explained before, Cezoram, the Chief Judge of Zarahemla, has been murdered. They don't know who assassinated him, so they've closed the city to Lamanites. Zeram and I spent the night working with our parents to help all of you prepare to return to your homes a little earlier than planned. As you know, my father makes a fine wine, which is sold everywhere. Knowing where you're from, we have put together some trustworthy merchants to take you home using the shortest routes possible. My father will be here shortly with the merchants. You will leave with them as soon as possible before things potentially get worse in the city."

"What about our stuff back at our room?" Melek asks.

"Sariah helped. She gathered everything from each of your areas and packed it all up. Your belongings are all here for you," Zeram informs them. "Plus, some added items from us." He grins.

"Sounds like you're trying to get rid of us," Jashon teases.

Zeram chuckles, "In a way it does sound like it." His smile disappears, "But . . . know that you are all welcome at our homes if ever you find yourself back in Zarahemla when times are more stable." He takes a breath. "You're my brothers," he looks over at Ziva, ". . . and sister."

"Even though you gave me such a hard time, if ever you're my way, please come and visit," Melek chokes, trying to control his emotions.

"Same here." Echoes within the group. A few sniffs are heard.

"Don't forget an old man and his wife." Nephi smiles as Tokal tweaks his nose.

Everyone laughs.

Nephi removes Tokal's hand. "You'll all make great astronomers and do your families and cities proud."

Turning to Lib, Amnor says, "Take care of our sister and Tokal."

Lib nods in agreement.

Amnor swivels his head to Ziva. "Take care of our brother."

Ziva smiles. "You know I will." A tear escapes her eye. She brushes it away. "I'm going to miss all of you."

"We know," Jashon grins at Ziva.

"Melek, I found your knife." Ziva sets down her empty bowl and digs in her pocket. "Let me give it to you." She pulls the knife out, handing it over.

"You keep it, Ziva. I already purchased another one at the market." Melek pulls it out to show her.

Ziva grins. The weapon is hidden in her pocket. "Thank you."

"Everyone."

All eyes turn to Paanchi. He stands next to an older version of himself. "This is my father, Ephah. As sad as it may be, the time has come for all of us to return home."

Everyone acknowledges the man.

Ephah gazes at the group sitting in a circle. "My son thinks well of each of you. He will miss your presence. When you're done with your parting, come see me and we will get you started. I will be over here with the merchants." He turns and walks a few paces away from the group.

The party stands as individual farewells are given. One by one, each student walks to Ephah, where he links them to a merchant, and they depart. Ziva and Lib stand back with Sariah and Nephi, watching the cluster get smaller.

"Give me Tokal while they ready themselves," Sariah tells Nephi.

Tokal is passed to her a final time.

Sariah hugs the little boy.

Tokal cries for his parents, thinking that they're leaving him again.

Sariah soothes him while Nephi and Lib load the pack with Tokal's things.

Ziva stands with Sariah, holding hands with Tokal.

Lib places the pack on his back.

"Lib, pass the cloth. I can carry him."

Lib scrutinizes Ziva. "Are you sure?"

"Yes. Put him on my back."

Sariah helps Ziva settle the boy on her back and tie him there.

"Thank you, Sariah." Ziva grabs Sariah's hand. "I will miss you."

Sariah squeezes Ziva's hand, trying to keep her emotions under control. "I'm so going to miss you both." She sniffs.

"Thank you for everything. Please let everyone back home know we wish we could have said goodbye to them too."

Lib gives Lib and Sariah a hug. He opens his hand and waits.

Ziva places hers in his.

Together they tread toward Ephah.

Ephah smiles at them. "This is Amos. I trust him to take you home. You can rest easy."

Amos has black hair with gray around the temples and a receding hairline. Crow's-feet around his sparkling brown eyes show his happy disposition.

The only person Ziva trusts right now is Lib. She palms the knife in her pocket.

Amos smiles at Ziva and Lib. "We'll have you back in Uthal in a matter of days."

Lib looks from Amos to Ephah. "Our supplies?"

"Already packed and loaded in the canoe," Ephah says. "Come this way, and you can see for yourselves."

Hand-in-hand Lib and Ziva follow Ephah and Amos to the river's edge.

Ten long boats full of supplies and a multitude of men wait for them.

Ziva stands closer to Lib, looking wary.

Ephah stops at the first canoe and points to the lashed-down mound. "Your things are tied there. You will be in this boat with Amos."

Lib nods.

Ziva and Lib share a look, fear evident in Ziva's eyes.

Lib places an arm around her.

Ziva stiffens.

Lib says to the men, "Will you give us a moment?" He drops his arm.

"Of course." Ephah smiles with understanding.

When the men are out of hearing, Lib speaks to Ziva. "I've traveled from Uthal to Zarahemla by canoe. It will take two days. We can do this for two more days."

"I'm not sure I can travel two more days."

"I will be with you and will help you." Lib squeezes her hand in a caress. "Our return isn't by foot. We're taking a canoe, which will be a lot easier for you."

"My concern is not only for traveling." Ziva's eyes won't me Lib's.

Lib peers at her thinking. "You fear the men."

Ziva nods. She exhales, relieved that he understands her.

Lib scrutinizes those under the merchant. "They will keep their distance. I won't leave your side unless you approve of it." He takes a breath. "Will that work for you?"

Tokal on Ziva's back watches Ephah and Amos.

After a few moments, Ziva raises her head. With a tense look she nods her assent.

Lib motions to the men to return. When they arrive, he explains the conditions which must be met.

Ephah and Amos agree to his conditions.

"Thank you, Ephah, for making all this happen."

Amos notifies the others that they are about to leave.

Lib helps Ziva into the canoe.

The other men in the party move toward their canoes.

Amos and Lib push the canoe out into the river. They climb into the boat and start paddling down the river.

Nephi and Sariah stand on the shore waving at them.

Ziva bites her lip. Her fingers clamp onto the sides of the canoe. She's unable to let go to wave, one last time, to the receding forms on shore because she worries the boat will tip over. After some time, she gets used to the movement. Her fingers relax some. She starts to look around.

The river is swift. Soon she can no longer see Zarahemla. This is so much better than the many days of walking to and from Arnac, though the canoe is confining.

Their transportation veers down a smaller river that forks off Sidon, taking them deeper into the forest. The soothing cadence of the oars and the peaceful scenery lull her. She closes her eyes.


SOMETHING WAKENS HER. THE CANOES move to shore for the night. The little family is fed and left to rest near one of the fires. The others stay away.

Tokal sleeps next to Ziva.

Lib leans against a tree on Ziva's other side.

Ziva stares at the river in the distance. Her arms are wrapped around her knees. "How did you find me?"

"Kelev. When I couldn't find you, I met up with the others. We separated into two groups. I retrieved Kelev and went back to the market with Paanchi and Zeram to see if we could find where they took you. The only things we found were your bracelet and necklace that a vendor had for sale." Lib takes a breath. He throws a rock. He is silent as he works to control of his emotions. "With help from Paanchi, Zeram, and of course Kelev, we were able to obtain some information from the merchant. We took your necklace and bracelet." He searches her face in the firelight to see if he needs to stop.

No emotions show on Ziva's face.

"With the information obtained, we knew you would leave the city that night. We gathered supplies and left at dawn.

Kelev found your trail on the bank. We ran to catch up to you."

Ziva tamps down her demons. "I'm glad you found me—us."

"Sleep, Ziva. You're safe."

"I can't." Ziva blows out a breath. "I'm scared. I'm trying not to be, but I am."

"Come here. Let me hold you." Lib lifts an arm for her to move into.

She scrutinizes Lib. She bites her lip. In slow, cautious movements she settles into his side.

Lib drops his arm at the same pace she moved.

When Lib's arm settles at her side, Ziva stiffens.

"Am I hurting you?"

"No." Ziva stares at the river.

"A man hurt you." Lib says with understanding as a combination of emotions sweep through him. He battles them down, trying to remain calm on the surface, to support Ziva. He thinks about what she endured. He wanted to keep her safe but failed miserably in the market.

Ziva doesn't say a word. She starts shaking.

Lib lifts his arm away.

A forceful "No!" is heard in the dark. "Don't take your arm away."

Lib settles his arm around her again.

A sob escapes from Ziva. She tries to stop it.

"Let it out, Ziva. Tell me what happened." he kisses her forehead.

She sniffs. "If I cry, I'll awake Tokal. Just hold me so I feel safe."

They sit together.

Lib holds Ziva while she shakes. He pulls a blanket up around her. He doesn't say a word. Just offers his support. When the shaking subsides, he whispers, "Did he breach you?"

Ziva stiffens at the question. A brittle laugh rips the air.

Tokal stirs.

The noise stops.

Tokal settles.

"He tried . . . I fought . . . he died. Please, just hold me."

Lib exhales in relief. "I'm here, Ziva. You're safe. Rest. I'll keep you safe." Lib kisses her forehead again.

Ziva snuggles down, hearing his steady heartbeat. She closes her eyes. The fresh, earthy smell of Lib combines to chase away her demons.

AFTER A HEARTY MEAL, THE canoe trip resumes.

Amos smiles in the wind at the front of the boat. "We are making good time. If things continue as they are, tomorrow morning, we'll be in Uthal."

By midday, Tokal is cranky from being confined to Ziva's back. They stop for a meal.

Tokal is removed from his mother's back. He runs around playing a game of catch with Kelev.

When Tokal gets tired, Lib bundles him to Ziva's back.

The canoe trip continues.

Later in the day, a thunderclap is heard from the blue sky above.

Frightened, Tokal cries.

Lib tries, unsuccessfully, to comfort him.

A steady sheet of rain falls.

"We have to find shelter." Amos yells over the noise of the storm and Tokal's wails. "The canoes will fill otherwise."

The boats head for the next nearest stretch of land to wait out the storm.

When they reach earth, Ziva is helped out of the canoe by Lib. He accompanies her away from the water.

A soaked Ziva sits under a tree.

"I need to help the others before our things are damaged." Lib says over the storm. "Kelev can stay to guard the two of you."

Ziva nods her approval.

Lib helps the others.

Kelev stands guard.

Ziva removes a miserable, wet Tokal from her back and holds him.

The men unload their haul, moving it toward the tree line away from the river. They return for the canoe, placing them upside down over their supplies.

The men huddle, shivering under the trees a distance from Ziva, waiting for the storm to pass.

Lib returns soaked to the bone. "It looks like we'll be camping here tonight. The spring storm has made it unsafe on the river. We don't have any dry kindling to even start a fire. I have some dried fruit and meat and a blanket for the night." Lib pulls the blanket out of the bag, laying it around a shivering Ziva and Tokal. "Get some rest, the best you can. We'll need to leave early tomorrow."

"Take off your shirt so you don't catch a chill, and come join us here." Ziva demands over the rain.

Lib, shivering, pulls off his shirt. He tosses it over a limb before settling next to Ziva.

She throws part of the blanket around him.

Tokal crawls into his arms.

After the rain stops, Lib keeps guard over his sleeping family, sitting against a tree while Kelev lies next to him.

Tokal is draped over the dog's stomach.

Ziva sleeps on her coat, cuddled up on the other side of Lib. The blanket covers portions of each of them.

While they sleep, Lib deals with a myriad of emotions regarding Ziva's abduction, abuse, and his failure to keep her safe. He swipes away the tears that escape his eyes. After some time, he finally finds some peace.

Kelev growls, informing Lib that someone is approaching.

Lib opens his eyes, allowing them to adjust.

Ziva moves to her feet and crouches next to him, ready to respond to the threat.

Lib touches her arm to reassure her.

Hearing the dog's growl, Amos stops. "Lib. It's Amos. Awaken your family. We need to continue our travel. Today, we reach Uthal."

Ziva extends herself to stand. "Are you sure?"

Amos chuckles. "Yes. As soon as you are ready, we'll continue."

Ziva, excited to hear that they are almost to Uthal, gets herself ready.

With Tokal in Ziva's care, Lib dons his shirt. "May I help them?"

"Yes."

Lib assists the men with the canoes.

Ziva and Tokal join Lib.

They continue down the river.

The morning birds' flit, singing in the trees, while the oars break the water in a rhythmic dance. The air smells fresh and clean.

To Ziva, it seems like she's been in the continue a long time. However, the early morning sun lights up the sky and warms the air. They are drifting around a bend.

Amos points and shouts back at them, "Look."

Ziva gazes up to see a city of vertical wooden walls away from the riverbank. They have animal carvings on the exterior. "Uthal!" she exclaims. "We're here!"

Lib grins at the excitement on her face.

The canoes make their way to shore.

# TOGETHER

Arriving at Uthal's gates deteriorates Ziva's mood, as memories of the past overtake her. She stops in her tracks.

The merchant stops on the other side of the gates with a questioning gaze.

Lib, realizing that Ziva has stopped, turns her to him. He lifts her chin seeking her eyes.

Ziva continues to look at the ground.

Lib waits.

Ziva's eyes find his.

He reads what is contained in their depths. Her memories, punctuated by fear, pain, and anguish are choking her. He pulls her into his arms. "Let it go, Ziva. You're safe," he soothes. "I'm here. I'm not going anywhere without the both of you." He pulls back and their gaze meets. "You are not alone."

An unsteady smile crosses her face. It's swallowed with the lump in her throat.

Lib kisses her forehead. "You've already conquered so much more. You can face this too." He holds her for a few moments before touching his forehead to hers and gazing into her eyes. "Are you with me?"

Ziva feels his warmth. It melts the fears in her heart. *Faith over fear* she reminds herself. She whispers, "Yes."

Lib takes her hand and kisses it.

Together, they cross into Uthal.

They travel through the streets.

Two men, sent by the merchant, follow at a distance with their belongings.

Lib stops a door and opens it. He ushers all to enter.

Once in the courtyard, Amos's men set their belongings down according to Lib's instructions and depart.

Lib closes the door behind them. He returns to Ziva's side. He takes her hand and kisses it. "Come." he takes a step.

Ziva doesn't move. "Where are we?"

"This is my parents' home. We'll stay here until I can make our own home."

"I shouldn't be here."

He takes a breath, exhaling slowly, trying to contain his excitement at seeing his family again, but instead deals with Ziva's fear. "You have every right to be here." He takes a breath. "Whatever happens, we'll deal with it together."

She examines him.

Lib's excitement is mixed with concern for her.

*He has always kept his word.* Ziva nods, trusting him.

"That's my girl." Lib smiles. He gives Ziva an affectionate squeeze. Opening the door to the home, he enters.

Two people greet him in the main room.

Lib's mother, recognizing him first, flies into his arms.

Lib feels like she's squeezing the air from his lungs.

"Easy, Mother. Let the boy breathe," Lib's father stands at their side.

Lib's mother releases him and swipes at the tears rolling down her cheeks.

When his mother steps back, Lib and his father embrace, patting each other on the shoulders before separating.

Both men work to contain their emotions.

"No letter letting us know you were coming?" Lib's mother chides.

Lib chuckles. "Didn't know we could be coming back as soon as we did." Turning his attention to Ziva, he calls her to his side. "Ziva, these are my parents." Pointing to his father, "This is Heth, and . . ." pointing to his mother, "this is Abana." Putting his arm around Ziva, he pulls her closer. "Ziva is my wife," he proudly announces. "And the little imp behind her is Tokal. Your grandson."

Abana, a woman with brown eyes and dark-brown hair sprinkled with gray, is the first one to react. "Oh. Oh!" She rushes forward. "Ziva, you must be so tired from your journey. Let's get your babe off your back. You're all probably tired from your trip."

Lib grabs Tokal, holding him while Ziva unties the heavy bundle from her back.

Abana tries to take Tokal from Lib.

Tokal's arms and legs move back and forth, trying to get into Lib's arms. He screams.

Lib holds Tokal to him, soothing him.

Tokal climbs further up on Lib's chest, holding tightly to his father's neck.

Lib loosens the strangulating hold around his neck. "Easy, Mother. You're scaring him." Lib holds out an arm to slow her down.

"I only want to hold my grandchild."

"They've both been through a lot. You must move slow until they get to know you better." Lib takes Ziva's hand and has her sit down. Once she's seated, he places Tokal in her arms.

Tokal stands in Ziva's arms and holds tight to his mother's neck.

Ziva pats his back. "Be still, Tokal."

Taking his mother's hand, Lib moves her to sit next to Ziva.

"Let Tokal come to you." Lib sets the heavy pack he's wearing on the floor next to Ziva. He touches her shoulder. "I'm going to get our things moved inside."

Ziva nods her approval.

Lib gives her shoulder a gentle, affectionate squeeze in thanks. Lib touches his father's arm. "Will you help me?"

"Of course." Heth follows his son out the door.

Ziva chooses a toy and gives it to Tokal.

He grabs it. He sits and plays.

Ziva pulls a clean cloth from the pack. She lays out the bundling cloth, then lays Tokal on it.

This he understands. He plays with his toy.

When Ziva is done, he rolls over and pushes himself to his feet, coming to stand next to his mother.

Abana breaks the silence. "Where are you from, Ziva?"

Ziva returns, keeping her attention on Tokal. "Uthal."

Abana examines the girl with wide eyes. "From here?"

"Yes."

"When did you go on the Journey?"

"Last season."

"I don't recall seeing you among the single women that returned from Arnac." Abana recounts more to herself.

"I didn't return with them. My mother's illness kept us at Arnac, so I started the Challenge there."

"The Challenge? But the single women are still at Arnac." Abana's voice rises. "The child?"

"Is mine!" Lib interrupts, walking to stand next to Ziva. He's ready to defend his family.

"But son, how can that be?"

"I'm taking my wife and child to my room where we can rest. We'll talk more later!"

"Easy Lib. Your mother is only trying to understand everything. She didn't mean any offense," Heth places a hand on his wife's shoulder.

Lib takes a deep breath, getting his anger under control before he tries again. "Look. We are tired. Let us get some rest and we'll tell you all."

"As you wish, son." Heth turns to Ziva. "I'm happy to meet you, Ziva." Lib reaches down and helps Ziva to her feet.

"I'm happy to meet you both." A quick smile crosses Ziva's face.

Lib takes Tokal from Ziva. He reaches for Ziva's hand.

Ziva follows as she's pulled down the hall.

Lib whistles.

Kelev jumps to her feet and trots to Lib.

When inside his room, Lib sets Tokal down. He turns to her. "Are you all right?"

Ziva pushes him away. "Your mother is only trying to understand how we came to be."

"You're right. I can't deal with any judgement at this moment."

"Judgement?"

He takes a deep breath and rubs his eyes. "My mother is quick to judge before knowing all the facts. I'm tired. I don't want any of us to deal with that at this moment."

Ziva notices how tired he looks. "You better sleep. I'll stay up with Tokal."

"But what about you?"

Ziva smiles. "We'll be fine."

Lib settles on his bed.

Ziva sits on the floor with Tokal.

Lib falls asleep.

Tokal is wide awake and full of energy, curious to discover what's in this new place.

Ziva grabs the rag ball. She picks up Tokal. Together they leave the room. She tiptoes, heading for the front door to the courtyard.

Kelev trotting behind.

Hearing talking coming from the main room, she makes herself known. "Tokal, we must be quiet so Dada can sleep."

The little boy looks at her with vague comprehension and innocent eyes.

Arriving at the main room, Ziva smiles and in a hesitant voice asks, "Lib's sleeping. Tokal has lots of energy. Do you mind if we play in the courtyard?"

"Of course you can," Heth stands, coming her way.

Ziva steps back.

Heth stops. "We're glad you're here, Ziva. Make yourself at home."

Ziva gives a brief smile and nods. Not knowing what else to do, she moves to the front door and exits.

Kelev trots behind.

Outside, Ziva takes a deep breath, trying to calm her beating heart. She closes her eyes and hugs the little boy to her.

Tokal squirms.

Ziva places on the ground. She gives him his ball.

Tokal smiles and tosses it. He chases after his toy.

Ziva smiles as she watches Tokal and Kelev play together.

Lib's father joins her outside.

Ziva takes a step back.

Heth stops. "My son is right—you do look tired, and . . . you have a myriad of bruises. Take a chair, Ziva and rest." He picks a seat that is nearest to him. His chin juts up. "Did my son do that to you?"

Ziva looks around and settles in the chair furthest away from him. "No."

Abana shows up with some water and cups on a tray.

Tokal, seeing liquid being poured, runs to Ziva.

Ziva helps him drink from her cup.

When Tokal finishes, he returns to his game with Kelev.

Ziva drinks. It quenches her parched throat. A grateful sigh escapes.

"Would you like to tell us your story?" Heth asks.

His words remind her of something Lib would say and how he would say it. One side of her mouth curves up. "My story is long . . . but I'll give you a brief version of it." She pauses, thinking.

Tokal comes her way, handing her the ball. She tosses it and Tokal squeals in delight, chasing after the ball with Kelev. "Last year, I went on the Journey from Uthal to Arnac." Ziva explains who she is and how Tokal and Lib came into her life.

The little boy plays with Kelev. He interrupts the story for more water or to touch his mother.

Ziva looks down and swallows before returning to face Lib's parents. "I made a mistake, and Lib and I were forced to Join." She searches their faces for any sign of rejection. "I'm sorry about that." Not finding any, she checks on her son.

Tokal throws the ball. With a smile on his face, he chases after it.

Ziva finds strength in her son and finishes her story.

Tokal reaches for the cup.

Ziva grabs the beverage before the contents spill. She helps Tokal drink.

When he's done, Tokal races back to his ball. He picks it up, bringing it to his mother.

Ziva tosses the ball.

Tokal flashes another smile. He chases the ball.

Lib's parents watch Tokal having fun. They digest Ziva's words.

Ziva doesn't break the silence. She fills the empty cup she has and sits down. She takes a drink.

Tokal runs back with the ball, dropping it in Abana's lap. He smiles up at her.

Abana smiles back. She tosses the ball.

Tokal laughs, taking off after it.

"So, you were Joined before winter? By whom?" Abana keeps her attention on Tokal.

Ziva glances at the woman. "Yes. Nephi joined us."

Abana meets Ziva's gaze. "The astronomy teacher?"

"Yes."

Heth scratches his head. "What of your father?"

Ziva glances at Heth. She looks at the ground. "He died long ago."

"You're mother?"

She shakes her head, answering Abana's question.

Tokal returns throwing himself at her.

Ziva picks him up, setting him on her lap.

Tokal reaches for the cup again. Water spills.

Ziva stops it. She helps him with another drink. When he's done, he turns himself around and lays his head on her shoulder, indicating he's ready for a nap.

Ziva pats his back.

Tokal falls asleep.

Heth marvels at what has been told him. He suspects what she said is true. Nevertheless, he would like to confirm it with Lib. "You've been through a lot, Ziva. With Tokal sleeping, perhaps you would like to join my son."

Ziva gives a tired sigh. "Thank you." Ziva stands with her heavy load and heads for the door.


WITHIN A COUPLE OF DAYS, life seems to settle into a routine.

"Ziva, I need to purchase some food at the market. Would you like to join me?"

The day is bright and warm, with a cool breeze.

In the room with Lib, Ziva says, "I don't want to go to the market with your mother."

"Why?"

"I just don't."

"Ziva, you've done a remarkable job overcoming every obstacle in your way. You can overcome this fear as well." He kisses her forehead. "I will go with you." He pulls out the necklace and bracelet.

Ziva looks at them. Her gaze meets his. She nods.

Without word, Lib ties the bracelet and necklace in place. He holds her. He breaks the connection with a tender kiss on her forehead.

When they reach the main room, Abana notices Lib's necklace and the intricate bracelet. "You have an exquisite bracelet. Who made it?"

Ziva touches the bracelet on her wrist. She smiles to herself. "My father."

"His love for his daughter shows in his work."

Ziva looks at Abana. She smiles in thanks.

The little family and Lib's parents take the trip to the market.

Tokal is attached to Ziva's back.

Lib holds Ziva's hand at all times.

Ziva faces another fear. She keeps Melek's knife in her pocket.

Lib encourages her to try new foods and to shop.

Ziva keeps her guard up, preferring to follow her mother-in-law. *Faith over fear, like Ami taught me.* She repeats it over and over, trying to overcome her demons.

"Ziva? Is that you?"

The familiar voice of Ami turns Ziva's head. Their eyes meet. Ziva releases Lib's hand and heads for Ami's arms.

Ami hugs Ziva. "When did you get back?"

"Who's this?" Tovah questions, seeing a child on Ziva's back.

"I'm happy to see you. I arrived back a few days ago. This is Tokal, my son."

"Tokal? Isn't that the guard the queen gave you. He was your best friend?" Chaya asks.

"Oh, you looked to be Joined." Mazal scans the area. "Where's your mother?"

Her friends notice a man and two others standing near Ziva.

Ziva's eyes falter for a moment. "She isn't here."

Frema frowns and gasps, "You're bruised, Ziva. What happened?"

"I was injured."

"It looks like someone beat you," Ami jokes.

Ziva's eyes drop again, and she chokes out, "Someone did."

"Oh, Ziva. I'm so sorry," Ami sputters.

Changing the subject, Mazal asks, "Who are these people behind you? Did one of them beat you?"

Ziva is startled by her question. "Oh." She turns including Lib and his parents. "No, they didn't hurt me." She motions for Lib and his parents to come forward.

Lib arrives at Ziva's side.

Ziva smiles at her friends. "This is my husband, Lib." She pulls him closer to her. "Lib, this is Ami, Tovah, Frema, Chaya, and Mazal. We met on the Journey last year."

"I'm happy to meet you all."

While they are talking some guards come. The gather around, then reach for Ziva.

Lib pushes them away. "What's going on?"

"She's to go to the palace." The guard points to Ziva. "It has been reported that she was overheard saying she took the Challenge and is back in the city before the others have returned from their Journey. She must stand before the king."

"She's, my wife!"

"She's my friend," is heard from multiple people.

"You can either come peacefully and stand with her, or you can stay here. The choice is yours, but *she's* to be presented to the king." The guards extricate Ziva from Lib.

Ziva loses her grasp on her husband's hand. "Lib!" Ziva shrieks.

She's hauled off in the arms of two guards, another guard in front and one in back.

Lib follows, trying to reach her. "I'm right here. I won't leave you."

The guard keeps himself between the woman and man.

Lib yells at the guards, "She has a child on her back, and she's already injured. Be gentle with them both."

The first guard slows his step, making it easier for Ziva to keep her feet under her.

Ami, Lib, and his parents to keep up with them.

On the way out of the market after running errands for his father, Prince Enon sees Lib. This is his close former school friend that has been away learning astronomy. "Lib. You're back?" he calls, trying to get his attention.

Hearing Enon shout his name, Lib turns his head and spots his good friend. Knowing that Enon will help, Lib stays with Ziva, following the guards. He hollers, "Enon. They're taking my wife!"

Enon drops what's in his hands. He jogs to catch up to his friend. His plain clothed guards bring up the rear. "What is going on?" Enon asks a worried Lib.

"They're taking her to the king."

"My father's a reasonable man. I'll go with you," Enon matches Lib's pace. "Why are they taking her to the king?"

"Because she took the Challenge and is back in the city before the next group of new women have returned from their Journey." Abana provides, loud enough so that everyone can hear.

"Quiet, wife!"

THEY ENTER THE GREAT HALL where King Gilgal sits, dealing with city issues. The building looks the same to Ziva as she recalls it from her last visit many years ago. She's brought forward to stand before the king.

King Gilgal recognizes who stands before him. His eyes widen. Multiple speak.

Gilgal can't understand. He flicks his wrist.

"Quiet!" bellows the chief guard.

A soldier steps forward. "King Gilgal, this woman was taken in the market. She stated that she took the Challenge and is back in the city before her year is up."

Ami shouts, "She spoke this to me, sir. Her friend. Our friends are getting my parents."

Gilgal's disapproving eyebrow lifts as he looks at the young female.

Ami humbles herself before the king.

Gilgal turns his attention to Enon. "Son, what brings you here?"

"Lib is my friend. His wife is the one accused. I know that you are a wise and honorable king who'll administer mercy."

"My son, a good king must also obey the law."

Enon opens his mouth to speak.

Gilgal cuts him off, saying, "Let me speak, and you listen." He turns his attention toward Ziva. "Guards, move away from Ziva. She will remain where she is." He waits until the guards have distanced themselves from her. "Ziva, who are the other people with you?"

"Ami is my friend. I met her on the Journey." Pointing to Lib, she says, "Lib is my husband. We were Joined during the Challenge." Waving to the rest, she says, "And his parents, Heth and Abana."

"It looks as though you have a babe on your back. Is he yours?"

Ziva smiles. "Yes. His name is Tokal."

"That is the name of the guard we sent with you. The same boy who brought you to the palace the first time. What happened to him?"

Ziva cringes. She looks at the floor. "Dead . . ." Her voice cracks, laced with melancholy. She swallows. "By Gadianton."

"Your mother?"

"Dead," she returns in a tighter voice. She struggles to keep her emotions in check.

"How?" The king queries.

To Ziva it feels like a knife to the chest. Ziva looks up at King Gilgal. Tears sparkle in her eyes. "Gadianton."

"I see." The king takes a breath. With empathy, he continues. "I'm sorry that happened to Tokal and your mother. I'm happy to report that the assassin that pursued you as a child was finally found and dealt with while you were at Arnac."

"How?"

"He followed you to Arnac. Tokal found him and he was sent back to Uthal. He was tried and executed. Didn't Tokal tell you?"

Ziva shakes her head, trying to figure out when and how. "No. I never knew. What was his name?"

"His name?" The king looks to his guard.

"Kish," the guard supplies.

"Kish? He was one of the guards protecting us on the Journey." She spoke to him in the Hall at Arnac. *He could have killed me.* "I didn't remember him."

"Yes. He was caught. He confessed everything to several of the guards before he was transported back to Uthal."

The king continues his inquiry. "Explain how this child can be yours?"

Pulled out of her shocked state, Ziva looks up. "Gadianton killed his parents and placed him in my care."

"Do you not want this child?"

Ziva locks eyes with the king. With great heartfelt emotion answers his question. "I want this child. I love him."

"When were you Joined?"

"Before the winter."

"Who Joined you?"

"Nephi Joined us. He's my husband's astronomy teacher."

"Did this Joining take place by mutual agreement?"

Ziva's head falls forward. "No."

Lib shouts at the same time. "Yes. Ziva, remember we are in this together."

Ziva swallows. She lifts her head, but doesn't meet the king's direct gaze. "I made a mistake by following him to a river to retrieve his shirt, which Tokal had dirtied, so I could clean it. We were found together."

Gilgal notices a rosy hue on her cheeks. "Do you not want him as your husband?"

Ziva's eyes light up. Her eyes meet the king's. "I want my husband. He's the nicest, most loyal, patient man I have ever met. He listens to me and understands me, even when I don't understand myself. He supports me. He makes me feel safe."

"Those are quite a list of compliments." King Gilgal glances at Lib, then returns to Ziva. "Ziva, who put the bruises on your body?"

As though she's seeing them for the first time, Ziva looks at the ugly green and black bruises still on her wrists and arms. "Gadianton,"

The eyes of the king widen for a moment. Something is missing. His eyes squint to daggers. "I don't believe you."

Fire lights Ziva's eyes. "I don't care what you believe. The truth is the truth. I have always told you the truth. But for clarification, I will explain further." She takes a breath. "Less than a week ago, I disappeared. Stolen from my husband's side at the market in Zarahemla, because I overheard a plan to assassinate Chief Judge Cezoram. When I awoke, they marched other captive women and myself out of the city. Like animals to be sold. During that time, the women and I learned that Nephites had joined Gadianton and had infiltrated the government in Zarahemla. We escaped with our lives. We ran back to the city. They pursued us. Nephi, Lib, and my other astronomy brothers saved us. Saved me. When we returned to the river Sidon, we were informed that Cezoram was killed, murdered by someone. Lamanites were no longer welcome in the city. We returned to Uthal with a merchant."

"What is the merchant's name?"

"Amos."

The king lifts a finger.

Two guards disappear.

"How did you escape your captors?"

"One of the guards got . . . careless and began to . . . hurt me. I . . ." Ziva stammers, trying to breathe, and her anger dissolves as she relives the experience. Ziva turns pale, drowning in the memory and unable to breathe.

Lib comes to her side. He touches her forearm, pulling her out of the past.

Ziva recognizes him. She swallows the knot in her throat, allowing her to inhale air.

Seeing the color return to her face after taking a breath, Lib squeezes her hand. He turns toward King Gilgal, standing protectively in front of Ziva. "She killed him with a knife before freeing the other women and escaping."

The king examines Lib for a long time before speaking. "I want her to tell me."

"Why?" Lib throws back.

Enon puts a hand on his shoulder to stop him.

Lib brushes off his friend's hand. He steps forward as champion for Ziva. "She has been through so much, and you can see she's still recovering from her injuries. I told her that she would be safe in the market today and here we are." He raises his hand and waves it. "She's the bravest woman I have ever met. When something she loves is taken from her, she finds a way to move forward. Even through all her fear and loss, she stands. I don't think I would have the fortitude to do what she has done and survive. So, again I ask why. Why do you want to hear it from her mouth, when she can barely even talk to me about it?"

Silence reigns.

The guards move forward to remove Lib from the king's presence.

The king halts the soldiers with a wave of his hand.

They return to their stations.

"I have known Ziva for a very long time. She has been under my protection for many years as she has grown. In order for her to move forward with her life, she must work through her past until she understands she's not defined by it. She must take the steps necessary to change, making her life happier and more fulfilled." His eyes flick to the woman on trial. "Ziva?"

Ziva meets his gaze. She nods, and swallows. She understands she must say what happened. "The captain of the soldiers—my captors—he . . . he hit me over and over again. He jumped on me, choking me." The tears roll down her face, but her eyes don't leave the king's. "I tried to stop him . . ."

Lib takes her hand in his, infusing her with his strength. Inside, he cringes, hearing what she had to endure because he couldn't protect her.

"Melek, a young astronomy student, lost his knife on our way to Zarahemla. While held captive I found the weapon and hid it in my pocket." Ziva swallows. "I pulled the knife from my pocket. I stabbed him. When I came to myself . . . I freed the others, taking with me a bow and arrows. We ran . . ." She swallows. "We ran and I shot as many of our captors as I could before they could overtake us. Lib, Nephi, and the others showed up, stopping the rest."

A commotion occurs as guards step into the Great Hall with Amos, who is moved forward toward the king.

Amos, recognizing the Great Hall, falls on his hands and knees, kneeling next to Ziva before the king.

"This is the man Amos, the Nephite merchant," the guard announces.

"Amos, the Nephite merchant, how do you know Ziva and Lib?"

Amos scrutinizes Ziva and Lib, trying to figure out how to answer that will save his life. "Oh, Great King, I brought them with me from Zarahemla."

"Why?"

Amos glances at Ziva and Lib again. *They seem upset.* He turns his attention back to the king. "My supplier paid me to bring them to their home in Uthal after the unfortunate death of our chief judge."

"Who killed the chief judge?"

"They found him stabbed, kind, wise king. No one knows who did it, but the gates are closed to anyone who is not a Nephite."

"Do you know how Ziva became injured?"

"I do not, great and good king," he simpers. "I saw other women that had bruises as well. Their families departed to Zarahemla after meeting on the bank of Sidon. That's all I know."

The king rubs his chin. He notices that Ziva and Lib are holding hands. "Ziva, do I have this right? You came with your husband back to Uthal and followed him into the city?"

"Yes." Ziva realizes she signed her death warrant. Her face falls, looking down at the floor. Her chin quivers.

Lib, no longer able to hold his tongue, squeezes Ziva's hand. "Please, Good King. Please let me speak."

The king moves his hand, palm up, in a short motion forward, indicating for Lib to continue.

"True, we were found together, thus forcing us into Joining, but prior to Joining, we had talked about it." He glances at Ziva. "We agreed to move forward, together." His eyes sparkle. He gazes into Ziva's eyes. "I have loved Ziva and Tokal since the day I met them in the woods pinned against a tree. To me, our Joining is the happiest day of my life. I know that life with Ziva isn't going to be easy, but having her by my side is going to be worth it. She makes me happy. They both make me happy. All I want is their happiness in return." He turns back toward the king. "She only followed me home from Zarahemla because I come to serve my king. Please spare her life, King Gilgal.  If any punishment needs to be given, I willingly take her place."

"No, Lib. I can't lose you too," Ziva cries.

The terror and anguish in Ziva's voice cause Tokal to wail. All eyes turn to him.

Lib and his parents try to soothe Tokal. The toddler is removed from Ziva's back and held in Lib's arm. He keeps his other arm around Ziva.

Ziva holds one arm around Lib and Tokal as they huddle together as a family.

Tokal quiets in the arms of his parents.

The king's eyes narrow toward the small family huddled together. "Lib . . . you freely offer your life for Ziva's?"

Lib stands tall and proud. "Yes."

Ziva's tears cascade down her face.

"Do you freely choose Ziva as your wife?"

"Yes."

"And you take her child as your own?"

"Yes. They are my life" Lib's voice cracks with emotion.

King Gilgal's gaze turns to Ziva once more. "Ziva."

She pulls her eyes from Lib's face. Ziva's heart swells with his words yet breaks with his sacrifice.

"Do you freely choose Lib as your husband?"

"Yes, my king," she sobs.

"I see." King Gilgal can no longer keep the smile from his face. "You are Joined as man and wife."

Ziva and Lib scrunch their eyebrows together and frown at the king, not understanding.

King Gilgal stands. He walks toward the small family. "The law I have in place is for a single woman who returns to the city before her time is up. You returned as a Joined couple. The fact that my guards didn't recall this will be dealt with." He waves the words away and is about to continue.

Those in the hall gasp.

Ziva and Lib's eyes widen. They stare at each other. They understand. Relief overtakes them, they envelope each other in a hug.

A cheer of joy is heard from those in the hall.

King Gilgal waits until the emotion has calmed. "I have admired Ziva's ability to state her truth even when the truth is difficult for her. I am glad that she found a champion in her husband." Gilgal smiles at Lib. "Since you have returned as an astronomer to serve me, your living should appropriately correspond. When you leave here, Enon will take you to your new home. Even though your return is early, the house is already stocked. Lib's parents can bring the rest of your belongings tomorrow. You can also expect a gift from the queen and me." He nods to himself before smiling at them. "It makes me happy to see that you have found each other." Turning to Amos, he says, "Get up from your knees, Nephite."

The man stands.

"Amos, the Nephite merchant. I want to thank you for returning to Uthal two of its citizens. As a reward, you will be further compensated. What did you bring to sell?"

"Sweet wine. The best that Zarahemla offers."

"Do you have a sample on you?"

Amos looks at the king for a moment before pulling out a wineskin attached to his belt. He explains how the wine is made>

A cup is brought forward by a servant and filled by Amos.

Heth, Abana, Ami, and Enon join Lib and Ziva. They offer congratulations and dispense hugs and pats on the back.

Tokal wails at being squished.

Everyone laughs, taking a step back to make sure that Tokal isn't crowded as they continue their conversations.

In the dark, Ziva nestles in Lib's arms. They lie on the comfortable large bed in their new home.

Tokal sleeps nearby in a basket on the floor.

Kelev lies next to the basket, guarding the little boy.

Lib strokes her arm. "This has been another stressful day for you. I'm sorry."

Ziva looks up at him, confused. "Why are you sorry?"

"I didn't keep you safe."

Ziva hears within the tone the blame Lib has for himself. Ziva turns to face him. "You kept me safe. You stayed with me through it all. Even when I was abducted, *you* were there when I needed you most. She smiles. "It's been a stressful day, but I think it has turned out rather well."

Lib's eyes widen in surprise. He's not able to see her face, even though he knows she's facing him. "You are all right with what you had to go through, including dealing with the king?"

She smiles to herself. "King Gilgal helped me understand the why behind telling him what happened. He helped me get to where I am now."

Lib tightens his arms around her, "The thought of losing you, again, after everything scared me." He takes a breath, caressing her face. "I love you, Ziva." As an afterthought he asks, "How did telling the king help you?"

Ziva smiles in the dark at his announcement. Her face changes to a frown at his question. "The thought of losing you scared me— so much so that I couldn't move forward." After a moment she continues, "I had to go through all my experiences including the explanation to King Gilgal to get me to a place where I can let go of the past and live in the present—to realize what I have. I feel like a heavy burden has been lifted from my shoulders." Ziva cups his face and gazes at him. "You're such a good man, but don't ever offer your life up for mine again, because I can't bear to lose the man I love."

Lib's heart leaps for joy at her revelation. He chuckles that it was contained in a reprimand. His eyes communicate his great love for her.

Her eyes sparkle in the dark. She caresses his face.

Lib turns so that she's lying on her back, but still in his arms. He leans down and kisses her.

Ziva's hands go around his neck, pulling him even closer to her. The kiss deepens.

When they come up for air, Lib leans his forehead against hers with hope in his heart, trying to formulate into words the many questions swirling in his head. Will you stay with us? Do you finally trust me? Are you happy? But the most important question on his mind is will you truly be my wife? "Together?" spills whispered from his lips.

With a twinkle in her eye, she responds to each and every one of them—including the one that asks if she'll be his wife in every sense of the word. "Together."

## THE END

# HISTORICAL FACTS

This novel is a work of fiction that attempts to identify what it was possibly like to be a young woman growing up in Book of Mormon times.

There are two geographical hypotheses regarding where the events in the Book of Mormon took place. The original location of the Book of Mormon was North America, as stated multiple times by Joseph Smith throughout his life.[34, 35, 36] The other popularly believed geographical location is in Mesoamerica. This opinion came about later in history[2, 34, 36] and has become prominent due in part to some beautiful artwork depicting persons within the Book of Mormon using Mesoamerican geography.[34] Furthermore, the Book of Mormon contains words that are not openly accepted as historical for North America, such as swords, horses, sheep, and linen. Below is some historical information that may corroborate the use of these words within this book.

An Ancient Civilization—According to the Book of Mormon, over 2,000 years ago lived an advanced civilization with a complex society. The people in the Book of Mormon were divided into two main societies who were geographically separated: the Lamanites and the Nephites.[3] The Nephites lived north of the Lamanites.[2] What remains of these societies today is an abridged 1,000 years of history, their posterity—the American Indians—and a few archeological items.

Hopewell Indians—The name *Hopewell* originated from a man named Mordecai Hopewell, whose land in Ross County, Ohio contained archaeological mounds that were excavated in the 1800s.[1, 2] The events of Book of Mormon, which was retrieved from the Hill Cumorah in Ontario County, New York,[37] and contains an abridged 1,000-year historical record translated in the 1800s,[3] were located in the region inhabited by the Hopewell Indians.[38] Both the Hopewell Indians and the peoples of the Book of Mormon built their cities using wood and dirt,[4, 5, 32] and over 2,000 years, the remains of their civilizations have all but disappeared. Since the Nephites were an advanced civilization, I gave them stairs and two-story buildings.

Weapons—The Hopewell culture knew how to work metal.[27] Swords are mentioned throughout the Book of Mormon as a weapon of choice during their wars between the two societies.[39] The sword type mentioned in this book is something similar to what is known as a *maquahuitl* sword.[11, 12] The practice of archery is also well-documented historically, and the ram's-horn bow is still used today.

Mulek—We have records stating that Mulek was the son of Zedekiah, the last king of Judah, circa 589 BC. [41] How he escaped death during the Babylonian invasion and came to America is unknown to us, but it is theorized that he came with some help from Phoenicians. [2, 41]

Eye Color—The perception is that Native American Indians only had black hair and brown eyes. While this coloring was a dominant characteristic, it was not the case for every American Indian. [6, 7]

Textiles—The industry of some of the Hopewell Indians produced fine clothing. [8] Linen is also mentioned multiple times in the Book of Mormon and thus is included in this book. [11]

Society—Utilizing the Book of Mormon and other historical sources for research, I found a complex society based on different tribes. [9, 10] I decided to use some of the differences between these tribes to develop differences between the cities mentioned in this book.

Sheep, Horses, and Dogs—The Book of Mormon mentions "horses" a multitude of times. [15] Bones of horses [16, 28, 29, 30] and sheep [17] have been discovered in North America and Canada from after the last ice age and before the arrival of Columbus. Dogs are mentioned in the Book of Mormon [42] and in historical accounts. [43] Dogs are still abundant in some native tribes.

Food and Herbs—The Book of Mormon contains many references to food, including corn, wheat, barley, and such seeds as *neas* and *sheum*. [18] I think the Nephites and Lamanites planted and harvested many other things as well, using the land's resources to create variety to their diet and improve health, just as we do today. I have provided some indigenous foods and herbs that are native to

North America in an effort to enhance the historicity of the story.[19, 20, 21, 22, 23, 24, 25, 26]

The Joining—There is no reference to the marriage ceremony within the Book of Mormon nor in any historical document that has been found for the time and region. Taking the context of some tribes' ideology and ceremonies for marriage, I have tried to move that back 2,000 years to create what possibly could have occurred with regard to arranged marriages, non-arranged marriages, and ceremonies in the Lamanite culture.

# REFERENCES

1. The Archaeological Institute of America. (2009). *Who were the Hopewell*. Archeology. https://archive.archaeology.org/online/features/hopewell/who_were_hopewell.html

2. Neville, J. (2016). *Moroni's America*. Digital Legend.

3. Mormon. (1989). *The Book of Mormon* (J. Smith, trans.). The Church of Jesus Christ of Latter-day Saints. https://www.churchofjesuschrist.org/study/scriptures/bofm/bofm-title?lang=eng

4. Mormon. (1989). *The Book of Mormon* (J. Smith, trans.). The Church of Jesus Christ of Latter-day Saints. https://www.churchofjesuschrist.org/study/scriptures/bofm/bofm-title?lang=eng City walls: Alma 53:4, Alma 49:2

5. Squier, E. G., & Davis, E. H. (2015 August 10). *The Project Gutenberg EBook of Ancient Monuments of the Mississippi Valley.*

https://www.gutenberg.org/files/49668/49668-h/49668-h.htm

6. DNA Consultants. (2018). U.S. Cherokee. https://dnaconsultants.com/cherokee-1/

7. Swancer, B. (2017 October 13). *The mysterious tribe of blue-eyed Native Americans*. Mysterious Universe. <u>The Mysterious Tribe of Blue-Eyed Native Americans (mysteriousuniverse.org)</u>

8. Kakima. (n.d.). *The Hopewell Culture of Ohio: Teaching Native American History*. Bright Hub Education. https://www.brighthubeducation.com/middle-school-social-studies-lessons/67881-teaching-students-about-the-hopewell-native-american-culture/

9. TeachingHistory.org. (2018). *American Indian women*. Teaching History. https://teachinghistory.org/history-content/ask-a-historian/23931

10. Encyclopaedia Britannica. (2019). The Hopewell culture: North American Indian culture. In *Encyclopaedia Britannica*. <u>Hopewell culture | North American Mound Builders, Artifacts & Trade | Britannica</u>

11. Mormon. (1989). *The Book of Mormon* (J. Smith, trans.). The Church of Jesus Christ of Latter-day Saints. https://www.churchofjesuschrist.org/study/scriptures/bofm/bofm-title?lang=eng
Cloth: Helaman 6:13, Alma 1:29, Alma 4:6; Mosiah 10:5

12. Native Languages of the Americas. (2015). *Native American Indian weapons*. Native-Languages.org. https://www.native-languages.org/weapons.htm

13. Squier, E. G., & Davis, E. H. (2015 August 10). *The Project Gutenberg EBook of Ancient Monuments of the Mississippi Valley*. Retrieved from Ancient Monuments of the Mississippi Valley; by E.G. Squier and E.H. Davis; A Project Gutenberg eBook.

14. Jeffcoat, T. L. (2013). Weapons and warriors: Gunstock warclub of the Native Americans. *Sailing on the Astral Sea*. http://mrtalkstoomuch.blogspot.com/2013/12/weapons-warriors-gunstock-war-club-of.html

15. Mormon. (1989). *The Book of Mormon* (J. Smith, trans.). The Church of Jesus Christ of Latter-day Saints. https://www.churchofjesuschrist.org/study/scriptures/bofm/bofm-title?lang=eng
Horses: Alma 18:9-10, 12, 1 Nephi 18:25, Alma 20:6, 3 Nephi 6:1, 3 Nephi 4:4, 3 Nephi 3:22

16. Jones, S. E. (2012). Were there horses in the Americas before Columbus? *The Wild Horse Conspiracy*. https://thewildhorseconspiracy.org/2013/07/02/exciting-article-about-by-phd-steven-jones-re-more-recent-surviving-native-horse-in-north-america/

17. National Bighorn Sheep Center. (2018). *About bighorns*. Bighorn.org. https://bighorn.org/about-bighorns/

18. Mormon. (1989). *The Book of Mormon* (J. Smith, trans.). The Church of Jesus Christ of Latter-day Saints. https://www.churchofjesuschrist.org/study/scriptures/bofm/bofm-title?lang=eng Food: Mosiah 9:9 19.

19. Bray, M. (2024). *Chiltepin Pepper: Heat, Flavor, Ingredient Pairings.* Pepper Scale. Chiltepin Pepper: Heat, Flavor, Ingredient Pairings (pepperscale.com)

20. Kiprop, V. (2019 July 5). Fruits native to North America. *WorldAtlas.* https://www.worldatlas.com/articles/fruits-that-are-native-to-north-america.html

21. Food Tank. (2016). 20 native North American foods with stories to tell. *Food Tank.* https://foodtank.com/news/2016/07/indigenous-foods-historically-and-culturally-important-to-north-americ/

22. Havard, V. (1895). Food plants of the North American Indians. *Bulletin of the Torrey Botanical Club, 22*(3), 98–123. doi:10.2307/2477757. https://www.jstor.org/stable/2477757?seq=1#metadata_info_tab_contents

23. MacWelch, T. (2014 May 27). *Survival skills: 14 wild medicinal plants.* Outdoor Life. https://www.outdoorlife.com/blogs/survivalist/2014/05/survival-skills-14-wild-medicinal-plants/

24. Kellner, J. (2016 November/December). *Native American plants and medicinal herbs: Discover the benefits*

*of five of North America's most-researched healing native plants*. Mother Earth Living. https://www.motherearthliving.com/health-and-wellness/natural-remedies/native-american-plants-zm0z16ndzfol

25. Polizzi, N. (2018 March 24). 3 Powerful indigenous herbs from North America. *The Sacred Science*. https://www.thesacredscience.com/3-powerful-indigenous-herbs-from-north-america/

26. Bergo, A. (2013 July 4). Using wild ginger. *Forager Chef*. https://foragerchef.com/how-to-find-and-use-wild-ginger

27. Mormon. (1989). *The Book of Mormon* (J. Smith, trans.). The Church of Jesus Christ of Latter-day Saints. https://www.churchofjesuschrist.org/study/scriptures/bofm/bofm-title?lang=eng
Metal work: 1 Nephi 17:11; Helaman 6:11

28. Johnson, D. (2015). "Hard" evidence of ancient American horses. *BYU Studies, 54*(3), 149–179. https://byustudies.byu.edu/article/hard-evidence-of-ancient-american-horses

29. Johnston, L. J. (2019). Yes world, there were horses in Native culture before the settlers came. *Indian Country Today*. https://ictnews.org/news/yes-world-there-were-horses-in-native-culture-before-the-settlers-came

30. The Horse Fund (2013). Indian horses before Columbus. *Tuesday's Horse.* https://tuesdayshorse.wordpress.com/2013/10/14/indian-horses-before-columbus/

31. 8 Humanities. (n.d.). *Woodland Indians: Iroquois and Algonquin.* 8 Humanities. https://8bishumanities.weebly.com/woodland-indians-iroquois-and-algonquin1.html

32. Weiser, K. (2020). *Cahokia Mounds, Illinois—Largest archaeological site in North America.* Legends of America. https://www.legendsofamerica.com/il-cahokia/

33. Platt, D. (2012). *Hopewell Culture National Historical Park: Seip Mound.* TrekOhio. https://trekohio.com/2012/07/27/seip-mound-at-hopewell-culture-national-historical-park/

34. Book of Mormon Evidence. (2019 October 11). *The smoking gun of Book of Mormon geography.* BookofMormonEvidence.org https://bookofmormonevidence.org/the-smoking-gun-of-book-of-mormon-geography-2/

35. Smith, J. (4 June 1834). Letter to Emma Smith, 4 June 1834. *The Joseph Smith Papers.* https://www.josephsmithpapers.org/paper-summary/letter-to-emma-smith-4-june-1834/3

36. Book of Mormon Evidence, (2019 October 14). *Joseph Smith knew Book of Mormon geography.*

BookofMormonEvidence.org
https://bookofmormonevidence.org/joseph-smith-knew-book-of-mormon-geography/

37. Mormon. (1989). *The Book of Mormon* (J. Smith, trans.). The Church of Jesus Christ of Latter-day Saints. https://www.churchofjesuschrist.org/study/scriptures/bofm/js?lang=eng

38. Legends of America (2020). *Hopewell Culture of Native Americans*. Legends of America. https://www.legendsofamerica.com/hopewell-culture/

39. Mormon. (1989). *The Book of Mormon* (J. Smith, trans.). The Church of Jesus Christ of Latter-day Saints. https://www.churchofjesuschrist.org/study/scriptures/bofm/bofm-title?lang=eng
Swords: Alma 17:7, Alma 44:8, Alma 60:2, to name a few.

40. Center for Digital Research in the Humanities. (n.d.). *Images*. Ohio Hopewell: Ancient Crossroads of the American Midwest. http://hopewell.unl.edu/images.html

41. Christianson, R. T. (1967). *The Phoenicians and the ancient civilizations of America*. Ancient America Foundation. Ross T. Christensen/THE PHOENICIANS AND THE ANCIENT CIVILIZATIONS OF AMERICA - Elias Bejjani News

42. Mormon. (1989). *The Book of Mormon* (J. Smith, trans.). The Church of Jesus Christ of Latter-day Saints. https://www.churchofjesuschrist.org/study/scriptures/bofm/bofm-title?lang=eng
Mulek: Omni 1:15, Mosiah 25:2, Helaman 6:10, Helaman 8:21

43. Mormon. (1989). *The Book of Mormon* (J. Smith, trans.). The Church of Jesus Christ of Latter-day Saints. https://www.churchofjesuschrist.org/study/scriptures/bofm/bofm-title?lang=eng
Dog: Mosiah 12:2, Alma 16:10, Helaman 7:19, 3 Nephi 7:8, 3 Nephi 14:6

44. LaFlamme, K (nd). *History of the American Indian Dog.* http://www.iidoba.org/history.htm

45. Mormon. (1989). *The Book of Mormon* (J. Smith, trans.). The Church of Jesus Christ of Latter-day Saints. https://www.churchofjesuschrist.org/study/scriptures/bofm/bofm-title?lang=eng
Money: Alma 11: 4-19

# OTHER BOOKS BY THE AUTHOR

Ziva's Challenge

Emara's Challenge

Palla's Challenge

# EMARA'S CHALLENGE

# EMARA'S

# CHALLENGE

*THIS IS MY ESCAPE!* SHE stands looking over the valley. *I can think here. It's high, hard to get to, and private. No one can see me except for the birds above.* She looks at Uthal, where she came from, in the distance. How small it looks. The wooden buildings with all their decorations look like little rectangular trees. Even the tall wooden wall around the city with all its elaborate designs seems so small that she could walk over it from up here. The people beyond the wall look like ants scurrying from one place to another inside a four cornered cage. She allows her mind to turn to the problem while her hands absently reach for her braid.

*At the Stand I'll have to announce my decision to be bound to a husband within a year or take the Challenge.* "I'm not ready for a husband." She paces around the plateau. Raising her hands midstride, she shouts at no one in particular, "It's not fair!" She exhales forcefully, recalling that there is a better way to solve problems. Pacing a few more revolutions, Emara finally sits, drawing her knees to her chest and wrapping her arms around them.

She watches as a bird soars overhead, singing a joyful melody while the fresh, cool spring breeze touches her skin. The smells of springtime fill the air even here on this precipice. With a mind of their own, her hands again reach for her braid. "My alternative to a husband is the Challenge, from which no woman has returned. What happened to them? Well,"—she bites her lip—"I can defend myself."

"Emara!" a male voice reaches her ears from below, invading her privacy. She wonders who it is and how he found her. "Emara, are you up there?"

Thinking that the guards have found her, she worries that her parents will be informed and what little freedom she has left will be gone. Quietly getting on her stomach, she looks over the edge, trying to see who's below while keeping invisible.

The irritated voice from below sounds again. "Emmy, answer me! I tracked you this far." Only a few people call her that and they are her brothers and her best friend, Selina. Looking down over the ledge, she sees a man standing far below and looking up, but his face is shaded. "Emmy, answer me! I'm worried something happened to you."

Emara backs away from the ledge and sits, weighing the pros and cons of not answering her brother. Her hands fiddle with her braid. The now quite familiar voice empowers Emara to hope that she can persuade him to not tell their parents. Making a decision, she looks over the ledge. "Enon, is that you?"

"Yes!" Enon looks up toward the sound of Emara's voice, but sees nothing. "Where are you?"

Waving an arm, "Up here."

Shielding his eyes to see better, he sees the moving arm.

"How did you get up there?"

"I climbed. I'll come down."

Enon grins, knowing his sister is trying to hide something. "You don't have to hurry down. I can come up. Just tell me where to start."

There is a pause that becomes pronounced. Enon hears, "First thing's first. You have to promise not to tell anyone about this place."

Looking up at where his sister perches, he hollers, "You've got to be kidding."

"I am serious! This is my place and I want to keep it private. Promise me."

Enon stands there for a minute, looking at the cliff face, back up to where Emara is, and back at the cliff face. He finally looks up, hollering back, "I promise not to tell anyone."

Even with Enon's promise, Emara sits back, contemplating sharing her world with her older brother. She needs his advice; there is plenty daylight left and she's not ready to return to the city. "Come up." She shouts. "Start in the groove where the rock face meets. I could use your help with something."

Enon follows his sister's instructions, finding where to start.

"Coming up." As he starts climbing, Emara's thoughts drift as her eyes catch the view in front of her. Her hand absently snakes up, snatching a braid.

"Emmy?" says a deep, concerned voice behind her.

Emara jumps up, ready for an attack. "You scared me!"

Laughing at her response, he says, "Serves you right. You invited me up here and knew that I was coming."

"I was thinking."

Enon's eyes fasten on the view around him. "What a strategic place." Enon looks at the city below. "This is a perfect place to hide while monitoring the valley and the back of the city. When did you find this place?"

"A few years past." Turning to her brother, she glares at him. "Just remember you promised not to tell anyone." Enon nods.

Enon watches his sister as she sits down, tucking her arms around her knees and fiddling with the end of her long black braid while looking out over the precipice. Enon sits down next to his sister. "You always did like to climb. How did you find this place?"

"As you know, Selina and I like to explore. We found a way to get out of Uthal without others missing us. It started off as a challenge to see who could climb the highest." Emara shrugs. "We made it to the top." She looks at her brother. "How did you find me?"

"I saw you leave with your guards after we took you home this morning. Being that it was still too early means you were up to something, so I followed you. I sent your guards home and they will tell anyone who asks that you're with me."

"Where are your guards?"

Enon grins at Emara. "Standing where you left your guards. That's pretty inventive, making a rope to climb out a window." He reaches over and retrieves the waterskin that is available. After taking a drink, he wipes his mouth and replaces the cap, deciding to get to the point of what is bothering Emara. Nudging Emara's shoulder with his own, he says, "What's bothering you? Is it a boy?"

"Stop it!" She glares at him. "You know I don't like anyone around here. They're stupid. If I did like someone, you all would know about it and tease me mercilessly."

Surprised by her reaction, Enon holds up his hands. "All right, Emmy, I'll stop. What's troubling you?"

Emara is quiet for a few moments, thinking of how to voice her concerns. "It's not fair."

"What's not fair?"

"Now that I'm in my sixteenth year, I have to choose whether to be joined to a man or take the Challenge. None of you have to do that."

"Wait a second, I'm not understanding."

"You, Helam, Hezekiah, and Telah are not being forced to be joined or take the Challenge. Why am I? I'm the youngest."

"As far as I know, you're not being forced. You have a year to decide who to accept to be your husband. Now, on the other hand, I feel sorry for Helam. His spouse has been chosen for him, and he's not even met her. He was supposed to be joined several years back. I don't know how he managed it, but has been a le to defer it until later this year. I think I know why he's waited so long."

Surprised, Emara looks up at Enon. "Why?"

"I'm pretty sure he loves Selina and he has waited because he's trying to figure out a way to be joined to her. I don't know how he's going to make that happen."

"I didn't know that he had an arranged Joining. We're all together every morning for my self-defense lesson. Why don't I know that?"

"I thought you were smart? We're not Nephites who can choose for themselves, Emara. We are Lamanites and sometimes have arranged spouses. Helam is crown prince. Of course it is arranged. Helam doesn't like to talk about it, so he doesn't bring it up."

"Of course, I know that Uthal sometimes has an arranged Joining, but I didn't know about Helam. It doesn't seem like something our parents would do to us. They haven't talked about it. Does Selina know?"

"No! And you're not going to tell her, even if she is your best friend." Emara frowns at her brother. "As commerce with the Nephites has grown, we have also accepted some of their beliefs. This was arranged many years ago and there wasn't a reason for you to know about it."

"Why can't I tell Selina? She needs to know. She loves Helam, and I know she wants to be joined to him."

"And he to her, but until Helam can figure out a way to make it happen, he doesn't want to get her hopes up. You know how Selina is. You've grown up with her. She will not be available to choose to be joined until after the Journey. We have until then to help Enon out."

Emara nods, "I will help where I can, but I don't know what to do. They should be able to be joined. Being second oldest, did our parents arrange a wife for you?"

"I'm so glad they didn't. I think I would be upset about it."

"But what about me? At the end of this year, if I still don't want a husband, Father will decide for me." She took breath. "I am not ready to be joined to any man, but the only other choice I have is the Challenge. None of the other women ever come back from it. Their guardian does, but they don't." Enon sits still, waiting for Emara to finish while Emara looks out at the scenery. "I'm scared." When she looks up at Enon, a tear streams down her cheek, which she quickly wipes away. "What is going to happen to me?"

Emara looks away from her brother, blinks a few times, and takes some steadying breaths. Enon's voice breaks through the silence between them. "You're going to have to decide for yourself. If you say you're not ready to be joined, I suggest you work on trying to decide who's going to be your guardian."

"What? I can't believe you'd say that knowing I won't return."

With a sigh Enon says, "Some return."

"They do?"

"Yes. They do. I happen to have a friend whose wife took the Challenge and returned. If you want, tomorrow I'll take you to meet her."

Emara watches her brother's face. "Would you really?" Enon nods his head seriously.

Emara's face lights up. "Yes. I want to go."

"Good. Let's go home." Enon stands up, picks up the waterskin, and looks at the view.

Emara doesn't move. "Not yet." Enon looks down at his sister, sighs, and sits down again next to her. "Who do I choose for a guardian? I'm told a guardian needs to be a trusted friend who can defend himself. All of you can defend yourselves. How am I going to pick?"

Enon laughs. "You are set on taking the Challenge?"

"No! Yes! Aww, I don't know. I don't want to be joined with anyone right now and the only other option available to me is the Challenge. I want to figure out my path and then decide from there."

"You can't plan everything, Emmy. Sometimes, life just happens."

"But I can plan this. Help me decide."

"Then will you be willing to return home?"

"Yes. I promise."

"I think Hezekiah and Telah are too young to be a guardian."

"So that narrows it down to Helam and you." Enon nods his head. "Selina will never forgive me if I take Helam."

"You know that if you asked Helam to be your guardian, he would do it even if Selina was upset."

"Yes, I know. It would make both of them miserable to be separated, and I don't want to do that to them. Aren't we trying to help them get joined?" Enon laughs. "Seriously, would you be my guardian?"

Enon looks at his sister. "I would like nothing better."

Relief rushes through Emara, and she gives her brother a hug. "Thank you."

"My responsibilities can be given to Hezekiah and Telah. It's time they grew up." Grinning, Enon looks at his sister. "Good. Now we can get back to the city. Ready?" Emara nods.

They climb down the cliff face and hurry back toward the brown rope that is hanging outside the window, blending with the wall. Emara takes the lead climbing the rope. She has done this many times, making quick work of it. Enon, however, takes more time working himself up the rope. When he gets in through the window, he sits on the floor. Emara pulls up the rope and hides it in a box that is sitting in the opposite corner from the window.

"It amazes me how well thought out all of this is," Enon says. "How did you find this place?"

"We wanted a place to go where we could talk—without someone listening to our conversation. Selina is the one who found this place and brought me here. We worked out a plan to keep it a secret. It's like everyone has forgotten this place even exists. We've cleaned it up just a little bit."

"What made you want to go outside the city?"

Emara shrugs, "Adventure."

"Emmy," Enon sighs, "It's not safe out there."

"Who says?"

"I say."

Emara glares at her brother. "I've been doing just fine for the last several years."

"You've been with Selina—"

"Until she got that governess. Even without Selina, I haven't had any problems and I've met no one."

"Promise me, Emmy, you will not go outside the city again on one of your adventures without me."

"Why? So, I can have a babysitter?"

"Because I am your brother and don't want anything bad to happen to you."

"I'm fine!"

"No, you're not! What if someone finds your rope and pulls it up while you're outside the city wall? What then?"

"What does that mean?"

"It means that a lot of people care about you and will be worried about your safety. Since you asked me to be your guardian, I would feel better if I were with you."

"Oh!" She looks out the window and her hand reaches for her braid. Enon grins, knowing that she is thinking it through.

Finally, the hand falls and Enon quickly wipes the grin off his face before Emara faces him. "I promise. Just so you know, it is because I decided. Not because you said so."

Enon chuckles at his sister's further display of independence. "Good. Let's get going. Do you have Helam's letter with you?"

"Yes."

"Selina is fortunate that she went to school with you so she knows how to read and write."

"She is, but it helped me having her at school."

"How so?"

"Selina is very smart. She's helped me so many times in understanding concepts that were presented. I couldn't have passed the classes without her. Furthermore, she is so gregarious that I didn't stand out with her next to me."

"How are you getting the letter to Selina?"

"I was going to visit her." Enon nods and gestures toward the stairs. Emara steps past her brother, leading the way down the stairs and out the door, closing it securely behind them. They stop for a moment, blinking as their eyes adjust to the bright sun. Enon's guards stop talking and quickly follow behind them as they move through the city streets toward Selina's home.

## **<u>Book Club Questions</u>**

### Character & Motivation

1. What drives Ziva's fierce independence, and how does it shape her decisions throughout the story?
2. How does Ziva's mistrust of others both protect and hinder her?
3. In what ways does Lib challenge Ziva's worldview? Do you think he succeeds in changing her?
4. How does Ziva's relationship with the infant she cares for reveal hidden aspects of her character?
5. Which secondary character stood out to you most, and why?

### Themes & Symbolism

6. The novel explores **trust versus self-reliance**. Do you think Ziva ultimately learns to balance the two?
7. How does the story portray **resilience** in the face of danger and isolation?
8. What role does **faith or divine guidance** seem to play in Ziva's journey?
9. How does the wilderness setting symbolize both danger and opportunity for growth?
10. The Gadianton robbers represent chaos and corruption. How does Ziva's struggle against them reflect larger moral or societal conflicts?

### Plot & Conflict

11. What moment in the story felt like the true turning point for Ziva?
12. How does the constant threat of pursuit heighten the tension and shape Ziva's choices?
13. Were there any decisions Ziva made that you strongly disagreed with? Why?
14. How does the survival aspect of the story compare to other survival or adventure novels you've read?
15. Did the ending feel satisfying? Why or why not?

### Personal Reflection

16. Have you ever experienced a time when you had to rely on others despite wanting to be independent? How does that connect to Ziva's struggle?
17. What lessons about **community and belonging** can modern readers take from Ziva's journey?
18. How does Ziva's story challenge or affirm your own ideas about resilience?
19. If you were in Ziva's position, would you have trusted the astronomy students? Why or why not?
20. What do you think the author wants readers to carry with them after finishing the book?

## About the Author

As a child, Monica Flores hated reading and all things that fall under the subject of English. She didn't become a bookworm until she was a teenager, when introduced to Jane Austen's *Pride and Prejudice*. Since that time, Monica has become an avid reader. During the day, she works as a nurse at the county hospital. She enjoys serving in her church and community, spending time with friends and family, doing family history work, eating chocolate and, of course, reading books. You can find her on Facebook, Instagram, or contact her at https://monicafloresauthor.com